LORD RAVEN'S WIDOW

LORD RAVEN'S WIDOW

LESLIE O'GRADY

ST. MARTIN'S PRESS / NEW YORK

Design by Lee Wade

Library of Congress Cataloging in Publication Data
O'Grady, Leslie.
   Lord Raven's widow.
   I. Title.
PS3565.G68L6   1983   813'.54   83-2893
ISBN 0-312-49870-5

First Edition
10 9 8 7 6 5 4 3 2 1

To Marlane Loersch,
a survivor

LORD RAVEN'S WIDOW

CHAPTER

I

"I never want to see Raven's Chase again," I said.

Amabel uttered a low groan. "Oh, Nora, surely you can't mean that. Why, the Chase is your home."

Rising in a soft rustle of black crepe, I walked over to one of the wide casemented windows and pretended to gaze out across the flat green lawn so she couldn't see the uncontrollable tears that sprang to my eyes. "Without Mark and Gabriel, all that house holds for me now is bitter memories. Do you know, every time I walk into the library, I expect to see Mark standing there, flipping through a book, or sprawled in a chair before the fireplace? And I never realized how deathly silent that house is without Gabriel's laughter. It's as though it's haunted—not by ghosts—but by a lack of them." My voice broke and trailed off as I sniffed and wiped my eyes with my ever-present handkerchief.

Amabel rose and rushed over to put a comforting arm around my shoulders. "You must give yourself some time, Nora. It's been only three months since—" She stopped herself, then added, "The hurt will go away. You'll see."

Would the knot of pain in my heart ever go away? I wondered. "I doubt it," I murmured stiffly, more to myself than Amabel.

Easily daunted by my refusal to be comforted, she dropped her arm and quietly returned to her corner of the sofa, leaving me to stare out the window.

I

Suddenly, a knock interrupted the long, awkward silence, followed by the sound of doors opening.

I turned and watched as Amabel's two children came charging into the drawing room, whooping at the top of their voices while loud, stomping feet caused every piece of porcelain in the room to tinkle and dance in place. The eldest, six-year-old Peter, was mounted on an old, battered stick horse, which he proceeded to ride with reckless abandon through the drawing room, maneuvering around antique tables and chairs as he made shrill neighing noises. He was pursued by four-year-old Timothy, red-faced and puffing to keep up.

"Come on, Timmy," Peter called scornfully over his shoulder, "you're too slow. You'll never catch me."

As the exuberant pair went careening around the room a second time, while their mother just beamed indulgently, I decided it was time to put an end to their antics, especially when Peter took a corner too sharply and his stick horse cracked against a piecrust table, sending a priceless old Wedgwood vase teetering precariously.

"Boys!" I admonished them, lunging for the vase and rescuing it just in time. "That will be quite enough."

It is not my custom to reprimand other people's children, but since Amabel could never bring herself to raise her voice to her sons, I felt perfectly justified in doing so now.

My presumption won me a sharp glance from their mother, but the boys stopped at once, quieted down, and snapped to attention, like eager spaniels awaiting a command. They were as handsome as their mother was beautiful, and their mourning clothes accentuated their straight, flaxen hair, blue eyes, and round, rosy cheeks. I took my seat in a wide, comfortable chair and wagged my finger at them in reproof. "The house is not the place to ride your horse, Peter."

"I was just racing Prince in the Derby," he explained, dismounting his stick horse and letting it clatter to the floor.

Instantly, Timothy reached down to make a grab for it,

but his older brother was too quick and shoved him away.

"I want to ride Prince!" Timothy wailed, his face crumpling.

"You can't ride him," Peter said cruelly. "You're just a baby and he's much too spirited for you."

I flashed Amabel a stern, imploring look, but again, no response, so I said, "Peter, let your brother ride Prince. You shouldn't be selfish with your toys."

Peter wore a mutinous expression as he protested, "But Timmy's just a baby, Aunt Nora. Prince would throw him and he'd get hurt."

Seeing that I was getting nowhere, I sought to divert him instead. "Peter, why don't you come here and sit on my lap?"

He grinned and came running toward me, his arms extended. Of course, Timothy, always afraid of being excluded, promptly lost interest in Prince and came rushing in his older brother's wake.

When the boys reached me, Peter stopped, turned, and pushed his brother away, causing him to lose his balance and sit down, hard. Timothy promptly started crying.

"Peter!" I cried, at my wit's end. "Don't fight, or I won't let either of you sit on my lap. There's room for both of you." And to prove my point, I lifted first one, then the other, onto my lap.

Peter stopped fighting with Timothy long enough to stare at me intently, out of his innocent blue eyes. "Aunt Nora, why are you always crying?"

Amabel finally sprang to life. "Oh, Nora, I'm so sorry." And she rose to take her children from me.

I stopped her with, "It's all right, really." When she sat back, I said to the children, "When someone we love dies, we feel very sad for a long, long time, because we miss them very much."

"Do you miss Uncle Mark and Cousin Gabriel very much?" he asked.

I nodded, my eyes brimming with tears again.

"I miss them, too," Peter assured me.

Not to be outdone, Timothy piped up, "I miss them, too, Aunt Nora."

"We all do," I murmured, hugging them fiercely.

Almost nothing could hold Peter's attention for long, and even now, he was scrambling out of my lap, sliding down my skirts and running to his mother. I fully expected Timothy to tail after him, but he didn't. He stayed nestled in my arms and rested his head against my bosom, grateful for any attention.

"Mama," Peter was saying with his most winning smile, "can I ride Star today? Will you go riding with me, Mama, please? And will you let me jump Star this time?"

"Of course I will, precious," Amabel crooned, hugging her handsome child while she brushed his straight blond hair away from his eyes. "After luncheon, we will go riding together, out on the moors, and perhaps I'll let you jump your pony this time."

"And you can't come," Peter called over to Timothy, "because you're just a baby and can't even ride a real pony, unless Mama rides behind you and holds the reins."

My aversion to playing favorites warred with my inclination to champion the downtrodden. I found myself saying to Timothy, "But you don't care, do you, because Aunt Nora will take you back to Raven's Chase and let you draw and paint like Grampa Stokes. You'd like that better than riding some old pony, wouldn't you, Timothy?"

The child's face glowed at being part of a conspiracy against his older brother, and he bobbed his head up and down enthusiastically.

Peter changed his mind quickly, as I knew he would. "Mama, I want to go to Raven's Chase too," he wailed.

Now even his indulgent mother was getting exasperated by his capriciousness. "But, precious, I thought you wanted to go riding with your mama?"

Before he could answer, there came another knock at the door, and the boys' nurse, Nellie, walked in. She was every mother's dream of a nurse—a plump, grandmotherly woman with huge soft arms that were made for cradling and comforting. And she loved the boys almost as fiercely as their mother. "Ah, there you are, you naughty boys, hiding from your poor old Nellie. It's time to come upstairs with me and have biscuits and hot chocolate."

Peter bolted off the sofa and rushed to her, but before Timothy slid off my lap, his sticky lips brushed my cheek, and he whispered, "Please don't cry any more, Aunt Nora. It makes me sad when you do." And he scampered off to join Nellie and his brother.

The child's compassion touched me deeply, and my eyes filled with tears. Peter could be an irritating, aggressive child whose main concern was getting his own way by fair means or foul. Timothy, however, wanted people to like him, and even at such an early age was developing compassion and empathy for others that would guarantee him admiration and approval.

Amabel said, "Will you please excuse me for a moment, Nora? I must discuss something with Nellie." And she followed them out into the hall, closing the door behind her.

As I sat alone in the too-silent drawing room, listening to the loud, monotonous ticking of the clock on the mantel, I wondered what I ever would have done during this time of deep sorrow had it not been for Amabel, her husband, Colin, and their two lively children. I first met Lady Amabel Gerrick five years ago, in 1863, when I came down to Devonshire to be her hired companion, and, at that time, I did not like her very much, finding her to be spoiled, self-centered, and occasionally cruel. Later, when I married her oldest brother, Mark, and she wed Colin Trelawney, we became neighbors. Instead of taking his wife and son back to Australia, where he had made his fortune some years before, Colin bought a piece of Gerrick land not far from Raven's Chase and built his adored Amabel a small replica of her family's ancestral home. She was delighted with it and named it the Little Chase. Being a mere ten minutes away, the Trelawneys and Gerricks were constant visitors, especially when more children came, and a close, strong bond grew between our two families.

Of course, from the day we met, Amabel and I have never enjoyed a smooth friendship, for we are both too strong-willed for that. She has mercurial moods and a volatile temper, and I am often blunt and outspoken when I think I'm right, qualities that do not make for a placid relationship. But, despite our differences, I like to think we are loyal, dependable friends.

Even now, as I waited for her to return, I feared what I had to say would strain that friendship once again.

When she came back, she smiled apologetically. "I hope the boys weren't too rowdy for you."

"Please, Amabel, I'm not some ninety-year-old maiden aunt who must be indulged and coddled. I can't tolerate silence these days. Lots of noise and laughter are what I need."

Amabel didn't say a word as she seated herself on the sofa once again, and, as usual, I couldn't help but admire her beauty. She was still lithe and slender, with silky golden hair that had never darkened with age, and wide, innocent eyes of a deep blue. Her skin was a flawless peaches and cream, and her features were delicate and well-proportioned. In her stylish mourning dress of jet-trimmed black crepe, and a matching cap of black lace, Amabel had an appealing vulnerability that made her even more beautiful, if that was possible. From the cradle, she had learned how to use that beauty to charm, disarm, and ultimately get what she wanted. Peter was certainly like her in that respect.

Like most people, I found it difficult to deny her anything or to be firm, when necessary. But I would not let her beauty sway me this time. I took a deep breath and folded my hands primly in my lap. "Amabel," I began, "there is something I must say to you, though I doubt you will find it pleasant."

Her eyes sparkled as they widened in mock horror. "Oh, I recognize that stern, hired companion tone of yours, Nora. What have I done this time?"

"Please, Amabel, this is quite serious." After she composed

her face, I took a deep breath and plunged right in. "I hope you won't take offense at what I'm about to say, but I think you are far too indulgent with the boys, especially Peter. And I'm worried about the way he abuses Timothy. He constantly criticizes and belittles him, and is always pushing him down or punching him or making him cry. You saw how Peter treated him just a few minutes ago. As much as I love Peter, his behavior makes me angry. And yet you refuse to put a stop to it."

Amabel just smiled benignly and dismissed my concern with a shrug. "All brothers fight, Nora. I'd be worried if they didn't. It's part of growing up, that's all."

"That's just an excuse absolving yourself," I retorted. "I would hate to see Peter turn into a friendless bully, and if Timothy feels his brother is your favorite, he'll grow up resenting him."

"As Mark resented Damon and me?" she snapped.

I nodded and waited for the explosion, but, surprisingly, none came. Actually, I would have preferred Amabel to lose her temper, for then her anger would evaporate almost as quickly as the mist on the moors. It was when she didn't get angry that I worried, and wondered what scheme was hatching behind those innocent blue eyes.

She was not angry now as she rose to pace the room, circling the sofa with quick, nervous steps. "I will admit that what you say is true, Nora. I know I do indulge Peter. But do you know why?"

"No, I don't," I replied, with customary bluntness.

"Because he's the one who will have the least in life," she explained, coming to a halt before me.

I leaned back and gave her a quizzical look, for I did not understand. "How can you possibly say that? Peter has everything a child could want—loving parents and relatives, a happy home, every material comfort. If anything, he has *too* much."

"Peter's illegitimate," she reminded me, "and even though his father and I are now married, as far as the law is concerned, he is still illegitimate. Oh, of course Colin has seen to it that the

7

boys will divide the Trelawney fortune equally, but Peter can't claim his Gerrick birthright because of his illegitimacy. As you know, with Mark and Gabriel . . . gone, the title passes to Damon."

I thought of the Honorable Damon Gerrick, my husband's mad younger brother, and sighed in despair as I shook my head.

Amabel nodded and seemed to read my thoughts as she said, "There's no question of Damon ever marrying, of course, so when he dies, my eldest son should become the sixth Earl of Raven and inherit Raven's Chase. But, since Peter's illegitimate, that means Timothy will inherit instead. So, for all intents and purposes, my younger son has all the rights of a firstborn. How do you think Peter's going to feel when he grows up and realizes that he's the one who should inherit Raven's Chase, but can't, because of an accident of birth? He has all the attributes of a firstborn—he's bright, aggressive, a leader—and yet, he'll have to step aside for Timothy someday."

Since I came from a solid, though somewhat unconventional, middle-class background, I was always forgetting how important such matters as titles and inheritances were to people like Amabel, a member of an old, titled Devonshire family. Though she no longer used her own title out of deference to her commoner husband, Amabel was still quite conscious of the privileges of rank, especially for her children. They were Gerricks by blood.

I shook my head. "All of that is years away. Perhaps it won't matter to Peter at all." In fact, I almost said, "I think it matters more to you than anyone," but I wisely held my tongue for once.

She looked down her patrician nose at me. "He's a Gerrick. It *will* matter to him. That's why I tend to spoil Peter, to make up for the loss of his birthright."

"It will only matter to him if you constantly remind him of what he will lose," I insisted. "I think you'll wind up hurting both of your children in the long run, Amabel."

Now the long-awaited explosion came, bright and fierce. "I

don't care what you think, Lady Raven!" she said with such vehemence that the jet beads on her bodice jumped and sparkled. "Peter is my son, and I shall raise him as I see fit!"

Scowling and sullen, she stalked over to the window, her head held high and her back stiff with anger. Suddenly, her mood changed, and it was as though the sun had pierced through storm clouds to spread its golden warmth across the land. "Colin's back from Plymouth," she announced breathlessly.

And without another word or a glance at me, she gathered her skirts and went running from the drawing room like an excited schoolgirl.

Minutes later, she returned, calm and smiling, on her husband's arm.

My brother-in-law was a slight young man, just as fair as his adored wife, but with a short, sandy beard that made him look much older than his twenty-nine years. While not physically imposing, he had a core of iron that gave him great spiritual strength. When all about him were falling apart, Colin managed to remain level-headed and strong. He was our anchor, our guiding star, and we always depended on him in times of adversity and sorrow.

He came toward me, his arms extended. "Good morning, Nora. How are you?"

I fought back the tears as I went to him and kissed him on the cheek. "As well as can be expected, under the circumstances."

He squeezed my hands, warming them. "I'm pleased to hear it. We worry about you, you know."

"There's really no need," I replied.

Amabel went to ring for tea, while we went to our seats. "And how was Plymouth?" I asked. "Is everything well with the Raven Line?"

Colin flipped back the tails of his black coat and seated himself on the sofa. Then he scowled. "I don't really know."

My brows rose in surprise at the baffled tone in his voice.

9

Colin had been managing my affairs since Mark's death, and when it came to finances, he was usually so decisive.

"Oh, the ships are fine," he hastily assured me, "but I heard something disturbing down at the docks."

"Well, don't keep us in suspense," Amabel admonished him as she sat down by his side and reached for his hand.

"Discreet inquiries are being made concerning the Raven Line and the information sought is quite detailed—the number and condition of the ships, tonnage capacity, profits, losses, that sort of thing—the kind of information a prospective buyer would want to know."

"Buyer!" I cried in alarm, going rigid. "I'd never sell my interest in the Raven Line. Why, Mark built that company from nothing, he—"

"I know, Nora, I know," Colin said gently, to soothe me. "No one is suggesting you sell. I'm just telling you that someone is making inquiries, that's all."

At that moment, a maid entered with the silver tea service, Royal Worcester cups, and a lardy cake, set them on the table, then left. While Amabel poured, Colin and I continued our discussion.

"Have you consulted with John Belding about this?" I asked. John was Mark's trusted, capable partner, and he handled all the business affairs from the London office.

Colin nodded. "I sent him a telegram at once, but John knew nothing, surprisingly, so I made further inquiries of my own in Plymouth. I did learn the interested party is none other than Drake Turner."

I could feel the blood drain from my cheeks. "Not Drake Turner!"

Colin nodded solemnly. "I'm afraid so."

I rose and pressed my palms to my cold face, trying to control the hysteria I felt was imminent. "I never met the man, but Mark spoke of him often, and not in congenial terms. They were bitter rivals. Colin," I begged, "Turner must not be allowed to buy the Raven Line. Mark would never forgive me for letting that happen. You must promise me, Colin!"

He came to my side and took my arm, his strength flowing into me. "Don't worry, Nora. All you have to do is refuse to sell."

Relief at such a simple solution overwhelmed me, and I murmured shakily, "Of course," as I sank back into my chair and accepted the proffered teacup from Amabel. Then I said to Colin, "Would you advise our solicitors to be on the alert, if he should approach them, and notify me at once?"

Colin nodded. "Of course."

That out of the way, Amabel spent the next fifteen minutes regaling her husband with tales of his sons' latest escapades. He beamed in approval when he heard of Timothy's progress with his lessons, such as they were, but scowled in disappointment when he learned Peter had run away from Nellie again, hiding in the hayloft above the stables for several hours, giving everyone a fright.

"I shall have to have a talk with that boy," he said sternly. Unlike his indulgent wife, Colin was a formidable and impartial paterfamilias.

I decided now was the time to make my announcement, so I set down my teacup and folded my hands. "Colin, I've already told Amabel this, but now I must tell you. I'm leaving Raven's Chase. I've decided to go to London for a while, perhaps even Paris or Vienna, wherever the mood takes me."

Two identical pairs of blue eyes stared at me in silence and dismay. Finally, Colin said, "I'm sorry to hear that, Nora. We think of you as a member of our family, and it's not the same when you're not here. There's nothing we can say that will change your mind?"

"Nothing," I replied. "My mind is quite made up."

"Where will you stay?" Amabel wanted to know. "The Mount Street house, or with your father?"

The house in Mount Street was a small but elegant gray

stone townhouse located just minutes away from Hyde Park. Mark and I had always spent part of each year there, whenever we grew weary of Devonshire's slow, rustic pace and yearned for the bustle and vitality of London, with the Royal Theatre, Regent Street shops, and evenings spent in sparkling, stimulating company with a crowd of artistic and literary friends. And as for going to live with my artist father in Chelsea . . . this was one time I didn't think we'd be good company for each other.

"Yes," I murmured, "I'll be staying at the Mount Street house."

Colin said, "We *will* see you again," and it was a statement rather than a question.

My smile was shaky as I replied, "Do you think I could bear to stay away from my two darling nephews for long?"

"Well, if Peter and Timothy are your only reasons for staying here, then you're welcome to go!" Amabel sniffed in mock indignation, but I knew she was teasing, so I laughed along in high good humor.

"When do you plan to leave?" Colin asked as he unselfconsciously slipped his arm behind Amabel.

That simple gesture of husbandly intimacy brought back painful memories, and I had to look away. "I thought I would leave next Monday."

"So soon?" Amabel asked in surprise. "It's April, and Dartmoor is so pretty in the spring, all golden and purple with the gorse and heather in bloom, and new lambs dotting the tors."

Mark had never loved the moors, with their sudden, hidden bogs and cold, impenetrable mists that could come up so suddenly, without warning. But he loved the spring because he claimed it rejuvenated him every year. Now, the thought of spending his favorite season without him intensified my grief, and the tears started to fall again, much to my embarrassment. But my black-bordered handkerchief was always ready, and I dabbed at my eyes. "I—I really must be going."

"Oh, I've upset you again," Amabel groaned. "Nora, I am

sorry. I didn't mean to say anything that would cause you pain."

"Don't apologize. It is I who should apologize to you for weeping at every little comment that causes me to remember Mark. But I just can't seem to control myself."

"You've lost your husband and son," Colin said sympathetically, rising. "You're entitled to mourn them. I'll have Simmons bring your trap around."

As usual, his strength was contagious and buoyed me. "Thank you both for being so understanding," I said, and bid them good day.

Soon I was seated in the trap, slapping old Bonnet's flanks with the reins to get her ambling down the circular drive. I turned and waved to Colin and Amabel as they stood in the doorway, arm in arm, as well matched as Darby and Joan. Then I concentrated on my short drive back to Raven's Chase.

As I approached the gate, a figure wielding a rifle sprang out of the bushes and grabbed Bonnet's bridle. Even the poor old mare, not known for her spirit, flung back her head and snorted in surprise.

"Damon!" I said sharply. "You shouldn't go leaping out at people like that. You frightened me, not to mention poor old Bonnet."

The blue eyes, so like Amabel's, were as vacant as the poor man's mind. "I can't let you pass," he said with great determination. "Cawnpore has been surrounded by sepoys, and supply wagons aren't allowed past this point. General Havelock's orders."

To listen to him, you'd swear Damon Gerrick was as lucid as I, but everyone for miles around knew his madness condemned him to relive the Indian Mutiny of over a decade ago, when, as a young soldier, he had found his fiancée butchered along with 205 other helpless women and children, their mutilated bodies thrown into a well. Since he was unstable to begin

13

with, this horrifying experience had sent him over the brink, and now his memory was frozen in that faraway place and time, refusing to budge backward or forward.

When Mark returned to England and became head of the Gerrick family, after wandering the world for several years, he committed his younger brother to a progressive private asylum called Goodehouse for a while; but once we were married, he wanted Damon to live with us at Raven's Chase, partly out of guilt for old childhood wrongs, and partly out of a sincere desire to see his brother well again. But Amabel had pleaded to have her favorite brother live with her at the Little Chase. Mark agreed.

Through the years, the best medical care on the Continent as well as England had been obtained for Damon, but all the king's horses, and all the king's men, couldn't put Damon Gerrick's mind back together again.

So now, Damon spent his days prowling around the garden or moors, shooting imaginary sepoys with his empty rifle and waylaying carriages, which he insisted were supply wagons. He was a harmless soul, who delighted in reviewing his troops— Peter and Timothy—but beyond being able to remember names, he remained locked in his own private little world and would never let anyone else in. I wondered if he would ever come out of the darkness of the past and rejoin the rest of us in the daylight of the present.

"Damon, where are you?" a sweet, trilling voice called, and I turned to see his latest nurse—a young woman with the improbable name of Angel Blessed—hurrying down the drive toward her charge.

Miss Blessed was a tall, dark Valkyrie of a woman who looked as though she could just tuck Damon under her arm and carry him away to Valhalla. But once one became accustomed to her intimidating presence, one found she was actually as kind and gentle as her name implied. Unlike her many predecessors, who had been nothing more than keepers, she treated her charge with compassion and respect and seemed to be trying to help him.

"Good morning, Lady Raven," she greeted me with a wide, white smile. "Is Damon detaining you?"

"The supply wagon isn't allowed past this point," I explained.

Her dark eyes sparkled in silent communion. "I see. Well, Damon, why don't you come with Miss Blessed? General Havelock wishes us to report to him immediately."

Damon's face brightened readily, as he let go of Bonnet's bridle to join his nurse. "General Havelock wishes to see us?"

"At once, so let's not keep him waiting, shall we?" And she led him away with a backward glance at me.

"Thank you, Miss Blessed," I called as I raised the reins and urged Bonnet on through the gates and out on the road that swung in front of the Little Chase. Once I pointed the mare toward my house, I sat back and relaxed, for she could find her way home on a pitch-black night, or in the thickest fog that Dartmoor could send rolling our way.

Ten minutes later, we slowly climbed the sharp rise in the road and the house came into view. For once, I stopped Bonnet so I could survey what had once been Mark's domain. Over to my right, I could see the gray, crumbling ruins of St. Barnabas' Abbey, the remains of a tall oriel window sharply etched against the clear April sky. I knew wild, untamed Dartmoor was lurking just beyond the wooded hill that swept away from the house in a long, lazy arc. And at the base of that hill stood Raven's Chase.

I felt my throat constrict and tears fill my eyes as I stared down at the place that had been my home. It was a grand, imposing manor house built in the early sixteenth century out of dark, weathered stone that made it appear as black and gloomy as the raucous ravens roosting beneath the eaves of those sharply pitched roofs. Even the beautiful gardens, now a cheerful profusion of yellows, reds, pinks, and blues, and the painted folly at the end of the lawn could not alleviate the oppressiveness of the place. Not long ago, just looking at Raven's Chase could cause me to shiver and draw my cloak more closely about me. But, of course, when Mark and Gabriel were alive, the Chase had no dark shadows or ghosts.

A day didn't pass without my thoughts turning to my son, Gabriel. He had been named after an old family friend, Dante Gabriel Rossetti, the Pre-Raphaelite artist and poet, but my son's artistic ability was limited to making obscure drawings with a stick in the garden's soft, muddy soil. Gabriel had his father's dark hair, my curls and amber eyes, and Grampa Stokes' round, jolly monk's face. What I wouldn't give to hear his bubbling laughter again, and feel the weight of him as I rocked him to sleep in my arms, his dark head lolling on my breast.

And as for Mark . . . I wiped my wet eyes with my sleeve, and brought the reins down on Bonnet's flanks, as the old mare started with a jerk, and trotted down the hill toward Raven's Chase, where she knew a measure of oats and a comfortable stall awaited her.

When I arrived, I went upstairs immediately to my private suite, removed my cloak and bonnet, and mulled over what Amabel had told me.

Although I disagreed with her preferential treatment of Peter, I could understand her concern for him. And I did have a soft spot for the child myself, in spite of his constant squabbles with his brother. "He will have so little in life," his mother had said. Well, if the Gerrick heritage mattered so much—and it did—then perhaps there was a way Peter could claim a greater share of it.

I flung myself down into a worn, comfortable chair, laced my fingers together behind my head, and started thinking about this problem. After a half-hour of careful deliberation, I had an idea.

Rising, I went to my desk, unlocked a drawer, and took out

my journal, a slender book of blank pages in which I could write anything I wished—the weather, something that made me angry, descriptions of people and places. Every year, Mark had given me a new one for my birthday, and this one was bound in gold-tooled maroon leather. Although I had earned a decent living as a writer before my marriage—having had several successful novels and dozens of short stories to my credit—I hadn't written anything since Gabriel's birth two years ago, being totally absorbed in the wonders of this tiny human being Mark and I had created, and watching him grow and change in so many ways with every passing day. But my journal had filled that gap, and I wrote something in it daily, faithfully recording events and impressions with an admittedly biased eye.

Now I took my pen and started writing, recounting my visit to Amabel, our heated confrontation, and her concerns for Peter. Just when I came to my plan, there came a knock on the door.

It was Fenner, my maid.

"Lunch, madam," she announced cheerfully, setting a tray down on a side table. "We have barley broth, breast of cold chicken, bread, water cake, tea . . . a lovely lunch."

"I'm not hungry, Fenner," I said, without looking up.

She would not be daunted. "But, madam, you've got to eat something, to keep up your strength. You're skin and bones as it is."

Fenner was one to accuse me of being skinny, for she herself was a tall, gangly young woman, all pointed angles of shoulder, elbow, and wrist. When she tucked in her chin and looked down her long, pointed nose, she reminded me of a pelican I had seen once at the shore. But she was fiercely protective of me—almost *too* protective—and very loyal.

"Just the soup will be sufficient," I insisted.

"As you wish," she replied with a disapproving sniff as she left me.

Now I started on my last paragraph:

I've decided to leave my nephew, Peter, my interest in the Raven Line, and the Mount Street house, in my will. Even though he'll never be the Earl of Raven, perhaps this will compensate him in some small way. Since I shall never remarry, I can think of no one more deserving. Needless to say, I shall tell no one what I've done. I wouldn't want Peter to be more spoiled than he already is.

I slipped my pen inside the journal, to mark my place, and left the book on the seat of my chair, while I turned to my lunch. The soup was hot and thick, and that's all I could force myself to eat. I was just about to pour myself a cup of tea, when someone knocked at my door.

"Come in," I called, expecting to see Fenner.

To my surprise, it was Amabel, dressed for riding in a smart black habit and hat with a narrow brim and gossamer veil. She may have been in mourning, but her clothes were expensive and retained the stylishness of her everyday wardrobe. "Why, Amabel, what a surprise."

"I'm sorry to interrupt you, Nora," she said apologetically, tapping her crop against her gloved palm, "especially since you just left the Little Chase. But Peter has started jumping Star today, and he is so proud of himself, he insisted his Aunt Nora come see him ride."

If Peter wanted me to see him ride, then his mother was going to ensure that he got his wish. But I didn't mind the interruption. "So, you've decided to let him jump after all. Well, a first jump is an important event in a young gentleman's life," I agreed with a rare laugh, as I rose. "Just let me fetch my cloak, and I'll be right with you."

And I left Amabel standing there while I disappeared into my bedroom to retrieve my cloak. Minutes later, I emerged, and we went off to witness Peter's dazzling display of horsemanship.

Late that day, after dinner, which was always sent up to me on a tray, so I could pick at it and send the leftovers back, I summoned my housekeeper, Mrs. Harkins.

A dour-faced woman whose steely eyes could spot a lazy housemaid or speck of dust from five yards away, Mrs. Harkins jingled the keys at her waist. "Yes, madam. You wished to see me?"

"Yes, Mrs. Harkins, I did." Then I told her I planned to go to London for a while.

"How long will you be away, madam?"

"Indefinitely, I expect."

"We'll miss you, madam."

I smiled, touched by the concern and respect in her voice, then added, "I especially want Lord Raven's study, and—and the nursery, locked. No one is to go into those rooms, even to clean, is that understood?"

Her steely eyes suddenly looked affronted. "Madam, those rooms have always been locked, since—" She stopped and looked away, blushing uncomfortably.

"Fine, Mrs. Harkins," I said. "I didn't mean to take your housekeeping to task, for you know we've always thought quite highly of your work here. I just wanted to be sure, that's all."

"Your instructions will be followed precisely, as always, madam."

"Thank you, Mrs. Harkins. That will be all."

When she left in a soft jingling of keys, I sat back and closed my eyes with a bleak sigh. I could picture Mark's study in my mind's eye—the huge, scarred old desk at the far end of the room, my portrait hanging nearby, "Where I can always look at it," Mark had said—and the tears flowed unbidden again. And when I thought of the nursery . . .

I bolted to my feet and poured myself a generous glass of Madeira from a bottle hidden in my desk.

True, repairmen had removed all traces of the fire, but without Garbiel . . .

I brought the glass to my lips with a shaking hand, swallowed the Madeira in two gulps, choked, and gasped. Then I hid my head in my hands and sobbed.

* * *

If Gabriel lingered in my thoughts during the day, then it was the night hours that turned them to Mark.

Each evening, when I was ready to retire, Fenner came and helped me to undress and put on my shift. She also brought me a cup of hot milk to help me sleep. I always drank it dutifully, more to please Fenner than anything, but it never helped me, for it was at night, when the house lay deep and quiet, that my longing for Mark would intensify, like some rampaging fever.

After Fenner left, I locked my door and just sat for a while in the spacious bedroom Mark and I had shared, an elegant, sensual room done in muted blues and golds that had been his before our marriage. When I eventually felt drowsy, I went to his armoire, and took out some article of clothing—a coat, usually, for the collar still contained faint traces of his spicy shaving soap—and took it to bed with me. If I closed my eyes, I could imagine Mark's long, lean body lying next to mine, and the warmth that would suddenly spring into his cold gray eyes as he reached for me.

Finally, I fell asleep with the coat in my arms. The next morning, I awoke to a lifeless, empty coat beside me, instead of my husband, and disgust at my own behavior overwhelmed me.

"You're as mad as Damon," I muttered as I put the coat back and unlocked my bedroom door, but each night, I repeated that pitiful performance, even though its comfort was so cold and fleeting.

Could I ever escape from the memories that bound me?

The week flew by, busy as I was making preparations for my departure, and, before I realized it, there was just one day left at Raven's Chase. Tomorrow morning, Fenner and I would be driven to the nearby village of Sheepstor, where we would board the train to Plymouth, and from there, it would be on to London.

That Sunday morning, after church services, Amabel, Colin, and the boys called on me to bid me farewell. It was an emotional visit, with none of us knowing quite what to say, and everyone on the verge of tears. Peter even ceased tormenting Timothy in my honor, and I was touched.

Finally, Amabel hugged me tightly and wished me well, while Colin kissed me on the cheek and promised to do his best to keep the Raven Line from being sold. It was harder for me to say goodbye to my nephews, but I somehow got through it and was soon standing at the front door, waving as their carriage disappeared down the drive.

The next morning, I rose before dawn and hastily dressed myself, for there was one more thing that had to be done before I left for London.

Young Corman, our head groom since his father, Old Corman, had died last year, was waiting for me in the stable's cobbled quadrangle. He tipped his hat gravely to me, nodded, and wished me good morning.

"The boys just wanted me to tell you that we'll all miss you, Lady Raven," he said.

"Thank them for me," I said, shivering in the cold morning air that smelled of the stableyard. "Is she ready?"

He nodded, as he rubbed his chinful of stubble. "Are you sure you want to do this, Lady Raven? I could fetch a fortune for her in Exeter, or even Mrs. Trelawney would jump at the chance to have her."

I shook my head firmly. "I want to make certain that no one ever rides her again."

He nodded, went to a stall door and came out leading a spirited black Arabian mare, who arched her neck and started prancing in defiance of the groom's tight hold on her halter.

"Odalisque," I murmured, offering her a carrot, which she accepted delicately from my outstretched hand.

She had been Mark's horse, a gift from a desert chieftain for saving his son's life. While I no longer feared horses as I once had, and was now a confident, capable rider, I was not good enough to handle this mettlesome creature, who was still full of vinegar, even though she was almost ten years old. Odalisque had never known another master and would belong to no other man. We were much alike, I thought wryly, in that respect.

So, on that cool, brisk Monday morning, our quiet trio filed out of the stableyard and started climbing up the wooded hill that led to the moors. When we reached the top, Young Corman and I panting and out of breath, the sun was poised just over the horizon, and Dartmoor a dramatic panorama as far as the eye could see. A sudden wind blew up, riffling the mare's mane and snapping through my black cloak, billowing it out behind me.

I reached up, unbuckled her halter and stepped back out of range of those sharp hooves. For a moment, the mare just stood there, regarding me strangely out of her luminous black eyes.

"Go!" I cried, slapping her shoulder. "You are free now."

She bolted then, bounding away from me with a toss of her head, before I could change my mind. She just trotted at first, but, when she realized she was actually free, she broke into a canter, running up the tor with strong, easy strides, her arched tail flying out behind her like a banner. When she reached the summit, she turned to me and reared and, for one instant, was silhouetted against the fiery, orange sun. Then she turned and disappeared down the other side.

"At least she'll improve the moor stock," Young Corman said with a smirk.

"No pony stallion will be able to come near her," I retorted with conviction, and he stopped smiling.

"I hope no one steals her," he said. "Lord Riordan has had his eye on her for years, and if he knows she's running wild on the moors . . ."

"Let him try," was my defiant retort. But I know Odalisque would be fine, just fine.

And I turned and hurried back toward the house, so I could bathe, change, and leave for London at long last.

Fenner, our mountain of luggage, and I arrived in Plymouth at ten-thirty, and, since our train wasn't due for another half-hour, we had something of a wait. So the porter piled our baggage on the platform, and my maid and I waited patiently.

There were about a dozen people at the station that morning, and several women gave me soft looks of pity, for I was heavily veiled. In my youth, I had had little use for mourning customs, thinking them barbaric and unnecessary. A year seemed like such a long time to wear unrelieved black right down to one's undergarments, and later, to switch to dreary gray and lavender. Death was so far away then, and life for the living to enjoy. Oddly enough, after Mark and Gabriel died, black comforted me, seemingly an outward expression of the deep despair I felt inside. By wearing it, I could hide, warning people to keep their distance, to leave me to my sorrow. Why, I could even weep in the middle of a crowd, and the long, black veil hid my misery from public view.

But, in spite of my camouflage, someone was noticing me, for a nervous Fenner whispered, "Madam, that gentleman over there has been staring at you most improperly for the longest time."

I needed to turn my head only slightly to see him without appearing to stare.

He was a tall man, dressed for the country in well-tailored brown tweeds that complemented his solid, broad-shouldered form. Although a round hat hid his hair, I presumed it to be the same light brown as his shaggy brows and full mustache. The man was pleasing to look at, with a fine, thin nose, prominent cheekbones, and a full lower lip of the kind that was often described as sensual. Fortunately, he was rescued from perfection by rough, pockmarked skin, the result of some inflammation as a youth perhaps, which he didn't try to conceal with a beard or whiskers, as another man might. That act of defiance intrigued me, and I studied him more closely.

I judged him to be intelligent and confident, yet there was something about him I did not like, an aloofness that discouraged closeness. This was a man who kept people at a distance until he was ready to reveal himself, and then only a little at a time. And, judging by the way he kept scowling at his pocket watch and scanning the horizon, patience was not one of his virtues.

My writer's imagination got the best of me, and I found myself wondering about him. Was he here to meet someone's train—a friend or lover, perhaps?—or waiting for the tain to take him somewhere? And why had he singled me out—a nondescript widow two years short of thirty—when there were several young, pretty women standing nearby, casting flirtatious glances in his direction?

He caught me staring, and a slight smile of amusement lifted one corner of his mouth, then he nodded at me with odious familiarity.

I felt the color rush to my cheeks, and I was thankful for my veils as I hastily turned to Fenner to ask her something inconsequential. When I looked again, the man had disappeared.

I did not see him again until we were boarding the train for London. As Fenner was reaching for the door to our reserved compartment, a resonant masculine voice said, "Allow me, madam."

I turned to come face to face with the stranger, and even through my dark veil, I could tell his eyes were an icy blue outlined by thick, dark lashes. He had the intense sort of stare that made me uncomfortable and very conscious of my appearance. I found myself wondering if my collar was crooked or a button missing at my wrist.

"Thank you," I murmured, as he swung the door open.

Strong fingers gripped my elbow, and he effortlessly steadied me while I climbed up into the train, then he assisted Fenner as well. Keeping my maid between us, I thanked him again and seated myself in the farthest corner of the compartment.

Suddenly, the man said boldly, "Do you mind if I share your compartment, ladies?"

"Of course we do!" I said rather rudely. "I reserved this compartment so my maid and I could travel in privacy."

For one awkward moment, the man looked as though he

was going to enter our compartment and just sit himself down. Then he smiled, murmured "I see," tipped his hat, and was gone.

When Fenner and I were settled, I gave a little sigh of relief as I lifted my veil and moved near the windows, where I could watch the soft, green landscape slide by, my last glimpse of Devonshire for a long time. Or so I thought.

CHAPTER

2

I stood before my bedroom window, sipping my breakfast tea and watching the banker who lived next door step into his carriage and drive off to his office in the City. Up and down Mount Street were large, well-kept homes, each housing a family and its army of servants who swept front steps and drives religiously, as though dirt were a sin, and washed windows inside and out until they gleamed and sparkled in the sun. Here, laughing, well-fed children played in spacious walled gardens under the watchful eye of a nursemaid or governess, while their stylish mamas paid leisurely afternoon calls to fellow members of their aristocratic social circle. Here, money bought peace, security, and freedom from fear.

Suddenly, a picture of another street in the East End flashed through my mind. I saw a row of unassuming terraced houses, their once-rosy brick façades faded to a muddy brown, and each surrounded by its own spiked fence that gave a false feeling of security. In some of the houses, panes were missing from upstairs windows, while paint was chipped and peeling on all the front doors. The steps were often littered with trash such as rotting apple cores carelessly tossed by passersby, and sometimes a greasy scrap of butcher's paper would become caught in the fence and flap in the breeze. In this neighborhood, hungry, hollow-eyed children tried to keep from getting run over by growlers and drays as they played unsupervised in the streets, while their haggard mothers trudged off to the factories at first light in hopes of earning a few shillings for food. Here, living in fear was a way of life, something each inhabitant accepted with a futile stoicism.

I sighed, and that street retreated into the past.

Fenner, busily setting out my clothes for the day, frowned at me and said, "What were you thinking of just then, madam, if I may be so bold to ask?"

"I was just thinking of another place where I used to live, that's all," I replied.

"You mean in Chelsea, with Mr. Stokes?"

I shook my head. "No, Fenner. New Holborn Street, in the East End, near the St. Giles rookery."

She stopped brushing lint from my dress and gave me a strange look. "The East End—that's the place the police patrol in twos during the day and never at night, isn't it? I've heard no decent folk ever go there. And if that's the case, madam, what were *you* doing *living* there?"

I didn't answer her at first, just sipped my tea, while debating whether to tell her of the tumultuous circumstances that had driven me to the shabby terraced house all those years ago. Mark's love had eradicated those deep scars of the past, so there could be no harm in satisfying my maid's curiosity.

"Would you really like to know?" I asked her. "I warn you, it's a very shocking, sordid story."

"I would be curious to hear it, madam."

"All right," I began. "You know, of course, that Lord Raven was my second husband."

"I had heard something to that effect below stairs, madam," she confessed, then added hastily, "Not that it's any of my affair, madam."

Suddenly, for the first time in years, I felt compelled to talk about my first husband, and Fenner was as good an audience as any. I was silent for a moment, to collect my thoughts, then plunged right in. "Well, I was very young and inexperienced when I first met Oliver Woburn, and so blinded by love I didn't realize he was nothing more than a ne'er-do-well and an opportunist. Once we were married, however, I discovered he was a violent man as well and would sometimes beat me, when life overwhelmed him."

"Oh, madam!" Fenner gasped, appalled.

"I stayed with him because I had convinced myself that I loved him, and he loved me, despite his rages. But, one day, he pushed me down a flight of stairs, and the fall caused me to lose our unborn child, though I myself managed to escape with only a few bad bruises." How dispassionate I could be now!

Fenner just stared at me, so I continued. "Of course, any love I had for him died along with that child, so there was no question of my staying with him after that. I left him."

"You're lucky you had your father to go back to," Fenner said.

"Ah, but I didn't. My father had disowned me for marrying Oliver, and I was forced to make my way in the world alone. I went to live in that East End house because the rent was cheap and I could support myself as a writer. I was luckier than most women in a similar situation. I had a skill and didn't have to go to a workhouse . . . or worse." I scowled at the memory as I studied my teacup's floral pattern. "And then, one day, my husband tried to force me to return to him by legally taking away my earnings as a writer."

"He didn't!"

"He most certainly did, and he had every legal right to do so. Poor Oliver was such a failure at everything he attempted, he needed me to support him, you see."

"And what happened, madam? Did you return to him?"

I found myself recalling the windy April day that Oliver had come to the house and brazenly tried to force himself on me in punishment for refusing to return as his wife. He had not succeeded, thanks to the timely intervention of a bellicose neighbor.

That same day I met Mark for the first time. I had returned from my incompetent solicitor's office, shattered and numbed by the news that all of my earnings—including the meager savings I had squirreled away for years—now legally belonged to Oliver Woburn and I was destitute. A stranger was waiting for me in my sitting room, a dark, distinguished man, with eyes as cold and gray as rainwater. He had a commanding presence and radiated wealth and power, and I think I fell under his spell from the first moment I saw him.

I smiled at my maid. "No. Lord Raven rescued me by offering me a position as Mrs. Trelawney's hired companion. Of course, she wasn't married then and was in disgrace because she had borne a child out of wedlock."

"Where is your first husband now, madam?"

"Dead," I replied quietly. Two husbands, two children. . . .

Fenner sighed audibly, obviously moved by my sorry tale. "It was fortunate you met Lord Raven."

"Yes, very fortunate indeed."

Our conversation dwindled, and she helped me into my lace-edged camisole and pantaloons of finest lawn. I was so thin I could blessedly dispense with a corset, which I considered to be an item of torture, like the iron maiden of centuries past. Once Fenner slipped a severe black walking dress over my head and buttoned it up the back, she asked to be dismissed, though a few minutes later she returned to tell me that my father was waiting downstairs to see me.

"Father!" I cried in delight when I saw his solid, bearlike figure standing in the Regency drawing room, so named for its neoclassical furniture of sixty years ago.

"Nora, girl," he said, extending his arms to me.

I rushed to give him a hug and was enfolded in his arms, his grizzled beard rough against my cheek and the faint aroma of turpentine tickling my nose.

When I stood back, I still held him and regarded him with profound love and respect. "How wonderful it is to see you. When did you return from Paris?"

"Last week," he replied. His round, monkish face was grave as he murmured, "And how are you?"

I moved away from him to hide the tears that sprang to my

eyes as I fumbled for my handkerchief. The hard knot of pain in my heart seemed to intensify, and all I could do was shrug helplessly. After several seconds, I was able to turn to him and say, "I thought time was supposed to heal all wounds, but I feel more wretched with every passing day. I feel as though I want to die, but can't."

He sighed deeply, and I knew he shared my sorrow. "Nora, I know what you're going through. Mark was like a son to me, and little Gabriel . . ." He stopped, as the words caught in his throat. "I know I should have stayed with you down in Devonshire, but I had to get away to Paris and just keep working until I thought I'd go blind. I hope you understand."

"Of course I do, Father." That was his way of dealing with grief, to escape to Paris or Vienna and paint from dawn until there was no more light. He had done that right after my marriage to Oliver Woburn.

"I felt the same way when your mother died, but, believe me, you will feel better with time."

Suddenly, I couldn't bear to discuss my loss any more. "So, tell me, Father, what are you doing here? I thought you were going to stay in Paris for the rest of the summer."

"I was," he replied, "but my—er, Muse has flown."

I chuckled at that. "What you mean is that your favorite model deserted you for another."

He giggled with an irrepressible twinkle in his eye. "I should know by now that I can't fool you, Nora, girl. I was commissioned to paint Madam Martine de Gramont's portrait and instantly fell in love with her. Poor thing . . . her husband is a stuffy wine king from Bordeaux, and she longed for a little frivolity in her circumscribed life." He sighed. "Alas, her husband suspected we were growing—er, close and whisked her away, back to his vineyard. When she left, Paris lost its glow for me, so I decided to return to London."

Stifling my laughter at my parent's amorous misadventure, I just shook my head. "Well, Madame de Gramont's loss is my gain. I am glad to see you, Father."

Suddenly, he stared at me, then held me at arm's length. I should have known I could hide nothing from his wise, experienced eyes. "Nora, girl, is anything the matter?"

I hesitated before answering, then hung my head. "Today, for the first time in years, I thought about the house in New Holborn Street, where I used to live before I met Mark."

"That's where you rented rooms after you left Woburn and we were—er, not on speaking terms."

I smiled as he blushed beneath his beard, for Ivor Stokes didn't like to be reminded of those years he had disowned me out of pique at my marriage to Oliver Woburn, whom he considered to be nothing more than a parasite, remorselessly living off women. It had never comforted him to be proved right.

I nodded. "Yes, that is where I lived."

"Whatever made you think of that place again?" he demanded, his brows raised in curiosity. "From what you told me, it was a shabby sort of place, inhabited by poor souls."

I shrugged as I turned away. "I don't know. Mark and I first met in that house. I suppose I wanted to see if I could recapture the past."

"You can't recapture it, daughter," he warned me. "The past is never quite the same country we left."

"Yes, Father," I said meekly, to force him to change the subject. Then I added, "Will you stay for breakfast? There's so much we have to talk about."

"I'd like that," he said.

So I had the cook make an omelet with tomatoes, and my father and I spent several pleasurable hours discussing art and avoiding all mention of Raven's Chase, Mark, and Gabriel. He could see I wasn't ready, and I appreciated his tact and sensitivity.

Finally, he rose and hugged me. "Remember, the Chelsea house is still your home, and you're welcome there at any time. In fact, I expect you to call soon."

"I will," I promised as I watched him walk out the door, down the front steps, and look for a hansom cab.

* * *

No sooner had my father left than faithful Fenner came stomping in, her arms laden with a long, narrow box that could contain only flowers.

I raised my brows in silent inquiry.

"For you, madam," she said unnecessarily. "A boy came to the back door with them a few moments ago."

"Who are they from?" I asked, as I lifted the lid and gasped. "Lilies . . . my favorite flower. Why, there must be two dozen of them! My father must have sent them." But when I read the card Fenner handed me, all it said was, "From an admirer."

I made a noise of consternation as I felt my cheeks grow pink. "Someone is certainly being mysterious. Well, put them in water and leave them in the drawing room, Fenner."

The lilies continued to prey on my mind as I dressed and had the carriage brought round so I could go to my solicitor's office and draw up my will, naming Peter my heir. I forgot about them while completing my business, but on the way home, they popped into my mind again. Who could have sent them? My father was the prime suspect, but perhaps Colin was the culprit. Such a gesture would certainly appeal to him, for he was a kind, thoughtful man, always thinking of the welfare of others.

"Madam," Grimes, the butler, said when I walked in the door, "there is a gentleman here to see you."

"You know I'm not receiving callers," I said flatly as I lifted my veil. "This house is still is mourning."

"It's Mr. Darwin, madam."

I brightened, for Lewis Darwin was my publisher and an old, dear friend. "Well, that is different," I said, and hurried off to the Regency drawing room.

"Lewis," I said, beaming, as I entered the room and extended my hands to him. "What a pleasant surprise."

He rose and came toward me, a trim, natty figure with a fresh pink rosebud in his lapel. "Nora, my dear, how *are* you?"

he greeted me, emphasizing certain words so that he seemed to speak in italics. "You *must* forgive me for flouting the most tiresome of conventions by coming to call on you when you're in mourning."

"Please, Lewis, don't apologize. You know you're always welcome here."

"And *shame* on you for coming to London and not calling on me *immediately*. You have *mortally* offended me and *sorely* tried our long friendship."

I knew him too well to take his words to heart, and I slipped my arm through his companionably as we strolled back to our chairs. "Oh, come now, Lewis, I refuse to believe a busy man such as yourself spent time wondering about me."

"My *dear* Nora," he admonished me severely in his raspy voice, "you *know* each and every one of my authors interests me."

What he said was true. Lewis Darwin had coddled and cajoled countless writers, both great and small, for he had a genius for discovering and developing literary talent, just as he had a talent for growing lovely hothouse roses. He had the energy of seven men, and I swore he got only five hours of sleep a night, judging by the pouches beneath his bright, lively eyes. And if a writer was down on his luck, Lewis Darwin's door and bottomless purse were always open to him.

"Well," I began, offering him a chair, "to what do I owe the pleasure of this visit? By the way, you didn't send me these lilies, did you?"

He wrinkled his nose in distaste. "Nora, *please*. How *could* you even suspect me of such a crass act? *Lilies,* indeed!"

I laughed. "So, you are not the culprit. I might have known. Do forgive me for such a lamentable lapse of judgment."

"You're forgiven," he said with a sniff, "but on *one* condition."

"And what is that?"

"That we have a *new* novel from you." His bright eyes sparkled with anticipation, and I had the feeling I was next in line for some coddling and cajoling. "You realize it has been more than *three* years since *Call of the Curlew* was published, and I think it's time your readers had another novel from you."

"Oh, the fickle public has surely forgotten me by now."

His eyes widened in genuine horror. "Forget *Nora Woburn?* Never! I *guarantee* you fame and fortune the moment we publish your new work."

As I said, Lewis Darwin is splendid for plumping up one's sagging sense of self-importance.

"Well, I did have an idea for a new novel, but when Gabriel was born, he commanded all of my attention, and I put it aside. Now . . ." My voice trailed off, and tears sprang to my eyes.

"Now you'll have the time to *finish* it," he said callously, in his raspy voice.

I dabbed at my eyes. "You may find this difficult to understand, Lewis, but I have just lost my husband and son, and I don't really feel like writing."

He reached over, grasped my hands and squeezed them tightly, until they hurt. "Nonsense. Writing is what you *need* to do now, what you *must* do. It will be your salvation, Nora."

I smiled tremulously. He was still the tyrant I remembered. "You're probably right."

"Not probably, *definitely.* I *know* I'm right," he replied, releasing me with a speculative look. "I am seldom wrong about *anything,* but *always* right when it comes to dispensing literary advice." The twinkle in his eyes took some—but not all—of the arrogance out of his words.

Then we had tea, and Lewis regaled me with choice morsels of gossip about the London literary scene, nothing ponderous, but light and frothy vignettes. Lewis was a master at providing just the type of conversation one needed, and when he was ready to leave, my spirits were considerably lighter. Thank heaven I had friends like Lewis.

I showed him to the door myself and wished him good day,

his admonitions to write ringing in my ears. Then I returned to the drawing room and looked at the lilies, wondering once again who could have sent them.

I soon regretted ever receiving the flowers—and those that followed daily for the next four days—when I learned who had sent them, and why.

The following morning, another two dozen lilies were delivered, with the same card and, at first, I was amused and flattered that someone had gone to such lengths to impress me. When still more flowers arrived the day after that, my amusement turned to irritation. There were lilies in the drawing room and lilies in the dining room. The entire house would soon be overflowing with lilies.

On the fourth day of my return to Mount Street, I was feeling particularly bereft and lonely. Mark and Gabriel were on my mind constantly, and I remained shut away in my room so I could weep unobserved.

I was sniffling into my third handkerchief when Fenner came flapping in, all elbows and wrists. "Madam, there is a Mr. Drake Turner downstairs to see you."

"Drake Turner . . . whatever on earth is he doing here?" My jaw tightened obstinately. "Tell him I'm in mourning and not receiving callers."

"He said if you refused to see him, he'd just keep calling every day until you did see him," Fenner said. "He also asked how you liked all the flowers he sent."

Oh, the man was certainly clever and shrewd. But if he thought gifts of flowers obligated me to receive him, he was mistaken, for I resented being manipulated, especially by my husband's adversary.

I rose, went to my desk and took out a sheet of black-bordered vellum, and started writing. After politely thanking him for the flowers, I nonetheless regretted I was not receiving callers. Then I signed it with a flourish and handed it to Fenner.

"Please give this to Mr. Turner."

"Yes, madam," Fenner replied, and went clopping off.

Minutes later, as I hid behind a curtain and watched from my bedroom window, Drake Turner walked down the steps and into a waiting carriage. Since I was looking down at him, I could not tell if he was short or tall, or even if I recognized him. All I could see was the top of a hat and broad shoulders.

But why was I left with the uneasy feeling I had seen the man somewhere before?

True to his word, Mr. Turner called daily, like his flowers, and was dutifully turned away, as promised. This game of cat and mouse continued for a week, and I was beginning to wonder when the man would give up. But, as I was later to learn, Drake Turner never gave up, especially when he wanted something.

One morning, after watching Mr. Turner trot down my front steps for the sixth time, I took pen and paper in hand and went out to the walled garden to write Amabel a letter. I was feeling somewhat guilty, for I had been in London a month and had not yet written her a letter, though I had received one from her. The day was one of those delightful May days poets rhapsodize about—not too warm, with a bright blue sky overhead and a profusion of flowers growing in beds and climbing up walls. I seated myself, cushioned by pillows, with a wool rug spread across my lap, and started to write. After a few moments, a great weariness overcame me. I tired so easily these days, probably because I found such blissful oblivion in sleep, a blessed respite from pain and grief. I leaned my head back and closed my eyes.

Minutes—hours?—later, a sudden noise jarred me out of my rest. I opened my eyes just in time to see a man drop down from my high garden wall and land on his feet noiselessly, with cat-like grace. Then he straightened, caught me staring at him, and smiled.

It was the man from the Plymouth train station.

He removed his round hat, revealing light brown hair streaked with golden lights that caught the sun. "Good morning,

Countess Raven," he said, his voice the pleasant tenor I recalled from our one meeting. "You are a most elusive creature." Then he stopped, paused, and added, "I am Drake Turner."

For a moment, I was so overcome by the man's daring, I could only gape at him. Then I found my tongue and quickly rose. "What impertinence! You were told I am in mourning, Mr. Turner, and not receiving callers. And even if I were, I wouldn't receive you! Now, will you please depart the way you came in?"

He frowned in dismay, but his pale blue eyes were laughing as he looked back at the wall. "That will be impossible, I'm afraid. Unless, of course, you propose to hoist me up?"

I did not smile at his feeble attempt at humor. "I will have one of the men bring you a ladder," I retorted, turning and starting for the house.

But Drake Turner was a persistent man and hurried after me. "Please, Countess . . ."

"I prefer to be called Mrs. Gerrick."

"Mrs. Gerrick, I apologize for my brashness, but I must speak with you, and since you have repeatedly refused to see me, you surely cannot blame me for taking such drastic measures."

"And surely you cannot blame me for not receiving you. Mr. Turner, I don't know why my husband disliked you so intensely, but he did. I am also assuming that you did not like him, either. So, since you both disliked each other, why do you have the effrontery to come to his house and accost his widow in his garden? You can't really expect me to welcome you under the circumstances. And then to try to flatter me with flowers. . . ."

Mr. Turner looked as though he were quickly revising his opinion of me. "But most women adore flowers."

"I am not most women, Mr. Turner. Good day." And I started walking up the flagstone path.

Suddenly, I felt a detaining hand on my arm and whirled around, furious at his familiarity. "Mr. Turner!"

"Please, Mrs. Gerrick. All that you say is true. Lord Raven

and I were bitter rivals in commerce, and not always—shall we say—cordial to each other. And I agree that it is quite presumptuous of me to come here, expecting you to receive me." His arm dropped. "But I wouldn't go to such great lengths to see you if it weren't important."

I know I should have stood firm and called for a footman to remove Mr. Turner forcibly from my garden, but I must confess I am always moved by men who have a boyish wistfulness about them, and the expression on Drake Turner's face was so crestfallen that I couldn't fail to be softened.

"Very well. Forgive my rudeness, Mr. Turner," I said reluctantly. "Please come inside and we'll talk."

His wide grin transformed him. "Thank you, Count—Mrs. Gerrick."

As he followed me through the back entrance toward the Regency drawing room, I could see him glancing into open rooms with their fine furnishings, paintings, and other art objects Mark and I had collected together over the years. "You have a beautiful home, Mrs. Gerrick," he said, those sharp eyes missing nothing.

After I thanked him, we entered the Regency drawing room, and I rang for tea. "I recognize you as the man who assisted me into the train in Plymouth, but I didn't know who you were." I indicated a chair, then seated myself across from him.

"If I recall correctly, you gave me no opportunity to introduce myself," he said. "You informed me quite matter-of-factly that you preferred your privacy."

"I am not in the habit of sharing my train compartment with strangers, Mr. Turner," I said coldly. "And if I had known who you were at the time, that refusal would have given me even greater satisfaction."

His mustache twitched just before he smiled. "As much as your husband and I disliked each other—"

"Not dislike, Mr. Turner. Hatred. It is not too strong a word in this case, I assure you."

"Hated, then," he agreed amiably. "As much as Lord Raven and I hated each other, I would not wish death on anyone. You have my condolences, Mrs. Gerrick. And as for the loss of your son—"

I thanked him quickly, before my eyes could fill with tears, and said, "Now, Mr. Turner, what did you wish to discuss with me?"

"I think you already know."

I gave him a level look. "You wish to buy the Raven Line."

"Yes, and I'm prepared to pay—" And he named a figure that made me gasp.

Nonetheless, I replied, "But I don't wish to sell my share, Mr. Turner. My husband started that company with only one ship, and he left it to me in trust. And, even if I did decide to sell, I would never sell it to you."

The icy blue eyes grew crafty, and colder. "You are brutally frank, madam."

"It's one of my many faults."

"So, you must keep your husband's company out of his rival's hands at all costs."

"At last we understand each other, Mr. Turner."

"And tell me. Do you plan to run it yourself?"

I smiled sweetly, refusing to be baited. "You don't think a woman is capable of running a shipping line?"

"Most women, no," he said candidly. "But then, from what I've learned about you, Mrs. Gerrick, you are not a conventional woman."

He was right. I did consider myself different from other women—not superior to them, merely unconstrained by the conventions that still bound members of my own sex. But I saw through Mr. Turner's ruse instantly. "More flattery, sir?" I snapped. "I should have thought you had learned your lesson."

"I was not trying to flatter you, Mrs. Gerrick, merely to state what is apparent to me."

"I like to think I know my limitations, so I leave the management of the company to John Belding, my late husband's partner, and Colin Trelawney, my brother-in-law. Both men are quite capable, and I trust them implicitly."

"I see." He did not look disappointed, as I thought he might, merely frustrated, like a man suddenly confronted with a fallen tree in the middle of the road.

"I'm sorry, Mr. Turner," I said, "but I have no wish to sell the Raven Line for any price. I fear you have wasted all of your efforts."

"The company of an interesting woman is never a waste of time, Mrs. Gerrick," he said, his eyes shining with such intensity that I suddenly felt uncomfortable even in my own home.

I was spared the necessity of replying by the entrance of a maid bearing the Spode tea service and a freshly baked apricot tart sliced into thick wedges. I thanked her, and when the girl left, I began to pour. That simple, gracious act of pouring tea always relaxed me, and I found I was even mellowing toward my adversary.

"The lilies are lovely," I commented as I passed him a cup and slice of tart. "Who told you they are my favorite flower?"

"But I know everything about you, Mrs. Gerrick," he said cryptically, without really answering my question.

"Oh, I doubt that, Mr. Turner," I replied, trying not to let him see how much he had disconcerted me.

He tasted the apricot tart. "A commendable attempt," was his pronouncement, "but the crust is a trifle tough and the filling not sweet enough."

I stared at him, dumbfounded. Good manners dictated that he should say something complimentary about what had been served, even if he didn't find it acceptable. "You are a culinary expert, sir?" I asked, my brows rising in irritation.

"Far from it, Mrs. Gerrick, but I do like to dine well, and feel good food is one of life's greatest pleasures. I shall have Antoine, my French chef, bake you the perfect apricot tart and send it to you tomorrow."

"I'm sure my cook will be mortified to learn she has baked

a less than perfect apricot tart," I muttered sarcastically, still awed by the man's rudeness.

"She should be," he retorted in earnest, setting his plate down, the tart barely touched. "Everyone should do his job well, or find another occupation, one at which he can excel."

He had finally silenced me, for there was a germ of truth in what he said.

After draining his cup, he murmured, "The tea, however, is excellent." Then he rose, obviously in a hurry to leave my presence, since he could not get what he wanted. "Well, then, Mrs. Gerrick, I shan't waste any more of your time. It was a pleasure meeting you, at long last. Thank you for receiving me."

Then he took my hand and drew it to his lips before I had the chance to pull it away. Once again, his touch made me shiver. As I watched him stride out of the drawing room, I had the feeling I had not seen the last of Drake Turner.

Screams of terror filled my bedchamber, waking me instantly. As I sat up in bed, my wide eyes darting around the darkened room in search of danger, I realized the screams had come from deep within me, not some external lurking menace. My skin felt cold and clammy with sweat, and my nightgown as damp as a wash towel. Though my heart was hammering against my ribs and my fingers were trembling, I managed to light the lamp by my bedside and fell back against the pillows in relief as its comforting light revealed only the familiar, friendly shapes of furniture in the room. Then I started shivering, so I rose, changed into a dry nightgown and crawled back beneath the covers, where I drew my knees to my chest and confronted what had terrified me so.

It had been a nightmare, of course, the same kind that had recurred since Mark's and Gabriel's deaths. In this one, I was running toward Raven's Chase, but as I approached the heavy oak door, Colin, Amabel, my father, Fenner, and even Oliver were reaching for me, seeking to restrain me. I could feel their cold fingers clutch and tear at my dress, like branches in a forest, but I pushed them away and ran inside, where no one followed. As I started up the familiar horseshoe staircase, my legs felt so heavy I could barely lift them. I moved with agonizing slowness, though I knew I must move faster if I was to save my husband and son from some nameless terror. Finally, I was able to reach the corridor that led to the nursery, but it suddenly filled with smoke, forcing me back. That's when I started screaming—when I realized I would never reach them in time.

Shivering as I lay huddled there, I squeezed my eyes shut to block out the nightmare, and when I opened them, there were fresh tears on my cheeks. My shaking hand poured a glass of water from the pitcher on my nightstand, and I drank it down. Then I rose, wrapped myself in the coverlet from the bed, and sat in the chair near a window overlooking the silent, deserted street.

I know it may be an odd admission for a bereaved widow and mother, but I tried not to think about my husband and son, not out of callousness, but because I couldn't bear the anguish. Often I didn't succeed, because love always won, and tonight was no exception. Tonight I saw Mark as clearly as if he were standing by my side, his tall, lean frame, dark, brooding countenance, and cold eyes that always warmed at the sight of me. Then Gabriel appeared, his chubby baby's face alive with mischief, his smile so radiant it could break your heart.

"Why?" I cried out to them, wounded and betrayed. "Why did you leave me?"

But neither answered, and they gradually faded away.

I cried again, my tears falling into the coverlet, and finally I slept. This time, there were no more dreams.

The next morning, I had only a cup of milky tea for breakfast, which earned me Fenner's pelican stare and a disapproving sniff, but I ignored her as usual, ordered a carriage brought round, and went for a ride in neighboring Hyde Park.

When I returned, one of the maids produced a wicker basket covered with a crisp, white linen cloth and said it had been delivered just moments ago. I had to smile as I read the enclosed card: "You'll see there is no comparison. Drake Turner."

Inside was the promised apricot tart, its smooth golden surface and aroma indicating it had been freshly baked.

I had the maid take it to the kitchen for slicing, and when she returned, I sampled Antoine's creation. While food is not one of my overriding passions, I had to admit the pastry was delicious, and superior to what my cook had prepared yesterday.

As I brushed the crumbs from my lips, I couldn't help but recall Drake Turner's visit and his generous offer for the Raven Line. I knew, if I sold out and invested the money wisely on the Exchange, it would provide me with a handsome, independent income for the rest of my life. But there were many things in life more important to me than money or security.

Tiring of thinking about Mr. Turner, I rose and went to the study to try to work on the novel I had started before Gabriel's birth, for I knew the determined Lewis Darwin wouldn't rest until I had something to show him. Perhaps all of my old friend's coddling and cajoling would work miracles once again.

I worked diligently through lunch and into the early afternoon, and when I emerged from the study, I had a great feeling of accomplishment. My scolding, demanding Lewis was right, as usual. Work was what I needed. I felt better than I had in months, and I decided a visit to my father was in order. So I put on my veil and ordered the carriage brought round once again.

My father's resi-
dence in Chelsea, in Upper Cheyne Row, is the house I grew up
in, a homey, whitewashed building with an outrageous green
front door visible from down the street, and cheery red gera-
niums growing in flower boxes beneath the windows on the
ground floor.

When I alighted from the carriage and tried the front door,
I was not surprised to find it unlocked, for Ivor Stokes was a
trusting man—too trusting—and liked to make his many friends
feel welcome. So there was usually a steady parade of people
coming and going at odd hours, day and evening.

As I entered the foyer and placed my gloves on the long,
battered table, I could hear loud voices and laughter coming
from the parlor. I had barely thrown back my veil before a
foppish young man holding a glass of wine came sauntering out
of the parlor and down the hall toward me.

"Hello there, miss," he said pleasantly. "Thought I heard
someone come in." Then he squinted at my black gown. "I say,
are you going to a funeral?"

"I am in mourning," was my reply.

The young man's face fell. "Oh. Sorry. But, do come in.
We're a cheery bunch in here, so I'm sure we'll lighten up your
spirits in no time at all."

"I'm Nora Gerrick," I said, as I followed him into the parlor. "I'm Ivor's daughter."

The young man looked at me in astonishment. "Ivor's daughter? I say! Didn't know he had one!"

Another young man appeared and said, "Severn, you dolt!" in a high, squeaky voice. "You know Ivor's got a daughter. You've seen his sketches of her enough."

Severn reflected on the matter for a moment, then said, "Yes. Quite right." Then he bowed to me. "Do forgive me. It's the claret. Always fuzzies the old brain a bit."

The gathering in the parlor was enough to give a proper matron an attack of the vapors, but typical of my father's free and bohemian household. Judging by the empty wineglasses and cigars scattered about, the two young men, barely out of their teens, were smoking and drinking in the presence of two young, beautiful—and unchaperoned—women. One, dark and dainty, held a stereoscope in her hand, and the other was lounging—there was no other word to describe her pose—on the sofa and fanning herself with a Japanese fan. Well, everyone knew artists were loose and immoral, so I should not have been surprised by their behavior.

The second young man took my hand and bowed over it. "Mrs. Gerrick, it is an honor to meet you. My name is Beeton, Kevin Beeton. You've met Severn here, and that's Louisa, the one with the stereoscope, and that's Marigold, who is shy."

Louisa nodded, and Marigold gave me a fleeting smile, her eyes downcast.

"Won't you join us?" Severn asked in his Oxford drawl.

"I would love to, but I haven't much time and I must see my father. He is here, isn't he?"

Beeton nodded, and said, "Upstairs, in the studio," in a reverential tone that would have made my father giggle.

I smiled and thanked them all, then left them alone to their claret, cigars, and laughter, and went upstairs.

As I hurried down the upstairs corridor to the closed door at the far end of the hall, I could smell the turpentine already, a familiar, pervasive odor that brought back many fond memories of my childhood. I remembered sitting quietly for hours on a high stool, watching my father work, and his lovely models would often smile or wink at me when he wasn't looking, then compose their faces just in time as he turned back. Thus inspired, I would run downstairs and attempt to sketch my mother, seated among her plants in the conservatory, quietly writing in her journal. As much as I yearned to be an artist like my father, it was my mother's literary leanings that I inherited.

This house held such pleasant, cherished memories that my black mood lifted for the first time in months, and I felt genuinely happy as I knocked, heard my father's gruff, "Come in. The door's open," and went inside the spacious, airy studio, flooded with bright light from the skylight overhead.

"Nora, girl," he said, his eyes shining as he looked up. "Calling on your old father, are you?"

I nodded. "I had the urge to have a whiff of turpentine again."

He giggled, an odd, feminine laugh for such a large man. "Well, it's good to see you out and about. You look positively radiant."

"Who could be anything but happy in your house, Father?" I replied, wandering around the room, inspecting the paintings he had done while in Paris.

He beamed. "I'm pleased this house holds such pleasant memories for you." Then he scowled and added, "Are my devoted followers still downstairs?"

I laughed at that. "Yes, and Marigold and Louisa appear to be enjoying themselves to the hilt, I might add. Who are they?"

"The boys are Oxford students escaping the rigors and tedium of academe to worship at the feet of the Great One." He rolled his eyes heavenward to deflate the vain, pompous words, then said, "I sense they're disappointed in me, though. I think they expect me to sleep in a coffin, or wear only green, or steal wild animals from the Zoological Gardens and bring them

46

home. Don't they realize one can still be an artist without behaving like a Bedlamite?"

"And the women . . . are they Oxford students as well?" I asked innocently.

"Nora, I'm surprised at you. You know they don't allow women to take degrees there." My father's round face reddened in guilt. "They're here, to, er—study other subjects with me." And he giggled.

"They look like apt pupils," was my only comment.

"Oh, most apt," he assured me.

I started prowling around the studio and discovered one painting tucked away in a corner, a depiction of John Keats' *Lamia,* complete with the hideous serpent-woman herself. I held it up and blew on it, to disperse the film of dust that dulled and coated its shiny surface.

"This is ancient and so gruesome," I muttered with a grimace, "it must be from your Pre-Raphaelite period."

My father actually looked sheepish. "One of these days I'll throw the damn thing out, because no one of taste and refinement would buy it." He shook his head in wonder at his own folly. "I can't believe I used to paint like that. Whatever possessed me?"

In the early days of his career, my father had been a devoted Pre-Raphaelite and one of Dante Gabriel Rossetti's closest friends. But several years ago, they had had an artistic and philosophical parting of the ways. My father had grown weary of painting "posed illustrations," as he called them, and instead turned to painting portraits and street scenes, saying he preferred to paint people and where they lived as they really were, not some mystical, mythical ideal. Today, he was in greater demand than ever and enjoyed a large measure of success, which I felt he richly deserved. Yet he always feared the corrupting influence of money and continued to live simply.

As I circled the room and came up behind him, I could see he was working on a portrait now. It was a huge canvas, and the subject was just lightly sketched in with charcoal. My father's method was to study his subject for hours, make dozens of detailed sketches and notes, then take them back to his studio and make a final sketch on canvas. Later, he would have the subject come to the studio once or twice for a sitting, to get the colors and lighting right.

Now, looking at this canvas, I had the strangest feeling that I had seen its subject somewhere before.

"May I see your sketches?" I asked.

"They're on the table," he muttered, without taking his eyes off what he was doing.

I went to the table, which was strewn with sketches, and picked one up. It showed a man standing with his hand resting negligently on a large globe, and a fat, furry cat at his feet. In the left-hand corner, part of a desk was visible, its top crammed with a half-rolled map, spyglass, and sextant. The large window that illuminated him overlooked a calm ocean and a three-masted sailing ship far in the distance. My father's sketch was so finely detailed, I could even make out the pockmarks on the man's face.

"Drake Turner," I muttered, flinging the sketch down in disgust.

Now my father did stop and look up at me. "Do you know him?"

"Know him? Of course I know him!" I had gone gray with anger. "Father, why didn't you tell me you accepted a commission from him?"

"Judging from that murderous glint in your amber eyes, I would say you don't like the man."

"That, Father, is an understatement." And I told him what I knew about the bad blood between the man and my husband.

When I finished, he stroked his beard and said, "If I had known how you felt about him, I never would have accepted his commission."

I dismissed his misgivings with a brusque wave of my hand. "Don't worry yourself, Father. What's done is done." I thought

48

for a moment, then added, "But tell me, what *do* you think of him?"

"What do I think of Drake Turner?" My father took a step back from his canvas, studied it for a moment with his head cocked to the side, then looked at me. His round monk's face twisted into an expression of bewilderment, as though he couldn't quite make up his mind. Then he scratched his chin with the end of his paintbrush. "You know I'm an easy man to get along with, an affable fellow who likes everyone—excluding your first husband, of course—until they do something reprehensible and fall from my high esteem." He shook his head slowly. "But I don't like Drake Turner, and I don't really know why. I just looked at the man and did not warm to him."

Now my curiosity overwhelmed me. "Did he later do anything to justify your initial feeling of dislike?"

"Well, he seemed a little too self-assured and proud of his wealth, but then, I suppose all of these merchant princes are that way. He was charming, smooth, and put me at my ease right away. But . . ." And he could not finish.

"But what, Father?" I demanded impatiently.

"But what disturbed me were his incessant questions about you, Nora. At first, I thought he was just making polite conversation while he posed for the sketches, so—being the proud papa that I am—I told him all about my daughter, the writer. I can't recall, but I may have mentioned you were a widow now, and how pleasant Raven's Chase was to visit." He frowned again. "But then he started to ask quite personal questions about your first marriage to that parasite. That's when I began to suspect his motives, and I began talking of other things. Minutes later, he'd start asking questions about you all over again. Finally, he could see I was becoming annoyed, so he stopped. I was on the verge of telling him to find someone else to paint his portrait."

Drake Turner had told me, "I know everything about you," and this was where he had learned, from my own father. Oh, the man was clever, all right.

Father turned his attention back to his canvas but continued speaking to me while he worked. "Turner seems to be the calculating sort who never does anything unless it's according to some plan. And from what you just told me about his hating Mark and wanting to buy the Raven Line, he probably sought to learn all he could about you to be better prepared to win you over."

"That he could even entertain the smallest notion of winning me over is surely a sign of his supreme arrogance," I muttered tartly.

"I assume you're not going to sell."

"Never," I said flatly. "That would have been Mark's wish."

"Good. It will probably be a pleasant change for Mr. Turner not to get something he wants so very badly." Father giggled at that thought. "Then you plan to run the company yourself?"

My knowledge of ships and sailing was so scant it could barely fill the head of a pin. "No, but John Belding has enough expertise to run it for both of us."

"A wise decision, Nora, girl, a wise decision."

I folded my arms and walked around the room, trying to concentrate on a plan of action for dealing with Mr. Turner. Finally, I stopped and turned to my father. "Is there anything else you can tell me about him? Anything at all would be of enormous help."

He hesitated for a moment, as though gathering his thoughts. "Well, his Grosvenor Street house is furnished expensively, though not ostentatiously. I would say he has the Frenchman's passion for good food—he even introduced me to his chef, Antoine, by the way—the opera, horses. . . . Oh, yes, and books. He's read yours, you know."

That disarmed me momentarily. "He has?"

"You'll be distressed to hear he said he learned a great deal about you from your books."

I groaned in dismay at that revelation.

"He also owns this huge black cat named Faust, after some

opera or other. This is the creature," Father said, tapping the cat's unfinished sketch with the end of his brush, then using it to scratch his chin again. "Turner is such a deplorably masculine sort—the kind of man the ladies always swoon over and chase in droves—" he added with just a touch of envy in his voice. "There's nothing soft or feminine about him, and yet he prefers a woman's pet. I thought it rather odd."

"Oh, Mr. Turner is just a study in contradictions," I muttered waspishly.

Always willing to find some admirable quality in even the blackest villain—except Oliver Woburn—my father added, "But I will say one thing for the man. He paid me in advance for this portrait, and you yourself know there are not many who are willing to do that. He said those who do their job well should be compensated for it. It's probably the only thing we agree on," he added with a sniff.

He wiped his brush, leaving a stripe of burnt umber paint on the rag, then gave me a long, level look. "Have you seen a doctor lately, Nora?"

I shook my head. "I'm fine, Father, really."

"Well, you're a grown woman, and I can't tell you what to do, but I think you should see one. You're so thin a good strong wind would blow you away, and those circles under your eyes . . ."

"They'll soon rival Lewis Darwin's," I said with a laugh. Then I went to my father, put my arms around him and gave him a hug. "Thank you for your concern, Father. I appreciate it."

"You are the most important person in my life, Nora."

"And you are the most important person in mine."

Then we said our goodbyes, and I left.

Mr. Turner called on me the next day, to charm me into selling, but I refused to see him and had Grimes give him a terse note thanking him for the apricot tart.

He returned to my doorstep every day for three more days,

but I remained adamant and would not receive him. I spent my days inside, writing, lest he make another attempt to drop in on me from my garden wall.

Yet four days after I had visited my father, I received the biggest surprise of all from Drake Turner, and it was not a pleasant one.

I was sitting in the library, busily writing, papers piled haphazardly on the floor near my comfortable chair, when Grimes announced Clement Charles, the young solicitor who had handled Mark's business affairs for the last several years.

"Good morning, Clement," I said, putting my writing aside to rise and greet him. "How kind of you to call."

He took my hand and bowed over it gravely. "Good morning, Lady Raven. I'm afraid this is not a social call. I have some disturbing news for you, I'm afraid."

Whenever I was in Clement's presence, I always had the urge to smooth his hair, straighten his tie, and brush lint or tobacco from the sleeve of his black frock coat, for he was the most unkempt man I had ever known. But he was an excellent solicitor, with a mind as orderly as his personal appearance was not.

"Please sit down, Clement," I said, indicating a chair. "Now, what is this all about?"

He seated himself, and there were no preliminaries, for Clement was a forthright man. He just plunged right in. "John Belding has sold his half of the Raven Line to Drake Turner."

I was so dumbfounded, all I could do was stare at Clement stupidly. When I regained my speech, the most I could manage was an incredulous, "What?"

"I know this must come as a shock to you, Lady Raven, and, needless to say, we were stunned ourselves. Mr. Turner's solicitors informed our office just this morning, and I rushed right over to tell you myself."

I rose, numbed and dazed. "But . . . but John can't!"

"Oh, he most certainly can," Clement contradicted me

with his usual candor. "Their transaction is legal and in order."
He stopped long enough to scowl up at me. "Lady Raven, are
you all right?"

I quickly sat back down before I collapsed. "But, why
didn't John *tell* me?" I demanded.

Clement shrugged as he attempted to straighten his tie. "It
was quite callous of him, I agree. Common courtesy dictates he
should have told you of his plans, but legally, he was within his
rights."

My hands were shaking so badly, I had to knot my fingers
together to keep them still. "Clement, isn't there something we
can do to stop this? Isn't there some clause in the partnership
agreement between Mark and John that one can't sell his half of
the company without the other's consent?"

The solicitor shook his shaggy head at the folly of it. "They
were friends, and I don't think either one of them foresaw this
happening."

"Why couldn't John have at least *told* me?" I wailed.

"Perhaps he remained silent under Mr. Turner's advice,"
Clement suggested. "Perhaps Mr. Turner didn't want you to
know until the transaction was completed."

Trust Clement to come up with a plausible answer, and it
infuriated me. I felt the blood rush to my face. "Of all the
deceitful, underhanded— I'm going to see John at once, and get
to the bottom of this."

Clement rose. "Would you like me to accompany you,
Lady Raven? If you'll forgive me for saying this, you're quite
distraught, and—and you don't look well."

"No, I'll go alone," I snapped. "And I'm just fine, Clement.
Thank you for your concern."

Then I called for my carriage, thanked Clement once again,
and set out for the offices of Gerrick and Belding.

John was evidently expecting me, for I was shown into his
office as soon as I arrived.

When he saw me, he rose with difficulty, for he was a huge

man, with a barrel-sized paunch and several chins. His one good eye—the other had been lost in an accident while he was still a sailor—did not meet my furious gaze as he said, "Good day, Lady Raven. I've been expecting you."

"Why, John?" I demanded irately, without preliminaries. "Why did you sell your half of the company to Drake Turner, of all people? I'm sure Colin informed you that I've been opposed to him and refused to sell. And why didn't you at least have the common courtesy to inform me?"

He indicated a chair, and when I remained standing, he flushed and seated himself with a weary sigh. I had never known a man with more physical ailments than John Belding. In addition to his missing eye and bloated body, he suffered from gout, and even mild exertion or excitement caused him to wheeze and gasp for breath.

"Lady Raven," he began, his chins shaking as he wheezed, "I had no other choice. My health began to fail after the death of my first wife, and though my dear Jessie does her best for us, God bless her, it is taxing on her as well. To be blunt, I also have eleven plain daughters, who will soon reach a marriageable age, one right after the other, and they will need generous dowries to make them attractive to some man."

"But the Raven Line has always been profitable," I protested. "You have always managed before."

His gaze slid away. "Mr. Turner's offer was just too generous to turn down. And, as my dear Jessie so cleverly pointed out—God bless her—that income would allow me to take a less demanding position with another company, and we could even afford a larger house in the country."

I might have known his "dear Jessie, God bless her"—John's young, vain second wife—was behind this. The few times I had met her, she was always complaining—the house was too small, the girls' dressmaker bills too large, her allowance a mere pittance. And she certainly had John dancing to her tune.

"I don't blame you for selling, if you haven't been in good health, John," I said, my voice injured, and for the second time asked him why he hadn't informed me of his plans. "If I had known you wanted to sell out, I'm sure Colin Trelawney would have bought your share for a fair price, and we could have kept the line in the family."

"But Mr. Turner approached me first. He said he wished the transaction to be done in secret, or he would withdraw his offer at once."

I could feel my mouth tighten into a thin, hard line, as I snapped, "Thank you, John, for your loyalty."

He looked sheepish as he muttered, "I'm sorry, Lady Raven. But there comes a time when a man's got to look out for himself and his own."

"I don't want to hear any of your excuses, John," I said. "Do you have Mr. Turner's address?"

He nodded and wheezed, "Thirty-nine Grosvenor Street."

I whirled on my heel, and his voice floated after me. "I'm sorry, Lady Raven, truly sorry." But it was too little, too late.

The London traffic was heavy and snarled by several accidents along the way, so by the time I arrived at Mr. Turner's grand house, it was late afternoon, and I was hot, tired, and angry. My carriage drew up to the door; I stepped down, walked up the steps and knocked.

The butler who answered the door stared at my heavily veiled face, but politely said, "Yes, madam?"

I handed him my card. "Lady Raven to see Mr. Turner."

"I'm sorry, your ladyship. Mr. Turner is dressing for dinner, then he plans to attend the opera. I know he would not wish to be delayed."

Was this his idea of vengeance for my not receiving him, I wondered? My jaw was thrust forward as I snapped, "It is urgent that I see him."

"Very well, Lady Raven. If you will be so kind as to wait here . . ." And he started down the hall.

But I was not going to risk being refused an audience with Mr. Turner. I waited a moment until the butler was at the top of the stairs, then followed him at a discreet distance, the thick, lush carpeting muffling my footsteps. Once upstairs, I watched him disappear through a door, so I scurried after him, determined to see Mr. Turner and vent my fury at him.

I stood before the closed door, took a deep breath to steady my shaking insides, twisted the knob and flung the door open so I could sweep inside, the very picture of righteous indignation.

Three men looked up to stare at me aghast, the butler, a valet, and Drake Turner himself, shirtless and dressed only in black evening trousers.

"Countess," he murmured with a smile, once he quickly regained his composure, "I've been expecting you, but not in my bedchamber."

The sight of his bare, muscular torso did not embarrass me as I marched right up to him, drew back my hand and swung it with all my strength.

But the man, who had discerned my intention at once, was too quick for me. His hand shot out and grasped my wrist, effectively stopping me. "Violence doesn't become you, Countess."

I flung him off and stepped back, glaring at him. "I couldn't wait a moment longer to tell you I think you are a deceitful, despicable—"

"Please, Countess . . ." he began, dismissing his red-faced menservants and reaching for his shirt.

"I'm not through with you, Mr. Turner. I've just learned what you've done, thanks to my solicitor. Why wasn't I told you were planning to buy out my partner? Surely it would have been common courtesy to inform me?"

"But if I had given you fair warning of what I intended, I'm sure Trelawney or Charles would have come up with some clever scheme to thwart me. And I couldn't have that." A smile of triumph flashed across his rugged countenance. "So now we are partners, Lady Raven."

"Partners?" I echoed stupidly. *"Partners?"*

"Partners," he assured me.

This was one shock too many. My head felt as light and hollow as an empty eggshell, and seemed to float off my shoulders. My last conscious thought was Mr. Turner's look of startled alarm as I pitched forward onto the floor.

From out of the velvet blackness, an insistent voice kept repeating my name. I tried to ignore it, but it wouldn't stop, so finally I just surrendered and opened my eyes.

"That's better," Drake Turner said, his face grim and surprisingly frightened. "How do you feel?"

"It's none of your concern," I snapped.

Someone had removed my veil and taken the liberty of unbuttoning the collar of my gown, then set me on the bed, for I could feel a soft pillow beneath my head and glimpsed a tall, carved bedpost out of the corner of my eye.

"But of course it's my concern," he said, rising from the edge of the bed to stare at me in irritation. "You turn as pale as paper and collapse in my bedchamber, and it's none of my concern? I've sent for my doctor, and he should be here shortly."

"Your concern is touching, and oh, so false," I replied, struggling to prop myself up on one elbow and sinking back, exhausted, as the dizziness hit me again.

"When's the last time you ate a decent meal, Lady Raven? You look as though you live on tea," he said with a snort. "You can't weigh more than seven stone."

"My weight is none of your affair, Mr. Turner."

"Oh, but it is, and I insist you dine with me tonight. Then you're sure to get an excellent meal."

Now I did find the strength to sit up and stare at the man. "I will do no such thing! You've no right to be peremptory with me, sir."

He just grinned again. "But you have no choice. I've already sent your carriage home."

Fury revived me quicker than sal volatile, and I swung my legs over the side of the bed. "Then I shall call a hansom cab to take me home, or, if worse comes to worst, walk. But I shall not remain in the same house with you, sir."

"Lady Raven—"

"Mrs. Gerrick, if you please. And you cannot keep me here against my will." I rose and started for the door, but, in my weakened state, I hadn't taken more than three steps before the room teetered ominously to one side, and I stumbled.

"Stubborn woman," Drake Turner muttered, lifting me in his arms as though I were a bag of feathers.

My face was just inches from his own, and I found myself staring into fierce blue eyes that made me blush as they roved boldly over my face. "Put me down this instant," I growled, suddenly going rigid.

He smiled wickedly. "With pleasure." And he dropped me onto the bed, then stared down at me, his hands on his hips. "First, you are going to be examined by my physician," he insisted, "and then you are going to dine with me. At that time, I shall explain why I bought out John Belding." When I opened my mouth to protest, he said, "Don't argue with me, Lady— Mrs. Gerrick. I won't have anyone accusing me of trying to kill you for your share of the Raven Line."

I glowered at him but acquiesced, for I was helpless and I knew it. It was a fine time to wish I had eaten something more substantial for breakfast.

His physician came a half-hour later, and though I have an aversion to doctors, this one was a gentle man who reminded me of St. Nicholas, with his snow-white hair and beard. Dr. Lautrec examined me, talked for a few minutes, then said I was suffering from a combination of exhaustion and melancholia and should try to eat more to build up my strength.

When I told him of my difficulty in sleeping, he said, "Some laudanum should remedy that situation."

I thought of Lizzy Siddal, Dante Rossetti's wife, who had died so tragically of a laudanum overdose some years ago, and I shook my head adamantly. "I won't take it."

He gave me an indulgent look. "Many women take it for a variety of female complaints. I assure you, it's perfectly safe, but I'll give you something else, if you prefer."

So he didn't force it on me and also gave me a tonic to build up my blood and tease my appetite. It was a vile-tasting liquid, and I wrinkled my nose as I swallowed a spoonful of it.

When the doctor left, Drake Turner came back into the room. He was now dressed for dinner and the opera, in elegant black evening attire that minimized his solid physique. "It's early yet," he said, "but I've ordered dinner prepared for us. Will you join me?" And he extended his arm.

It would have been childish to create a scene, so I took his profferred arm without a word and accompanied him downstairs. He led me, not to the formal dining room, but to a small conservatory, where a drum table had been set with soft rose linens, fine crystal, and gleaming silver. Fresh flowers and candlelight were conducive to intimacy, and I found myself wondering cynically how many other women Drake Turner had sought to charm in this manner.

"I visited my father several days ago," I said, as he held my chair. "That was most clever of you, Mr. Turner, to commission him to paint your portrait so you could gather information about me."

He smiled as he seated himself. "I assure you that was not the sole reason for my commissioning him. Every successful man wants his portrait painted, and Ivor Stokes is the best. I admire people who excel at their professions. I might add, that is why I admire you."

I bristled. "Please, Mr. Turner, I'm quite weary of your flattery."

"Why must you turn every honest compliment into an accusation of flattery?" he demanded harshly, growing suddenly angry as he shook out his napkin with a snap.

"And are they honest compliments, sir?"

"Yes!"

"Why should I think you are honest this time, when you have been less than honest on other occasions?"

He was silent as those pale eyes studied me for a moment. "You're right," he said softly, "and I apologize."

I was spared commenting by the arrival of a footman, who served us a cream soup made from lobster that was delicious.

"And was it my father who told you how much I love lilies?" I asked.

"I learned that from another source."

"And what else did you learn from my father? You certainly took advantage of his love of conversation, did you not?" I said bitterly.

"He told me all I needed to know."

I felt myself growing tense and set down my soup spoon.

"You must finish it," my host said. "If it is returned to the kitchen, Antoine will be inconsolable. He won't cook another meal all week if he thinks his talent is not appreciated." His eyes twinkled mischievously. "You wouldn't subject me to a life without food, would you, Mrs. Gerrick? I assure you, I would rather die than go without Antoine's cuisine."

"Perhaps that would be one way of eliminating an unwanted partner," I shot back, but I did finish the soup.

By the time the fish course was served—several pieces of flaky sole rolled and stuffed with crabmeat—I found the wine had mellowed me a little and loosened my tongue. Since my host had taken such pains to learn all he could about me, I thought this would be the perfect opportunity to turn the tables on him. So I asked, "How did you get into shipping, Mr. Turner?"

"I started at the bottom rung of the ladder, as a humble clerk in the Bidwell Company, which is rather a large line with agents scattered all over the world," he replied. "I worked eighteen hours a day, seven days a week, and caught the eye of its founder, Maurice Bidwell. He became my mentor, and when he died, he left me a share in the company. I sold that to his grasping children, who were anxious to be rid of me, and made some careful investments. The profits from that enabled me to start my own company."

"You are very ambitious, Mr. Turner."

"I've always worked hard for what I have," he stated

proudly. "I wasn't born into wealth. My father was a headmaster of a public school up Norfolk way, and he saw to it that I was well educated."

"Does not being born into wealth make you a better merchant?" I asked.

"I think so," he replied smoothly, his pale eyes glittering with that disconcerting intensity again. "It drives me to succeed, you see, for if I fail, I lose all, and don't have the family fortune to cushion me against losses."

"As my husband did," I murmured, to let him know I had not missed the point of this conversation.

He just shrugged.

Falling silent, I turned inward to my own thoughts, and Drake Turner respected my silence, saying nothing throughout the rest of the meal, of which I tasted little. Before I knew it, the footman was coming around for the final time with a tray of pastries, which I had to refuse, for, although I had eaten little, I felt as bloated as a hot-air balloon.

"We'll have coffee in my study," Drake Turner said and rose to hold my chair.

"My compliments to Antoine," I said. "Dinner was delicious."

He beamed, and his eyes sparkled as he showed me to his study, an orderly room, with a huge mahogany desk and the globe I recognized from my father's sketches. The footman followed with a silver coffee service, left it on the desk and departed.

Then Drake Turner offered me a chair that at first glance looked as though it had a fur cushion on it.

"Faust," he murmured, reaching for it. "Down now."

The pillow suddenly stirred and came to life, unrolling itself to reveal a shaggy black cat the size of a small dog who eyed us with supreme disdain as he took his time stretching, then bounded off the chair.

No sooner had I seated myself than Faust sniffed the hem of my dress and startled me by leaping into my lap.

61

"Where are your Sunday manners, cat?" Mr. Turner scolded as he poured two cups of coffee and added milk and sugar at my request before handing me a cup.

Faust ignored his master, turned around several times, then tucked his legs beneath him and settled himself in my lap, where he began to purr so loudly I was sure he was hiding a small engine in his chest.

As I stroked the soft black fur with my free hand, I recalled what my father had said about Drake Turner's preference for a woman's pet being at odds with his absolute masculinity. And there was certainly nothing feminine about the strong, forceful man seated before me.

"What kind of man would prefer cats to dogs?" I mused aloud.

"A man who prizes independence," Mr. Turner replied, sipping his black coffee. "Dogs are such stupid, slavish creatures. Even if you beat them, they'll quickly forgive you and lick your hand afterward, as though thanking you for punishing them. But a cat? Never. They have too much sense."

I thought of the hound I had owned as a child and said, "I do not favor cats, Mr. Turner, for I find many of them capricious and untrustworthy. You can feed them, give them love and a home, and they'll turn on you without provocation if it suits their fancy."

"I'm surprised, Mrs. Gerrick, for you yourself have cat's eyes, golden and slanted. You could be a golden-eyed witch, and Faust your familiar."

"Golden-eyed witch" . . . that had been my husband's favorite term of endearment for me, and hearing those same words spoken by his hated rival devastated me. "Don't call me that!" I snapped, bolting to my feet so fast I spilled my coffee into its saucer. Poor Faust didn't even have time to dig his claws into my skirt to steady himself before toppling onto the floor with an indignant yowl.

I turned my back on Drake Turner and stalked over to the

cold fireplace at the other end of the room, where I stood for a moment trying to compose myself.

"I'm sorry if I offended you," he said gravely.

"No harm done," was my curt reply as I took a deep breath and turned to face him. He looked both startled and alarmed by my odd behavior, but he said nothing else as I walked back to my chair. "Now, I believe you have some explaining to do," I said, seating myself. "I want to know why you secretly bought out my partner."

I could see by the furrow between his brows that he wanted to discuss my outburst of a moment ago, but finally he shrugged. "It was quite simple. I offered to buy your half of the Raven Line, and you repeatedly refused to sell it to me. I'm not one to bang my head against a stone wall, so I approached John Belding instead, to see if he would sell to me. He accepted my offer."

"But why wasn't I told?" I demanded, leaning forward as my voice rose.

"This is *commerce*, Mrs. Gerrick, not some child's nursery game," he said scornfully. "Colin Trelawney is no fool. He knew how Lord Raven felt about me, and if he also knew I was planning to buy out Belding, he would have moved first to acquire those shares himself. I knew I was taking a risk by telling Belding to keep our transaction secret. He could have gone to you at any time and exposed me. But, with his ambitious wife and homely daughters, I didn't think he'd be in a position to risk my withdrawing the offer." He leaned back and gave me a self-satisfied smile. "And I was right."

My face reddened as my eyes narrowed in dislike. "You are unscrupulous, Mr. Turner."

"Oh, come now, Mrs. Gerrick, haven't you ever wanted something so badly you'd do just about anything to get it?"

I looked away in embarrassment, for I knew he spoke the truth. I had once wanted my freedom from Oliver Woburn so badly I would have done anything short of murder to obtain it.

"Now that I've bought out your partner, will you now sell me your half of the company?"

"That's just what you're counting on, isn't it? Well, I hate to disappoint you, Mr. Turner, but no, I will not sell out to you."

He raised his heavy brows at this unexpected turn of events. "You know, of course, what this means?"

"We're partners, you and I."

"Are you sure you want that, since you hate me so much?"

"It's the last thing I want, but there's nothing else I can do, is there, short of selling out? Yes," I said, with greater calm than I felt, "I suppose we shall remain partners. And I expect to be an active one, so don't think you'll be able to run the company without interference from me."

Drake Turner did not look at all pleased, which gave me great satisfaction. "Can you put aside your animosity and work for the good of the company, Lady—Mrs. Gerrick? We must cooperate, because if we don't, we'll soon be bankrupt and there'll be nothing left for us to fight over."

"I realize that," I replied, bristling. "I'm the first to admit I am quite ignorant about running a shipping line, and while I'll cooperate with you as much as possible, don't think for one moment that I'm going to give you license to do as you please with the Raven Line."

"The company would be better off if you did," he replied, "but, since we must work together, I suggest we declare a truce, put our personal feelings aside, and work for the good of the company."

"And you think me incapable of that?"

"I would be delighted to be proved wrong," he said with that infuriating, patronizing smile.

Then, as if to soften the harshness of his words, he began telling me about his great passion for the opera, which began seven years ago when he saw Adelina Patti's Covent Garden debut in *La Sonnambula*. Listening to him talk so enthusiastically about his favorite operas and performers, I realized Drake

Turner cared intensely about whatever interested him, whether business or pleasure, a quality Mark had also possessed.

Suddenly he glanced at a small gold clock on his desk and rose. "I don't mean to be rude, Mrs. Gerrick, but a certain young lady of my acquaintance is going to be quite out of sorts with me if I don't call for her soon. We're attending the Royal Opera, where I have a box, and I am never late for a performance."

I took his hint at once and rose. "Far be it from me to detain you, Mr. Turner."

Remembering my veil was still in this man's bedchamber, I said, "Will you please send someone for my veil?"

He started to say something, changed his mind and murmured, "Of course."

Later, a maid brought me the veil and the brown glass bottles of tonic Dr. Lautrec had given me. I draped the veil over my head, feeling secure as it hid me from the world once again, then my host returned me to Mount Street and departed for his lady's house.

As soon as I was back in my own home, I thwarted Fenner's attempts to foist more food on me and went right to the library to write Colin a long letter, detailing the startling events of this day. How I longed to hear his calm, soothing voice and feel his great strength enveloping me, giving me courage. But Colin was at the other end of the country, with his own concerns, and I did not like to be too dependent on him. He was an attractive man, and I a vulnerable widow, a potentially dangerous combination that could have disastrous results.

Still reeling from the shock of what Drake Turner had done, I berated myself for my naïveté, my childish cry of "But why didn't John Belding *tell* me?" ringing in my ears. Why hadn't I suspected a man like Turner would resort to any deception to gain his own ends? I had expected him to play as fair as Mark would have, and that had been my undoing.

"Always expect your adversary to do his worst," was Mark's

golden rule, "because he usually will do that and much more."

As a result of underestimating the opposition, I had failed. Now I had acquired a partner I neither liked nor trusted and felt like a helpless lamb chained to a mighty lion.

Once I posted my letter to Colin the next morning, I rushed right over to Upper Cheyne Row to tell my father about Drake Turner's audacious ploy. He turned livid and stormed about his studio, raving, "I knew it! I knew there was something underhanded about that man from the moment I met him!" until his considerable fury was spent. At one point, he brandished his palette knife and was on the verge of slashing the half-finished portrait of Mr. Turner, but I caught his arm just in time and restrained him, pointing out he shouldn't let personal feelings deprive him of a handsome commission. Both of us finally calmed down, and, because my father's house encourages high spirits and hope, we enjoyed a pleasant lunch together, laughing about many things, and I finally left in a much better mood.

Thankfully, there was still a Clement Charles to look after my interests, and, in the days that followed, he diligently prepared me to make intelligent decisions concerning the Raven Line. Oh, I knew a little about the company. One couldn't be married to Mark Gerrick and not take an interest in the ships that were his whole life. But there was still much to learn.

During the course of my studies, I discovered why a shipowner such as Mark was so fiercely competitive with his chief rivals, such as Drake Turner and George Thompson, owner of the huge Aberdeen White Star Line. It was a matter of pride. The fastest and best ships were rewarded with the choicest cargoes, and he wanted the Raven Line to be the best there was.

I also learned about the various trades that engaged Raven ships, such as the China tea trade, the Indian jute trade, and the San Francisco grain trade, and, in my quest for knowledge, I even learned about the ships' construction. For example, I was surprised to discover that only American clippers were built entirely of wood. Our English ships were composite-built, which meant that wooden hull planking was bolted to iron frames.

There was so much more to learn, but I never once doubted my ability to do so and became Clement's apt pupil.

Several weeks passed. I received a long, reassuring letter from Colin, reviling Turner and telling me he would come to London as soon as some pressing matters of his own were taken care of. However, I was beginning to wonder if Colin's presence was even necessary, for my new partner was surprising me with his patience and cooperation.

Drake Turner called almost daily on mercantile matters, and while we were both suspicious at first, each expecting the other to be uncooperative and hostile, he soon began to convince me of his sincerity, and I won his grudging respect for my impartiality and flexibility. For the first time in weeks I was cautiously optimistic about this partnership.

And then came the day I received a visitor who called herself Mrs. Mark Gerrick.

CHAPTER

4

How could I have ever thought Drake Turner cooperative and reasonable? But then, I suppose I felt he should be given the benefit of the doubt if our forced partnership was ever to be a success.

The day began innocently enough, with Mr. Turner walking into the library for our daily meeting, and I remember thinking grudgingly how distinguished he looked in a plain, dark blue coat, checked trousers, and burgundy silk tie.

"Good morning, Mrs. Gerrick," he greeted me politely as he set a sheaf of papers before me on the desk. But I should have suspected something was wrong by his aloof demeanor, that air of keeping the world at arm's length. "Are you ready for some work this morning?"

"Of course, Mr. Turner," I replied, wondering what was the matter. "But, before we begin, would you care for some breakfast or tea?"

"No, thank you. Antoine made me a hearty breakfast this morning." Then he sat down and cleared his throat, and it was as though a wall had suddenly sprung up out of nowhere between us. "Last night, I studied the staff lists of the Raven ships very carefully, and I've discovered each one is overstaffed by three or four men."

I sat up straight, on guard now. "Oh?"

Those intense blue eyes met mine, and I had to resist the impulse to reach up and straighten my collar, as he said, "So, with eight ships, that means we have twenty-four men we really don't need."

"What are you suggesting, Mr. Turner?" I asked, though I think I already knew.

"I feel the excess crew should be dismissed at once."

I sat back in my chair, turned and looked out the window at the backyard, where my gardener was busily raking and weeding one of the flower beds, his back bowed as he worked. My thoughts were on those loyal sailors, most of whom had been in our employ since Mark had started the company. Many had wives and children who didn't see them for months at a time while they were sailing to faraway places like China and Argentina, making money for the Gerrick family.

I turned back to the man seated across from me. "I don't think they should be dismissed."

His brown, shaggy brows rose in surprise at my dissension. "And may I ask why not? They're unnecessary. The other men can do their work easily enough."

"That may be true, Mr. Turner, but many of these men have families. What would become of them if their providers were out of work?"

"Their providers would sign on with other ships."

"Can you guarantee that?"

"No, but what happens to them after they leave our employ is not my concern."

"Well, they are *my* concern, Mr. Turner," I retorted, upset, but not surprised, by his callousness. "These are people we are discussing, sir, not numbers on a page."

The man's smile was offensive and patronizing. "Mrs. Gerrick, you are just too softhearted to play a man's game."

"I wonder if you want these men dismissed because we really are overstaffed, or because they've worked for my husband for years and are loyal to our family?"

A muscle twitched in Mr. Turner's jaw, and he looked as though he were making a great effort to control himself. "Mrs.

Gerrick, I believe we both agreed to put aside our personal feelings for the benefit of the company. That applied to me as well. Believe me when I say these ships are overstaffed. If I wanted to be rid of all men who were loyal to your husband, I would have dismissed captains and entire crews and replaced them with men of my own choosing."

He sounded so sincere I looked away in embarrassment. "Still, I will not agree to the dismissal of those men."

He sighed and regarded me indulgently, as one would a stubborn child. "Mrs. Gerrick, if you are going to be an active partner in this company, you're going to have to put aside your kindhearted, feminine impulses and be more hardheaded."

"And if we are going to run the Raven Line together, Mr. Turner, you are going to have to stop being so hardheaded and display a little compassion toward your fellowman."

Now he rose to glower at me across the desk, and I could almost see sparks fly between us. At that moment, I realized Drake Turner expected me to defer to him on all decisions concerning the operation of the company, because I, after all, was a mere woman, lacking the intellect and experience to manage a shipping line. As long as I cooperated, our meetings would run smoothly, but if I dissented, as I had today, I would be the recipient of his considerable wrath. Well, if he expected me to quake in my shoes, he was mistaken.

I suspect he was trying to reduce me to tears, and with his black scowl, icy gaze, and rough, pockmarked countenance, he did look fierce. But, although I barely came up to his chin, I stood my ground and glared right back at him. Years ago, destitute and at Oliver Woburn's mercy, I had been forced to swallow my pride and retreat many times in a world dominated by such men. Now, wealth and independence allowed me to stand up without fear to men like Drake Turner, and I relished that power.

"Compassion has no place in commerce, Mrs. Gerrick!" he roared.

I knew it was pointless, but I tried to reason with him. "Mr.

Turner, what harm would come of keeping these men after all these years? The line is not going to go bankrupt because we retain those men. Surely it would make no difference."

He rolled his eyes toward the ceiling in exasperation. "We are running a company, Mrs. Gerrick, not a charitable institution. Next, you'll be wanting to increase the sailors' wages so their daughters will all have dowries and their sons an Oxford education!"

I resented his depiction of me as some witless Lady Bountiful, and I felt my resolve to oppose him grow stronger. "I will never agree to the dismissal of those men," I said flatly. "Never."

We argued like my two nephews, our voices rising as each tried to convince the other of the rightness of his position, and we probably would have spent the entire morning locked in verbal combat if someone hadn't knocked at the door and interrupted us.

At my terse command, Grimes entered, white-faced and distressed. "Begging your pardon, madam, but there is a lady waiting to see you." He hesitated, as though gathering his courage. "Madam, she says her name is Mrs. Mark Gerrick."

I glared at the hapless butler. "Is this some sort of jest, Grimes?"

"No, madam. She says she is Mrs. Mark Gerrick."

"Well, tell this Mrs. Mark Gerrick that I resent her impersonation of me and I will not receive her. Make certain she leaves, Grimes."

"Yes, madam."

When the butler left, I turned my attention back to Mr. Turner. "Now, where were we?"

But he was regarding me with an odd expression. "Aren't you in the least bit curious as to what that was all about?"

"Why should I be?" I replied. "It's obviously someone's idea of a prank, and in very poor taste, I might add. Shall we resume our discussion and try to settle this matter once and for all?"

Suddenly, we heard raised voices outside the doors just before they were flung open with such force they crashed against the walls. We looked to see Grimes trying to restrain another man, who was equally intent on entering the library.

"Stop fighting this instant!" I shouted. "Grimes, what is the meaning of this?"

"I'll tell you," the other man replied in a broad American accent as he shook off my butler and strode into the room.

I studied the intruder, and my first impression was anything but favorable. Physically, the man was not imposing, being of my height and almost as thin, while his clothes were poorly cut and not well coordinated. Longish black hair, parted in the middle and flaring away from his eyes like wings, contrasted sharply with white skin, and dark eyes seemed to burn with some fierce, internal fire.

He stopped before my desk and said, "My sister crossed the Atlantic to see you, and you turn her away as though she's some lowly servant. That's not very hospitable, madam."

I regarded the presumptuous intruder with a mixture of anger and disdain. "I am Lady Nora Gerrick, Countess of Raven. Who are you?"

"My name is Mason, Seth Mason," he replied with an ingratiating smile. "I'm here with my sister, Ella, the *real* Mrs. Mark Gerrick."

His words caused me to go livid with rage. "Mr. Mason, I don't know who you are, or why you're here, but I deeply resent your invasion of my privacy."

"My sister and I came to discuss this matter like civilized people," he said, "and if you won't talk to us, by God, we'll let our lawyers do the talking for us."

"And just what is it you wish to discuss?" I snapped, my remaining patience sorely tried.

"My sister was once married to Mark Gerrick," Mason insisted, "and we can prove it."

At that moment, I wished I were Medusa and could turn him to stone with a mere glance. "I have never heard anything so absurd in my entire life."

"I assure you, it's true."

"Mr. Mason—"

"If you will just see my sister, she will explain."

"I'm sorry," I said with great finality. "What you are saying just isn't true. I don't know what you hope to gain by coming here, but—"

"I don't blame you for not believing me," he said earnestly. "If someone came into my house and told me the woman I was married to had been married to another man, I'm sure I would feel as you do. But, please, you've got to talk to my sister. She will explain."

I stood there for a moment, taking his measure, trying to assess his strengths and weaknesses. He reminded me of a small, scrappy terrier, one that barks and worries your leg, demanding to be noticed. I read aggressiveness and determination in the proud way he carried himself, and I could see I would not be rid of this man unless I did as he requested and talked to his sister.

"Very well, if you insist on carrying out your tasteless little jest . . ."

"I assure you this is no jest. My sister is waiting in your parlor." He smiled, friendliness itself now that he had gotten what he wanted from me.

As I came around my desk, Mr. Turner, who had been wordlessly observing our heated exchange, said, "May I come with you?"

"As you wish," I replied curtly, and the three of us followed Grimes out of the library.

My prevailing emotion as I marched down the hall toward the Regency drawing room was outrage. Mason's words were so ludicrous I didn't dignify them with a second thought. I just wanted to learn what his game was, then have him and his sister thrown out.

The woman was standing near the Duncan Phyfe drum table, studying the mark on the bottom of a rare Sèvres porcelain dish, a wedding gift from Lewis Darwin. When Miss Mason saw she was being observed, she nonchalantly placed it back on the table without so much as a guilty smile or blush. I must admit she was beautiful, with the same jet-black hair and pale skin as her brother's, but it was her eyes that were so arresting. They were dark, like two lumps of coal, yet, unlike most brown eyes, lacked warmth and softness. When she looked directly at me without ever once blinking, I felt like a hapless rabbit being eyed by a cobra, and I shivered involuntarily though I could not draw my eyes away.

But I recovered myself immediately. How clever, I thought as my eyes raked her over mercilessly, to be dressed in mourning, as was I. But, on closer inspection, I could see that her dress was clumsily handmade and repeatedly dyed. I would guess that Miss Mason and her brother had fallen on hard times and were seeking to remedy the situation.

"My name is Nora Gerrick," I said, my voice as cold and hostile as this woman's eyes. "This is Drake Turner, my partner."

"I am Ella Gerrick," she said in a soft, refined voice that held just a hint of a challenge. She scrutinized me just as carefully, and I could tell by the way her lips tightened imperceptibly that she resented and disliked me as much as I did her.

"Will you tell me what you've come for, and then leave?" I said.

"May we sit down?" Mason asked, going to his sister's side and placing a protective arm around her, though she did not seem to need any protecting. "Seeing you has been a great blow to Ella."

I indicated the sofa, while Mr. Turner and I seated ourselves across from them.

"Now, Ella," her brother said gently, patting her hand. "I know this is painful for you, but you must tell these people everything."

She needed no encouragement and began at once in her soft, cultured voice. "We live in New York City and come from a modest, though genteel, background. Eleven years ago, when I was only seventeen, I met a young English sailor named Mark

Gerrick, whose ship, the *Neptune,* was in port at the time. He seemed like such a well-educated, refined young man, not rough and coarse like so many sailors, but kind and considerate."

"How did you meet him?" I demanded. "Most genteel young ladies don't frequent the docks in any port."

Her thick, dark lashes fluttered, and she replied, "I was taking some lunch to my cousin, who worked as a clerk in a shipping office. That's where I met Mark."

Seth Mason reached over and patted his sister's hand again, as if to encourage her to continue.

"Mark happened to be there, and my cousin introduced us," she went on. "Later, he brought Mark to our house for dinner. We were attracted to each other instantly, and he called on me every day after that." She shrugged. "We fell in love. I don't know what else to say."

"Oh, come now, Miss Mason," I said, my voice sharp and heavy with sarcasm, "do you really expect me to believe that my husband fell in love with you while his ship was in port for several days?"

The dark eyes regarded me without emotion. "It's true. Not only did we fall in love, we were married within two weeks of our meeting."

I threw back my head and laughed, a harsh, bitter sound that caused heads to turn. "That's absurd. Mark was not the sort to make hasty decisions. He would never marry a woman he had known for so short a time."

"Are you calling my sister a liar, madam?" Seth Mason said, clutching her hand.

Leaning forward, I looked him straight in the eye and said, "Yes, sir, I am. I think the pair of you are nothing more than swindlers."

His eyes narrowed as his sister drew herself up like one girding herself for battle. "But we have proof," he said. "We have a marriage license signed by Mark Gerrick."

I extended my hand, palm up. "I want to see it."

"It is with our lawyers—or, solicitors, I think you call

them—Squires and Appleby, who will present our case to you in their offices tomorrow morning at nine o'clock, if you would be so good as to attend."

"You're lying," I said.

"Mrs.—Gerrick," Ella said, making a face as though calling me that name were a bitter pill on her tongue, "I can understand your hostility and reluctance to believe me. How do you think I felt when I learned my husband had been alive all these years, never once contacted me, and even married someone else?" She hesitated for effect, then said, "But you must believe that we are telling the truth."

Suddenly, Mr. Turner, who had been strangely silent during all this, spoke up for the first time. "Madam, what did Mark Gerrick look like?"

Her face brightened at the memory. "He was tall, with dark hair and light gray eyes, and so strong."

"And he had no infirmity?" I asked, praying she would mention that Mark walked with a limp.

Her brow furrowed in confusion. "He had no infirmity." Then she looked at her brother in alarm, and back to me. "Why do you ask? Did something happen to Mark? Had he been injured in some way?"

So this woman had known Mark before the accident that had lamed him, but even that did not prove they had once been married. "He was crippled in a tavern brawl in Rome," I replied crisply.

The woman's hand flew to her mouth in distress, while her brother patted her arm.

But Mr. Turner wasn't through with her yet. "And how did you discover Mark Gerrick had been alive all these years? Why didn't you come forward before now? If you were so much in love, why did he leave you? And why did he marry this lady, when he already had a wife in America?" His smile was most disarming as he said, "Why did he never try to contact you in the eleven years that have passed?"

I regarded Ella Mason closely. Mr. Turner's questions were

certainly valid, and I wondered if she would try to wriggle out of answering them.

But she didn't, and never lost her composure. "After we were married, Mark had to put out to sea again, though he promised to return for me." Her dark eyes grew bright with tears, and her voice wavered convincingly as she said, "Months later, we heard the *Neptune* went down off the Cape of Good Hope and all the men were lost."

I suddenly went cold all over, for I seemed to recall Mark telling me he had been shipwrecked once, but managed to cling to a piece of flotsam before being plucked out of the sea by fishermen a day later. How had this woman known? Well, I suppose anyone could read of a shipwreck in the newspapers, and this pair had done their research very, very carefully.

"I assumed he was dead," Ella Mason said.

"But he wasn't," Mr. Turner persisted, "so why didn't he try to contact you when he returned to England?"

Her brother interrupted. "I can answer that. My father was a very stern, overbearing man, Mr. Turner, and he hadn't approved of Ella's marriage to a sailor, especially one who left her within a week of their wedding. When our father died last January, he confessed to me on his deathbed that he had intercepted many letters from Mark during that first year, and finally wrote back, saying Ella had died, and not to bother writing any more. Mark wrote him one last letter of condolence, then never wrote again. He thought Ella was dead, you see."

"How convenient," was my only comment.

"It is the truth," Ella said calmly, ever in control.

"Our family wasn't wealthy, Mr. Turner," Mason said, with a toss of his head when hair fell into his eyes. "I made a little money working for the *New York Tribune,* and my father owned a store, but we didn't have enough money to scour the world for Mark."

"How did you hear of his . . . death?" I asked, curious.

"A co-worker returning from London brought a copy of the *Times* back with him, and while reading it, I noticed Mark's obituary. Naturally, we were shocked to discover he had been alive all these years, though our father had known and kept it from us."

"Naturally," I said.

Ella took offense at my caustic tone. "I'll have you know I was devastated!"

"Miss Mason—"

"I wish you wouldn't call me that. My name is Ella Gerrick, Mrs. Mark Gerrick."

"I find it difficult to believe Mark never told you about his home in Devonshire and his aristocratic family," I said. "He never told you he would become the Earl of Raven upon his father's death?"

"He told me he lived in England, but that was all. We knew each other for such a short time, there were many things we never had a chance to share with each other. But he was very reluctant to speak of his family and always changed the subject whenever I inquired. I sensed he didn't get along with them very well."

Now that was certainly the truth, I thought to myself as I knotted my fingers together. "It's a very interesting tale, and I congratulate you for putting so much thought and effort into it, but what is your real reason for coming here?"

"Why, to claim what is rightfully my sister's," Seth Mason said, sounding like a noble Knight of the Round Table about to embark on a quest for the Holy Grail, "a share of the Gerrick estate."

So that was it. "I should have guessed," I said, with a sweet smile. "Mr. Mason, as an American, you may not be aware of English laws of inheritance. Since Mark and his—his son are both dead, the estate of Raven's Chase passes to his younger brother, Damon. Your sister would receive nothing, even if she had been married to Mark, which I doubt."

Mason grinned in triumph. "But my sister and Mark had a child—a son. I think that alters the situation slightly, don't you?"

"His name is Brentwood," Ella added, with a soft smile of pride, the first sign of emotion she had displayed.

Brentwood . . . the middle name that Mark hated with a passion. How had this woman known?

I rose to my feet, trembling with rage. "Get out!" I shouted. "Get out of here this instant!"

Seth rose and started to protest, but Mr. Turner could see that I was too upset to listen any more. "I think you and your sister had better leave, Mr. Mason."

Ella rose, and by the smug looks on their faces I could tell they were pleased that they had needled me at last. As they departed, Mason said, "Remember that our lawyers wish to see you tomorrow morning at precisely nine o'clock." And he handed Mr. Turner their card. "Perhaps you will believe *them* when they tell you my nephew is Mark Gerrick's rightful heir."

"Good riddance," I muttered savagely when I heard the front door close on the Masons. Then I walked over to the decanter of Madeira on the sideboard and offered Mr. Turner a glass, but when I tried to pour, my hand was shaking so badly, I couldn't do it without fear of spillage.

"Allow me," he said, taking the decanter so I could sit down.

"You should be pleased with today's turn of events," I said, as I leaned back in my chair and closed my eyes.

"What do you mean?"

I opened my eyes to stare at him defiantly. "You have such a low opinion of my husband that you're willing to accept that woman's accusations, aren't you?"

He crossed the room to hand me my glass and looked quite put out with me. "Mrs. Gerrick, I have my own reasons for hating your husband, and yes, I am quick to believe that he was capable of doing what that woman has claimed. But if you think I'm gloating over your misfortune, you're wrong."

I sipped the Madeira, which was a stream of liquid fire as it slid down my throat, but it soothed and strengthened me. "I still can't believe someone would have the impudence to claim my husband had been married to another woman and just—just *forgot* about her! Preposterous!"

Drake Turner studied me intently for a moment, then his gaze fell to the floor as he said, "What if the Masons are telling the truth?"

I started, splashing some wine onto my dress, but I ignored the dark, widening stain. "You would say that," I sneered.

"I merely posed the question," he said. "You are hardly in a position to be objective, Mrs. Gerrick."

I set my glass down, then jumped to my feet, and started pacing the room. "No," I said, adamantly shaking my head. "I refuse to believe Mark was ever married to that woman no matter what you or anyone else says."

He made no comment.

"Damn it!" I cried in anguish, whirling on him. "Mark would have *told* me!"

He was at my side in two strides, taking my arm, steadying me. Although I did not like to reveal any weakness to Drake Turner, I was forced to lean against him or collapse, grateful for the warmth and strength of his arm around me.

"I know you loved your husband," I heard him say quietly from far away, "but the Masons could be telling the truth."

"It's just not true!" I shrieked, pulling away from him and bunching my hands into fists. "It can't be true."

But, deep within me, a tiny seed of doubt was beginning to grow even as I made my vehement denials.

That night, I was lying awake in my darkened bedroom, listening to the clock chime twice, while the events of this day played over and over in my mind.

Finally, I rose, put on my slippers and wrap and padded downstairs through the dark, quiet house. Then I unlocked the back door as quietly as possible, lest the servants think there was a prowler about, and let myself out into the garden.

It was a lovely night, calm and still, with so many stars visible that the Milky Way looked like a wide, spangled belt overhead. All around me, my neighbors' houses were dark and silent, heightening the eerie feeling that I was the only person left in the world.

I breathed deeply, savoring the garden's sweet scents of flowers, moss, and grass, and shivered, more from fear of what the future held than the warm May air.

After Drake Turner had reluctantly left me that afternoon, I locked myself in my room and noisily fell apart, sobbing and wailing hysterically. When I was finally able to pull myself together and think rationally, I wrote a note informing Clement Charles of my summons tomorrow morning and requesting him to accompany me.

As I stood there in the darkness, I thought about that woman. Earlier today, I had refused to admit there was even a possibility she was telling the truth, but now that seed of doubt had flowered, and I was willing to concede there could be some truth to her claim.

And if she was the real Mrs. Mark Gerrick? Tears trickled down my cheeks. Then a man I had loved deeply and trusted for five years would suddenly become a stranger to me, and I would wonder for the rest of my life why he had hidden the truth.

The warm breeze gently blew against my face, drying those tears, but it felt like the icy lash of winter. I started shivering uncontrollably, so I went back inside, locked the door after me, and trudged upstairs to await the morning. This was one dawn I was not looking forward to.

The next day, I left the offices of Squires and Appleby in a state of shock, and had it not been for Clement Charles' guidance, I surely would have stumbled and fallen down the stairs, or been run down by a carriage in the street. Later, after stopping to leave Clement at his office, I told the driver to take me to Upper Cheyne Row, and when I arrived, I was startled to find my father's house locked and the curtains drawn. Luckily, I had a key, so I was able to let myself in.

The house was so very silent—no voices, giggling, clinking

wineglasses—I began to get alarmed. Had something happened to my father? I wondered, as I dashed from room to room, calling his name.

I went limp with relief when I heard a faint voice reply, "I'm here, Nora, in the conservatory," and found him in his shirtsleeves, humming to himself as he watered the plants that had been my mother's delight.

"You frightened me half to death by locking the front door," I admonished him. "The house is so quiet I thought you had—I thought something had happened to you."

He chuckled. "Even a gregarious old soul such as myself craves a little solitude every now and then, so when that happens, I just lock the front door, draw the curtains, and people assume I'm not at home. Then they just go away." He set down his watering can and scowled at me. "Nora, is something wrong?"

I nodded wordlessly and burst into tears. He took me in his arms and I pressed my face into his shirt, which smelled faintly of turpentine, as comforting in its own way as the scent of my mother's soft violet perfume had been in my childhood.

Then I looked up at him. "Father, yesterday a woman came to my house claiming to be Mrs. Mark Gerrick. She says she and Mark were once married."

My father turned white beneath his grizzled beard, and his eyes widened. When he gained control of himself, he stepped back and bellowed, "What!"

I nodded. "It's true. I've just come from her solicitors' office."

And that meeting had left me shattered. To my way of thinking, I was the injured party, defending myself and my late husband's honor against two reprehensible swindlers. Yet to see those two fawning old men, Squires and Appleby, hanging on that woman's every word, treating her like Joan of Arc and me her loathsome tormentor . . . It enraged me with its flagrant injustice.

"Let's go into the parlor, Nora, girl," my father said. "I think I need to sit down and have a drink."

We went to the parlor, and while he poured claret for me and whisky for himself, I recounted everything that had happened since yesterday. When I finally finished, he looked as though he had aged twenty years, and his normal loquaciousness had deserted him.

"Nora," he began in hushed tones, "I'm speechless."

"You should see those two, Father," I said with a shudder of disgust as I pictured the Masons in my mind's eye. "They try to hide their baseness by assuming postures of gentility, but I can see through their ruse. Seth tries to look the poet with his dark, flowing hair, but underneath that façade is a calculating mind. And Ella . . ." My eyes narrowed at the memory. "She is so cool and contained, I can't imagine her having a genuine emotion. And she's so still. All through our interview with the solicitors this morning, she sat with her hands in her lap and never once moved them. All she does is regard one out of those unblinking snake's eyes." I shivered as though she were in the room, watching me.

"They sound like formidable adversaries," my father mused.

"Oh, they're very clever. They would have to be, to conceive such a bold scheme and think they can get away with it. They seem to know a great deal about Mark, and have answers for everything. They even had a marriage license with Mark's signature on it!" Even when I closed my eyes I could still see my husband's plain, bold signature scrawled on that piece of paper. "They must have forged it," I insisted. "Mark's signature is very easy to copy. A child could do it."

"And you say this woman has a son?"

I nodded, fighting to keep back the tears that threatened to fall at any moment. "He would inherit."

"Everything?"

"Oh, yes, Father, everything—Raven's Chase, the Raven Line, the Mount Street house, the fortune—everything."

"But where would that leave you?"

I laughed, a shaky, hollow sound. "Why, with nothing, of course. Destitute. All I would have is my income from my writ-

ing, as I did when I left Oliver. Of course, since I haven't published anything in years, who knows how large even that income
would be?"

He came to stand beside me and took my hand in his bear's
paw. "You know you could always come live with me, Nora,
girl. I'm successful now and could support us both quite comfortably."

I thought of shy Marigold and Louisa and shook my head
quite firmly. "Thank you, Father, but no. I'm twenty-eight years
old and too independent to return here and become your daughter again. We have our own lives to lead, and we're used to
coming and going as we please. Ultimately, we would wind up
resenting the restrictions we would place on each other."

He shook his head. "Now, Nora, you know I would gladly
give up my independence to help you."

"I appreciate it, Father, but let's hope I'll never need it."

"You're much too proud and stubborn for your own good,
Nora, girl," he said.

I sighed as I folded my arms and walked away from him,
then turned and cried, "I'm so afraid! First, Mark's longtime
rival manages to secure half of our company, and now this
American woman claims her son is the rightful Gerrick heir. I
just don't know what to do next."

"Surely your clever solicitor—the one who never combs his
hair—has come up with a solution?"

"Clement insisted he wanted an investigation of our own
conducted in New York City, otherwise, we would fight the
Masons' claim in court—which we may still do, anyway. I have
to give credit to that woman and her brother. They weren't
intimidated by the threat of an investigation and even welcomed it, they said, because it would prove they were telling the
truth." I took a deep breath to steady myself. "And they want to
stay at Raven's Chase until their claim is proved or disproved.
Can you imagine? I suppose they want to examine the spoils
beforehand."

My father was aghast. "And your solicitor *agreed* to this?"

"We had no choice. The woman's solicitors were adamant on that point. It seems the Masons used what little money they had to make the voyage here, and have nowhere else to stay, so I plan to go back to Devonshire with them."

Actually, I was not being totally truthful with my father on this point. Clement had protested strongly when Squires and Appleby made this demand on their clients' behalf, urging me to stand fast and refuse. He pointed out that by the time the case came to court, an investigation would have been completed, and I would be spared the Masons' company at Raven's Chase. And if they were out of funds, let them eke out a living as best they could in London. Their fate was no concern of mine, as Clement so bluntly reminded me.

And yet, what if the boy *was* Mark's son? That heretical thought flitted through my mind and ultimately caused me to agree to the Masons' terms, despite vocal opposition from Clement.

There was something I had to ask my father. "If they are telling the truth, why didn't Mark tell me about this woman he had once loved? Didn't he trust me to understand?" My voice was filled with hurt and betrayal. "How could he have just forgotten her like that?" I turned and looked out the window at a serving girl from next door, standing on tiptoes and flirting with my driver.

"Perhaps it's because Mark was never really married to her," he pointed out.

I made an exasperated noise as my mind became too befuddled for me to think clearly any more. "I don't know, Father, but, whatever the reason, I am going to find the answers to all of my questions."

"Be very, very careful, Nora," he warned me. "These brazen colonials have more to lose and I suspect they know it. If they've come this far with their outlandish scheme, they're not going to give up easily and let it fail."

I took a deep breath. "I realize that, Father."

He came up behind me and set his hands lightly on my

shoulders. "Just remember one thing. Even if Mark did marry this woman, don't let it sour your love for him. I know he loved you deeply, and you had five wonderful years together. Gabriel was living proof of that. Mark was happy and content with you, so please, don't let the past destroy that memory."

The tears started again. "Mark and I did have a wonderful life."

"Always hang on to that." When I turned to hug him, he had tears in his eyes, too. Then he said gruffly, "Come upstairs. There is something I want to show you."

Once inside the studio, he whipped off the canvas that covered a painting, revealing Drake Turner's completed portrait.

"Well?" he said. "Do you think I've captured the essence of the beast?"

I stood there, rocking back and forth on my heels as I studied my father's creation for a few minutes. Every so often, I nodded silently to myself in approval.

"Well?" he prompted impatiently.

"Perfect," was my pronouncement. "You've caught his air of confidence and accomplishment, and, at first glance, it's a flattering portrait of a successful merchant. But look more closely, or stare at it for a while, and you see a certain aloofness in his demeanor, an arrogance in the tilt of his head. And you've captured that icy, unsettling stare of his perfectly."

He bowed. "Why, thank you, Nora, girl. You know how I value your criticism." As he swung the canvas covering back over the painting, he said, "I can't tell you how shocked and angry I was when you came here and told me what Drake Turner had done. I fumed all night and was ready to go to Grosvenor Street and fling his money in his face."

"I'm glad you didn't, Father. That would only make matters worse."

As we went back downstairs, he asked me how Drake Turner and I were getting along after the trick he had played, and I replied, "Understandably, there's a great amount of tension between us, but both of us have managed to declare an uneasy truce of sorts and have resolved to put our feelings aside to work together."

"But what are you going to do about running the Raven Line while you're in Devonshire?"

I stopped halfway down the stairs and rubbed my forehead. "I had quite forgotten about that. I shall have to discuss it with Mr. Turner and make other arrangements. Perhaps Clement can take charge in my absence." But even as I said the words, I doubted that my overworked solicitor would have the time to do it.

As I departed, my father grasped my hands and squeezed them. His round monk's face was grave as he said, "Please be careful in your dealings with that man, Nora. If Mark didn't trust him, for whatever reason, neither should you."

I tried to reassure him, though I was not convinced myself. "Don't worry, Father. I have friends to guide and protect me."

Then why did I feel so alone—so helpless—against Drake Turner?

All the way back to Mount Street, a black cloud of gloom hung over me, sinking me deeper and deeper into despair.

What was I going to do about Drake Turner?

During the meeting with Squires and Appleby this morning, I had completely forgotten about him until my father reminded me just moments ago. How could I possibly go down to Raven's Chase to try to expose the Masons, when another wolf was at my door right here in London, waiting to swallow up my share of the Raven Line? And could I trust someone else to replace me?

By the time the carriage pulled up to my front door, I knew what I had to do.

The first words out of Grimes' mouth were, "Madam, Mr. Turner is waiting for you in the drawing room."

I thanked him and went inside. Mr. Turner was by the window, rocking on his heels and consulting his pocket watch impatiently.

As soon as he saw me, he growled, "Where in the hell have you been? I've been waiting here for the last four hours." When he saw my mutinous expression, he became apologetic at once. "I'm sorry. Forgive me for snapping at you, but I'm just eager to learn what happened at the solicitors' office this morning."

"I don't see how it's any of your concern, Mr. Turner," I said, angry with the man's familiarity. "You are my business partner, not my husband."

He rolled his eyes skyward and clenched his hands into fists. "Of course it's my concern. You are my partner, and I can't afford to have your unstable female emotions hampering our arrangement and jeopardizing the company."

"Well, Mr. Turner," I began, my lower lip trembling, "since the Raven Line is of paramount importance to you, then you'll be pleased to hear you've won."

I had the satisfaction of seeing him thrown off balance for once. "What do you mean?"

"You heard me," I replied. I may have been defeated, but I was not going to cower before this man. I straightened my shoulders, thrust my chin out belligerently, and spoke in a loud, decisive voice. "I said, you've won. Even I know when I'm beaten, Mr. Turner. I must leave London for Devonshire, so I won't be around to interfere with you any longer. I trust you won't bankrupt the company in my absence." When he said nothing, I murmured, "What, Mr. Turner, at a loss for words, are you? You should be rejoicing. You've won." Then I had to turn away, for while my words were glib and brave, I was terrified of what the future held for me.

He moved so softly I didn't realize he had come up behind me until I was startled by the sound of his voice. "What happened this morning?"

I turned, nearly bumped into him, and jumped back.

"What the Masons said was true—at least, the solicitors think so, and I can't prove otherwise." Then I told him about the marriage license with Mark's signature on it.

"Nora, I am sorry."

I was so upset I didn't even notice his use of my Christian name or reprimand him for that familiarity. "Thank you," I said stiffly. Then I explained about the investigation and how the Masons wanted to live at Raven's Chase while it was being conducted. "Since I don't want them wandering around, stealing the furniture and silver, I'll go back and stay with them until this is settled one way or another. So you're free to dismiss those sailors, paint all the ships red or yellow . . . do whatever you wish. I won't be around to interfere."

"So you're giving it all up, just like that. I might have known a woman couldn't handle such a responsibility."

I whirled around, scowling furiously. "This may be difficult for you to understand, Mr. Turner, but the Raven Line isn't as important to me as learning the truth about my late husband."

"And what if I insist that you run the company with me?"

There was a strange gleam in his eyes that I did not like or trust. "I'm not asking you to remain in London," he said. "In fact, I've got an idea. Why don't you let me come down to Devonshire with you, and we could manage the line from Raven's Chase, or even Plymouth?" He smiled. "I wouldn't want anyone to accuse me of trying to take advantage of a lady."

"Oh, that *is* amusing, sir, since you've taken advantage of me at every opportunity," I countered, "buying out John Belding, gleaning information about me from my father—"

"Will you stop being so prickly? Either you agree to my proposal, or not."

"But Devonshire would be so deadly dull for a gentleman such as yourself, Mr. Turner, used to lively London society. Are you sure you wouldn't miss your opera, or Antoine's exquisite cuisine? Or your women?"

His smile was arrogant as he retorted, "There are women in Devonshire, are there not? In any case, I would insist that Antoine be allowed to accompany me—and Faust, of course, even though you prefer canines to felines. Those are my conditions, madam. Take them or leave them."

As I stood there, I stared at the floor and searched quickly for any other excuse that might dissuade him. Finally, I said, "Devonshire is a long, long way from London, Mr. Turner, and Raven's Chase is rather isolated out near the moors. How do you propose to run your own company without access to your offices?"

He dismissed my objection with a wave of his hand. "Mr. Featherstone, my second-in-command, knows the company almost as well as I do, and can assume much of the responsibility for routine matters in my absence. I'll have him send down messengers twice a week to keep me abreast of new developments. And, in a crisis, there's always the telegraph." His mustache twitched and he smiled. "Minor problems, surely."

I finally realized the man was serious. Still, I was reluctant to commit myself, perhaps because I didn't quite trust Drake Turner, and for the best of reasons. "I'll have to think about it," I said.

"Fine," he replied, reaching for his round hat and briarwood cane. "I don't think I need to outline the advantages of such an arrangement to you." Then he wished me good day and left, humming some operatic tune.

I spent the better part of the early afternoon agonizing over Drake Turner's offer. The thought of having Mark's rival and enemy as a guest in our home sent my spirits plummeting. Still, I realized it was in my own best interest to comply with Mr. Turner and remain an active partner in the company.

And yet, as always, I found myself questioning the man's motives. While Drake Turner should have been delighted I was offering to step down and leave control of the company in his hands, here he was, going out of his way to ensure that I would still be a participant. Why? Now that he had partially conquered the enemy, was he looking forward to residing in his house as the ultimate triumph? The man could be so secretive, so withdrawn, who could tell what he was thinking?

And how could I possibly live with myself if I invited my husband's rival to live with us, even for such a short time? What would Colin and Amabel think? Yet if I didn't, there was a good chance Drake Turner could encroach on my authority and gain even more control of the Raven Line by taking actions I wasn't aware of. At least if he was with me, I could ensure that didn't happen. So, faced with the choice between having the man under Mark's roof and losing the company he had worked so hard to establish, I found my decision quite easy after all.

I went to my desk and wrote Mr. Turner a brief note, asking him to be ready to leave for Raven's Chase the next morning at eight o'clock.

CHAPTER

As the soft green landscape of southern England slid by my window, I found myself remembering the countless times Mark and I had sat together, alone, in a first class compartment on our return to Raven's Chase after spending months in London or Europe. Odd, but with him seated close by, his large hand covering mine possessively, I never really noticed the lazy green meadows of Somerset rolling away from the tracks or the slate rooftops of villages visible just above the trees in the distance. Even after five years of marriage, when many of our friends had become as familiar as old shoes to their spouses, Mark and I were as absorbed in each other as newlyweds and never failed to take advantage of any private moment to hold hands or kiss. Once, he had even tried to persuade me to make love in our railroad compartment, between Exeter and Plymouth, but the risk and embarrassment of discovery had inhibited me. How the rogue had teased me about my uncharacteristic prudishness!

"You're blushing," a voice said, and I started, for those had been Mark's exact words when I declined his bold, immodest proposal.

But when I snapped out of my daydream, I realized they were now being spoken by Drake Turner, seated across from me and wearing an inquiring look.

"I wonder what you were thinking just then," he said.

"Something personal and very private," I replied coolly, looking out the window again.

His gaze was direct as he smiled and said, "Thank you for inviting me to be your guest at Raven's Chase, though it was on somewhat short notice."

Despite that short notice, the man had been waiting for me at Paddington Station promptly at eight o'clock the following morning, with a pile of luggage, a grumbling Antoine, and a sleepy-eyed valet carrying one disgruntled, yowling cat in a small, portable cage. Mr. Turner's entourage, plus my own Fenner, were now ensconced in the compartment adjacent to ours.

"I apologize for that," I said, "but the Masons will be arriving in Devonshire the day after tomorrow, and I want to get there first to warn Colin and Amabel and the household staff at the Chase."

"Why didn't you ride down with them?"

I stared at him as though he were daft. "I'm sure they are capable of reading a train schedule and finding their own way."

"So you haven't met the boy yet?"

"No," I replied, turning my attention to a smart carriage with yellow wheels as it disappeared behind a bend in the road. "I'll meet him on Thursday, I suppose."

I was not looking forward to meeting a ten-year-old boy some people claimed was my husband's legitimate son. To me, Mark had only one son, and that was Gabriel. A vision flitted across my mind's eye of Mark laughing as he tossed Gabriel almost up to the nursery's high ceiling, then caught him as he came down, kicking and squealing with glee. Never had a man loved a child more.

I heard Mr. Turner murmur, "Amabel . . . that's Trelawney's wife, isn't it?"

Nodding, I replied, "She's my sister-in-law."

"Your father told me you first came to Raven's Chase as her hired companion."

I nodded again, wondering just how much my garrulous father had told Drake Turner about my first acquaintance with the Gerrick family.

When he saw I wasn't going to enlighten him further, he

added, "He also started to tell me some wild, fantastic tale about Amabel's child being kidnapped."

I couldn't win. With a sigh of resignation, I said, "You may as well know the entire story, Mr. Turner, since you're bound to hear it sooner or later.

"It actually began some years ago with Damon, Mark's younger brother. At that time, he was a spoiled young man used to doing whatever he liked, whenever he pleased, no matter who happened to be hurt. Well, when he was a high-spirited Oxford student, he seduced a young girl from the town. The innocent misinterpreted his intentions, shall we say, so naturally she was distraught when she discovered she was going to have his child. Of course, he did what any upstanding young gentleman would do—he repudiated her." I took a deep breath before continuing. "Her shame was so great that she took her own life. The girl's father—a physician—was grief-stricken and came down to Devonshire demanding justice from Damon's father. The then Lord Raven just laughed in his face and enlisted Damon in an Army regiment bound for India."

I quickly related the death of Damon's fiancée at the battle of Cawnpore, and his subsequent madness, and watched Mr. Turner's icy eyes melt with pity.

I continued with, "Damon was useless to the Army after that, so he was discharged and sent home. About that time, Mark returned home from his travels, and their father died. But little did they know that the physician had not forgotten the wrong done to him. So, he had his sister-in-law installed as housekeeper at the Chase to spy on the family, and he himself replaced the village doctor in Sheepstor, who was retiring. Then he set out on a diabolical plan of revenge against the Gerricks that included driving Damon deeper into madness, and—"

"How in the world did he accomplish that?" Mr. Turner demanded.

"By having his sister-in-law impersonate Damon's dead fiancée." I explained how the doctor had discovered a secret passage in the nearby ruins of St. Barnabas' Abbey which enabled them to appear to Damon, then disappear before they could be discovered. "With the doctor in a perfect position to influence Damon's unstable mind, he lured him out to the abbey night after night, where his 'fiancée' waited. The plan worked beautifully, Damon's mind became progressively worse, and Mark had no other choice but to commit him. Meanwhile, Colin returned from Australia a wealthy man, to discover Amabel had borne him a son in his absence. We were all devastated when the housekeeper kidnapped Peter and placed him with a baby farmer in London."

Mr. Turner just shook his head in disgust.

"Colin and I went to London together, and through the aid of a . . . friend, we found the child."

"You were very fortunate."

I thought of that harrowing time and replied, "Very fortunate indeed." Then I shuddered. "To this day, I find it very difficult to trust doctors."

He smiled at that, then turned away without further comment, and instantly, a chasm yawned between us.

Suddenly feeling chilled, I reached for my paletot lying on the seat and slipped on the stylish jacket that Amabel had had made for me. Mark had always liked me to wear pretty clothes, and the paletot and dress I now wore were elegant and expensive, far different from the one or two faded, darned garments that had accompanied me to Raven's Chase all those years ago. It was so unfair the way even clothes could remind me of my late husband.

Now Mr. Turner turned to me again and said, "Will Trelawney be meeting us at the station?"

I shook my head. "He doesn't even know I'm coming."

My thoughts raced back unbidden to the last time Colin had met me at the station. I was returning home from a brief visit to a sick friend in Plymouth, and Mark was supposed to meet my train. It was dark when I arrived, with fat snowflakes drifting down, but no tall, comforting figure searched the platform for me. Puzzled, I waited for a full half-hour, shivering in the snow, wondering what was keeping my husband.

And then I saw the Gerrick carriage come thundering into the yard, the driver barely able to stop the horses in time. It was not Mark who flung open the door and bolted out, but Colin, hatless as he came running and sliding toward me. When I saw his face, I knew something dreadful had happened.

Now I squeezed my eyes shut and covered them with my hands, but I could not blot out Colin's white tormented face.

A viselike grip on my wrists and a firm, "Nora!" snapped me back into the present. My hands were gently pried away, and I opened my eyes to find Mr. Turner's face inches from my own, those blue eyes bright and intense.

"Are you all right?" he demanded.

"Please let go of me," I ordered, offering nothing more.

He looked as though he were about to ask the reason for my odd behavior, then just released me and sat back in his seat. "We should be arriving in Plymouth soon," he said, his voice cool and distant as he consulted his pocket watch, "and then Sheepstor."

Once we reached Sheepstor, I hired a carriage to transport our entourage to the Little Chase, and when we arrived there half an hour later, I sent the servants on ahead to Raven's Chase after giving Fenner instructions to relay to Mrs. Harkins concerning our guests. Then Drake and I went inside.

We found Colin and Amabel in the drawing room, and when they saw me, their mouths dropped open in astonishment.

"Nora!" Colin cried, leaping to his feet.

"What are you doing here?" Amabel added, her blue eyes wide. "We thought you were staying in London all summer."

"I'm sorry to startle you like this," I apologized, entering the room and kissing her on the cheek, "but I was too distraught to send a telegram."

"Is something wrong?" Colin demanded, flicking a curious glance at Drake Turner.

"Before I tell you, I'd like you both to meet Drake Turner, my new partner. Mr. Turner, allow me to present Colin and Amabel Trelawney."

Colin's blue eyes narrowed, and I could see him redden beneath his sandy beard. He made no attempt to murmur a greeting or extend his hand as Mr. Turner came forward.

Amabel looked incredulous, as though she could not believe the man who had inspired such loathing in her brother was standing in her drawing room. But she recovered herself enough to nod briefly and say, "Mr. Turner," in a tone so cold it made me shiver.

He, however, seemed to relish the effect he was having on everyone, for he grinned impudently and bowed. "Mr. and Mrs. Trelawney . . . my pleasure."

"Now," Colin said, "what is all this about?"

While the men sat down and eyed each other with hostility and Amabel rang for tea, I began pacing the floor to calm myself.

"Several days ago, I received some visitors from America," I began, "a brother and sister named Seth and Ella Mason." I took a deep breath and laced my fingers together, but even that couldn't quell the tremor in my voice and limbs. "The woman calls herself Mrs. Mark Gerrick, and she claims she was married to Mark eleven years ago."

The Trelawneys stared at me, thunderstruck, for what seemed like an interminable time, and both turned deathly pale. Then Colin rose to his feet. "Nora, this is . . . preposterous!"

"I agree. When they first came to the Mount Street house and told me, I was as dumbfounded as you are."

"This is absurd," Amabel echoed her husband. "She must be lying, Nora."

"She has a marriage license with Mark's signature on it," I said, "which, of course, must have been forged. But the Masons have the solicitors convinced they are telling the truth, and I can't prove otherwise at this point."

"But how did this ever happen?" Amabel cried. "Where did Mark meet this woman and supposedly marry her?"

I related all that the Masons had told me about Mark and Ella's meeting, and when I finished, the Trelawneys were more white-faced and grim than before.

"But even if her story is true," Amabel said slowly, "even if she was my brother's wife, she still can't inherit Raven's Chase." That was Amabel, always thinking of inheritances and securing the Gerrick fortune for her son.

My eyes filled with tears as I said, "But this woman has a son, Amabel."

Her mouth dropped open in astonishment. "What?"

"He is ten years old, and his name is Brentwood. He is the sixth Earl of Raven, unless we can prove otherwise."

Rising in agitation, her hands fluttering helplessly, Amabel went to her husband's side for strength and support. "No, that can't be true! Raven's Chase belongs to Damon, and someday to Timothy." Her wide, desperate eyes were filled with pain and supplication. "Colin, we've got to *do* something."

We were interrupted by the maid serving tea, but once she left we ignored the tray and picked up the thread of our conversation.

"Are you sure, Nora?" Colin asked, slipping his arm around his wife's waist.

"Do you think I want to believe those people?" I cried, my voice rising in anguish. "How do you think I feel, hearing that my husband may have been married to another woman and had a child by her?"

Colin's gaze fell to the floor, but Amabel was still too shocked to say anything. Mr. Turner, meanwhile, who had been silent so far, took the liberty of pouring a cup of tea and handing it to me. I accepted it gratefully and murmured my thanks.

As I sipped the strong brew, I related the Masons' reasons

for not coming forward all these years and saw Colin's face lengthen in hopelessness.

Finally, Amabel, on the verge of hysteria, cried out, "And what are we supposed to do, just sit back and turn over Raven's Chase and the Gerrick fortune to these—these usurpers? There must be something we can do to fight them." She looked imploringly at her husband, but he would not meet her gaze.

Able to stand no longer, I sat in the nearest chair and explained how Clement Charles had insisted on an investigation before any titles or moneys were turned over to the Masons. "I've been thinking about this all the way down here from London," I said, "and I have an idea." Hope suddenly sprang into the Trelawneys' eyes, though Mr. Turner regarded me with skepticism. "Colin, would you be willing to go to New York City and investigate the Masons' claims?" Before he could comment, I rushed on, speaking hurriedly in my effort to convince him. "I would be fully satisfied with the outcome. If you learned that this Ella Mason and Mark were married and had a son, I would accept it more readily than if some American solicitor—who does not know, or care about us—told me so."

Colin frowned, and I could almost hear him thinking. I had obviously caught him off guard. "I don't know, Nora," he said slowly. "It would take me about three weeks to cross the Atlantic, several months to conduct such as investigation, and another three weeks to return."

"I know I'm asking more than I have a right to," I confessed. "I'm asking you to leave your wife and children for three, perhaps four, months, and your business as well. And it may be all for naught. You may learn that the Masons are telling the truth after all." I glanced down at the narrow gold band on my finger. "But there is no one I trust more than you, Colin. I know you will keep digging until you unearth the truth, whereas another man might stop when he thought he had all the answers."

Drake Turner suddenly spoke up. "I don't think I need to

remind you, Trelawney, that your family will ultimately benefit if you can prove the Masons wrong."

"Mr. Turner!" I cried indignantly, but even as I reprimanded him, I grudgingly admired his keen perception. He had seen what it would take to convince Amabel her husband should go to America.

Colin glowered at him. "I don't need you to remind me of that, Turner."

Amabel waved her hand in a bored fashion. "Let's not be hypocritical, my friends. Mr. Turner is merely saying what we are all thinking. He's right, my dear," she said to her husband, squeezing his hand. "Our sons will benefit if you can prove these people are frauds."

Colin looked into his wife's eyes, then sighed in surrender. "I suppose I must, but there is much we have to discuss, Nora, before I leave."

"Then you will go to America?" I asked excitedly, my hopes rising.

He glanced at Amabel again. "If my wife can do without me for several months . . ."

"You know I can't bear to be parted from you, Colin," she said, "but in this case, I'm afraid we must both make the sacrifice."

I felt as though Colin had just lifted the world from my shoulders. Everything was going to be all right now. "Thank you, Colin. I don't know how I can ever repay you."

A smile of irony touched his mouth. "I hope your faith in me is justified, Nora."

"You've never once let me down."

Was I imagining it, or did Amabel's eyes narrow slightly as I said those words? But then her face took on its wide-eyed innocent look, and I decided I must have been mistaken.

"Well, Mr. Turner and I must be taking our leave," I announced, rising. "I know you both will need time to become accustomed to what I've just told you. It took me a while to adjust to the news myself. And, by the way," I added, "you'll soon have the chance to meet the Masons and judge for yourself."

"They're coming here?" Amabel asked. When I explained their solicitors had insisted I take them as guests until the matter was resolved, she turned an unflattering shade of red. "Why, I never—!"

"There is nothing I can do about it," I lied and held my breath when I saw Colin frown. But he didn't challenge me, and I breathed a sigh of relief as Mr. Turner and I said our goodbyes and departed.

Once we were seated in the Gerrick carriage, I turned to him and said, "That was very rude of you to remind Amabel that she would benefit if Colin agreed to go to America."

He smiled at me. "Come now, Mrs. Gerrick, righteous indignation does not become you. As Mrs. Trelawney herself said, I merely voiced what you all were thinking."

"Still, it was rather forward of you."

"I didn't get where I am by always being polite and doing what is expected of me."

"How well I know that, Mr. Turner," was my tart reply.

He laughed at that, a deep rich sound filled with mirth. Then he said, "I wonder if Antoine has taken over your kitchen yet."

I stared at him in horror as I thought of my cook, a small matchstick of a woman named Mrs. Baker. She was fiercely proud of what she called her "good, simple English fare," which was more likely to stick to one's ribs than to excite one's palate. Antoine and his "foreign ideas" would not be welcome in Mrs. Baker's kitchen.

"But you've only just arrived!" I sputtered.

He replied, "Do you expect me to miss even one of Antoine's delightful meals, Mrs. Gerrick?"

I shook my head in consternation, but before I could utter a word, the carriage rolled to a halt and a footman was opening the door to assist us down.

As soon as we entered the foyer, I watched Mr. Turner

carefully to gauge his reaction to Raven's Chase, the house he never would have been allowed to enter during Mark's lifetime. Did I expect to see his eyes light up in pleasure and see his mustache twitch in a smile of satisfaction? If I did, I was disappointed, for all he did was look startled and exclaim, "Why, this is exactly like the foyer in the Trelawneys' house!"

"You have it backward," I replied, then explained how Colin had copied the Chase as a wedding gift to his bride.

The foyer was twice the size of the one at the Little Chase, and I watched Mr. Turner's eyes rove over it, from the dark, slate flagstone flooring to the sweeping horseshoe staircase of polished oak that met in a balcony on the floor above. He was admiring the two huge brass pots filled to overflowing with colorful spring flowers from our own extensive gardens, when sharp, impatient footsteps echoed down the hall toward us.

I looked up to see Mrs. Harkins approach in a soft jingling of keys, her steely eyes alarmed and her mouth drawn into a thin line of displeasure.

"Welcome home, Lady Raven," my housekeeper said with a slight inclination of her head.

"Thank you, Mrs. Harkins," I replied. "I trust that a room has been made ready for Mr. Turner here, and suitable chambers found for his valet and chef?"

"Of course, madam. I've put Mr. Turner in the Green Room, and his valet in the servants' quarters." Now Mrs. Harkins jingled the keys rapidly, a sure sign of her distress. "But, madam, the . . . the other person in his party . . . he insisted on being shown to the kitchen immediately, and he's reduced poor Mrs. Baker to tears! And he just won't listen to me, madam. The kitchen is in chaos."

Drake Turner tried to keep from snickering as he pretended to study himself in the foyer's mirror, but I was more concerned with placating Mrs. Harkins, who was not used to having anyone usurp her supreme authority.

"That is Antoine, Mr. Turner's French chef," I explained,

my voice calm and soothing. "He expects to prepare all of his employer's meals. As soon as I go to my room and change, I shall go down to the kitchen and resolve matters with Mrs. Baker."

"And one other matter, madam."

"Yes, Mrs. Harkins?"

She trembled so violently her keys jingled of their own accord. "When I showed Mr. Turner's valet to the Green Room, he turned a *cat* loose, madam. You know I won't tolerate filthy animals in the house."

"The cat is our guest's pet," I explained, and before she could say another word, I dismissed her with, "Will there be anything else, Mrs. Harkins?"

Rebellion flared in her steely eyes for just a second, then she remembered her place and murmured, "No, madam," in surrender. I watched her stalk off, the very picture of displeasure and indignation.

As soon as she was gone, Mr. Turner said, "So, Antoine has taken over your kitchen, and Faust your house. I suspected they would."

"They're like their master," I retorted, then said, "If you'll follow me, I'll show you to the Green Room. Later, I would suggest we go down to the kitchen together and resolve this matter before I lose my cook. Then I'll show you the rest of the house, unless, of course, you'd rather wait until tomorrow."

"Tonight will be fine," he said and followed me upstairs.

Hours later, as I sat in a tub of hot, rose-scented water, letting the rising steam coat my skin and crimp my hair even more, I let today's events run slowly through my mind.

Drake Turner and I had succeeded in calming an agitated Mrs. Baker and even had her agreeing to share her kitchen with the temperamental Antoine. When I returned to my rooms, I found my clothes unpacked and put away, and my medicines arranged on the nightstand near my bed. Then I shocked poor

Fenner by informing her that I would be dining with Mr. Turner tonight, not alone in my room, as usual, and to please set out a suitable dinner dress.

Now, as I sponged the grit and grime of travel from my arms, I thought about Colin. I felt guilty about asking him to go to America to investigate the Masons, but he was the ideal choice. Yet, was I growing too dependent on him, taking advantage of his good nature and high regard for me? Probably. But if there was any way I could prove Mark had never been married to that Mason woman, I would take it, no matter who was inconvenienced. In my own way, I was as unprincipled and ruthless as Drake Turner, and powerless to stop myself from being so.

Again, I wondered what Mark's reaction would have been had he known his enemy was a guest under this roof, but somehow, I think he would have understood why I had to have Drake Turner here with me. I needed to believe that, otherwise I never would have been able to live with the guilt.

After stepping from my bath and drying off, I went into my bedroom to find a dress already set out for me. It was more Amabel's style than mine, a dinner gown of crisp black taffeta, trimmed with deep flounces of soft lace at the hem, and a neckline I could see was cut way too low for a decorous widow. But tonight, I felt in need of something to buoy my flagging spirits, so I summoned Fenner and had her help me dress.

Later, upon seeing Mr. Turner's unabashed look of appreciation, I wished I had not decided to dress for dinner after all.

When we finished eating Antoine's superb meal in the Garden Room, with its French doors overlooking the terrace and gardens beyond, Drake Turner held me to my promise to take him on a tour of Raven's Chase, though I was bone-weary and yearning to slip between the sheets and just sleep all night.

We had been down to the kitchens earlier today, and since

the potboys would be up to their elbows in soapy water and greasy pans, I decided to begin our tour with the ground floor. As I showed my guest the library, with shelves of familiar, favorite books, and the game room, where Mark and I often sent those billiard balls spinning all evening, I felt as though I were seeing Raven's Chase for the first time, through new eyes, and I suddenly realized how dear this old house had become to me.

We did bypass Mark's locked study, however, and went upstairs to the first floor, where there were mostly bedrooms with such descriptive names as the Print Room, with its pink floral wallpaper, and the Yellow Room, hung with heavy yellow draperies that gave the room its name. Mr. Turner especially liked the Ming Room, with its majestic chinoiserie pagoda bed, and tried to impress me by informing me that the coromandel screen at the far end of the room was very rare.

As we discussed the pair of blue-and-white china vases flanking the fireplace, I found myself filled with raw determination to keep Raven's Chase at all costs, and not just for Peter. This had been Mark's home, and later, mine as well. We had left indelible impressions of our personalities everywhere, and it seemed as though these very walls had absorbed our happiness and contentment. I could not lose it.

We left the Ming Room, and as we continued down a darkened corridor, I realized we were approaching the nursery. Suddenly, I couldn't breathe, and the lamp I carried began shaking uncontrollably. If I dropped it, I could start a fire . . .

"Let's go this way," I said, turning abruptly to go back the way we came.

"Something's wrong," Mr. Turner said, stopping to take the lamp from me.

My teeth were chattering so badly I could barely reply, "The nursery is this way."

He seemed to understand at once, so I assumed my father had told him about the two locked rooms that caused me the most pain.

"It's so cold," I muttered, as he drew me away from that dark, terrifying expanse of hallway. "So cold."

"Why don't we stop by your room for a shawl, then?" he suggested.

After I had fetched the wool shawl and savored its warmth, I said, "I don't think you'd be interested in the attics, so all that's left to see is the portrait gallery."

"Ah, the Gerrick rogues' gallery," Mr. Turner commented with a sardonic smile as he walked beside me.

When we started down the long, narrow gallery, he held the lamp high, so he could examine the many portraits in heavy, carved frames that took up the entire wall from floor to ceiling. As I looked up into these faces crazed with age as familiar to me as my own, this motley collection of Gerrick ancestors seemed to regard me with benevolence and acceptance. Each one, from the buccaneering Elizabethan Gerrick in his pointed beard and velvet doublet, to the Georgian bluestocking in her straw hat and silk panniers, looked down at me as though they knew I had won the right to belong here. I knew it was only my imagination, but the feeling of their approval heightened my determination to fight for what was mine.

I smiled.

"Why are you smiling?" Mr. Turner asked, those pale eyes missing nothing. "Do you find these people amusing for some reason?"

"I'm smiling because, no matter what happens, this is my home, and this is my family."

When we approached the end of the gallery, where Mark's portraits hung—one with Amabel and Damon, painted when they were children, and another of Mark and me done when we were wed—my heart began to hammer against my ribs, and I felt chilled again, despite my voluminous shawl.

"Lord Raven," was all Mr. Turner said, as he stood there and stared up at the foe he could never vanquish in life.

"Yes," I murmured and hurried past, so he was forced to follow me and not linger as I'm sure he would have liked.

On the way back to our rooms, I said, "Well, you've seen all of Raven's Chase. If you need anything, feel free to ask. As a guest, the house is at your disposal, but I would advise against trying to take advantage of our hospitality."

"I wouldn't dream of it," he said when we arrived at the Green Room. He was so close to me, his eyes appeared dark and inscrutable as they lingered for just an instant on my low neckline. "Good night."

When he opened his door, a black streak slipped past us, stopped in the hall and regarded us out of disdainful golden eyes.

"Beware, mice," Mr. Turner said with a laugh, "Faust is on the prowl. I hope your formidable housekeeper won't object."

I smiled. "I think Faust will be too quick for her." Then I wished him good night, but as I turned to leave, he stopped me with, "Mrs. Gerrick?"

I turned back. "Yes?"

"Please call me Drake," he said, his voice low. " 'Mr. Turner' makes me feel a hundred years old, and I'm not yet thirty-two."

I resented his attempt to ingratiate himself, and felt myself stiffen. "I prefer to go on calling you Mr. Turner," I said coldly, "and expect the same courtesy from you."

"As you wish," he snapped, then stepped into his room and slammed the door behind him.

Late that night, when the rest of the house had long been abed and Fenner's hot milk stood untouched by my bedside, I stole down to the portrait gallery in my nightgown and bare feet, my shawl wrapped snugly around me for warmth.

Setting my lamp down on a deep windowsill, I leaned against the opposite wall and regarded Mark's portrait with a mixture of yearning and bitter regret. He looked so magnificent, I felt the deep ache of longing growing in my heart until it seemed to fill my chest to bursting. My father had captured Mark's dark, Byronic good looks, the devilish glint in his cold gray eyes and the arrogant smile that would often cross his mouth. Intangible qualities had been captured as well—strength, intelligence, sheer power; they were all on canvas for the world to see.

I tried to picture Mark as a young seaman, sailing the oceans of the world from port to port, seeking riches and adventure. How convenient it would be to enjoy the local women for a few days, then sail away, never to be seen for months, often years. And I didn't doubt that Mark availed himself of such pleasures, for he was no monk. But to marry one of his flirtations, then leave her so callously, never to think of her again? I thought I knew my husband well enough to know that he would never do such a dishonorable thing.

Scanning the gray depths of his eyes, I could find no answer.

I don't know how long I stood there, staring at him, but when I realized it was deathly cold in this long tunnel of a hallway, I shook myself, took my lamp, and padded back to my own room.

Once inside, I ignored the sleeping draft, went straight to Mark's armoire and took out a long wool coat he had often worn in the winter. I pressed it to my face, desperately inhaling the faint, spicy scent of shaving soap and, suddenly, it was as though Mark's strong arms were about me once again. This was the only medicine I needed.

I could sleep at last.

The following morning I rose before daybreak, put my phantom lover back in the armoire, and hurriedly dressed for a ride. The house was just beginning to stir, with most of the activity centered in the kitchen. I could hear the low voices of Antoine and Mrs. Baker working in harmony, and smell the tantalizing aromas of bacon and strong coffee as I passed the kitchen and let myself out the back way without being observed.

The flowers drooped with dew this morning, and there was still a gentle ground mist swirling in the fields, but the cool morning air was crisp and invigorating as I hurried down the flagstone path toward the stables. When I arrived, I had Young Corman saddle my horse, Curlew, a frisky chestnut mare with flashy white socks on her hind legs.

As he helped me to mount, I asked, "Have you seen Odalisque?"

The groom rubbed his chinful of stubble and looked puzzled. "None of the men have seen her recently, madam."

I scowled as I settled myself in the saddle and gathered the reins. "They haven't? Where could she be?"

"Maybe Lord Riordan finally caught 'er."

"I'm sure she'll appear," I said, touching my heel to Curlew's ribs and moving her out of the stableyard at a brisk walk.

As I rode closer to the abbey, I slowed Curlew and kept her on a tight rein, for she didn't like this place and always pranced and shied when we came here, ready to flee at the touch of my heel. Amabel attributed her skittishness to being startled by noisy children playing out here one day, but I liked to think the mare sensed something evil about this place that made her wary and afraid.

And I could understand why, for even though St. Barnabas' Abbey was a ruin of crumbling stone walls open to the sky, there was something eerie about it. Perhaps there were ghosts of monks long dead still walking its cellars, a warren of dark cells and secret passages. I shivered, instantly communicating my uneasiness to Curlew, who snorted and tossed her head as though trying to shake off her bridle.

"Oh, come now," I chided, patting her glossy neck. "There's nothing to be afraid of."

I thought taking a jump would calm her down, but just as I turned her head toward a low stone wall, a horse and rider came cantering toward me. It was Amabel on her mettlesome blue roan stallion.

"What are you doing up so early?" I asked as she reined in her horse by my side.

"I couldn't sleep very well," she replied, "after your shocking news yesterday." She looked at me long and hard, as though she could see the truth written on my face. "Everything you told us . . . it's true, isn't it?"

I nodded. "Unfortunately."

"For a while, I thought it might have been a nightmare."

"Oh, no," I said bitterly. "It's certainly not that. Ella Mason, her brother and a boy they claim is Mark's rightful heir will be arriving tomorrow."

"They must be lying, Nora," she said in desperation.

It was odd to see Amabel's reaction paralleling my own, when we were not alike at all. "Of course they're lying. But they're a very clever pair. They've got everyone convinced they're telling the truth, and until Colin can come up with evidence to the contrary in America, I'm afraid the Masons are going to be your new neighbors."

Her delicate mouth tightened. "They will never take what is rightfully my family's."

And what about me, I wondered to myself? You will still have the Little Chase, but I will be left with nothing. I did not voice my thoughts, but said, "Thank you for agreeing to let Colin go. You two love each other so much, I know it will be difficult to be separated for several months. I can't tell you enough how much I appreciate it."

"You know me, Nora," she said wryly. "My motives are not entirely unselfish."

I laughed at Amabel's blunt assessment of herself. "Oh, I realize that."

She said she wanted to run her horse, so we fell silent as we urged our mounts up the sharply sloping path that led to the moors beyond. I leaned forward, giving my mare her head, and settled in to enjoy our gallop as we streaked past oaks and low evergreens that grew so thickly on the hillside. Finally, when both horses were out of breath and Amabel and I panting, we broke from the trees at last to come out to Dartmoor.

The panorama fanning out below us never failed to move

me with its wild, haunting majesty. The moors seemed to extend out to the ends of the earth in giant patches of green and brown cut by wide swaths of purple heather and golden gorse and dotted by white, woolly sheep. Off to our right was a rocky, ragged tor, and to our left, lowland bogs of green, stagnant water that bubbled up between clumps of razor-sharp marsh grass.

As we walked our horses side by side down the hill, Amabel said, "I didn't have the time to ask you last night, but what is that man doing here with you? He's not your lover, is he?"

I was so shocked and angry, my mouth formed words of indignation, but they never came out. When I finally regained some semblance of composure, I railed at her. "Amabel Gerrick Trelawney, how could you even think such a thing! Your brother is the only man I've ever loved, and for you to even hint that I had formed an . . . an attachment with his bitterest enemy . . ." Words finally failed me, and all I could do was let helpless tears course down my cheeks.

As usual, she was contrite in an instant. "Oh, Nora, I am so sorry. I didn't mean to offend you, but . . . well, it was just the way Mr. Turner kept staring at you when you weren't aware of it. I must have been mistaken, and I do apologize."

She fumbled in the pocket of her habit until she produced a handkerchief and offered it to me. "Forgive me for being such a fool."

After I wiped away the tears, I said, "Drake Turner is only interested in me as a partner, nothing more. I'm sure he has more women than he knows what to do with."

"Oh, I don't doubt it," she agreed complacently, brushing a fly from her mount's neck with a flick of her crop. "He reminds me of that portrait of Greyston Gerrick hanging in the gallery at Raven's Chase." At my puzzled expression, she said, "The Elizabethan. He and Mr. Turner don't look alike, of course, but they have that air about them. Men like that just take what they want and damn the consequences. They can break a woman's heart, but are so clever at it she doesn't hate them for it afterward." Amabel furrowed her brow and watched a hawk lazily riding the wind overhead. "Have you ever noticed how life is so unfair to us women?"

I gave her a wry look out of the corner of my eye and muttered, "On several occasions."

"I've seen them all in Hyde Park at the fashionable hour of five, the fine gentlemen taking a carriage ride with their wives and daughters on a warm spring day. When they pass their mistresses, they stare straight ahead and pretend not to see them, but everyone—except the gentleman's poor wife, of course—knows that he's probably keeping her in grand style somewhere." Amabel's lip curled and her blue eyes lost their innocence. "But let me take a lover and I'm labeled a harlot and ostracized by everyone in Devonshire."

This outburst from Amabel startled me, for she usually accepted her place in the world without questioning. I wondered what had brought this on, and said so.

She looked somewhat sheepish as she shrugged and said, "I know it's quite out of character for me, Nora, but every so often I do think about more than expensive dresses and my children."

"I'm glad to hear it."

"But, getting back to Mr. Turner . . . Colin detests him, even more so when he learned how Turner secretly bought out John Belding and gained control of half the Raven Line. Colin says you and he are going to have to fight Mr. Turner every step of the way because the man's unprincipled." She patted her stallion's neck, then began chattering about how she was just yearning for the day she could come out of mourning and wear a red silk petticoat. Immediately, she apologized for her lack of respect for Mark's memory, but I assured her that I was not offended.

Finally, she gave a little sigh that heralded boredom, and said, "Well, I'm famished, so I think I'll be getting back to the Little Chase. The boys are sure to be awake and clamoring for their mama. Good day, Nora. Do call on us later today, won't you?"

I wished her good day, then sent Curlew racing for home.

What could Amabel have been thinking of when she asked if Drake Turner were my lover? She had known me long enough to know that I would never, ever do such a thing to disgrace Mark's memory. To even suggest such an impossibility . . .

I shook my head as I returned Curlew to Young Corman, and went back to the house. I had much to do before the Masons arrived tomorrow, and worrying about Drake's fictitious interest in me was not one of them.

Later that afternoon, while in Colin's study for a council of war, I watched Drake play croquet with Miss Blessed, Nellie, and the boys. His round hat, tie, and coat were left draped over the back of a white wicker chair, and his shirtsleeves were rolled up to his elbows, revealing forearms surprisingly muscular for a man who sat behind a desk all day. I found myself wondering if perhaps he exercised in one of the many gymnasiums popular in London, as Mark so often did when we were there.

Then I shook myself in consternation. What did I care if the man exercised in a gymnasium?

"He's certainly made himself at home, hasn't he?" a voice said behind me.

The sound of Colin's voice made me start and turn around. "So I see. When did he meet the boys?"

"He came to call late this morning, and they rescued him from Damon," he replied. "It's unfortunate my brother-in-law's gun wasn't loaded, for once."

Colin's bald statement startled me, for he was a fair, genial man who rarely had an unkind word to say about anyone, unless it was well deserved. "I've never heard you speak so harshly about anyone before."

His blue eyes danced. "Mark must have had his reasons for

113

not trusting the man, though he never came out and told me what they were. Perhaps I have judged him unfairly, but I do disapprove of his business methods with you, and that would naturally color my opinion of him." Colin looked reflective and stroked his beard. "I wish I didn't have to leave you at his mercy, Nora."

I smiled as I walked away from the window and crossed the room. "Well, you can't be in two places at once, Colin, and you'll be of more use to me in America."

He walked over and seated himself on the edge of the desk. "I'm looking forward to meeting the Masons tomorrow."

I grimaced as I related my impression of the Masons to him. Finally, I said, "They're determined to win at all costs, and they've rehearsed their roles well." I looked him squarely in the eye and said, "I'm frightened, Colin."

"Don't be, Nora," he said kindly. "Your servants are loyal to you, so you have nothing to fear in my absence." Then he tapped his fingers against the desk top and frowned. "How are you going to behave toward them while they're here?"

When I looked puzzled he elaborated with, "Are you going to give them rooms in the servants' quarters and let them dine below stairs, or are you going to be cordial and treat them as any other guests?"

"I confess I hadn't thought much about what to do, but to expect me to be cordial and welcoming to them . . ." I thrust my chin out aggressively. "That is asking too much of me. I plan to stay away from the Masons as much as possible."

Colin looked thoughtful for a moment. "I don't know if that would be wise, Nora."

My mouth dropped. "What are you saying, Colin, that I should treat these people as *friends?*"

"Well, you know the old saying about catching more flies with honey than vinegar."

"Oh, I see. You think I should try to trap them."

A slow smile spread across his face as he nodded.

"I don't mean to discourage you," I said, "but I think it's impossible. If they have perfected such a convincing case for themselves that none of us can challenge, I'm sure they're too wily to be trapped. The Masons aren't stupid, Colin, and I think it would be foolish of us to underestimate them. We'd only be putting ourselves at a disadvantage."

Colin seemed disturbed by that, for he liked neat solutions to any problem. "One of them must have an Achilles' heel somewhere."

"Well, it's certainly not Ella," I declared. "Her nerves are made of iron. I think she could sit through an earthquake or typhoon without blinking."

"And her brother?"

"Oh, he tries to disarm everyone with his ingratiating smiles and attempts to make his sister look like a helpless, grieving widow, but I think he's as strong as she is, just more able and willing to hide it."

Then I handed him a packet of papers I had brought with me from London. "This was compiled by Clement Charles and contains information about the Masons—where they lived, the names of people they gave as references. You should find it most helpful."

"Splendid. Then I can leave on the first ship bound for New York from Plymouth—after I meet the Masons, of course."

His mention of ships suddenly reminded me of the sailors Drake Turner wanted to dismiss, so I decided to ask Colin if he thought our ships were overstaffed.

"Definitely," he replied without hesitation, "by three or four men per ship. I've always thought so, but it never seemed to disturb Mark."

"What would happen to the men if they were dismissed?"

"They're experienced seamen. They'd find work the next day with another line." He studied me for a second, then smiled. "I know what you're thinking, Nora, and I can assure you their families wouldn't be destitute."

I blushed and looked away. "You know me too well, Colin."

Then we rose and walked to the door. Before Colin could open it for me, I stopped and grasped his hand. "Thank you for everything, Colin," I said warmly, trying to to express the deep gratitude I felt.

"You're most welcome," he replied, then turned and went back to his desk.

"I won!" Peter shrieked, jumping at least two feet into the air. "I won!"

"But you played a good game, Tim," I heard Mr. Turner say as he tousled my nephew's head.

Timothy's bleak little face glowed. "Do you really think so, Mr. Turner?"

"A fine game," Drake insisted. "Why, once you get a little older, you'll even be able to beat me."

Peter, who saw any compliment to his brother as somehow lessening his own worth, scowled and protested, "But I *won*, Mr. Turner."

"Peter," Nellie said, stepping into the middle of the fracas, "I think it's time you boys went inside now."

He wasted no time. "I'll race you to the house, Timmy," and was off and running before his brother could give it a second thought. But Timothy went running after Peter, as I knew he would. We watched them go racing across the lawn to disappear into the house, while Nellie followed her charges at a more sedate pace.

Drake's kindness to Timothy touched me. "Thank you," I said, "for saying what you did to Tim."

He looked at me, and in the bright afternoon light, his eyes were as blue as the sky. "They're charming children, but I hate to see Peter treat his brother as though he's the runt of the litter. Does he do that all the time?"

"Constantly," I replied.

As Drake went to retrieve his coat, I turned to Miss Blessed. "And how is Damon today?"

She smiled as she indicated her charge napping in the shade of a tree at the far end of the lawn. "His battles have exhausted him," she replied in her beautiful voice.

"Poor Damon," I said with a shake of my head.

Then Drake joined me, we bid Angel Blessed good day, and started walking back to Raven's Chase.

"I hope Damon didn't frighten you," I said, as we went down the long drive.

"Well, I'm not used to having a man spring out at me and wave a gun in my face," he replied, "but when he started babbling all the gibberish about India, I knew who he was immediately. And then the boys and the angelic Miss Blessed rescued me." He looked back over his shoulder at the nurse busily pulling up the croquet wickets. "Will Damon ever be well?"

I shrugged. "Who knows? He's been this way for so long. The mad Earl of Raven. . . ."

As we followed the road back to the Chase, Drake told me how welcome everyone had made him feel, and how much he appreciated it, under the circumstances. But before long, talk turned to ships and the companies, with Drake telling me of the qualified men he had left in London to see to the day-to-day operations of the Raven Line. As he assured me that we would be consulted at once on important matters, I found myself wondering what drove this man. Was he just a typical man of our times, preoccupied with success and material wealth, or did something else drive him, some inner demon he never revealed to anyone?

When we arrived at the Chase, I stopped on the front steps and said, "By the way, I'll agree to the dismissal of those sailors."

He stopped, placed his hands on his hips and regarded me in astonishment. "What made you change your mind?"

"I discussed the matter with Colin, and he agreed with you."

"And, since you trust his judgment more than you do mine, you decided to agree to my proposal?"

The spitefulness in his tone took me aback, but all I did was reply, "Exactly," before disappearing into the house.

CHAPTER
6

The Masons had arrived.

From my sitting room window, where I had been stationed since rising early, I watched an unfamiliar carriage top the rise and slowly descend toward Raven's Chase. When it rolled up to the door, I hastily stepped away from the window before the vehicle's occupants could descend and catch me staring. Then I waited for the summons.

It was not long in coming. A knock at my door revealed the butler, who said, "Mr. and Miss Mason have arrived, Lady Raven. They're waiting in the Chinese drawing room."

I thanked him and went downstairs. As I stood before the closed door, I stopped and took a deep breath to steady my quaking insides. Anger and resentment bubbled up and threatened to boil over, but I knew if the Masons saw me red of face with eyes narrowed, they would know they had bested me. When I finally composed myself, I flung open the doors and went to meet them, the very picture of defiance and hauteur.

Seth was standing by a window, carefully examining a large ivory carving in the strong morning light. "Good morning, Lady Raven," he greeted me, friendly and smiling as always. "What queer heathen geegaw is this?"

"That is from China," I replied, "as are most of the furnishings in this room. My husband and I bought them during a visit to Hong Kong. That particular carving is quite rare."

The carving's worth obviously impressed him, for he regarded it with new respect as he set it down gingerly. "Who would've thought it?" he muttered.

I looked around the room for his sister and found her sitting on a chair near the fireplace. As our gazes locked, she called, "Brent, my dear, where are you? You must come and meet Lady Raven."

"Yes, Mother," a voice answered, and a boy dressed all in black stepped from behind the carved lacquer screen at the other end of the room, and came toward me.

I disliked him on sight.

My first impression was one of excess. He was too tall for his age, too thin to be healthy, and his skin too pale. A thatch of dark chestnut hair topped a head too large for his body, and brown eyes too large for my taste regarded me with interest way beyond his years. There was something about the child that made my flesh crawl, and it had nothing to do with the fact that he could be Mark's legitimate son.

"How do you do, Lady Raven?" he said to me with an exaggerated bow, in a voice excessively polite. "I am Brent Gerrick."

I ignored him, and said to the Masons, "If you will follow me, I'll introduce you to my housekeeper, Mrs. Harkins. She will show you to your rooms." I turned to leave, but that woman's voice stopped me.

"And where are those rooms, Lady Raven?" she inquired coldly as she rose. "A few rooms in the attic, perhaps?"

I turned and made no attempt to hide my dislike, in spite of Colin's warning. "You will be staying in the Ming Room, and your son next door. Mr. Mason has the Yellow Room across the hall. Most of our guests have found them most comfortable and satisfactory." I turned to go again.

"Lady Raven." Now it was Seth who spoke, smiling and conciliatory, as always. "We would like to see the house and grounds once we're settled."

So you can see what you're trying to steal from me? I

thought. But I fought to control myself, and replied, "Mrs. Harkins will show you."

"And what times are meals served?"

"Mrs. Harkins will tell you all you need to know."

Then I left the drawing room and led them out to the foyer, where my housekeeper waited with several footmen to transport the Masons' bags to their rooms. I watched them all disappear upstairs, then stormed off to the library, unable to control myself any longer.

As soon as I closed the doors behind me, I collapsed against them with a heavy sigh.

"I take it the Masons have arrived," came a deep voice from the vicinity of the fireplace, and I looked across to see Drake rising from one of the red leather wing chairs.

"Oh, yes," I replied, trying to smile and failing.

"You've seen the boy, then?"

I nodded. "I can't see that he resembles my husband at all, except for his dark hair. One just had to see Mark and Gabriel together to know they were father and son." I took a deep breath to stop the tears from falling. "This child is . . . strange. He seems too old for his years, like a little old man trapped inside a child's body."

"Why don't you come and sit down?" Drake said gently. "This hasn't been easy for you."

His concern both touched and surprised me, but I followed him back to the fireplace, sank into one of the chairs with a sigh, and rested my forehead against the heel of my hand. "He just can't be Mark's son!"

"Here, drink this," Drake commanded, offering me a glass of sherry.

After I took one large swallow, I said, "I resent their being here about as much as I do yours, but there's nothing I can do about it."

"Take heart," he advised. "No one can keep up such a pretense for long. If their claim is false, they're bound to let down their guard sometime and give themselves away."

"That's what Colin says," I muttered.

Drake was silent for a moment, as he downed the rest of his sherry, then said, "I've been meaning to ask you, is there a desk somewhere that could be placed at my disposal? I'll need one, if I'm to conduct business here."

I stared up at him. "The only other desk is my husband's, in the study, but that room is always locked. And even if it weren't, I'd never allow you to use his desk. You'll just have to make do."

His voice held a noticeable chill as he said, "I see," and suddenly, there was great distance between us again.

"Now, if you'll excuse me," I said, setting down my glass. "I am tired and must rest."

And I fled from the library.

As I passed the Ming Room, where I myself had stayed when I first came to Raven's Chase, I noticed the door was wide open. I could see Ella Mason busily unpacking her bags, which were set on the pagoda bed.

I would have liked to walk right by without being noticed, but it was not to be. The woman glanced up, saw me, and called my name. "Yes, Miss Mason?" I inquired from the doorway.

She came around the bed to stand before me, those emotionless eyes brazenly holding mine. "I just want you to know that we saw through your little ploy this morning."

I raised a brow. "Oh?"

"I'm sure you thought you could intimidate my brother and me by not sending a carriage to meet us at the train station, forcing us to hire one ourselves, and by keeping us waiting in the drawing room until you deigned to receive us. And if you think having a servant show us the house and grounds is going to insult us, you're quite wrong." For the first time, her eyes showed emotion, and it was pure hatred. "I just want you to know that nothing you can do will dissuade us from claiming what is rightfully ours."

"Oh, I'm sure nothing will, Miss Mason," I retorted

blandly. "But Raven's Chase isn't yours yet, so don't expect any preferential treatment from me."

Her eyes roved over me insolently. "Whatever did Mark see in you? You're not even pretty, and that hair . . ." She reached out and actually would have flicked at a curl had I not jerked my head back and glared at her. This caused her to smile—a mere tightening of the lips—before she said, "So wild and curly, like sheep's wool. . . ."

With a supercilious look on her face and as collected as ever, she went back to her unpacking. I was just about to whirl away when her voice stopped me.

"And, by the way, I heard your housekeeper mention that your 'partner,' Mr. Turner, is also a guest here. You are such a hypocrite, Lady Raven. You pretend to be, oh, so devoted to Mark, and all the time you're living here with your lover."

Livid with anger, I had to restrain myself from rushing into the Ming Room and clawing the woman's eyes out. But I managed to control myself enough to say, "That is so preposterous it doesn't even merit a reply," before turning and storming off down the hall.

When I returned, fuming, to my sitting room, I found my favorite chair already occupied by Faust, curled into a furry black ball with disdainful golden eyes somewhere off to the right.

"Up!" I commanded. "That is my chair, and I want it."

He blinked once, then nonchalantly began licking one paw in flagrant disregard of my orders. It wasn't until I made a threatening gesture that the cat streaked off my chair, only to sit on his haunches a few yards away and regard me with supreme disdain as I took the chair he had claimed for his own. The minute I was seated, he bounded back into my lap, demonstrating that I had not really won at all.

"Faust," I chided him in dismay but hadn't the heart to disturb him again. So, while I sat there, I slowly ran my hand down the cat's soft fur and felt suddenly calmer.

Now I could rationally analyze the conversation I had just had with the unflappable Miss Mason. What she had told me was that, if I attacked her, or her brother, she would retaliate in kind. I had insulted them by not sending the Gerrick carriage, so she derided my appearance. She had clearly stated her terms for any ensuing battles. All of my attacks would be returned with a vengeance. Without realizing it, Ella Mason reinforced my image of her as a viper, harmless if allowed to go its own way, dangerous if stepped on.

But I was not going to allow her to have her own way at Raven's Chase without a fight, no matter how stinging her bite. I had learned something else about Ella Mason today; I knew that I must never give her the satisfaction of seeing how much her words wounded me, for that would only increase her confidence in her ability to best me.

As for the woman's accusations that Drake Turner was my lover . . . "How dare she!" I muttered to Faust, who purred and settled himself more firmly in my lap. First Amabel, and now Ella. . . . I shook my head. Some women had only one great love in their lives, and I counted myself among their number.

I closed my eyes, feeling suddenly tired and drained, and before I realized it, my head fell forward and I was sound asleep.

The sound of someone calling my name dragged me back into consciousness, and I opened my eyes to find Mrs. Harkins standing there, her keys jingling rapidly in agitation and her steely gaze locked on Faust, the enemy of cleanliness, as he lay sleeping, curled in my lap.

"I'm sorry to wake you, madam," she said, "but you did instruct me to report to you as soon as I had finished showing the house to the Masons."

"Yes, Mrs. Harkins, thank you," I said, rubbing the sleep from my eyes with a knuckle, then dislodging Faust, who shook himself, stretched, and stared at my housekeeper out of golden eyes. "What was their reaction? And please be candid."

"To be quite frank, madam," she said, chasing Faust away, though he never made a move toward her, "they seemed very impressed. In fact, I thought Mr. Mason got quite a proprietary gleam in his eye when I directed them through the rooms. He asked many questions about the furnishings, paintings, china, and silver. He was especially interested in the Georgian silver coffee service on the sideboard in the main dining room."

I snorted in derision. "I'm not surprised. He's probably calculating what price they would bring." Then I was silent. "And what was his sister's reaction when you showed her the portrait gallery?" I held my breath as I waited for her reply.

"She was visibly moved by Lord Raven's portraits, madam. She recognized them at once and began crying."

"Ella Mason cry? The woman doesn't know how, Mrs. Harkins. I'll wager her handkerchief was dry the entire time," I muttered. "And anyway, she would recognize them because they are the only portraits draped with black crepe." I shook my head. "Did you explain the rules of the house to them?" When she nodded, I said, "You didn't mention anything about a personal maid for Miss Mason or a valet for her brother?"

"No, madam."

"And you told them the study and nursery are always locked and no one is allowed in there?" When she nodded a second time, I added, "Fine, Mrs. Harkins. I would appreciate it if you'd tell the staff they are to be polite to the Masons, but not to be drawn into confidences with them, and they are to obey them without being overly enthusiastic. I also want to know about any specific requests they make, is that clear?"

"Yes, madam."

I thought for a moment, then said, "I'd like dinner to be rather elaborate tonight—five or six courses, at least—and we'll eat in the main dining room. Perhaps Antoine and Mrs. Baker can once again work together to dazzle us with a feast."

My housekeeper's steely eyes widened in surprise, for she knew we never dined there except when entertaining a large group, since I considered the main dining room too formal and forbidding for the intimate dinner parties I favored. But she inclined her head and murmured, "Yes, madam." Then I dismissed her, and after giving Faust one last frozen glance, my housekeeper left in an agitated jingling of keys.

When I was alone, I went to my desk, took out a sheet of paper and wrote:

Dear Amabel,
If you and Colin would like to meet the Masons, please come to dinner tonight. I know I don't need to ask you to wear something dazzling.

Nora.

Then I rang for Fenner and had her deliver the note to the Little Chase, while I plotted the social demise of the Masons.

Amabel did not disappoint me that evening.

"You look beautiful!" I exclaimed as I swept into the Chinese drawing room before dinner. She wore a black faille dinner dress with narrow sleeves, high neck, and a skirt liberally trimmed with grosgrain ruffles and knots. Her hair had been cut so she sported a fringe of curls on her forehead, a new style that looked quite becoming. The only jewels she wore were drop earrings and a necklace of black onyx that had been Colin's Christmas gifts to her. My sister-in-law looked elegant, wealthy, and intimidating, which suited my plan perfectly.

If I was pleased with her appearance, she was astonished by mine. "Nora!" she gasped, rising to stare at my gown. "Wherever did you get that dress? Not Plymouth, I'll wager."

"Do you like it?" I asked, whirling around so she could see the back, with its newly fashionable slim skirt caught into a small puff of material.

"I'm positively green with envy," she declared. "I must have my dressmaker make me one just like it."

Colin, who looked quite handsome in formal evening attire, was standing by the fireplace, regarding us with wry amusement. "Now, if you two ladies are through complimenting each other to death, I would like to know what happened when the Masons arrived today."

We sat down, and I quickly told them all about the Masons' first day at Raven's Chase.

Amabel listened attentively, her eyes sparkling at the prospect of intrigue. Then she announced, "I've been thinking about this quite carefully, and I've come up with a plan to expose these people."

"What devious machinations are hatching in that pretty golden head of yours, my darling?" Colin asked, chucking her under the chin.

Amabel, who thrived on plots and schemes, leaned forward and lowered her voice conspiratorially, for effect. "Why don't I pretend to be friendly toward the Masons and accept them? I'll make it quite clear that I don't owe any allegiance to Nora, but just want to see justice done. Perhaps if they trust me, they will let something slip."

Colin looked skeptical. "We thought of something similar this afternoon, but Nora says they'd see through such a scheme at once."

Amabel pouted and raised her head a proud notch. "I can be quite convincing an actress, I'll have you know."

"You don't need to convince me," Colin replied with an affectionate smile. "You would be so subtle and devious, poor Mr. Mason wouldn't know what hit him."

"You can poke fun at me, Colin, but I think it's a good plan. I would make an excellent spy."

Trying to keep peace between them, I said, "If Amabel can learn something—anything—what harm can it do?"

There was no time for further discussion, for the drawing room door opened, and our guests were announced. Drake entered, followed by the Masons, who, I was pleased to note, were not dressed for dinner.

"Good evening," Drake said. "I found your guests wandering through the halls, so I took the liberty of directing them to the drawing room."

"Thank you," I said, as we three rose to stare at the Masons.

When they reached us, Seth smiled and said jovially, "Good evening, everyone."

"Mr. Mason . . ." I murmured, trying to fight the resentment that was building within me, "and Miss Mason."

"Mrs. Gerrick," she corrected me coldly.

I ignored her and introduced them to the Trelawneys, then stood back to observe their reactions to one another.

The tension hung on the air like a thick Dartmoor fog, and I could tell that everyone, save Drake, was ill at ease. Colin had his hands jammed into his pockets, his head thrown back a little, like a wary animal, and Amabel's innocent blue eyes were studying that woman, then her brother, in frank curiosity. Such scrutiny had no effect on the cool, composed Ella, though I saw her glance at our elegant gowns with interest and perhaps just a touch of envy. Seth was giving Colin measure for measure and seemed to be assessing the Trelawneys just as frankly, but he kept smiling all the while, and I could tell that at any moment he would reach out to pat his sister's arm reassuringly.

Once again, I found myself wondering cynically just how long it had taken them to polish and perfect their performance.

"I wish we could've met under more pleasant circumstances, Mr. and Mrs. Trelawney," Seth said with his charming smile, "since we are in-laws."

"Perhaps," Colin said. Then he smiled. "You must forgive my wife and me for our hesitancy in accepting your claim, but you must realize that you place us in a very awkward position."

It was the perfect thing to say and put Seth at ease at once. "Of course we understand. We would feel the same if someone suddenly turned up on our doorstep, claiming to have been married to our brother."

Ella managed a smile totally devoid of warmth and sincerity as she approached Amabel. "You must be Mark's sister. I'm afraid he didn't speak of you, but I am glad to meet you at long last."

"And I you, my dear," Amabel said warmly, touching the other woman's arm in a gesture of friendship that I resented.

"I'm sure Lady Raven has explained why Mark never mentioned us," Seth said smoothly, tossing his hair out of his eyes.

"Lady Raven has told us everything," Colin said cryptically.

When an awkward silence descended once again, we were saved by a footman announcing that dinner was served in the main dining room. Drake stepped forward to escort me, followed by Colin and Amabel, then the Masons.

When we entered the dining room, a smile of satisfaction played about my mouth. If I had been in Ella Mason's shoes, I would have turned and run back to America. The two huge crystal chandeliers were ablaze with light, and beneath them stretched that forbidding twenty-four-foot table, set for six with a bewildering array of china, silver, and crystal needed to serve the six-course meal I had requested. A liveried footman stood at attention at the sideboard, presiding over a collection of covered dishes, ready to serve the meal *à la Russe,* while another stood behind my chair, waiting for orders.

As Drake led me to the head of the table, and my guests came around to take their places, I watched the Masons very carefully to see what effect all this splendor was having on their simple colonial souls. They, to my chagrin, approached the table as though they were accustomed to dining like royalty every night, and their eyes appraised the silver and china, lingering on the ornate silver epergne that divided the table as effectively as a hedge, and moving on to the half-dozen spoons on one side of each plate and all the knives and forks on the other.

If I had wanted to intimidate Ella, I could not have chosen a better means. A social quagmire as deep and deadly as the Dartmoor bogs had been set in motion, and I was curious to see if the Masons were going to be able to extricate themselves.

"I understand I have a nephew," Amabel said with a warm smile as she was seated.

"Yes," Ella replied conversationally. "His name is Brentwood—"

"Mark's middle name," Amabel said.

Ella nodded. "He's ten years old. Mr. Turner has already met him, but perhaps you would like to, after dinner."

"I would love to," Amabel replied. Then she widened her eyes in a gesture I knew was calculated to make her seem guileless, as she said, "Brentwood . . . how odd you should give Mark's son the name he himself hated."

"Did he hate it?" Ella replied smoothly. "I never knew that. He just mentioned it once, and when our son was born, I thought it would be perfect."

Seth added, "But, then, there was so much about Mark you didn't know, my dear."

Amabel just smiled politely. "We have two sons of our own, you know. Peter, the eldest, is six, and Timothy four. They are charming boys, but, as their mother, I'm afraid I'm prejudiced."

"I'm sure they are just as charming as you are, Mrs. Trelawney," Seth said, unfolding his napkin. "Why, our boys can be playmates together. They should get to know one another, since they are cousins."

Colin noticed my look of irritation, coughed and said, "Well, we don't know that for certain, yet. Your claim has yet to be proved."

"Oh, it will be," Seth said with easy confidence, as a soup bowl was set before him.

While the six of us ate the light chicken consommé with pearl barley, our conversation was of the tentative, exploratory kind one usually finds among people who are strangers.

"Where did you live in New York, Mr. Mason?" Colin asked.

"Seth, please," he replied with his ready smile. "There should be no formalities, since we are practically brothers-in-law."

"Seth, then," Colin said.

"We lived in a comfortable brownstone on Fourteenth Street," Seth said.

"Brownstone?" Amabel murmured, with a puzzled frown. "What is that?"

"Oh, I don't suppose you know what those are," he said indulgently. "They're houses—usually five stories high—faced with brown stone. Quite elegant, but not as elegant as your house on Mount Street, Lady Raven."

"*In* Mount Street," I corrected him automatically, then felt myself fill with resentment that I'm afraid I let show. "Oh, I'm sure you took copious notes the day you called there, Mr. Mason. You probably can't wait until the day you move in."

Seth's white skin reddened, and his mouth twisted in anger. "I resent your tone, Lady Raven. My sister and I only want what is rightfully Brent's."

Colin smoothly intervened before we had a raging argument. "I understand your father was a shopkeeper, Seth. Was his store very large?"

The tense moment passed, and Seth talked of his family's store and how it had been looted and burned by rioters protesting conscription during their country's Civil War. While Colin and Drake seemed intensely interested in this conflict, I found my attention flagging, so I remained silent and endured Ella's black looks darted toward me now and then.

Amabel, also tiring of all this talk of blood and battles, delicately stifled a yawn and said to Ella, "It must be extremely difficult for you to raise a son without a father."

"Yes, it is," she replied, dabbing at her lips with her napkin, "especially since my son is such an extraordinary child."

I almost choked on my soup, but Amabel just widened her blue eyes innocently and asked, "In what way?"

"He's highly intelligent, like his father, and quite advanced for his years. Naturally, other children sense his superiority and resent him." She sighed with genuine sadness for her son. "I can't tell you the number of times my poor Brent has come home crying, because the neighborhood children threw stones at him or pushed him in the mud."

Growing weary of listening to Ella extol the virtues of her odd child, I turned my attention to what the men were discussing. Seth was telling Drake about his adventures as a novice

131

reporter for the *New York Tribune,* and, as I listened, I became more convinced they were greatly embellished for our benefit.

I managed to keep my opinions to myself, however, but not for long. I felt my temper soar dangerously when Seth turned to me and said, "So, you see, Lady Raven, we do have something in common after all. We're both writers."

I deeply resented his attempt to ingratiate himself with me, so I just looked at him and said, "A nightingale and a crow are both birds, Mr. Mason, but they are as different as you and I."

He colored as he tossed his hair out of his eyes, but chose to ignore my comment. "As a matter of fact, I was thinking of writing a series of articles for my paper about England. They'd be my personal impressions of this country and its people for American readers."

"And what would anyone care what you thought of England and its people?" I retorted, which won me a sharp look from Drake.

Amabel fluttered her eyelashes coquettishly and cooed, "Oh, Seth, I trust you will be kind to us."

"Who could fail to say anything kind about you, Mrs. Trelawney?" was his gallant reply.

I had never heard such a sickening exchange in all my life.

The soup bowls were cleared away and replaced by the second course, a baked turbot with caper sauce. Glancing at Ella, I noticed with satisfaction that she had picked up the wrong fork. It was the moment I had waited for, a chance to draw everyone's attention to the Masons' lack of breeding. But, at the last moment, I couldn't do it. To berate Ella for using the wrong fork would have been too petty and cruel, so I just sat back and said very little through the remainder of the meal.

Later that evening, when my beautiful dinner gown was back in its closet and I was seated in my favorite chair, writing in my journal, a soft knock sounded at the door. When I called, "Come in," Drake entered, still in evening attire, though his tie had been loosened comfortably.

I closed my journal and rose, upsetting the cat, who had been curled quite contentedly on the stool at my feet.

"So that's where my cat has gone," Drake muttered, bending down to stroke him beneath the chin. "Has he brought you burnt offerings yet?"

"Burnt offerings? What do you mean?"

"Dead mice . . . fruits of his nocturnal labors to be laid at your feet."

I swallowed hard and made a grimace of distaste. "No, I have not yet had the pleasure."

"You will, since it appears he has adopted you, despite your lamentable preference for canines, and you seem to have accepted him as well."

"It's not his fault that you're his master," I muttered, walking over to the window. "And I suspect Faust stays here to annoy me, just as you do."

Drake's blue eyes twinkled, but he made no comment, so I sighed and said, "Well, to what do I owe the pleasure of this visit, Mr. Turner? It is rather late."

"I thought you might be curious to learn what happened after dinner, when you left for your room and the rest of us retired to the drawing room."

"I'm sure I'll hear all about it from Mrs. Trelawney tomorrow," was my smooth reply. "You needn't have bothered."

"You don't bend at all, do you?"

I just shook my head. "I believe in letting my adversaries know just where they stand with me, Mr. Turner."

He was staring at me with that intense look in his eyes again, and I found my hand straying self-consciously to my hair, which I had tied out of the way, so it flowed down my back in a soft cloud.

"Is there something wrong with my appearance?" I demanded.

The man looked startled. "There is nothing wrong with your appearance. Why do you ask?"

I shrugged lamely. "It was the way you looked at me."

"And how was that?"

I looked out the window, but the darkness backed the glass, turning it into a smoky mirror that reflected Drake's head beside my own. As his face grew larger and larger and seemed to hover over my shoulder, I realized he had crossed the room to stand behind me.

"And how do I look at you, Mrs. Gerrick?"

He spoke so quietly I almost didn't hear him, but I was quite aware of his presence. He was standing so close I could feel the soft warmth of his breath on my ear. Suddenly, the face in the glass changed, and I found myself staring at Mark. In another moment, my husband's fingertips would be on my shoulder, and his lips brushing my neck.

This is madness, my mind cried out as I jerked away and went to pick up Faust, who had climbed onto the back of my chair and stood poised there on all fours. It was a swift, simple movement, yet it broke the spell and put distance between Drake and me.

Did I imagine it, or did he sigh in regret? I must have, for he said brusquely, "Well, I must be going. I must study those contracts tonight and dispatch them back to London tomorrow morning. If you would be so kind as to give me my cat . . ."

I placed Faust in his arms and bade him good night.

Early the next morning, Colin departed for America.

Amabel and I stood together on the front steps of the Little Chase, watching the Trelawney carriage until it disappeared around a bend in the road, then went inside for a long visit.

When I returned to Raven's Chase, I found Drake waiting for me in the library and consulting his pocket watch impatiently. He informed me that a messenger had just arrived with a heavy parcel of papers from his offices in London, and when I expressed surprise that one should have arrived so soon after our own departure, he just smiled. So we sat down with our papers to discuss the possibility of an agreement to ship railroad ties to

Brazil, and, as usual, Drake dazzled me with his shrewdness and business acumen. But he was so detached, I decided I must have imagined the look of longing in his eyes last night, and was greatly relieved.

We worked diligently through the morning, had lunch in the library, and worked while eating so we would finish in time to send the young messenger back on the afternoon train. Finally, when my eyes began to see double and a knot of stiffness formed between my shoulders, I decided I had had enough for one day. I left my partner studying contracts, while I retired to my room for a much-needed nap.

Hours later, I awoke feeling rested and refreshed, so I decided to read for a little while before tea. When I hurried to the library, I was startled to find Drake gone and that woman's son standing on a stool in an attempt to secure a book sitting just out of reach.

He turned and stared at me out of those huge brown eyes, as if expecting me to say something, but I just ignored him and hurried to select a book.

"Would you please help me?" he asked. "I am having difficulty reaching this particular volume."

"Have your mother get it for you," I replied, running my fingertips along a row of leather spines. "I'm in a hurry. Besides, those books are much too advanced for you."

The child jumped off his stool and ambled toward me. "You hate me, don't you?"

My stare was cold and contemptuous as I looked down into his old man's face. "Why would you say that?"

"My mother told me," he replied matter-of-factly. "She also told me why."

"Oh? And why is that?" I demanded, curious to learn what that woman had been saying about me.

"Because I am really the sixth Earl of Raven and this house belongs to me." He grinned unpleasantly, revealing small, pointed teeth, like some badger or otter. "So perhaps you should be asking *my* permission to take a book from this library. Also," he added, before I could utter a sharp reprimand, "you hate me because your own child died, and I am alive."

My eyes narrowed in contempt as I said, "You have a lively imagination," but my questing finger stopped and trembled.

"Oh, I doubt that," he replied with adult nonchalance. "I am quite bright for my age, you know, and cleverer than most children. I see the world through adult eyes."

That revelation left me speechless.

Suddenly, he straightened his jacket in a strangely adult manner. "How did my father die? I know it was in a fire, but I am curious as to the circumstances surrounding his death. My mother said she didn't know, but I think she may be trying to spare me."

I know I should have ignored his deliberate baiting and not let him know he had deeply wounded me. But it took all my self-control just to keep from grasping his shoulders and shaking him until his teeth rattled.

"Since your mother tells you everything," I hissed, "ask her."

And I fled from the library as fast as I could.

After that disturbing encounter, I left the house by the back entrance, hurrying through the garden in the golden light of late afternoon. The folly beckoned like a beacon at the end of the lawn, and I climbed the steps of my sanctuary and seated myself inside, feeling my spirits lighten immediately.

Leaning back against the cushions and listening to the ravens and crows squabbling overhead, I found myself thinking of that strange child in the library, and the stranger conversation we had had. Hearing such adult words come out of a child's mouth was disconcerting to say the least.

I hadn't been sitting there for fifteen minutes when I saw Ella, her son in hand, come strolling toward me. She was dressed in a different black day dress, but her heavy black tresses were wound across her head in that unbecoming coronet.

And she had the audacity to criticize *my* hair, I thought, as I watched them approach.

"Good day," she mumbled, while eying me warily.

I said nothing, just glared at Brent as his mother dragged him by. Our gazes remained locked until he was way down the path. They finally disappeared into a grove of trees.

I leaned back once again, closed my eyes and was granted a few moments of peace before a shrill scream of terror split the silence. My eyes flew open as I realized it was coming from the vicinity of the grove of trees, where Ella and Brent had just gone.

I dashed out of the folly and bolted across the lawn toward the trees. When I finally emerged from the copse, with a sharp stitch in my side for my efforts, I stopped when I saw what all the commotion was about.

There stood Ella, all semblance of composure gone as she screamed again, while shielding her son with her own body. A few feet away stood Damon, pointing his rifle right at the terrified woman.

I stopped and walked slowly toward them, but my heart was racing out of control. "Damon?" I called, smiling tremulously at him.

"That man was going to shoot us!" Ella cried.

"I was not!" he insisted, frowning as he attempted to digest what was being said about him. "I was just trying to protect them from the sepoys."

"There's no one here to protect us from!" Brent shouted, coming out from behind his mother's skirts. "You just started waving that gun in our faces, and—"

"Stop it!" I snapped, when I saw that Damon was bewildered and on the verge of tears.

"I was just trying to protect them, Nora," he insisted, whimpering, his vacant blue eyes widening in alarm.

We all usually humored Damon to keep him calm and controllable. To have someone contradict him with such vehemence only caused him to become befuddled and frightened.

"This is Damon Gerrick, who became the Earl of Raven on his brother's death," I said sharply. "He is mad, and we all try to humor him. His gun is not loaded, so he wouldn't have harmed you and your son, even if he did happen to pull the trigger."

"He's mad?" Brent said, staring at Damon as though he were some exotic specimen in a butterfly collection.

I turned away from Ella, for I could see that Damon was distressed more than I had ever seen him. His breathing was quick and shallow, and the whites of his eyes showed. "I was just trying to get them away before the sepoys took them to the House of Women."

The House of Women . . . the place where his fiancée had been taken a decade ago, then slaughtered. I could see the dangerous turn his mind was taking, and Damon became my overriding concern.

I advanced on him slowly, as I would on a restive horse that might bolt or shy at a moment's notice.

"You've saved them, Damon," I said softly, always smiling. "All the sepoys have run away, so they will not be taking these people to the House of Women. You've saved them," I repeated, reaching out to touch his arm in reassurance.

At first, he looked as though he didn't believe me. "But I saw them coming, over that rise, hundreds of them, screaming and shooting."

"Do you see them now? I don't. You've frightened them away. Look for yourself."

He frowned and put his hand up to his forehead, as if to shield his eyes from the blazing Indian sun, then scanned the horizon. I fervently prayed he would see no sepoys.

"You're right, Nora," he said with a sigh, dropping his hand. "They have gone."

"See. I told you." Then I turned to Ella standing there so still and quiet, watching. "Now, would you like to be properly introduced? After all, he may be your brother-in-law, and he did save you and your son from the sepoys."

Without further urging, she strode forward confidently, her reluctant son in hand, and approached Damon.

"Lord Raven . . . Damon," she began, "how do you do? I am Ella Mason, and this is my son, Brent." It was sweet, simple, and quite convincing.

"Thank him for saving your lives," I whispered under my breath.

The woman looked at me sharply, as though I were the one who was daft, but she added, "Thank you for saving our lives."

"Quite all right," Damon replied, shaking her hand. "It was my pleasure."

Then Ella turned and started walking back to the house without another word. However, I noticed Brent kept looking back at Damon in morbid fascination. Whatever the child was thinking, I was sure it didn't bode well for Damon.

"Come, Damon," I said to him. "Let's walk back to the house together. It's almost time for tea."

CHAPTER

7

Three weeks had passed since the Masons had come to Raven's Chase, and, compared to what followed, it was a peaceful time indeed.

Every day, I made an extraordinary effort to seek out the Masons, not because I enjoyed their company, but because I hoped to catch them revealing some discrepancy in their story that would give them away. If I saw Seth reading in the library, or strolling alone in the garden, I would join him and engage in conversation, but, while he smiled and was politeness itself, he revealed nothing. I even began going downstairs for meals instead of having them sent up to me on a tray, but those mealtime conversations were pointless, especially since Ella was there with her expressionless eyes that always watched me.

My favorite measure was to challenge every statement with, "But I thought you said . . ." or, "Didn't I hear you say. . . ?" in an attempt to confuse and coerce them into contradicting themselves. But it never worked. Both were just too smooth and unflappable.

Mrs. Harkins and her faithful staff kept their eyes and ears open, though, and reported to me faithfully. Unfortunately, she usually had little to report, for the Masons' activities were quite unremarkable and above suspicion. In addition to walks around the grounds, they sometimes went riding on the moors or took a picnic lunch out to St. Barnabas' Abbey. They were model guests, always following house rules and never making demands on the servants. If they ever let their masks slip and discussed their deception between themselves, they made sure no one was around to hear it and report to me. They never gave anyone the opportunity to eavesdrop, either, though I would have done so without any qualms.

I often visited Amabel, but she wasn't having any more success than Mrs. Harkins in learning the truth about the Masons. Privately, I thought them too clever to be fooled by Amabel's transparent scheme, though she seemed determined to keep up the pretense.

When I wasn't calling on her and the boys, I was ensconced in my sitting room, trying to write that novel I had promised Lewis Darwin. I had received three letters already from my old friend, one every Wednesday, each cajoling me to get to work and demanding a weekly progress report. I smiled as I read his small, cramped script, with many words underlined for emphasis just the way he spoke. I could almost hear his rasping voice in my ear and smell the single rosebud in his lapel as I wrote about the adventures of a spirited young woman named Cordelia.

Though not as diligent a correspondent as Lewis, my father also wrote one brief letter informing me that he was taking shy Marigold to Paris for a few weeks to further her education. I just smiled and shook my head. Some things never changed, thank goodness.

During the first two weeks of my return to Raven's Chase, I did battle not only with the Masons but with Drake as well during our daily meetings for the management of the Raven Line. He constantly tested me just to see how far I would allow him to go before objecting, and, as usual, if I agreed with him, the meetings ran smoothly. If not . . . There were days when I was amazed we got anything resolved at all.

But I found myself eagerly anticipating the arrival of messengers from London and the long, involved conferences with Drake that followed. The more I learned about the day-to-day operation of a shipping line, the more I wanted to know.

Then, just a week later, Drake received a telegram informing him that one of his own ships, the *Traviata*, which had been placed on the overdue list, was now reported lost in a storm off the coast of India, and this news sent him hurrying back to London on the next train. At last I would receive a respite from Mr. Turner's presence.

The day after he left, I put all thoughts of ships and the Masons out of my mind and looked forward to uninterrupted time I could devote to the novel I was writing.

But it was not to be.

Actually, Fenner was responsible for what later occurred, for she said something that sent me down a path I hoped would not lead to disaster.

That morning after breakfast, she had just come up from the laundry with an armful of lacy lawn camisoles and petticoats, which she proceeded to sort. We began discussing one of Brent's more appalling characteristics—his instinctive ability to determine a person's most vulnerable spot, then play on it—and I told her how Brent had badgered me for details of Mark's death. She mentioned she thought Brent enjoyed making Peter lose at games because he knew how much Peter needed to win, and delighted in thwarting him.

We continued to discuss the odd child for a few more minutes, when Fenner said suddenly, "Madam, did I tell you that two of my younger brothers have decided to emigrate to Australia?"

"No, Fenner, you didn't," I replied, taken aback by the sudden shift in the conversation. "When did they decide to do this?"

"About a month ago, madam. There's more opportunity for a pair of strong lads out there, so they just decided to pack up, kiss our mother goodbye, and leave the farm."

"That's what Mr. Trelawney did years ago, you know, and just look at him today. When do your brothers leave?"

"At the end of the week," she replied. "They wanted to book passage on a Raven ship, madam, since I work for the family, but were told there were no passenger ships on the Raven Line going to Australia."

"That's correct. The Raven ships are all merchant clippers, and they only take several first-class passengers on their voyages."

Fenner looked down her long nose at me in dismay. "First class is too rich for the Fenners' blood. Why can't they carry more people? My brothers told me the ship they'll be sailing on will be taking two hundred fifty others to Australia."

"Passenger ships are built differently," I explained. "You can't just throw people in the cargo hold like cattle, though it was done during the slave trade. A proper passenger ship is designed for comfort."

Fenner turned to leave. "It seems a shame that the Raven Line doesn't even have one passenger ship. My brothers would have been proud to sail on one."

She left me, but I couldn't concentrate. In the old days, I would have returned to my writing without another thought, but since I was now as least partly responsible for running the shipping company, I was training myself to listen carefully and glean any information I could use for the company's betterment. I slowly set my pen and paper down, folded my arms and sat back to mull over what Fenner had just said.

Why *didn't* the Raven Line have passenger ships? I knew the answer to that right away. It was because there were other, more profitable cargoes to be had. I bit my lip in deep concentration. What had Fenner said about 250 people leaving for Australia in one ship? Now I rose and paced the sitting room, thinking that perhaps it could be possible to make a profit from a passenger ship.

Once the idea was firmly rooted in my mind, I could not dislodge it, and it grew more intriguing by the minute. Who could I ask about the feasibility of such an undertaking? Colin was in New York and Drake en route to London for an indefinite period of time. I drummed my fingers against the desk top, trying to decide what to do. Perhaps I should wait for Drake to return and discuss it. Then I thrust my chin out stubbornly. No, I was a full partner in our joint venture, and if I wanted to investigate something that could be beneficial and profitable to the company, I didn't need Drake Turner's permission to do so.

I wanted answers today, and I knew just where to turn. I rang for Fenner and told her to pack, because we were going to catch the next train for Plymouth.

Early that very afternoon, I was seated in Hamish Pengelly's office discussing the prospects of acquiring a passenger ship for the Raven Line.

Pengelly, our agent in Plymouth, was a shrewd Cornishman who had the nervous habit of cracking his knuckles before and after he spoke, as though enclosing his words in audible quotation marks.

After listening to him express his shock and chagrin that Drake Turner now owned half the Raven Line, I outlined my proposal and asked for his opinion on the feasibility of such an undertaking. He turned his chair away from me, stared at a framed watercolor sketch of the *Black Raven* for a few minutes, then turned back to me and cracked his knuckles.

"There's no doubt in my mind that the colonial trade is on the verge of a boom, your ladyship. Our countrymen are emigrating to Australia by the thousands, and from what I've gathered, in a few more years, it's going to increase even more. And with more settling in New Zealand . . ." He cracked his knuckles again.

I gripped the arms of my chair and leaned forward in excitement. "If that's the case, I think it's time the Raven Line had a passenger ship, don't you? I'll discuss it with Mr. Turner and commission one."

Pengelly's countenance seemed to brighten as he looked at me thoughtfully for a moment, then cracked his knuckles once more. "If you're bent on acquiring a passenger ship, Lady Raven, fortune may be smiling down on you."

I cringed at the popping sound as I said, "What do you mean?"

Pengelly leaned forward, his eyes sparkling, and for once kept his hands still. "It takes time for a good ship to be built. But at this moment, there's a passenger ship for sale right here in Plymouth."

I perked up. "For sale?"

He nodded, "It's an iron clipper called the *Nancy Malone* built two years ago by Barclay, Curle and Company."

Now my eyes narrowed in suspicion. "Why is she up for sale? Is there something wrong with her? Has she been damaged?"

"No, no, Lady Raven. I've seen her myself, and she's as sound as the day she came out of the stocks. She was the only ship owned by a Captain Fergus Malone—an independent shipper. The good captain died recently, and his widow wants to sell his ship. Too many memories, you know."

I felt a corresponding twinge of sympathy when I heard that, but I was too excited to think of my own sorrow just now. "Tell me more about the *Nancy Malone*," I said.

I stood in the center of the *Nancy Malone*'s spacious eighty-foot-long saloon, staring up at its magnificent double skylights and tingling from head to toe with enthusiasm.

"I want her," I said, turning back to Pengelly. "I'll have to consult with Mr. Turner about the purchase, of course, but I'm sure he'll agree."

The agent's face fell. "Unfortunately, your ladyship, the *Nancy Malone* will be sold tonight at auction."

My heart sank as though it were an anchor. "Tonight?"

He nodded solemnly and cracked his knuckles.

"There's no possibility of the auction being postponed?"

Pengelly shook his head. "No, your ladyship. News travels fast. There are several interested buyers eager for such a prize."

His words drove the hope right out of me, and I had to knot my fingers together to keep them from shaking. "So what you're saying is that I have to make a decision immediately."

"Yes, your ladyship, I'm afraid so."

I looked around the beautiful saloon, with its gleaming mahogany woodwork, polished brass appointments, and those skylights overhead, and wondered if I could ever contact Drake in time and receive a reply. Even a telegram might not be delivered to him personally, if he was out of the office, and he could be anywhere in London. I swallowed hard and thought fast. No, if I wanted the *Nancy Malone,* I would have to make this decision on my own and suffer the consequences, good or disastrous.

Well, Nora, girl, I said to myself, you're about to learn if you have a head for shipping.

"Mr. Pengelly," I said with all the authority I could muster, "I want you to get me this ship. I'm counting on you to pay a fair price for her, but if you think the bidding is going higher than she's worth, then desist."

He blinked rapidly, looked stunned and pleased at the same time. "But, your ladyship, what about Mr. Turner?"

"What about him? This is my decision."

"Yes, your ladyship." I had never seen the Cornishman so pleased, and I suppose it was because Drake Turner was not going to be consulted for once.

Suddenly, another thought crossed my mind, so I said, "Mr. Pengelly, do you know why Lord Raven hated Drake Turner so much?"

The knuckles popped with irritating precision. "I won't bore you with details, Lady Raven, but I will tell you that your husband suspected Drake Turner of planting spies in our midst. He always seemed to know just what we were going to do next, you see."

"Yes, that would explain it," I murmured. Mark had always been a fair man, and I could see where such underhanded methods would earn his animosity.

Then I rose, thanked Mr. Pengelly for this bit of information, and returned to my hotel.

That night, I acquired a ship.

I did not tell Amabel about my purchase when I returned to Raven's Chase, though I was bursting with excitement, because I felt Drake, as my partner, should be the first to know. Exactly one week after he left for London, he returned to Raven's Chase.

I was in the library at the time, sitting by the window and reading, when the doors suddenly swung open and he was standing there, deep lines of fatigue etched in his cheeks and his eyes red-rimmed, as though he hadn't slept all week. When he saw me, a mocking smile touched his mouth and he bowed. "Mrs. Gerrick."

"Mr. Turner," I replied pleasantly, closing my book and rising to meet him. "How was London? Did you settle the matter of the *Traviata*?"

He nodded. "It was a grim business, but it had to be done." Now he stripped off his gray kid gloves and said, "I trust all went smoothly here. You didn't bankrupt the company in my absence, did you?"

"No-o-o," I murmured, and plunged right in. "I bought us a ship."

Drake just stood there in silence, staring at me blankly out of those icy eyes, as though I had spoken in a foreign tongue. I watched in some dismay and trepidation as his face turned white, then a dark, angry red.

"You did *what?*" he bellowed, his arms going rigid at his sides. "You bought a *ship* without consulting me first? Have you so quickly forgotten, madam, that we are partners? Or did you plan this all along, behind my back?"

I refused to bend before the force of his anger, like a willow in a gale, and became calm myself, though my confidence was beginning to evaporate and I was beset by grave doubts about my action. "If you will be so kind as to stop ranting and listen to me, I'll explain everything."

He glared down at me, and there was no mercy in his eyes. "I am eager to hear any explanations you have to offer, madam, and they had better be sound ones." Without another word, he crossed the room, flung himself into one of the wing chairs, stretched his long legs out before him and looked as though he would have liked to throttle me.

Clasping my hands together for courage, I slowly went to the cold fireplace and stood a safe distance away from him, for he was so very angry and therefore unpredictable. Then, calmly and rationally, I explained how Fenner's comment about her brothers had set me thinking about adding a passenger ship to the Raven Line.

"A passenger ship? Whatever for? You *do* know that all our ships are merchant clippers?" he asked as though he doubted my capabilities to understand even that.

"We could become part of the colonial trade," I replied, ignoring his scathing tone. "Do you realize a good passenger ship can carry three hundred and fifty or even four hundred emigrants to Australia and New Zealand?"

"Of course I realize it," he snapped. "I've been running my own company for years and know a great deal more about it than you ever will."

"And they say the boom is just beginning." I searched his face for any sign of relenting, but he was implacable, so I continued trying to convince him. "Our return cargo would be wool, of course. I consulted with Pengelly and discovered we don't have any ships in the wool trade."

"I did have one," he corrected me with relish, "but it capsized because some fool hadn't ballasted her properly. It was composite-built and could run circles around any iron ship."

"Well, we have one now."

Drake gave me a hard, deprecating look intended to make me feel small and foolish. "How could you be so—so *stupid* as to buy a ship without consulting me? You're green, Mrs. Gerrick, green! You haven't been at this game two months and already you have the audacity to think you can buy a ship!"

His biting words cut like acid, and I could keep my temper in check no longer, because deep inside, I knew I was right. I raised my chin a stubborn notch and said, "And you are put out because it galls you to think a green *woman* could come up with a better idea than the great Drake Turner!"

He jumped to his feet and regarded me with contempt and anger, and for a moment, I thought he was going to grasp my shoulders and shake me. "Don't provoke me, Countess!"

I stood up to him and continued in my steady voice, "The ship I had Pengelly buy for a mere £17,000 is named the *Nancy Malone*. She's a fifteen-hundred-ton iron clipper built by Barclay, Curle and Company. She's never been out more than eighty days from Sidney to London, which even someone as green as I knows is excellent time, and she's never once been on the overdue list." Which is more than I can say for the *Traviata*, I almost added, but didn't.

Now I sensed him waver and thought I detected a softening in his demeanor, so I managed a bright, enthusiastic smile and pressed my point home. "I've seen her, and she's such a beauty. There are berths for sixty first-class passengers, and plenty of room in the 'tween decks for emigrants. She's comfortable enough for people on the voyage out, and she'd fly on the way home with a wool cargo."

"But why didn't you inform me?" he demanded, his tone wounded. "You could have sent me a telegram or at least contacted Featherstone for advice."

Now I understood all too clearly. The point was not that I had bought the ship, but that I hadn't consulted him first, leaving his male pride battered and bruised.

"There was no time," I protested. "She was going to be auctioned off that very evening. How did I know if you'd even receive my telegram? I didn't know where you were and, I must confess, I didn't think of contacting Mr. Featherstone. I had to make the decision on my own and suffer the consequences if I made the wrong one."

"And you *will* be responsible for your actions," he declared ominously, still furious with me.

He went to a side table, where decanters of spirits stood, poured himself a glass of whisky and drank it down in one swallow. Drake had once said he would be surprised if a woman were capable of running a shipping line, and I think it galled him to be forced to consider that he might be wrong.

Now he turned to me, lines of anger still deeply etched in his face, his eyes as icy and contemptuous as ever. "Since you bought her, I want to rename her."

"Of course."

He stared at me hard. "I want to rename her the *Mary Glover,* after one of my mistresses."

If he sought to wound me, he was wasting his time. I steeled myself and said coolly, "If she flies the Gerrick house flag, she must have the word Raven somewhere in her name."

"Then let her be *Lady Raven's Folly*," he said. "I can't think of a more appropriate name."

"*Lady Raven's Folly* it is, then," I snapped, turned, and walked away before he could notice the pain that sprang into my eyes.

When I returned to my sitting room, I was shaking so badly I couldn't even pick up a pen to write, so I crossed my arms and went pacing about the room, while Faust stared at me with an expression of supreme disdain from the depths of my chair.

"*Lady Raven's Folly,* indeed," I addressed the cat, who blinked once in disbelief, then yawned. "He knows my acquiring that ship was a wise move, but he won't admit it because he didn't think of it first." I took another step, then stopped. "I'll wager every time we argue, he sees himself battling Mark, so he has to win. Well, cat, this is one time he's not going to." When Faust looked skeptical, I exclaimed, "He's *not!*"

Suddenly, there came a knock at the door, but when I called out for the person to enter, there was no answer, so I went to open it.

There was Drake Turner, one arm braced against the doorjamb, his head bowed as close to contritely as I would ever see.

"Mr. Turner," I said coolly, still smarting from the lash of his tongue.

"May I come in?"

"Why? I thought we had said everything we needed to say to each other down in the library a few minutes ago."

"Not everything." He took a deep breath and said, with great effort, "I have come to apologize."

That threw me off balance for a moment, and I felt my anger dissipate. "Come in, then."

When the door closed, he stood before me as nervous as Peter when facing his father for some well-deserved reprimand. "Your decision to buy the *Nancy Malone* was an excellent one."

I was so shocked, I actually stepped back a pace and couldn't think of a snappy retort quickly enough.

"As a matter of fact, I myself have been planning to add passenger ships to my own line for the colonial trade, but you, madam, bested me. And to pay only £17,000 for her is a coup indeed." He smiled, and the warmth filled his eyes. "Her name should be *Lady Raven's Fortune,* for that is what she will bring you." Now he looked even more uncomfortable, hunching his shoulders and shuffling his feet. "I'm also sorry I was so insulting to you. I was furious that I had not been consulted, and sought to denigrate what you had done."

As we faced each other, I wondered cynically if Mr. Turner was sincere, or just staging the performance of his life to engage my sympathy. I still did not trust him, but to refuse his apology would be ungracious.

"I accept your apology, Mr. Turner," I said levelly, "though I must confess it surprises me."

"Oh? And why is that?"

"You're a proud man, and I don't think apologies come easily to you."

"You're right, they don't, Mrs. Gerrick. But you can believe me when I say I only want what is best for the Raven Line, and if we're always bickering and at odds, or unwilling to make concessions when one of us is wrong, then the company will soon suffer. I admit my method of acquiring half of your company was questionable, but now that I'm a partner, I will do what's best for her." He extended his hand to me. "You have my word."

I took it, albeit reluctantly, and felt the warmth and strength of his clasp. When I searched his eyes for a corresponding look of sincerity, I was startled even further to find it. With that understanding, a bond, however tenuous, seemed to be forged between us.

When I withdrew my hand, he said, "I'd like to discuss your plans for the *Lady Raven's Fortune,* but first, would you like to go riding with me? I've been sitting on trains for hours, and the exercise would do me good."

My initial response was to refuse, but I was feeling so elated about the *Nancy Malone* I threw caution to the winds and accepted, a decision I was later to regret bitterly.

After Fenner dressed me in my riding habit of lightweight black serge, with its flattering peplum jacket, I joined Drake downstairs in the back entrance foyer, and we walked toward the stables. Once outside, I realized how one's mood affected one's perception of the world, for today, since I was so pleased with myself—my sorrow set aside, at least momentarily—the summer sun seemed strong and warm on my back, and the air smelled sweeter as it gently brushed tendrils of hair against my face. The sky was a shade of blue so vivid even Constable couldn't capture it, and the flowers in our gardens were a riot of yellow, pink, white, and blue.

As we approached the folly, I noticed Brent sitting on its steps, all alone, as usual, deeply absorbed in the pebbles he was piling atop one another. Peter or Timothy would have just flopped down on the grass without any concern for stains on their clothes, but not fastidious Brent, who was preoccupied with cleanliness.

Brent grinned at Drake and welcomed him back with more warmth and enthusiasm than I had seen him display toward anyone else, and I wondered what the man had done to charm him so. Drake stopped for a moment to talk to the boy, but I hurried on ahead, having no desire to spoil my day by submitting to the child's sharp, dissecting tongue.

Drake caught up with me in the stableyard just as Young Corman came forward leading our mounts, Curlew for me and a sedate bay gelding named Jester for Drake. Nothing more was said between us as he helped me to mount, and we rode out to the moors.

As the wild, untamed moorland rolled out before us, and the horses went crashing through the purple heather growing in abundance along the tor's slope, a sense of peace and tranquillity washed over me. I felt the tension flowing out of my body, and I relaxed in the saddle, letting Curlew's gentle gait soothe me.

My spirits soared. I was so jubilant over my success that nothing was going to be allowed to spoil my perfect day, and, for an afternoon, I was going to forget that Drake Turner was my husband's enemy and enjoy my happiness, since life had meted out so little of it to me lately.

So I smiled and conversed with him as I would any acquaintance, and I think he was startled to hear me speak without sarcasm or bitterness. We discussed this perfect weather, London, and the portrait Ivor Stokes had painted of him, then stopped the horses and watched in silence as a moorhen and her chicks scuttled out of our path to hide beneath a furze bush. A little farther off, on the other side of a tor, we discovered a ewe separated from her flock and entangled in some brambles, so Drake dismounted to free the terrified, bleating animal, while I gazed on anxiously as I held the horses.

When he remounted and we rode on in companionable silence, I found myself trying to study the man objectively, without the haze of prejudice that so often colored my impression of him. Physically, he was an attractive man—"the sort all the ladies swoon over and chase," as my father had said—in spite of his rough, pockmarked skin. He cut a dashing figure in a dark blue riding coat tailored perfectly across his broad shoulders, and buff-colored breeches and top boots fit him as well as the chamois gloves he wore.

But beneath that dashing figure was a man of great complexity. True, he had been unscrupulous in his acquisition of half the Raven Line, but he still possessed the integrity to run it to the best of his ability. Drake was proud and arrogant, like Mark, yet his apology to me indicated a certain generosity of spirit and humility. His championing of Timothy and his kindnesses toward Brent—a thoroughly unlikable child—could not fail to raise him in my estimation.

Yet, there was always that wall between us, that wariness of his about revealing himself completely to another person. It kept me at a distance, yet challenged me to break it down and confront the man just out of reach. I wondered if any of his many women had penetrated that wall and won his heart? Somehow, I doubted it.

In spite of my resolve not to dwell on Mark today, I began to wonder once again why he had hated Drake Turner so. He had never given me a reason, but then, I had never really asked. I always assumed it was just a trade rivalry that caused Mark to sputter and revile the man so often. When your rival bested you, you cursed him roundly and vowed to turn the tables in the next foray. But I began to wonder if their mutual dislike ran deeper for some obscure reason that was lost to me.

Finally, after riding in silence for so long, Drake said, "You love these moors, don't you?"

I smiled and nodded. "Mark and I used to . . ." The words slipped out, but I stopped myself just in time. "Yes, I love this place. There's a great sense of peace here—can't you feel it?— away from civilization, away from worries. Many people find it desolate, and it can be dangerous, especially when the mists roll in so suddenly they obliterate the paths, but I've always loved it here. It's a refreshing change from the noise and dirt of London." I fell silent, as I watched a hawk dip and whirl on the air currents overhead. Then I said, "How was your trip to London?"

While we rode, he told me about his sad task of settling the loss of the *Traviata,* the first ship he had ever owned, a sleek, thousand-ton clipper built by the great Walter Hood of Aberdeen.

"I'm going to replace her, of course," Drake said, "but with a steamship."

I stared at him in astonishment. "Replace a China clipper with a steamship? I've never heard of such a thing."

"You will," he replied, his eyes sparkling with excitement. "The Suez Canal should be complete next year, and when it opens the Mediterranean as a trade route from China, it will be the steamships that make the best time, you mark my words. It will mean the death of the China clipper, and I, for one, don't intend to be left out in the cold."

"And what about all of our other ships?" I demanded in alarm. "They're all clippers as well. What will happen to them, if steam comes into general use?"

"Oh, that won't happen for years yet. But when a ship is lost or damaged beyond repair, I think steamships should replace them."

I could not help but admire the man for his foresight, and grudgingly admitted to myself that the Raven Line couldn't be in more capable hands.

As he continued talking about the value of the *Traviata*'s lost cargo, insurance claims to be haggled over and resolved, and the cost of replacing the vessel itself, I noticed there was no mention of the human misery brought about by the loss of the ship.

"And what of the crew?" I asked.

"There were no survivors."

I reined in Curlew and turned to face him, my tongue giving vent to all the anger and frustration I suddenly felt. "An entire crew was lost, and all you can talk about is the value of the cargo and the cost of replacing the ship?" I shook my head in disgust. I almost added, "No wonder Mark thought so little of you," but didn't want to spoil my perfect afternoon.

I fully expected to see him lose his temper and give me a tongue-lashing in return, so I was taken aback to see his icy eyes warm with mirth.

"Well, Lady Raven, since you think so little of me, I don't see why I should tell you that I made a special stop in Plymouth on my way back here. Would it please you to know that the sailors we dismissed have all found other employment?"

This considerate and totally unexpected act moved me so deeply, I didn't know what to say, and I hid behind a façade of light banter and mockery. "What, Mr. Turner, putting people before commerce? Perhaps there is a glimmer of hope for you yet."

"Must you mock me, madam?" he asked, with a shake of his head.

"But you so often deserve it," was my blunt reply. I smiled, however, feeling charitable. "Thank you for investigating the welfare of those sailors. They were loyal to us, and I was worried about them."

"I know."

An awkward silence fell between us, so I touched my heel to my mare's side and started walking her around a flock of sheep blocking our path. Then I said to Drake, "Did you at least take some time to go to your beloved opera while you were in London, or did you spend all your evenings pouring over contracts?"

"I did manage to attend an excellent performance of *Rigoletto*," he replied, "though when it was over, I discovered that Featherstone had been waiting outside my box for over an hour with an important matter to discuss."

My brows arched in surprise. "Why didn't he just knock and interrupt you?"

Drake regarded me with mock severity. "My dear Lady Raven, no one dares interrupt me at the opera, unless it's a matter of life or death."

I thought of poor Mr. Featherstone, waiting in the corridor, counting the minutes as they dragged on into hours, and I burst out laughing. "You're a hard taskmaster, Mr. Turner."

He tried to look stern, but failed. "I suppose I am." Then he said, "Actually, as stimulating as London was, I was eager to return to Raven's Chase. Oh, you needn't look so astonished, Mrs. Gerrick. After all, my cat and chef are here, and I suppose I even missed your animosity toward me. In fact, I was surprised to discover I missed you a great deal."

My head jerked around in surprise, and when I looked into his eyes, what I saw in their sea-blue depths frightened me. The wall of reserve was down, revealing Drake's desire for me. Amabel had seen it all along, but I had been too wrapped up in my grief for Mark to recognize signs every woman knows instinctively.

My happiness had dulled both my wits and waspish tongue, making me unable to put the man in his place for speaking so freely and out of turn.

Instead, I handled that dangerous moment by feigning ignorance and not responding at all. Standing in my stirrup, I shielded my eyes from the sun and scanned the horizon. My attention was caught by a dark horse in the distance, galloping wild and free through the heather, and I used it to break the tension that crackled about us, like the air before a storm.

"Odalisque!" I murmured excitedly.

"What?" Drake demanded, obviously expecting some other response from me.

"Odalisque . . . Mark's horse," I replied impatiently, then explained how I had set her free. I urged Curlew into a canter. "I'm going to try to catch her."

As I rode off, Drake followed, and we didn't need to ride far before the sleek, swift Odalisque turned into nothing more than a rangy old moor pony who was no match for our speedy thoroughbreds.

I reined in my horse, my voice thick with disappointment. "Fooled! It's not Odalisque at all."

Without another word, I dismounted, picked up my skirts and started to walk up a hill, ostensibly to pick heather, but in reality to gather my wits about me so that I could deal with Drake. He dismounted as well and removed his round hat in order to wipe his brow with a handkerchief, then led the horses after me.

When he caught up, he said, "While I was in London, I found it difficult to keep my mind off you, Mrs. Gerrick. I'd be haggling with the underwriters about the *Traviata* and find myself thinking about how your hair shines in the sun and your tawny eyes darken with anger . . ."

"Do they, now?" was my tart comment as my perfect mood shattered and fell apart.

"Yes, they do," he said amiably, confident of his powers to charm and woo me. "And even that dry, mocking wit of yours is really a most attractive quality." Then he added, "Most men would find your candor unseemly and unladylike, but not I," as he reached out and ran his gloved fingertips insolently down my arm.

I reared back as something inside of me exploded, and this time, when I raised my hand, he was not quick enough to stop me, and I slapped him so hard my palm tingled briefly.

Suddenly, I felt strong fingers grasp my wrist, causing the heather to tumble from my hand. When our gazes locked, his pale eyes were blazing, his sensual mouth trembling.

"If a woman dares strike me, madam, she had better be prepared for the consequences."

Without warning, he pulled me toward him and took me in his arms, crushing me helplessly to him. Before I could struggle or even scream, his mouth came down on mine ruthlessly.

It was a quick, punishing kiss that startled me with its fervor, and when Drake released me, I could still feel the pressure of his lips on mine.

As I stepped back, my first reaction was to slap him again as hard as I could, but instead, I deliberately drew the back of my hand hard across my mouth, as if to erase what he had just done. "You are despicable!" I cried, shaking uncontrollably, as I stepped on my fallen flowers and crushed them in my haste to take Curlew's reins and clamber unassisted into the sidesaddle. Then I flung my head back and looked down at Drake. "I want you to leave Raven's Chase as soon as you can have your valet pack your bags."

A sardonic smile was just visible beneath his mustache as he crossed his arms arrogantly and shook his head in defiance. "I'm not leaving. We're running the Raven Line together whether you like it or not."

I jerked Curlew's head around, pinching her soft mouth and causing her to squeal in surprise. "You can take the Raven Line and go to hell!"

Then I dug my heel into the mare's side and galloped back to the house.

When I returned to Raven's Chase and went up to my sitting room, I was startled to see Damon, of all people, wandering the halls like a lost soul.

I'm afraid I took my anger out on him as I snapped, "Damon, what on earth are you doing here?"

The vacant blue eyes stared at me, and his face crumpled in bewilderment. "I—I'm looking for my sister, but I can't find her anywhere."

Then I realized why he was confused. "Damon," I began gently, "this is Raven's Chase. Amabel is at the Little Chase. You have to go home."

He stared at me for a full minute before saying, "Oh," and ambling off down the hall.

I shook my head sadly as I entered the sitting room and

removed my gloves and bonnet. Who could blame the poor man for mistaking one house for the other, since they were identical?

Faust was curled in my favorite chair, waiting for me. He mewed in greeting and actually relinquished the seat before I had to ask, and I sank down in relief.

My thoughts were fixed on the moors today, and I recalled the look of bald passion in Drake's pale eyes as he drew me to him. But, once again, he metamorphosed into Mark. Suddenly, the years rolled back, and I was seated across the pommel of Odalisque's saddle, wrapped in Mark's heavy wool cloak. He held me securely around the waist while gently plucking twigs and bits of heather from my hair. Then his long, strong fingers entwined themselves in my curly locks, so he could pull my head back and reach for my mouth with his own.

And, if I live to be ninety, I'll never forget the words he said to me when we finally parted: "My golden-eyed witch . . . I've wanted to do that for a long, long time."

The sound of the cat's impatient yowling jerked me rudely back to the present, and my beautiful daydream popped abruptly, like a burst bubble, leaving me empty and bereft, yearning for Mark with a hunger that tore at my insides with the pain of a long-standing disease. It was a hunger no man would be able to satisfy, especially Drake Turner.

Forced to think about him now, I racked my brain to determine the reason for his forward behavior this afternoon. Had I unwittingly encouraged him in some way? Impossible, for from the day I met Drake Turner, I had always made my feelings for him quite obvious. I disliked and resented him. I couldn't make those feelings any plainer and had always treated him with utmost coolness.

"The conceit of the man!" I muttered to Faust, whose slanted golden eyes followed my progress around the room.

Drake's honey-tongued lies kept flowing through my brain. "I find myself thinking about how your hair shines in the sun and your tawny eyes darken with anger. . . ."

My heart was racing now and my cheeks burning from our

confrontation. Did he think he was so superior to Mark that just his touch and a few words of flattery would drive me into his arms? Or did he regard me as he had the Raven Line, his enemy's possession to be conquered?

The experience had so shaken me, I had to talk to someone about it, so I rose and hurried over to the Little Chase.

But by the time I arrived there, I changed my mind and decided against telling Amabel about Drake's behavior on the moors, for she would only delight in saying, "I told you so."

I found her in the drawing room doing embroidery, but judging by the expression on her face, she wasn't concentrating on the task at hand.

"What are you doing?" I asked, coming over to examine her handiwork.

She wouldn't show it to me and thrust it aside, saying irritably, "Oh, I've ruined it. You wouldn't want to see it anyway."

My brows rose in surprise, for Amabel excelled in such feminine accomplishments as embroidery, sketching, and playing the piano, while I could barely thread a needle without pricking a finger and drawing blood. So I found it difficult to believe she had ruined her embroidery. No, something else was irritating her, and I was determined to find out what it was.

"What's the matter, Amabel?" I asked gently, my own problems forgotten, as she rose to pace the room in agitation.

"Oh, it's nothing, really. My head groom just accused one of the undergrooms of stealing sacks of grain and selling them, or some such nonsense. The undergroom insists he's innocent, so they've come to me to settle the matter, like King Solomon." She groaned in anguish. "I wish Colin were here to handle the men. I just don't know what to do. Dismiss the undergroom? If I don't, the head groom will feel his authority has been usurped, but what if the other man is innocent?" She threw up her hands in despair. "How I wish my husband were here!"

I felt a little twinge of guilt, for if it hadn't been for me, Amabel's husband would have been here to handle this annoying domestic dispute.

To take Amabel's mind off her crisis, I told her all about my acquisition of the *Nancy Malone,* and the plans I had for her. Amabel was surprised and excited for me, though I think she would have been more interested if I had spent the £17,000 on a new wardrobe.

When she asked how Drake had reacted, I replied, "He was none too pleased, as you can well imagine. In fact, he was so furious, there were times I feared for my safety." I shook my head at the memory of his wrath. "He first wanted to name her the *Mary Glover,* after one of his mistresses, but—"

"Did you say Mary Glover?" she interrupted me sharply.

"Why, yes. Why do you ask?"

She plucked at her fringe of curls and looked puzzled for a moment, then shrugged it off. "Never mind. I thought we had a distant cousin named Glover, that's all."

Then I told her how Drake had apologized to me and finally admitted I had made the right decision, but Amabel's eyes had glazed over and I knew she wasn't really listening.

My suspicions were confirmed when she said, "Where do you think Colin is right this minute?"

I considered for a moment, then replied, "He should be in New York City."

Her pretty face glowed. "Just think. Soon he will be conducting his investigation, if he isn't already. I just pray he's successful." Then her eyes hardened. "Timothy's inheritance is at stake, and I'll be damned if I'll see it turned over to that odious little monster."

I nodded in agreement, though I was thinking more of keeping Raven's Chase for myself. Timothy would come into it eventually, as was his right, but until that time, I wanted to enjoy the home that Mark and I had shared.

Amabel went on with, "Do you know that when the boys first met Brent, they got along beautifully? Now, every time I allow them to go to Raven's Chase to play with him, Peter always comes home in tears, though Brent doesn't seem to hurt Timothy at all." Amabel virtually bristled with maternal indignation as she thought about the injustices done to her children. "And Miss Blessed has been watching Damon like a hawk, trying to keep that child away from him."

"What happened?" I asked sharply.

Amabel pursed her lips, then said, "He knows Damon is mad and must be humored, but he deliberately taunts him by telling him there are no sepoys or supply wagons."

I was aghast. "Oh, Amabel, he doesn't!"

"Miss Blessed nearly throttled the child when she first caught him doing it. Damon was so agitated she had to send him to his room and give him medicine to calm him down."

"As my maid said to me, that child knows where all our wounds are, and he just keeps turning the knife."

Amabel shivered as she sat back down. "I wish I could tell you that I'm on the verge of exposing the Masons, Nora, but I'm not."

I could tell her lack of success was bothering her. Amabel was accustomed to using her copious charms and beauty to make others do her bidding, but this was one time it wasn't working. It was a novel experience for her, and it rankled.

She turned to me. "You know as well as I, Nora, that when we tell one lie, we have to tell even bigger ones to cover up the initial lie."

I nodded. "The truth is always best."

"Well, I have yet to catch the Masons in a lie," she said, and flashed me an apologetic look. "You don't suppose they're telling the truth, do you?"

I just gave her a look that spoke volumes.

"Well, I can see that you don't. But, don't you think that if they weren't telling the truth, they would have given themselves away by now?"

"They're very clever and cautious, Amabel," was my only explanation.

"Well, I just think it's uncanny the way their stories remain consistent," she muttered, then wisely changed the subject. "Oh, by the way, I decided it's time I had the Masons to dinner. Will you and Mr. Turner come tonight as well?"

"Oh, I don't think so, Amabel."

But she badgered me, as I knew she would, and finally, I relented and promised to see her at six o'clock.

I went over to the Little Chase an hour early, so I wouldn't have to share the Gerrick carriage with the Masons and Drake, and when the three of them arrived, they were laughing and chattering away like old friends.

I had decided the best way to handle Drake was to pretend nothing had occurred between us out on the moors today. True, I could have forced him to leave but, much as I was loath to admit it, the Raven Line bound us together. So, that night at dinner, I was as cordial toward him as ever.

The dinner went smoothly, until Seth said, "And where is Mr. Trelawney? I don't think I've seen him for the last several weeks?"

"Brent said that Peter told him his father was away," Ella added.

"Actually," I said, after dabbing at my lips with my napkin, "Colin is in New York City, trying to prove you're swindlers."

Out of the corner of my eye, I saw Amabel shake her head in warning, and Drake look at me strangely. Ella's unblinking, expressionless eyes affixed themselves on me, but I held them and did not look away.

Seth just smiled his infuriating wide, white smile as he said, "Well, then, I'm afraid his trip will be for naught, because he will learn we're telling the truth."

I tried to look enigmatic as I murmured, "We shall see."

Amabel made an attempt to rescue the evening by saying,

"Well, ladies, shall we leave the gentlemen to their port and cigars, while we retire to the drawing room?"

"If you'll excuse me," I said, rising, "I think I shall look in on Peter and Timothy and perhaps read them a bedtime story, if Nellie hasn't put them to bed already."

Then I made my excuses and left.

Timothy was sound asleep when I opened his bedroom door and looked in on him, but that rascal Peter was still awake and greeted me with a winning grin when I came in and told him I would read to him. I read one book after another, hoping that if I remained up here long enough, the guests downstairs would finally leave, and I would be spared the carriage ride back with them. And, sure enough, three books later, I heard a carriage pull away from the front door.

"Aunt Nora, will you read me the story about the little blue soldier?" Peter asked, rubbing his eyes and trying valiantly to keep awake.

I nodded. "Where is it?"

"I think I left it in the drawing room."

"All right," I said, and left.

The drawing room was empty when I entered and started searching for the book. I looked under cushions and pillows on the chairs, and those on the window seat, but to no avail. I was down on my hands and knees, peering under the sofa, when I heard the drawing room door close.

"Mrs. Trelawney," Drake said, "how did Lord Raven and the boy die?"

I knew I should have popped up right then and there, or made some sound to warn them of my presence not ten feet away, but I didn't. I just froze, crouched there on my hands and knees, hardly daring to breathe lest I give myself away.

Amabel was silent, and I interpreted this as reluctance on her part. Finally, she said, "They died in a senseless, tragic fire, Mr. Turner. Surely you learned that when you were considering buying the Raven Line. It was in all the papers."

"Of course. But I'd like to know those details the newspapers and rumor omit."

"If you're so curious, why not ask Nora yourself?"

I heard Drake make a derisive noise. "Mrs. Trelawney, even an insensitive clod such as myself would never do that. The mere mention of her husband's name causes Nora great anguish."

"She loved Mark very much, Mr. Turner—perhaps too much, if that's possible."

"How well I know that." They were silent for a moment, then Drake begged, "Please, Mrs. Trelawney. Won't you tell me what happened?"

"All right," was Amabel's reluctant reply.

My mind formed the word "No!" but my plea remained a silent one as I crouched there, hardly daring to breathe.

"Nora was spending the day in Plymouth, visiting a sick friend," Amabel began. "For some reason, Mark didn't accompany her, but remained at the Chase. On the evening of the tragedy, most of the servants were away celebrating the birth of a footman's first child. So, the only people in the house at the time were Mark and Miss Bridges, Gabriel's young nurse." Amabel was silent, and I could imagine her wrinkling her pert nose in disapproval as she said, "I never liked Miss Bridges. I thought she was much too young and flighty to be a nurse, but you know Nora's soft heart. The girl gave her some hard-luck tale and Nora hired her.

"Anyway, after the tragedy, the nurse claimed someone slipped a note under the nursery door, telling her Mrs. Harkins had returned and wanted to see her in the kitchen immediately. The baby was sleeping, so she left him and went downstairs, but there was no one in the kitchen. When she returned to the nursery and opened the door, smoke came pouring out. She ran for Mark, who was in his study at the time, and he sent her for the stablehands." Her steady voice wavered as she said, "Mark shouldn't even have attempted to save his son. It was just too late, but he didn't realize it. He wouldn't give up, and paid with his own life."

"Was the note ever found?" Drake asked.

"Yes. Later, Miss Bridges produced the note, which she said she had stuffed into her pocket before going downstairs to the kitchen, but it is believed she later wrote it herself, to provide an alibi."

Scorn filled Drake's voice as he said, "Come now, Mrs. Trelawney, doesn't that sound a trifle implausible? Why would the nurse leave the child in the first place, make up such a tale, and even write the note herself? It sounds rather farfetched to me."

"Who else would have done it?" Amabel demanded peevishly. "No one else was around, except Damon and myself, and I can assure you, both of us were at the Little Chase that night. Constable Tibbins questioned me at great length on that point, and it was most insulting." Amabel was silent for a moment, then went on with, "Miss Bridges was quite flighty, as I told you. She probably left the room to fetch a book, or even to try on Nora's dresses while she was away. Who knows? And when she returned to find the nursery in flames, she panicked and had to fabricate a story that would make herself appear blameless. It is believed that Gabriel woke up while Miss Bridges was out, threw his ball, and knocked over the lamp. When—it was over, workmen found the lamp shattered on the floor. Help came in time to contain the fire and keep it from burning down the Chase, but the damage was done. Mark and Gabriel were gone."

"Oh, my God!" Drake moaned. "No wonder Nora—"

"Now can you understand why she keeps those rooms locked and refuses to talk about Mark and Gabriel? She blames herself for not being there when they needed her. The day of their funeral, all she kept saying, over and over, was, 'If I had been home, they would still be alive.' She was inconsolable for weeks. After the repairmen cleaned and fixed the nursery, Nora refused to allow anyone to throw away Gabriel's toys, so they were all left in a corner, and the room locked."

Drake sighed, a dismal, drawn-out sound, then was silent for a while. When he spoke again, he said quietly, "What happened to the nurse?"

"Miss Bridges? She was dismissed, of course. And do you know what Nora did? She actually gave the girl a letter of reference. Can you imagine that? The girl caused the deaths of her husband and child, and Nora gave her a glowing letter of reference. When I expressed my shock and disapproval, do you know what she said to me? 'If I don't give her one, she'll never be able to work again. She'll starve, or worse. So, as much as it pains me, Amabel, I must do this.' I couldn't dissuade her, either. You know Nora. She's kindhearted to a fault."

"I'm not surprised," Drake said, and there was no contempt in his voice. "I would expect Nora to do something like that."

Amabel sniffed. "So, thanks to Nora's generosity, Miss Bridges is in London, serving as governess to the family of Lord and Lady Creighton."

Reliving that night made me sit back and hug myself as hot tears streamed down my face, and great, shuddering sobs racked my body. I heard Drake exclaim in surprise and footsteps hurry toward me.

Then he was pulling me to my feet and into his arms, one hand stroking my hair. But my eyes were closed tight, and I refused to open them, even though he begged me.

"Oh, Nora, I am so sorry," I heard Amabel's remorseful voice say. "If I had known you were here . . ."

"Go away," I said. "Both of you. Leave me alone."

"I'm taking you home now," Drake said, swinging me into his arms as though I were a limp rag doll.

But I kept my eyes tightly closed and cried out just once against the blackness that enveloped me.

The sound of flames crackling awoke me, but when I opened my eyes, I knew I was in my own bedroom, for I could discern the slender fluted urns of the bedposts silhouetted against the darkness. I sat bolt upright, my heart racing in panic as I sniffed the air for smoke, but when I realized the flames were nothing more than the hiss of a heavy rain pouring outside my window, I fell back in relief.

I remembered little of what happened after Drake swept me out of Amabel's drawing room. As I sat up again, my thoughts were filled with hazy recollections of a short, wild carriage ride home, followed by Fenner's frantic efforts to undress me, give me a sleeping draft, and get me into bed.

But I couldn't go back to sleep now, for I knew if my head touched the pillow, the nightmare would begin again. My mind would force me to relive the horrible night that Amabel had so dispassionately described to Drake.

Flinging back the cumbersome blankets, I rose groggily, wrapped a shawl around me, and fumbled in the darkness until I found a lamp. After lighting it with unsteady fingers, I left my room, oblivious to the cold floor beneath my bare feet as I padded off to the portrait gallery. Passing the Green Room, I noticed a crack of light beneath Drake's door. So, he was working late as usual, I thought, and moved on silently, like a wraith.

When I reached my destination, I held my lamp aloft and stared up at Mark lovingly, then traced the strong line of his jaw with my fingertips, but felt only hard, dry paint, not the warm, living flesh I craved.

"God, how I miss you!" I whispered to him, my head lolling on my chest.

Then I set my lamp on the windowsill and tortured myself still further by imagining what had happened on that fateful night. I could see Mark turn gray as the hysterical Miss Bridges came screaming into his study, sense his rising panic and fear as he limped toward the nursery and was confronted by a wall of billowing black smoke and the sound of greedy flames crackling in triumph. Did he scream Gabriel's name before plunging into that inferno in a futile effort to save his son? What were his last thoughts when he realized he was going to die?

I placed my hand to my cold, clammy cheek, for such

thoughts sickened and depressed me. But I could no more keep them at bay than I could stop breathing. Everyone meant well when they reassured me such thoughts would disappear in time, but I knew they would always be there, crouching beneath the surface of my consciousness, waiting to spring when I least expected it.

Suddenly, I had the uneasy feeling I was not alone in the gallery, and I started, aware and wary. The lamplight, while strong, reached only halfway down the long hall, leaving the rest in darkness, and I could sense someone there, waiting in the shadows, watching me.

"Who's there?" I demanded, my voice a clear, strong challenge.

No answer, just the faint pattering of rain against the windowpanes.

I swallowed hard, as the backs of my hands tingled in apprehension. "Brent!" I said sharply. "Stop trying to frighten me. I know you're there."

In response to my brave command came a noise—a sound that puzzled me because my brain was too fuzzy from the sleeping draft to identify it immediately. When I did recognize it as the soft whirring sound of motion, the spherical object came rolling into the arc of light, then slowed and stopped just a few feet before me.

My brow wrinkled in puzzlement as I bent down to examine it, but as soon as my fingertips touched its crumbling, charred surface, I leaped back in horror.

It was my son's favorite ball.

I filled my lungs to scream, but all that came out was a strangled gurgle as I bolted out of the gallery and down the nearest corridor. I just ran blindly, trusting my senses to keep me from crashing into walls and injuring myself. Was that the sound of someone following me, or just the wild thudding of my own heart?

Then, as I rounded a corner, a sudden light blinded and

disoriented me, and a strong hand came out to grip my arm.

"Nora! What's wrong? What are you doing out of bed at this hour?"

The light fell away, and I stared up into Drake's white, concerned face and could see my wide-eyed, terrified countenance mirrored in his eyes. Despite my chattering teeth, I managed to blurt out, "Gabriel . . . in the gallery."

His eyes narrowed in disbelief for a moment, then he took off his green velvet dressing gown and wrapped it around my shoulders. "Now, tell me what happened," he began calmly. "What frightened you in the gallery?"

I told him as coherently as possible, but it still didn't make sense, even to my own ears. When I finished, I had never seen a man so angry.

"Damn that child!" he swore. "He has gone too far this time. When I find him, I'll— Come, follow me," and before I could hang back, he took my cold hand and pulled me after him.

But when we reached the gallery, neither the ball nor Brent was to be found, even though Drake searched the entire gallery thoroughly, while I stood shivering before Mark's portraits. Finally, when he came back, he said, "Where did you last see that ball?"

"It—it was left in the nursery."

"Fine. We'll see if it's still there."

I shook my head and shrank away from him in fear.

"Please come with me, Nora," he begged. "You can wait outside, if you want. You won't have to go inside the room itself. Leave that to me."

Reluctantly, I agreed, and we walked in silence to the nursery. As we approached that ominous closed door, my will nearly failed me and I stopped, but Drake urged me on.

"Wait here," he whispered with a reassuring smile.

"You'll need a key," I said between chattering teeth.

To our mutual astonishment, the door swung open easily

when he turned the knob. "Now, this is interesting," Drake mused before disappearing inside.

I don't know how long I stood there, propped up against the wall, as memories assailed me. Finally, Drake slowly emerged, looking puzzled as he stopped before me.

"There is no ball in there," he said.

Later, I was to wonder why Drake had been wandering the halls at the same time that malicious trick was being played, but when I returned to my room, I was convinced one of the Masons was the culprit.

At ten o'clock, I summoned the three Masons to the Chinese drawing room for the confrontation. As they filed in, I could tell they were curious as to why they had been summoned into my presence this morning.

"Lady Raven . . ." Seth said genially, tossing the hair out of his eyes. "Here we are, as you requested. Now, what is all this about? I must say, you look as though there's a thundercloud hanging over your head."

"There is, Mr. Mason," I replied, staring at Brent, whose huge dark eyes seemed to sparkle slyly. I looked from one to the other as I told them about my dead son's ball rolling down the gallery toward me last night, and surprised myself that I could sound so calm. I concluded with, "It was a terrible, vicious trick, and I think Brent did it."

Ella's pretty face turned even whiter as her hands came down protectively on her son's shoulders. "How dare you stand there and accuse my son of such a thing!"

"Now, just a moment, Ella," Seth said soothingly, patting her arm. "Let's be fair."

"Seth!"

He held up his hand for silence as he kneeled down to his nephew's height. "Brent, is what Lady Raven says true? Did you try to frighten her last night?"

"No, Uncle Seth," the child mumbled, looking his uncle straight in the eye.

Ella's unblinking stare met my gaze, and she gave me a look that promised swift retribution.

"Of course he would deny it," I said scornfully.

Seth rose. "Where would he have gotten this ball?"

"From the nursery," I replied, and repeated my theory.

He raised his dark brows in a gesture reminiscent of my first husband, Oliver Woburn. "But I was told that room is always kept locked."

"The door was open last night. Someone picked the lock with all the skill and efficiency of a London cracksman."

"A what?" Ella demanded.

"A thief," I said pointedly, looking at Brent.

"Lady Raven, my son is not a thief. He—"

"Ella . . ." Seth interrupted his sister with a warning glance. When she was silent, he went on. "Tell me, Lady Raven, did you actually see Brent in the gallery last night?"

"No. The other end of the hall was in darkness, and I was too enervated to confront the culprit."

"Aha, so you never actually *saw* Brent there."

"He must have run away as soon as he rolled the ball at me, and gone back to his bedchamber after he retrieved it."

Seth threw back his head and laughed, a mocking, patronizing sound that infuriated me. "So what you are saying is that you have no proof Brent frightened you, madam."

I folded my arms and said, "As soon as one of the maids finishes searching Brent's room, I'm sure I'll have all the proof I need, Mr. Mason."

"Why, I never—" Ella exclaimed in a rare burst of emotion. "May I remind you that we are *guests* here, Lady Raven? You have no right to search my son's room as though he were some common thief!"

"I have every right," was my reply. "This is still my house."

Ella turned to her brother again. "Seth—"

"I know it's annoying and degrading, sister dear," he said, "but I'm sure Brent will be vindicated."

Brent's dark eyes were filled with malice as they rested on me just once before he tugged at his mother's skirts for attention. "Mama," he said, "I promise you I didn't do it. Lady Raven may search until Doomsday, but she will find nothing to incriminate me."

The miserable child was right. Minutes later, Mrs. Harkins appeared at the door, and I could tell by the rapid, nervous jingling of keys that she brought bad news. She announced she herself had searched Brent's room and had found nothing.

Seth couldn't wait to gloat. "Lady Raven, we know you're grief-stricken by Mark's death, but I'm afraid it's affecting your mind."

"You'd like everyone to believe that, wouldn't you?" I retorted, clutching my hands into fists until the nails bit into my palms.

"I think you owe Brent an apology," he said, tousling his nephew's hair.

I thrust my chin out belligerently and strode toward the drawing room door. "It'll be a hot day in December before I do that, Mr. Mason."

And I left with what little dignity I had.

Once outside in the balmy air of late spring, I kept walking away from Raven's Chase in short, clipped strides. I listened for footsteps behind me as I passed the empty folly, but there were none.

Why had I allowed my rage against the Masons to eclipse rational thought? I had struck out at them blindly, and they merely used my distressed state against me to make me look the fool. Once again, the three of them were the very picture of wronged innocence, and I their vengeful tormentor.

I could have used some comforting right now. If Mark had been here, he would have extended his arms wordlessly to me, and I would have run to him. But he was not, and it was useless to torment myself with wishful thinking. I had to fight my battles alone now.

I skirted the stables, taking time to wave to an undergroom walking several horses, and started climbing the hill that rose sharply behind the barns. It was a steep climb along a narrow path, with brambles catching at my skirt and the fierce sun beating down on the top of my bare head, so that by the time I reached the summit, I was hot, sticky, and out of breath.

But the exertion was well worth it. Walking briskly, I plunged into cool, velvet shadows made by ageless oaks spreading their strong, leafy branches in a canopy overhead, and breathed deeply the natural perfume of wild flowers and ferns. I could hear the faint, merry gurgle of a brook in the distance, as water splashed over rocks, and I knew I was nearing the Eyrie, a high, secluded place on a cliff where we often came for picnics or just solitude.

As I marched down a sun-dappled path, the sound of voices rose above the chugging of the brook, and I was so startled to see Miss Blessed here, with Damon, that I just stopped and stared.

Damon was lying in the grassy clearing, his hands folded across his chest as he conversed with his nurse sitting by his side. Ordinarily, I wouldn't give such a scene a second thought, except for the fact that Angel Blessed's hair was unpinned and flowed freely down her back in a most unrestricted fashion, making her look quite young and carefree. Then when I myself saw her reach down to gently stroke Damon's golden head in a gesture more befitting a lover than a nurse . . .

Suddenly, a look of terror transformed his placid face, and he jumped to his feet. "I—I don't know what happened next!" he cried. "I can't remember! You mustn't make me remember!" Then he picked up his rifle and bolted away in the opposite direction, and I could hear him crashing through the underbrush like a startled deer.

Miss Blessed watched him disappear, then began to pin up her hair in a more decorous style. Just as she was slipping in the last hairpin, I stepped out of the shadows and made my presence known.

"Good day, Miss Blessed," I called out brightly, as though I had just this moment come up the hill. "I see you, too, sometimes need a little solitude."

She did not seem surprised to see me, and her lovely face was free of guilt as she said, "Good day, Lady Raven. Yes, sometimes I do need a bit of solitude."

Evidently she did not realize that I had seen her with Damon.

"And where is Damon today?" I asked innocently, looking around as I sat down beside her and settled my skirts about me.

She glanced over her shoulder and replied, "He was here just a few moments ago, but I fear I upset him and he ran away."

"Oh?" I murmured in surprise, for I was expecting her to deny Damon's presence.

She nodded, and her smile was as gentle as her voice as she said, "I often bring him up here to try to remember what happened to him in India."

I looked at her askance. "Oh? But everyone has been doing their utmost to help him forget India."

"I know Mrs. Trelawney would never approve, if she knew," she confessed somewhat sheepishly, "but I believe confession is good for the soul, and reliving one's unpleasant experiences can be beneficial. So, when Damon and I are alone, and no one bothers him, I can talk to him about India."

"And have you been successful?"

A look of chagrin flitted across her gentle features. "We always reach a certain point, and then Damon's mind refuses to go further. He retreats and won't come out."

"Poor Damon."

As we fell into a companionable silence, I surreptitiously studied the woman seated next to me and came to the conclusion that this "stunner"—as my father would say—could have every artist in London worshiping at her feet and vying to paint her. Her height was arresting in itself, but with thick, glossy chestnut hair, delicate white skin, and velvet brown eyes as well, Angel Blessed was beautiful. And there was nothing self-conscious about her, either. In fact, she seemed to regard her splendid looks as something to be endured with patience and stoicism.

Why, I wondered, did such a rose choose to blush unseen in Devon, when the world awaited?

The more I thought about it, the more curious I became. Finally, I said, "Do you mind if I ask you a personal question, Miss Blessed?"

"Of course not."

"I have often wondered why you became a nurse, which must surely be a taxing profession, seeing people sick and dying. You are certainly lovely enough to have your pick of suitors."

That amused her, for she laughed, a gentle, tinkling sound, like a soft breeze blowing through chimes. "I know life can be so easy for well-favored women, but I yearned to *do* something with my life other than decorate some gentleman's parlor."

Then she relaxed and became even more talkative, telling me of a childhood spent mending the broken wings of birds who strayed into her garden and patching up stray cats badly clawed in fights. As she grew older, the local doctor let her accompany him when he visited sick patients, because her calm presence and gentle hands seemed to soothe them. At the same time, he discouraged her, telling her that women were not admitted to medical schools, and she could never hope to be a doctor, like him.

She rolled her dark eyes skyward. "We used to argue endlessly about the physical and mental fitness of the female sex to attend medical schools, but even he could not stop me from daydreaming that I was Miss Nightingale, going to Scutari to tend the sick and wounded of the Crimea."

"And what did your parents think of this dream of yours?" I asked.

Her face clouded, and she looked away. "They were outraged, of course, as any proper parents would be. They wanted me to marry the Honorable Maurice Basingstoke as soon as I turned eighteen, but I refused and fought them bitterly." She laughed at some remembered battle. "I was beastly! I think they finally acquiesced because they were tired of fighting with me and loved me too much to see me married against my will."

Then I thought of Mark, our deliriously happy years together, and my son, and I could not help asking Miss Blessed, "But don't you yearn for the love of a husband, and children?"

The dark eyes sparkled. "Oh, I am not so dedicated as you would suppose, Lady Raven. There is someone I have deep feelings for, though who knows if we shall ever marry."

I was about to press her further, for she intrigued me, but she abruptly rose and shook her skirts, thus ending all confidences. "I've enjoyed talking with you, Lady Raven, but I'm afraid I must be getting back to Damon, or I'll incur Mrs. Trelawney's displeasure."

"Before you go, Miss Blessed, there is a question I must ask you."

She hesitated, then murmured, "Yes?"

I swallowed hard as I gathered my courage, then looked up at her and asked, "Is it possible for a person to go mad from grief?"

She nodded. "You have only to look at Damon."

"Something happened to me last night that made me doubt my sanity."

The nurse's brows rose in surprise. "Oh?"

I am not usually one to make confidences so readily, but there was something about this gentle, sensitive woman that set me at ease, and I found myself spilling out my story of what happened last night. "But when Drake—Mr. Turner—went to the nursery, he found the door unlocked and the ball missing." I reached up to touch her hand in desperation. "I know what I saw!"

Her fine brows came together in a frown. "It sounds to me as though someone was trying to frighten you."

I sighed as I rubbed my eyes, suddenly feeling very tired, though it was not yet noon. "I don't know how that child did it, but I'm sure he's the culprit."

"Well," she said with a comforting smile, "I cannot believe you are losing your mind, Lady Raven. You are one of the strongest women I have ever known, and I greatly admire you for that."

Her admission startled me with its frankness, for in the short time I had known Angel Blessed, she had never had such a frank conversation with me. "Why, thank you," I said, absurdly pleased, "and I admire you as well, for your devotion to Damon."

She looked away and her face glowed. "I am devoted to all my patients, Lady Raven." Then she wished me good day, and I watched her hurry away from the Eyrie.

When I was finally alone, sitting in the clearing while the brook gurgled at the base of the steep, rocky cliff, I felt oddly comforted by the nurse's words. Her simple confidence in me and her assertion that I wasn't going mad relieved me and buoyed my spirits. No wonder she was such an excellent nurse— she was soothing, gentle, and optimistic. Yet I had glimpsed another side of Angel Blessed as she told me how she had resisted and surmounted family opposition to her becoming a nurse. She was an angel with wings of steel. And there was even a third Miss Blessed, a vibrant, sensuous woman, with hair unbound, stroking Damon's golden head.

Rising, I banished the thought from my mind as I brushed away the grasses clinging to my skirt, then turned and started down the hill, feeling better for having spoken to Angel Blessed. Instead of going home, I decided to walk on to the Little Chase, for a visit to Amabel.

I hadn't seen her this furious in years. Her eyes flashed like angry sapphires and her perfect features were distorted by rage as she demanded, "Who would ever, *ever* play such an evil, malicious trick like that?"

"Brent," I replied, picking at a lunch of cold roast beef and salad.

"That little monster!" she sputtered, battering her tiny fist against the table so the silverware jumped. Then she stopped to stare at me. "How do you suppose he did it?"

I told her my thoughts on the subject, while Amabel made noises of indignation.

She shook her head. "The child is a menace. I shan't let my children play with him again, that's all. Did you confront the Masons?"

I grimaced. "Of course. But it was a fiasco."

"What happened?"

"It was just as I had feared," was my bitter reply. "Seth twisted everything around to his advantage, and they soon had me looking like a bitter, hysterical woman out to rob poor Brent of his inheritance."

Calmer now, Amabel took a delicate sip of wine. "I hope Colin learns something that will discredit them. Just the thought of those people getting what rightfully belongs to my family . . ." She cast several nervous glances in my direction before saying, "I'm sorry you overheard Mr. Turner and me talking last night, Nora."

I sat back, my appetite vanishing. "It's not your fault, Amabel. You didn't know I was there. I could have made my presence known at any time, but I didn't."

"I wouldn't have said anything at all, but the man has been so persistent."

I froze. "Persistent? What do you mean?"

"He's called here quite often, you know. Well, I can see by the look on your face that you didn't. He came ostensibly to play croquet with the boys, but he always managed to seek me out and engage in conversation about you."

I thought of Drake's forward behavior out on the moors that day and felt my mouth go dry. "What does he want to know?"

She raised one shoulder in a careless shrug, and appeared to rack her brain. "He was mainly concerned about the fire," she said. "He surprised me by seeming to know quite a lot about you already."

"Oh, Mr. Turner went to great lengths to learn all he could about me."

She pulled at her fringe of curls. "He pays you such flattering compliments, Nora. One day, he raved on and on about your beautiful eyes until I was positively green with envy."

I smiled at that. Amabel liked to be complimented herself, not listen to another woman being extolled.

"He also said he admired your fighting spirit and fierce independence. Then he got quite moody, as though saddened by something. I asked him what was wrong, but he wouldn't tell me." She hesitated. "I'm now convinced your partner has other interests in you, Nora, besides the Raven Line."

"Please, Amabel, I wish you wouldn't say that."

"You needn't use that harsh tone with me, Lady Raven," she admonished me with a sniff. "I was merely telling you what I thought."

Then she asked me if I'd like to accompany her to Sheepstor shopping for the afternoon, but I declined, and after we finished our lunch we went our separate ways.

Any thoughts of Drake Turner fled from my mind when I returned to Raven's Chase and walked into my sitting room to find my manuscript gone.

Whenever I wrote, I followed a prescribed routine. I sat in my favorite chair, with my feet up on a footstool for comfort and my lap desk before me with a fresh sheet of paper on it. After completing a page, I set it, face down, on a small piecrust table to the left of my chair. I began this ritual every morning, except Sunday, and by the time I was through in the evening, the pile had grown by five or ten pages. Then, when I was ready to retire, the day's efforts were collected and locked in my desk drawer along with the previous day's output. However, during the day, the completed pages rested on that table, and all the maids had been warned not to disturb that pile of papers on penalty of immediate dismissal.

The papers had been there this morning, but they were not there now.

At first, I just stared at the bare tabletop stupidly, in shock, then searched my desk and even beneath all the chairs, thinking that perhaps one of the maids had mislaid them. My efforts revealed nothing.

"What did you do with my writing, Faust? Eat it?" I asked the cat, who eyed me from the depths of my chair and volunteered only a weak "meow."

Finally, in desperation, I rang for Mrs. Harkins.

She arrived quickly, in a furious jingle of keys. "Yes, madam? One of the girls said you were ringing for me."

"My manuscript is missing, Mrs. Harkins. I believe one of the maids disturbed my papers when she was cleaning this morning, and I'd like to know what she did with them."

The housekeeper's cold eyes widened in surprise. "Why, madam, Cecily, the housemaid who always cleans your room, was not in here today, except to make your bed. And, besides, she knows full well she would be dismissed at once if she disturbed those papers."

"Ask all the staff if they have seen them, Mrs. Harkins. It is crucial that I know what happened to them."

"Yes, madam."

Confident that my papers would be found, I sat in my sitting room and waited, but when Mrs. Harkins returned a half-hour later, the grim look on her already dour countenance began the first stirrings of panic within me.

"I've spoken to the entire staff, madam. It is as I told you. Cecily did not clean here today. She said she made your bed, but that when she passed through the sitting room, she noticed your papers were on the table in their usual place. And all the other servants swear they haven't seen them."

And then I understood.

My knees turned to water, and Faust managed to streak off my chair before I sat down in a daze and crushed him.

"Are you all right, madam?" Mrs. Harkins asked, her brow furrowed with worry.

But I didn't hear her. All I knew was that someone had deliberately taken my manuscript, and I had a sickening feeling I never would see it again. Over one hundred sheets of hard, painstaking work had disappeared and was probably torn to shreds or burned by this time.

This morning, I had wondered how Ella Mason was going to retaliate after my accusation that Brent had tried to frighten me last night, and now I knew. She couldn't have hurt me more if she had struck me.

Of course I found the Masons and accused them of stealing my papers, and they vehemently denied it, as expected. Ella just sat with unnerving stillness, her blank dark eyes never leaving my face, while her brother was properly indignant for them both and insulting to me in return. Tempers flared, harsh words were thrown back and forth, and it all ended when I went storming out of the Chinese drawing room with nothing resolved.

During this interchange, I had not once thought of Drake Turner as a possible suspect, and yet, when I was back in my sitting room, I noticed that I had not seen him. I had Mrs. Harkins check with his valet, who said his master had gone off for the day, but had not enlightened him as to his destination.

So, Drake had once again been gone from Raven's Chase. Then I did begin to wonder . . . could *he* have taken my papers? How easy for him to slip into my sitting room when I was confronting the Masons this morning, take my papers, ride off, and destroy them. No one would be the wiser. Perhaps this was his way of punishing me for spurning his advances on the moors.

I left word with the butler that I wanted Mr. Turner to come to see me as soon as he returned. An hour later, I heard a knock at my door, and when I said, "Come in," Mr. Turner entered. He was still in riding clothes and must have ridden hard, judging by the way his hair was tousled and his cheeks still flushed.

"You wished to see me?"

I nodded and watched his face closely while I told him what had happened. He looked too startled to be the culprit, but then, I thought cynically, any man so adept at hiding his true feelings would probably be adept at feigning surprise. With lower lip trembling, I said bluntly, "Did you take my papers, Mr. Turner?"

A muscle twitched in his jaw and his shaggy brows almost came together in anger before he crossed the room and roared, "No, Countess, I did not steal your papers!"

The strain was too much, and I couldn't muster any anger to combat him this time. In spite of my best efforts to prevent it, my face crumpled and hot tears fell. Drake Turner was the last person I wanted to see me cry, but I just couldn't help it. I turned away from him and hurried over to the window.

I was startled to find a handkerchief pressed into my hand and to hear Drake say, "I know you have scant reason to believe me, Mrs. Gerrick, but I mean it when I say I did not steal your manuscript. I would not stoop so low as to destroy someone else's work. I admire your writing. Why would I want to destroy it?"

I wiped my eyes and put my hand to my mouth to stifle the sobs. "I apologize for accusing you, but it came as such a shock to find those papers gone. All that work . . . destroyed. It's a writer's nightmare. I'll never be able to duplicate it exactly, word for word. It's lost . . . gone." And my voice trailed off.

Drake suggested that perhaps one of the maids mislaid it, but I related to him what Mrs. Harkins had told me. Then I said, "No, I suspect the Masons had a hand in this, and I confronted them about it, but, of course, they denied it, just as they denied that Brent frightened me in the gallery."

Drake was silent for a moment, patted my shoulder in sympathy, then turned and left, but this time, his touch did not enrage me as it had on the moors yesterday.

CHAPTER

9

Later that afternoon, Drake and the Masons were in the drawing room, where a cart was laden with the usual small sandwiches and—since the arrival of Antoine—delicious iced French cakes and pastries.

". . . and where can he be?" Ella was saying to the men as I walked in. "He adores these little iced cakes your chef makes so superbly, Mr. Turner."

If my hostess had spoken to me the way I had spoken to the Masons this morning, I would have been too mortified to show my face at tea. The Masons, I was beginning to realize, were too brazen and obnoxious to be mortified by anything. Even now, as I entered the drawing room and glared at them, they just regarded me with a mixture of hostility and pity.

"Good afternoon," I said with a stiff nod in their direction as I poured myself a cup of tea.

"Good afternoon, Lady Raven," Seth said genially. "I see you're in a much better frame of mind than this morning. Have you come to apologize for your hysterical accusations against us?"

Just the patronizing tone of his voice was enough to infuriate me, and I longed to toss my cup of hot tea right in his face. But I realized that was what he wanted, to provoke me, and this time I had learned my lesson. I wasn't going to play into his hands.

Smiling brightly, I helped myself to a watercress sandwich from the tea cart. "As I told you this morning, Mr. Mason, it will be a hot day in December before you'll get an apology from me. I am here because this is still my house, and I am free to go where I please in it."

Drake's mustache twitched, and I suspected he was smiling.

"There's something I've been meaning to ask you, Lady Raven," Seth said, looking puzzled. "If Damon Gerrick inherited the title from his brother, why isn't he living here, instead of you?"

"Because he's happier with his sister," I replied. "He's incapable of managing this estate."

"So," he said smoothly, "couldn't one say that you have stolen his birthright from him, just as you have accused us of trying to steal from you?"

I set my teacup down too hard in its saucer, causing the hot liquid to spill. But I ignored it as I snarled, "It is not the same at all, Mr. Mason. I have stolen nothing. When—and if—Damon Gerrick regains his sanity, the Chase will be his again."

Drake, ever the peacemaker, glanced at his watch and said, "I wonder where Brent can be?"

Concern for her son furrowed Ella's brow as she glanced uneasily toward the window, where the golden light presaged dusk. "I don't know. He loves those cream buns your chef makes, Mr. Turner, and he's usually so prompt for tea."

"I'm sure he's just forgotten the time," Drake said. "Small boys love to go exploring, and this house must be fascinating to a curious child."

Ella gave a worried sigh. "I'm sure you're right, Mr. Turner. I'm sure Brent will be here soon."

But Brent did not appear.

Dusk had fallen, filling the landscape beyond my sitting room window with cool, blue light, and I myself was just about to light the oil lamp to work on my manuscript, when a knock at my door revealed a grim-faced Drake.

"Brent's disappeared," he said, without ceremony.

I raised one shoulder in an unconcerned shrug, for I was

still smarting from Seth's insinuation that I had stolen the Chase from my brother-in-law. "Has he? I'm afraid I can't find it in my heart to be too concerned," I replied, then turned away to go back to my writing.

"Ella has just searched the entire house, and he's nowhere to be found."

"Oh, he's probably hiding," I replied, not lifting my eyes from the sheet of paper in my hand.

Drake was staring at me with an unfathomable expression in his pale, cool eyes, and there was a vestige of impatience in his tone as he said, "This is serious, Nora. The child is missing."

"Good riddance."

"And what if he were your child?" Drake snapped.

Now I did look up at him, suddenly feeling betrayed. "That's not fair, Mr. Turner."

"I can't believe you'd be more concerned for some dismissed sailors than a child who could be in danger."

He was right, of course. I could no more bring myself to abandon a lost child than take a life. With a long, resigned sigh, I set my papers in a neat pile on the side table, tossed the protesting Faust from my lap, and rose.

"All right," I said in resignation. "Where are the Masons?"

"In the library, consoling each other."

I rang for Fenner, and when she came, I told her I wanted Mrs. Harkins to assemble all the staff in the library within ten minutes. Then I walked there with Drake.

Ella was sitting rigidly in a chair by the window, her hands clasped in her lap and unblinking eyes staring out into the darkness. She was so still, she looked like a marble statue.

"I understand Brent hasn't returned," I said, without smiling.

Seth nodded and for once did not smile. "We've searched the entire house for him, and he's nowhere to be found."

Just then, there came a knock at the door, and Mrs. Harkins entered, her keys jingling with every step. "I have the entire staff with me, madam," she said, and they all filed in after her.

When the footmen and maids were assembled around us, I spoke to them like a general addressing his troops. "Brent Mason has disappeared," I said, scanning the rapt faces. "Has anyone here seen him?"

The servants looked at one another with blank countenances, and all remained silent, until Gilly, one of the newer underhousemaids, timidly raised her hand. "As I was comin' from the dairy, I seen the boy, madam, going toward the folly. But that was hours and hours ago, just after lunch."

"And no one has seen him since?"

Again, shrugs and mumbles, but no answer.

"All right," I said, and began barking orders. Mrs. Harkins was to take several of the maids and scour the house from the attics to the cellars once again, while a footman rode over to the Little Chase to inquire about the boy, in case he had wandered over there. Another maid was to go to the stables and have Young Corman send men to search the moors, and the rest of the staff was to take lanterns and search the grounds.

Then I dismissed them and was left alone with Drake and the Masons once again. If I thought I would get any thanks from them, I was hoping for a miracle. Ella continued to stare out the window wordlessly, and Seth stood watch behind her chair.

I turned to Drake. "You and I will search St. Barnabas' Abbey. I can't think of a more intriguing place for a child to explore."

I didn't elaborate, for I didn't wish to panic the Masons further. The crumbling walls of the decaying abbey were known to give way without warning, and a village child had once been killed in such a manner, buried under stone while exploring the old ruins. But, in spite of the dangers, the place drew children like a lodestone, and many were the times I had had to scold Peter and Timothy for wandering unsupervised too near there. I was just hoping the place had not exerted its fatal attraction on the curious Brent.

"Are you coming, Mr. Mason?" I called over my shoulder.

"I think I'll be of more use here, comforting my sister," was his reply.

I said nothing, just walked out with Drake right behind me. We went upstairs for lamps and a shawl for my shoulders, for there wasn't a dram of daylight left, and, even so close to summer, it could become quite chilly outdoors when darkness fell.

As we walked out into the night air, we were silent with our own thoughts. Finally, Drake voiced his as he shortened his stride to match mine. "I wonder what happened to the boy?"

I shrugged in the darkness. "Someone should have been keeping a closer watch on him," I said, my censure of Ella fully apparent. "With the ruins, and the moors beyond, this is no country to let a child roam without some supervision."

"You needn't be so hard on Ella. I'm sure she's learned her lesson."

"And you needn't be so quick to defend her," I snapped, quickening my pace.

He made no reply as we passed the folly, took a sharp right and headed toward the ruins. In a matter of minutes, the dark silhouette of an empty arch that had once held a beautiful oriel window rose black against the moonless night sky, and suddenly, a low wall rose before us in the lamps' arc.

"This must have been magnificent in its day," Drake mused, staring up at the arch appreciatively.

"An order of monks lived here once, but they were put to death when Henry the Eighth dissolved the monasteries. The basement is full of cells, and there's even a secret passageway leading from the cellars to that stone cottage up on the hill."

"The secret passage the doctor and his sister-in-law made such good use of."

"The very same," I replied. Then I suggested we walk around the ruins, and if we couldn't find Brent there, we'd brave the darkness of the cellars below.

190

Drake agreed, and we started searching the abbey, calling the child's name at the tops of our voices, first in one direction, then another. Suddenly, the loud, bass strummings of frogs stilled, as though they, too, were listening.

I was scrambling over a pile of loose stones, when suddenly they just seemed to crumble and break beneath my feet as they went rolling away in a clatter. I cried out, but before I could lose my balance and drop my lamp, Drake grabbed my arm and held me steady while I got more secure footing.

"Are you all right?" he asked.

I nodded a wordless reply, but my mind had flown back to another time, when Mark and I had explored these ruins together for the first time. He had held my hand just as tightly as Drake was holding it now, and when a huge stone had come catapulting down on us, Mark had pushed me out of danger, saving me from serious injury or even death. I smiled bitterly to myself. The old abbey was haunted by more than ghostly monks.

"What were you thinking?" Drake demanded suddenly, scowling at me. "You seemed a thousand miles away."

"I was just thinking of my husband, as usual," I replied, then took a deep breath and called out Brent's name, hoping that would deter Drake from asking any more questions.

When we came to the cellar entrance, I hesitated, for the gaping black hole that was revealed by lamplight made me shiver. One expected some gruesome monster from one's childhood to be lurking just out of sight, waiting for the unsuspecting to venture down and be devoured in one swallow.

"I feel as though I'm about to be some monster's dinner," I muttered, as I peered down into the blackness and called Brent's name once again.

Drake laughed, and when the echo of my voice died away, he, too, called out Brent's name.

Then, very faintly, I heard something in reply.

I forgot myself and grasped Drake's arm. "Did you hear that?"

"No," he replied, and as we both listened attentively, a loud "Who-o-o-o" came from up above. "It's only an owl out hunting," he said.

"This wasn't an owl," I retorted, staring down the steep, narrow steps, taking care not to lose my balance on the smooth, well-worn stones. But, as the entrance yawned before me, black and forbidding, my resolve failed me, and I stopped, turned, and held my lamp high so I could look up at Drake. "Well, are you coming?"

His mustache twitched and I knew he was smiling. "What? Afraid to go alone, Lady Raven?"

"Very."

The cellar of St. Barnabas' Abbey was a living nightmare. It smelled musty and dank, of age and death, while gossamer cobwebs hung like sheer curtains from the low ceiling. I shuddered as one caught at my sleeve, broke off, and disintegrated, and I immediately brushed myself to make sure no spider had come off with it. Our footsteps reverberated against the damp, moss-covered walls and came back to us, magnified. I tried to ignore the sounds of sharp claws scrabbling and scraping against stone, but I knew red-eyed rats were watching us warily from their hiding places, rodents that would be a match even for the fearless Faust. I wanted to get out of this place as quickly as possible.

"Brent?" I called in a normal tone of voice, lest anything louder bring the roof down on our heads.

And then, from the other side of the cellar, came the child's voice. "Help me! I'm here!"

Drake and I hurried as fast as we could, zigzagging between cobwebs and treading cautiously to keep from slipping and losing our precious lamps, our only means of keeping fear at bay.

"He must be trapped in one of the cells," I said as we hurried along past shattered kegs that had once held spirits.

My worst fears were confirmed. As we approached the row of cells, dark little rooms no bigger than cupboards, where the monks were once punished, or did penance, Brent's high, babbling voice rose to a hysterical pitch, and we were soon able to follow it directly to a cell door. While there was some sign of rot, it was still a solid oak door, with only the smallest of barred windows high above. It was a wonder we had heard the child at all.

In my haste to free Brent, it did not occur to me that anything was amiss as Drake drew back the rusty iron bolt. While I held my lamp aloft, Brent came wriggling through the crack even before Drake had time to throw the door open.

"Brent, are you all right?" I asked, forgetting my previous animosity as I reached out to draw the sobbing child to me.

But the boy just looked at me with such unabashed loathing that my arm fell to my side in surprise as the rumpled, grimy little figure hurled himself at Drake.

"She did it!" he sobbed, pointing an accusing finger at me as he clung to Drake. "She locked me in there! She wanted me to die!"

I was so shocked, I could only stare at him with my mouth hanging open.

Drake patted his back and chose to ignore Brent's outburst. "Come," he said, "let's get you out of here and back to your mama."

"But Lady Raven did it," Brent continued, one hand clutching at Drake's coat while his eyes were riveted on me in terror and suspicion. "She locked me in there because she wanted me to die."

I whirled around without a word, held my lamp high and led the way out of the cellars. I was so furious I ignored the cobwebs this time, the shadows, and the glittering red eyes observing our departure. But the full implication of the child's words did not penetrate my numbed brain until we were back at Raven's Chase.

As soon as we stepped into the library and Ella saw her bedraggled, but safe, son, she uttered a shriek of joy and ran to the child, dropping to her knees and enfolding him in her arms as though she'd never let him out of her sight again.

"Thank God you're safe!" she murmured. "Thank God!"

"Brent, where have you been?" his uncle demanded. "You had us worried half to death."

"We found him in the ruins," I explained. "He was in one of the cells."

Seth scowled first at me, then Drake. "And what in the hell was he doing there?"

Brent disengaged himself from his mother long enough to pipe up, "I was locked in there, Uncle Seth, and Lady Raven is the one who did it."

"What?" Ella said incredulously, her tears stopping suddenly as she sat back on her heels and glared at me.

"It's true, Mama," Brent insisted. "I was exploring the cellars with a candle, when she came up behind me, blew my candle out and pushed me into that cell. When I tried to get out, I found she had locked it from the outside. Mama, I was terrified!"

Ella rose to her feet, her pale face now twisted into a mask of hate. "You tried to murder my son," she said, the words made more chilling by virtue of the fact they were uttered so dispassionately.

"That is a lie," I said coldly, my voice rising in anger.

"If you did this to Brent," Seth said between clenched teeth, "I'll see that you pay for it, Lady Raven."

"Your accusation is so absurd, it doesn't even merit a reply," I said, thrusting my chin out.

"Of course she did it," Ella insisted, her eyes on her brother. "With Brent dead, she would keep Raven's Chase for herself."

I was fast losing what little patience I had left with these people. "You're hysterical," I said flatly.

The three of us were so busy hurling accusations back and forth, no one noticed Amabel enter the library until she was almost in our midst, a lithe figure wrapped in a black wool cloak.

"Am I interrupting anything?" she inquired innocently, and immediately, all argument ceased. "Oh, Brent's been found!" she cried, rushing to the boy and kneeling down to hug him with what I thought was an overabundance of enthusiasm. "Whatever happened to you, my dear?" she asked. "You gave us such a horrid fright."

"Lady Raven locked me in the abbey, Mrs. Trelawney," Brent told her, while glaring at me out of huge dark eyes.

"The child is lying, Amabel," I said tartly.

This prompted a denial from Ella, and before we knew it, we were all shouting and squabbling again.

Finally, Drake raised his hands and bellowed, "Quiet!" When we fell silent, he proceeded to tell Amabel all that had happened.

She listened politely and attentively, then said, "But Nora couldn't have done it. She hasn't been near the abbey all afternoon. I know, because I spent the entire afternoon making watercolor sketches of the ruins." Amabel turned to the Masons with an apologetic smile. "I did see Brent playing near the ruins, but no one else."

The Masons were finally at a loss for words. I knew they valued Amabel's friendship too much to risk alienating her by calling her a liar to her face.

"Well," Seth said, trying to hide his displeasure behind a ready smile, "it seems you were mistaken, Brent."

Before Brent could protest, he found himself ushered out of the library with apologies to everyone from his uncle and mother.

When Drake, Amabel, and I were alone, I breathed a sigh of relief. "Thank you, Amabel."

"I was glad to be of assistance," she replied, her eyes sparkling as she tugged on her black kidskin gloves. "Well, I only came here to see if that tiresome child had been found, and since he has, I'll go home and call off the search." She bade us good night, then left.

I eased myself into the nearest chair, grateful for some silence at last. "I'm glad that's resolved."

"Is it?" Drake said.

I stared at him. "What do you mean?"

"Someone did push that child into the cell, Nora. The cells lock from the outside. I had to throw the bolt before I could open the door to let Brent out."

"What are you saying?" I inquired coldly.

"I'm saying that the boy couldn't have locked himself in that cell."

I sprang to my feet. "I did not do it!"

"I didn't say *you* did," he replied, his voice calm. "But someone did."

"Who?" I wondered aloud.

Drake shrugged. "Seth, perhaps, to pin the blame on you."

I wrinkled my nose in disbelief. "To his own nephew?"

"It's possible. Perhaps Mrs. Trelawney did it, to warn Brent not to torment her children any more. She was, after all, by her own admission, sketching at the ruins."

I shook my head vehemently. "Amabel would never do such a thing to a child, even one she dislikes. It's not in her nature." Then I rose as I stifled a yawn with the back of my hand. "Well, I'm not going to worry about it any more tonight."

But, even as I bade Drake good night and went upstairs to my sitting room, I found I could not get the day's events out of my mind so easily. They plagued me as I wrote in my journal, undressed, and got ready for bed. They stopped only when I finally fell asleep many hours later.

A week passed, and June was nearly over.

I spent most of my days in my sitting room, with Faust crouched on a stool at my feet and a blank sheet of paper before me, trying to recapture what had been stolen. Every so often, a soft, summer breeze, filled with the heady scents of roses and newly cut grass, would coax me out-of-doors for a game of croquet on the lawn, with Amabel and the boys, or a short ride on the moors alone. But, unless a messenger arrived from London with work for Drake and me, I stayed shut inside and wrote as though the devil drove me, as indeed he did in the form of one

Lewis Darwin. A four-page, rose-scented letter continued to arrive every Wednesday without fail, its underscored words alternately cajoling and demanding. I could envision Lewis' natty presence peering over my shoulder as I wrote, and hear his raspy voice say, "That paragraph is simply *beautiful,* my dear Nora," or "Strike those words *at once.* They positively *offend* my esthetic sense." And, as always, he was right.

Amabel called frequently with the boys, though she was adept at keeping them away from Brent, for no one must be allowed to antagonize her children. I noticed that Peter had resumed tormenting Timothy, now that he didn't need his younger brother as an ally against Brent. Timothy, however, always eager to win anyone's approval, tolerated this abuse good-naturedly. I wondered if he would ever learn he was fighting a losing battle, for Peter would always remain their mother's favorite, even if he grew up to be a thief.

Often, my thoughts would inadvertently stray to the night someone had rolled Gabriel's ball toward me in the gallery, and I would stop whatever I was doing and shiver. I had been so quick to condemn Brent, it had never occurred to me that Seth, his sister, or even Drake could have done it just as easily, and I chastised myself for not having had their rooms searched as well at the time.

Then, during the last week in June, I received word from Hamish Pengelly that minor renovations on the *Nancy Malone* were proceeding as planned, but someone in authority was needed in Plymouth to make several major decisions. At first, I was reluctant to leave Raven's Chase, citing all the writing I had to make up and the necessity of keeping a watchful eye on the Masons, but Drake surprised me by insisting that I go. The *Nancy Malone* was my purchase, he said, and my responsibility. He also pointed out I could take my manuscript with me and work on it in the evenings, and Mrs. Harkins was perfectly capable of watching the Masons in my absence. I further objected when he said he wanted to accompany me, but he just gave me that wry smile and pointed out I would have loyal Fenner as chaperone to observe the proprieties, since I would be traveling with a bachelor gentleman.

So I relented, and Drake, Fenner, and I went to Plymouth. Everywhere we roamed—from the noisy, vigorous docks teeming with life to the quiet, refined tearooms with superb views of the ocean—memories of Mark rose vividly to haunt me. In fact, my thoughts were constantly of my husband. I recalled his tender concern for me on our voyage to the Orient aboard the *Raven's Pride,* when seasickness plagued me, and his high spirits that unforgettable Christmas we spent in Vienna, where I'm sure Gabriel was conceived. I never recalled him losing his temper, being stubborn or argumentative, though, in truth, he had done all of those things at one time or another during our marriage. It was as though I selected only pleasant memories and conveniently forgot the rest.

But I found that by plunging into work, my sorrow was made more bearable. I spent my mornings consulting with glass workers, and we pored over drawings of scenes of Plymouth that I wanted executed in stained glass for those magnificent skylights in the saloon. They listened attentively to my suggestions, made a few of their own, and we all left satisfied. Then I inspected all the first-class passenger cabins with a workman at my elbow, who listened carefully as I dictated how I wanted the rosewood wainscoting refinished and pilasters gilded for a more sumptuous effect. And, since I wanted to make travel on the *Lady Raven's Fortune* as elegant as possible, I commissioned new china featuring a tasteful raven motif so the passengers could dine as if they were at home.

During this time, Drake never once argued about my proposals and was cooperation itself, even going so far as to praise me generously for them. I found myself mellowing and relenting toward him a little, trying to give him the benefit of the doubt by seeing another side of him.

Still, despite our truce, I couldn't bring myself to accept his invitation to attend performances of Plymouth's excellent provincial theater, though we did attend dinners in our honor given by several associates.

So Drake usually went out by himself in the evenings, while I sat in my hotel room working on my manuscript. He never said where he was going, and I did not ask, though he never returned before I myself retired for the evening, usually at midnight. No doubt he availed himself of some local female companionship, for, as he had once said to me, "There are women in Devonshire, are there not?"

When our week was over and business attended to, we packed our bags and went back to Raven's Chase.

"Did you have a pleasant stay in Plymouth, madam?" Mrs. Harkins inquired several hours after I had arrived home.

"Yes, Mrs. Harkins, quite pleasant," I replied, wondering where Faust had gone.

My answer came almost immediately, when the cat slipped through the door, which my housekeeper had left ajar, and came trotting over to me, purring and chirping with delight.

"Good cat," I crooned, tickling him under the chin and watching his yellow eyes narrow in feline ecstasy. "Did you miss me, you old reprobate?"

Mrs. Harkins ignored my behavior and said, "I'm pleased to hear it, madam. As you will recall, you requested that I keep a close watch on our guests in your absence."

"Yes?"

Before she could reply, Faust left my side to stroll over to her and attempt to rub against her skirts, but she jerked them away and moved to the other side of the room. I could see I was never going to have a complete conversation if the mischievous cat kept distracting her, so I rose, picked him up, and put him out into the hall again.

Mrs. Harkins made a sound of relief, then took a moment to brush imaginary cat hairs from her skirt before continuing.

"As I was saying, madam, I have tried to do my duty, but it's been most difficult. Even though you informed the Masons before you left that I would be in charge and able to answer any of their questions, they have flouted my authority." Her stare hardened. "The woman who calls herself Mrs. Gerrick tried to appropriate Merry for her own maid. When I confronted her about it, she became most argumentative and told me that I would be the first to be dismissed when she became the new mistress of Raven's Chase. We've been having the most frightful tug-o'-war, madam. She insists that Merry dress her, and I countermand that order and have the maid go about her duties."

My lips tightened in anger. "I shall speak to Miss Mason about this right away. Thank you for bringing this to my attention, Mrs. Harkins. You've done a fine job." And I dismissed her.

After she left, I sat there for the longest time, staring into space and wishing I had never agreed to have the Masons here. They were taking advantage of every opportunity to push me just a little further and gain a stronger foothold at Raven's Chase. Well, I had reached the point where I would be pushed no further. When I had myself under control, I left my sitting room in search of Ella Mason.

I found all three of the Masons sitting in the folly, fanning themselves languidly in the summer heat, sipping lemonade and nibbling on Antoine's pastries. As I approached, I noticed Ella's thick black hair was arranged in a dignified chignon, a style more becoming than the plain braid she had always worn in a coronet, and I knew this to be Merry's handiwork.

Brent, who looked hot and uncomfortable in his black suit, eyed me with unabashed hostility as he sat there, a book open in his lap. Most children would be in their shirtsleeves tearing about in the sun, playing games, but not this one.

Seth, fanning his flushed face with a hat, smiled genially at me as he tossed the hair out of his eyes and said, "Welcome back, Lady Raven. We trust your trip to Plymouth was a pleasant one. I've always wanted to visit Plymouth and see the port our ancestors departed from, to escape the tyranny of British rule."

I ignored his remark as I halted at the base of the folly's steps and didn't go in. I squinted in the sharp sunlight as I looked right at Ella and said, "Mrs. Harkins tells me you tried to appropriate Merry as your maid in my absence."

"Yes," she said defiantly. "I need someone to help me with my clothes and hair. I feel it's only right, since I soon will be mistress of Raven's Chase—until Brent comes of age, of course."

I shook my head. "Until you do become mistress of Raven's Chase, you shall do without Merry's services."

And I turned and walked away without another word.

I heard footsteps cross the folly and skip down the steps, but I took no notice and continued marching across the lawn, back toward the house.

"Lady Raven," Seth began, as he fell into step beside me, his voice soft and ingratiating, "what harm would it do to let my sister have a maid? It wouldn't cost you anything. Why, all the girl would have to do is spend some time in the morning helping Ella to dress and fix her hair, then she could go about her regular duties."

"Mr. Mason," I replied, not slowing my step or looking at him, "it would cost me a great deal. It's a matter of principle, though I know that may be obscure to you. You are all here because your solicitors said you must, not because I want you. It is not my obligation to make matters simple for you people, because I believe you're swindlers, out to defraud me and besmirch my husband's good name with your foul lies. I was told I had to offer you my hospitality, or face a legal battle, and, since I wish this matter resolved as soon as possible, I agreed. However, it did not specify that I had to treat you like royalty while you're here."

Now my anger burned out of control, like a brush fire, and I did stop and turn on him. "How do you do it, Mr. Mason?

How are you and your sister able to keep up the pretense so well?"

He raised his dark brows and widened his eyes in affronted innocence. "Why, by telling the truth, Lady Raven."

"Perhaps you are telling the truth, and your sister will be mistress of Raven's Chase one day. But, let's get one thing clear, Mr. Mason. Until the day that I am forced to leave, you and your sister will not get one concession from me, not one."

A sardonic smile twisted his mouth as he murmured, "We shall just see about that, Lady Raven, we shall just see."

And he whirled on his heel and went hurrying back to the folly, where his sister waited expectantly.

As usual, a confrontation with any one of the Masons ruined my day, so I changed quickly into my black riding habit, ordered Curlew saddled and rode over to the Little Chase, where I found Amabel in the music room playing one of those popular lachrymose ballads I hated on the piano.

She rose and greeted me warmly and asked about my trip to Plymouth, adding a few reminiscences of her own about our first trip there together, when she'd bought Peter the cloth pig he still slept with. I related the Masons' latest attempt to bedevil me, joined Amabel for lunch, and left the Little Chase in a much better frame of mind.

After leaving Amabel, I went for a long hard gallop on the moors before returning to Raven's Chase.

I was walking back to my room from the rear entrance of the house and, as always, had to pass by Mark's locked study. I always quickened my step and averted my eyes when passing this room, for it was here that memories of my husband were their strongest and most vivid. But, today, something made me stop as I approached his study.

The door was open.

For a moment, I was so paralyzed I couldn't move or utter a sound. But then my mind awoke with a snap, and I lurched forward, furious that anyone would dare disobey my orders and enter that room.

Suddenly, those powerful memories, like so many ghosts lying in wait, seemed to fly at me, so that I actually recoiled and swung my arm across my face to shield myself. When nothing assaulted me, I dropped my arm and noticed the man for the first time, standing behind the desk and watching me.

"Mark?" I cried, bewildered, hopeful.

Before I could catch my breath, he came around the desk, and when he towered over me, I blinked stupidly, realizing that I had been seeing what wasn't—what never could be—there.

Strong hands gripped my arms, and icy, angry blue eyes held mine. "Not Mark, Mrs. Gerrick," Drake said, giving me a shake to bring me back to the present.

I just stared up at the rough, pockmarked face for a moment, unable to collect my scattered wits. Finally, I was able to murmur, "What are you doing here?"

He released me with obvious reluctance and stood there wordlessly, looking troubled, for what seemed like an eternity. Finally, he said, "I was passing by and noticed the open door."

"Open!" I cried. "This room is to be kept locked at all times. Who would dare—?"

I walked around him and started striding through the study, where dust coated everything like a thin layer of dirty, gray snow. Even my trailing skirts raised a cloud that tickled my nose, causing me to sneeze repeatedly.

When I raised my head, I glanced up at the room's dominant feature, a portrait of myself entitled "The Edge of Experience," painted by my father many years ago, when I was just sixteen. It showed me dressed in a loose-fitting white dress that looked cream-colored in contrast to the stark white bunch of lilies I was arranging in a tall, cut-glass vase. But, as I stared as it, I realized there was something very odd about that painting.

"Nora . . ." Drake began in warning, but I foolishly didn't heed him, and hurried closer to study the painting.

When I stood before it, my eyes widened in horror, for my

face had been deeply scored by some sharp instrument so that my features ran together like the face of a wax doll held too close to a fire. The rest—hair, hands, lilies—was untouched. Someone had coldly and deliberately defaced the portrait.

I must have whimpered in shock, for I felt Drake's hands fall lightly on my shoulders as he came up behind me. "I found it this way when I came in a few moments ago."

Tears welled in my eyes as I reached out to touch the damaged canvas. "Mark always said he first fell in love with me when he saw this portrait. He said it was the beginning of a grand obsession. And now . . ."

"I am so very sorry," Drake said quietly.

Unable to face it a moment longer, I whirled blindly away, and as I did so, came up behind Mark's desk. What I saw there was even more shocking than the damaged portrait.

Neatly written in dust across its surface were the words: "Nora will die."

The room dipped and lurched crazily to one side, and had it not been for Drake, I would have fallen. He swung me into his arms and carried me to the Chinese drawing room, where he set me down on the sofa and went in search of spirits to revive me.

"It has to be Brent's doing," I moaned, as I placed my hand on my forehead and struggled to sit up.

"I don't know about that," Drake said, crossing the room to press a glass of sherry into my hand. "I suspect I got there only moments before you. The dust on the rug had been disturbed, but not on the chairs. In order for Brent to reach the portrait, he would have had to stand on a chair."

I thought about what he said while I sipped my sherry. "Tell me what happened."

Drake seated himself across from me. "I was coming from the library when I noticed the study door was open. I thought this odd, since I was told the room is kept locked at all times. When I went in, the first thing I noticed was the portrait, then the writing on the desk. You walked in just seconds later."

"My portrait . . ." I moaned, trying to keep the tears from falling. "Mark loved that painting so much."

"As I said," Drake went on, "I, too, suspected Brent at once, but then I realized he's not tall enough to reach the portrait's face without assistance. When I checked the chairs, I noticed that the dust was not disturbed on any of them."

"So, it had to be an adult," I muttered. "Well, that leaves Seth or Ella. They tried to talk me into letting Ella have a maid, and they were not at all pleased when I refused."

"Now, that is interesting," Drake said. When he saw I had finished my sherry, he said, "Before you confront the Masons, I want you to be sure you're strong enough to face them. Shall I take you back to your sitting room? We have to talk."

Once back in my sitting room and settled in my favorite chair, with a knitted throw covering me, I should have felt better, but I didn't. I was afraid.

I shivered as I saw the words "Nora will die" written in dust, and thought of the portrait's face, scored and scarred beyond recognition. "Do you think whoever did that will try to harm me?"

Drake saw the direction my thoughts were taking, and he broke into a reassuring smile. "I think whoever did this was just trying to frighten you."

"They succeeded admirably," was my wry comment, as I trembled and tried unsuccessfully to draw more warmth from the throw. "It's so easy to have an accident around here. A fall from a horse . . . getting lost on the moors . . ."

"I promise nothing is going to happen to you, Mrs. Gerrick."

As I looked up into his eyes, now soft with kindness, I believed him. I have never considered myself a weak, helpless female, but there were times—and this was one of them—when I needed to be sheltered and protected by a man. In a moment of weakness, I just wanted to go to Drake and hide within the circle of his arms, feeling his strength, but I resisted the impulse, for he was my husband's enemy, and I was still not sure of him.

Suddenly, Drake's eyes narrowed as he said, "If you think the Masons are responsible for these tricks, why don't you send them packing?"

"The solicitors said I had to have them here." But I could not meet his gaze when I said it and instead pretended to be absorbed in Faust, who had come trotting into the room to jump boldly on my lap.

"Oh, I know that's what you tell everyone, but you can't fool me, and I suspect you didn't fool Trelawney, either. It's always puzzled me how a fighter such as yourself could give in so easily on this point. You could have refused to have the Masons here and forced their solicitors to take you to court. Yet you didn't. Why, I wonder?"

I hugged myself beneath the throw, suddenly weary of lying any longer. I couldn't fool this man who had become so adept at reading my thoughts. "I agreed to have them here," I began slowly, forcing every word out, "because if Brent is his son, Mark would have wanted me to."

It cost me a great deal to admit that tiny doubt about my husband, and it left me feeling drained and very, very tired. Not wanting to see the pity in Drake's eyes, I closed mine and murmured, "If you'll excuse me, I'm greatly fatigued."

He said nothing, and I thought I heard him leave quietly, but minutes later, almost asleep, I heard him whisper, "Poor Nora. One day you shall not grieve for him."

I tried to rouse myself to ask him what he meant, but I could not, and just drifted off once again.

In the end, I wiped the words of warning from the desk top, had the study locked again, and said nothing to the Masons about the incident, though I was convinced of their guilt. I could not prove they had vandalized my husband's study, and, listening to them recount their delightful visit with Mrs. Trelawney that afternoon, I could see they had a ready alibi. People like the Masons always did. I knew if I confronted them, they would only twist my words around until I would appear to be the one in the wrong.

Later, I went to my bedroom, wrung out a cloth in cold water and made a compress, which I applied to my throbbing forehead while I rested. I closed my eyes and tried to blot out the events of this day, but they kept creeping back to torment me.

Who was responsible for these malicious tricks? In my mind, the Masons were already guilty, but I began to wonder if perhaps Drake wasn't the culprit.

I thought of the defaced portrait and the words written in the dust. When I went inside the study to investigate, Drake was already there. What if I had caught him in the act? Perhaps he had finished damaging the portrait and was writing on the desk with his finger when I walked in on him. A sharp instrument could have been easily concealed in his coat pocket and dust wiped off on his trousers. Then all he had to do was smile, look innocent, and pretend he had just discovered the damage himself.

And what about my stolen manuscript? At that time, he had been away from Raven's Chase for almost the entire day, and despite his convincing protestations, he could have taken it.

I sat up, the compress falling unheeded from my brow, as I then recalled the night the ball had come rolling toward me.

My mind pictured the scenario. Earlier that day, perhaps Drake had broken into the nursery and searched for something of Gabriel's that would frighten me. He found the ball and, later that night, waited for me to pass by his door, since he must have known I often visited the gallery when I couldn't sleep. Then he hurried to the other end of the gallery, rolled the ball at me, and watched me run off, scared out of my wits. Then he retrieved the ball and ran through the halls until we met, pretending to be solicitous to throw suspicion from himself.

I put the compress on my forehead again and lay back with a groan. But if that were the case, where had he hidden the ball? I recalled him slipping his green robe around my shoulders, but I had felt nothing concealed in its pockets. Then again, he could have hidden it somewhere.

Yes, Drake Turner could be my tormentor.

Galvanized into action, I pulled the compress from my head, rose, and hurried over to the Little Chase, to discuss these latest developments with Amabel.

When I arrived, I found her in the drawing room, just finishing tea herself, her brow furrowed in irritation.

"Have you seen Miss Blessed and Damon?" she asked me, without a word of greeting.

"Why, no," I replied, removing my bonnet. "I saw them this morning, on my way over here, but that was the only time."

Amabel looked vexed, and I prepared myself for an outburst, but all she said was, "That woman . . . she's supposed to be watching my brother at all times. That's what she's paid for."

"Oh, I think she does a splendid job of watching Damon," I said, stoutly defending the nurse.

Amabel just shrugged. "Well, I suppose she's certainly an improvement over all her predecessors. But, do forgive me for my rudeness, Nora, in not greeting you. How are you, and what brings you out to the Little Chase twice in one day?"

"Another mysterious occurrence," I replied, seating myself next to her on the sofa.

And while she listened raptly, I told her all about the defaced portrait and the warning written in dust.

At first, Amabel was so stunned she just sat back without a word. Then she twisted a curl around her finger and murmured sadly, "Mark so loved that portrait. I take it you suspect the Masons?"

I nodded. "But there's also someone else I suspect."

"Oh? Who?"

"Drake Turner." And I told her why.

She listened to me attentively, then was silent for the longest time, as if searching for an answer of her own. Then she said, "Well, Colin did warn me not to trust him, and, after these strange incidents, I can see why." She reached out and grasped my arm. "You must not trust him either, Nora."

"I know that better than anyone."

"He wants the Raven Line. You've refused to sell out to him, but if something should happen to you . . ."

"He still wouldn't get it," I pointed out. "The company would go to my heir."

"That's true," she admitted reluctantly. "I would never sell Peter's—" She caught herself and her pale cheeks turned bright pink with guilt.

I stopped and stared at her, but Amabel, who could usually look someone in the eye and glibly lie her way out of any situation, could not look at me now. "Amabel," I began softly, "how do you know I named Peter my heir? Only Clement Charles knows."

For once she did not try to disarm me by widening her innocent blue eyes and fluttering her lashes helplessly. She actually hung her head in shame as she said, "The day I came to your sitting room to invite you to see Peter's first jump . . . you left your journal open while you went to fetch your cloak." Her tone became defensive as she said, "Your secrecy about that journal only made me even more curious, so you can't blame me for taking a little peek when I had the opportunity. I wanted to see if you had written anything about me. Then I read you were going to make Peter your heir. I think it was quite a splendid thing for you to do, Nora." Then she said, "But why didn't you tell me?" Now she was affronted.

"Because I don't want you to spoil him any more than you already do," I replied in my best severe tone. Although I was annoyed with Amabel for reading my journal, what was done was done. I shrugged the entire matter off with, "I don't want to hear another word about it."

"But can't I at least tell Colin, when he returns?"

"Yes, but no one else. Wills can be changed," I reminded her ominously. "Now, you were saying . . ."

She was silent while she picked up the thread of her thought. "Well, if you were proved mentally unstable, perhaps Drake Turner could get a greater share of the company."

"Is that what you think he's trying to do, drive me mad like Dr. Lade did to Damon? Oh, come now, Amabel," I scoffed, "I find that a little farfetched."

"The deeply grieving widow starts seeing things that aren't there . . . her portrait is slashed and dire warnings written in dust. Perhaps she even did those things herself. People will start to wonder, you know."

I shuddered violently at the implication of her words. "Lord, how I wish Colin were here! I could use his sensibility and strength at a time like this."

Amabel's eyes narrowed into slits, and she said, somewhat harshly, "Well, he's not, so we must manage alone this time, mustn't we?"

Her tone surprised me, and I thought it prudent not to remind her of her husband's absence. "There's something else I haven't told you," I said, then told her about Drake's forcible kiss that day on the moors.

To my complete surprise, Amabel did not seem startled by this bit of news. "Now that is another matter entirely," she said mysteriously.

"What do you mean?"

A cynical smile touched her mouth. "Well, if one method of getting the Raven Line doesn't work, try another. If you became his wife, he'd have what he wanted, wouldn't he?"

"Wife!" I scoffed. "You think Drake Turner has set out to *woo* me? Nothing could be further from the truth!"

She plucked at her fringe. "It would be a perfect way to gain control of the company, you must admit that."

"Perfect, but hardly likely to occur."

"But don't you see? That just proves my point. Since you haven't been very obliging in that respect, perhaps he thinks he must resort to other means. You yourself said he was un-scrupulous and devious."

"But I have offered him control of the Raven Line on sev-eral occasions, and he's refused," I protested.

"Perhaps he doesn't want to appear eager." She stifled a bored yawn with the back of her hand. "Well, I don't know what to say, Nora. Perhaps I am just imagining things. But it makes sense to me that Drake Turner could be your culprit."

And it was beginning to make sense to me as well.

Later that night, after the rest of the house had long gone to bed, I was still awake in my sitting room, Amabel's words running over and over through my mind like some monk's chant.

Amabel is grasping at straws, I told myself as I rose impa-tiently and went to the window, where a heavy, impenetrable mist shuttered me in, adding to my sense of confinement. First she had intimated that Drake was attracted to me, and now she insisted he had intentions of controlling the Raven Line by play-ing such tricks on me.

But when I forced myself to be logical, I had to admit she had a point. Was that why Drake had wanted to come down to Devon, to court me? And when he saw I was unresponsive, de-cided to try less scrupulous means of getting what he wanted?

Somehow, I could not equate buying out John Belding in secret with the cruel, vicious tricks that had been played on me recently. As much as I didn't trust him, I could not believe Drake was responsible.

Yet, I could not help but wonder if I had been *too* trusting and played right into his hands. I knew from past experience that if my life was in danger, I could not afford to be compla-cent about anyone.

Was Drake innocent or guilty? There were only a few times in my life when I had felt so torn, so uncertain.

Suddenly weary and tired of thinking any longer, I locked the doors of my sitting room and went to Mark's cavernous oak armoire to select my companion for the night. As I opened the doors and the faint, fresh scent of cedar wafted out, something struck me as odd. The clothes seemed disturbed and out of order, but I didn't give it a second thought. Perhaps Fenner or one of the other maids had rearranged them after cleaning.

I selected a frock coat, ignored the sleeping medicines on the nightstand, and slipped into bed. As I hugged the fine wool to me and inhaled deeply, I was dismayed, for the spicy scent of Mark's favorite shaving soap was almost gone from the collar. Still, it was powerful enough to banish Drake Turner and conjure Mark lying next to me, and I quickly fell into a deep sleep plagued with dreams I couldn't remember on waking the following morning.

CHAPTER

10

Upon waking, I decided that Drake had to leave Raven's Chase for my own peace of mind and safety. But I knew I couldn't just summon the local constable and have him arrested. I had no proof he was trying to frighten me or cause me harm. And if I commanded him to leave, I was sure he would take increasing control of the Raven Line from the London office and involve me in exhausting, expensive legal battles to regain it. No, I had to be subtle and finally knew just how I was going to accomplish this feat.

Later, while Fenner dressed me after a meager breakfast of tea and toast, I found myself wishing I were out of mourning and wearing my favorite colors of rich gold and yellow again. This fleeting, heretical thought caught me unawares, and I instantly chastised myself for being unfaithful to Mark's memory as Fenner slipped the somber black walking dress over my head and buttoned it quickly.

Once dressed, I gathered my courage and went downstairs in search of Drake Turner. I found him in the game room engrossed in billiards with Seth Mason.

"Good morning, Lady Raven," Seth greeted me, peering out from behind his forelock as he deftly sent a ball spinning straight into a corner pocket.

Drake stopped and wished me good morning.

"I'm sorry to interrupt your game, gentlemen," I said coolly, without smiling, "but I need to speak with you right away, Mr. Turner."

"Of course," he said congenially, hanging up his cue stick and following me to the library.

Once inside, I was blunt, as usual, and did not stand on preliminaries. "I've decided to sell you my share of the Raven Line. Does your former offer still hold?"

His pale eyes widened in astonishment for just an instant, then narrowed suspiciously, for Drake Turner was not a stupid man and saw through my ruse instantly. "Why, all of a sudden, do you wish to sell your share of the company to me? You've been so adamant about keeping it, despite my many attempts to persuade you to sell."

I didn't tell him that losing the Raven Line would be worth it if my life depended on his being out of my house. But I had to turn away from that penetrating stare before my resolve crumbled once again. "I would just rather devote more time to my writing and not have to be bothered with contracts and refurbishing the *Nancy Malone*. Running the Raven Line has been too time-consuming and a barrier to my creativity."

"It never seemed to inconvenience you before. In fact, you were becoming quite good—for a woman, of course," he added, using words calculated to rile me. "You made the decision to buy the *Nancy Malone* without my guidance, and you got her for an excellent price. When we were in Plymouth for renovations, you went beyond basic changes and came up with brilliant ideas for our passengers' comfort. Stained-glass skylights, special china . . . I never would have thought of them."

I turned back to him and shrugged. "I'm quite a dilettante, you see. One day something interests me, and the next, I'm on to something else. Running the company was novel for a while, then it began to bore me."

"Bore you!" he cried. "The responsibility has been the making of you, for God's sake! When I first met you, you were lost, always so sad and forever grieving for your husband. Now look at you. You have confidence in yourself, and your spirit is restored."

Drake looked displeased now and placed his hands on his hips in an aggressive posture. "I don't know why you're pretending to be a dilettante. When you undertake something or believe you're right, you're quite tenacious and far from flighty." His mustache twitched as he smiled sardonically. "No, I'm afraid I can't believe you'd just agree to give up the company after you've fought me so hard to keep it. And I don't think it's because you've lost interest in it, either."

"But it's true," I insisted. "Now, do you wish to buy it from me, or don't you?"

His voice was heavy with sarcasm as he threw my own words back at me. "Sell the company that Lord Raven started with only one ship? Your legacy, Mrs. Gerrick? No, there's some other reason you want to sell, and I'd like to know what it is."

I could meet his gaze no longer and walked over to the fireplace. "My reasons are personal."

He took a few steps and stood before me, his voice strangely gentle as he said, "And can you tell me what they are?"

"No, I can't," I retorted, suddenly angry with him for being so persistent and forcing me into a confrontation I wished to avoid. "Now, would you please just agree to my terms and leave?"

I regretted the impulsive words the instant I said them, for comprehension dawned on his face. "So that's it. You don't really want to sell the Raven Line, you just want to be rid of *me*. Now I wonder why you want me to leave Raven's Chase so desperately that you would sacrifice your husband's company in order to accomplish it?"

I felt so frightened and confused I was not handling myself well at all. "Please," I moaned, "I would like you to leave."

His hand touched my arm, then fell away when I flinched. "I think I have the right to ask why."

"I don't have to explain my actions to anyone!"

"Well, I'm not leaving until you do."

I thrust my chin out angrily. "Why on earth should you

want to stay? I've agreed to sell you the Raven Line. It's what you've wanted all along, isn't it? There's no need for you to remain here any longer."

"Oh, isn't there?"

"No, there isn't."

We wordlessly faced each other, gazes locked combatively, and all I was aware of was the clock on the mantel ticking relentlessly, while outside, Peter called to Timothy in a shrill, querulous voice. Then Drake came over to me and thrust one arm out so he could lean against the mantel and effectively bar my escape. Standing so near we were almost touching, he let his eyes rove over my face and linger on my lips deliberately, as though wanting to kiss me as he had that day on the moors, but this time holding back. My heart was hammering so loudly I was certain he could hear it, but I held my ground and resisted the urge to dart away from his close, disturbing presence.

"Why do you suppose I kissed you that day?" he asked softly, a smile playing about his mouth.

As loath as I am to admit it, I must say he very nearly fooled me with this convincing performance. But when I searched the depths of his eyes and found them devoid of sincerity, I knew his actions for what they were—a polished exercise in seduction.

"You kissed me that day because I struck you, and you wished to hurt me in return," I said sweetly.

His face fell and he stepped back, my truthful answer obviously not the one he had expected or wanted to hear.

I didn't give him time to recover before I straightened my shoulders and let my tongue voice the strong feelings welling up inside of me. "Did you really think I am such a fool, Drake Turner, that I can't see through your scheme? Do you think that because I am a bereaved widow, I am so—so *desperate* for a man I would succumb to your blandishments like some schoolgirl? Do you think you're so devastating to women all you need to do is give me a smoldering look, utter a few silver-tongued phrases, and I will swoon into your arms? Well, I am so sorry to disappoint you, sir!"

He flushed deeply, more in pure anger than embarrassment at having been exposed and mocked.

I was in full career now and couldn't stop myself even if I had wanted to. "And if you do want me, I can't help but wonder why. It certainly cannot be for my beauty, for I have no illusions on that score." I hesitated just long enough to give my words time to penetrate his mind. "Or do you want me because I am your enemy's wife, and you see it as another victory over Lord Raven to possess me?"

Drake Turner now turned gray and dropped his hand from the mantel.

"But no matter how hard you try, you'll never be a better man than my husband. He was sensitive, sincere, and kind—qualities you sadly lack."

A muscle twitched in Drake's jaw, and I could see he was expending a great effort to control himself. When he finally spoke, his voice was calm, though edged with acid. "I should take this opportunity to enlighten you about your paragon of a husband, but since I am so insensitive and unscrupulous, I will leave you to your illusions, Countess. Good day." And he walked out of the library without looking back, slamming the door behind him.

When I was finally alone, except for his anger still hanging heavily on the air, I collapsed into the nearest wing chair. I felt drained and unsatisfied by our confrontation. I should have accused Drake of playing those tricks on me, not become embroiled in a personal emotional battle. Now, he had stormed off, and I would have to wait for another opportunity to send him packing.

His failed attempt to woo me still rankled. "Men," I muttered.

The words he had said about Mark just before storming out

of the library kept running through my mind. *I should take this opportunity to enlighten you about your paragon of a husband, but since I am so insensitive and unscrupulous, I will leave you to your illusions.*

I shrugged them off at once. They probably meant nothing. The man had just sought to hurt me with cruel, spiteful words and insinuations about Mark.

When I was sufficiently composed, I left the library and wondered what Drake Turner would do next.

In the week that followed—gloomy days beset by heavy mists, pouring rain, or dreary, sunless days—Drake was always polite to me, but never sought my company, even to discuss business matters when a messenger arrived. Mrs. Harkins told me that he ordered a horse saddled nearly every morning and rode off somewhere, returning quite late at night, if at all. Since I now took all my meals in my room again, I wasn't there to notice that Drake hadn't been present for dinner.

Every morning, I waited hopefully for news from Fenner or Mrs. Harkins that Mr. Turner had ordered the carriage to take him to the Sheepstor station, and he, his chef, cat, and valet were departing for London. But no such news ever came, and Drake stayed on.

I became more isolated from my own household and spent most of my days writing in my sitting room. Lewis Darwin would be pleased to learn that I had almost completed the first draft of the adventures of Cordelia in spite of my major setback when the manuscript was stolen.

On these bleak, gloomy days, so raw and wild for July, I would often happen upon Brent in the library, seated on one of the red leather wing chairs that dwarfed him. I found myself comparing him to Mark in spite of myself. He was such an *indoor* child, preferring to keep his clothes neat to running and riding like a normal boy As I watched him reading or playing chess alone in the game room, I caught myself thinking, "Yes, he is like Mark, an outsider, a loner." Then I would recall his dubious talent for playing upon the weaknesses of others, and I knew such an appalling characteristic could never have come from my husband. I would select my book, then leave quickly, before the child had a chance to speak and torment me.

When the isolation became too much even for me, I rode over to Amabel's. I would often see Damon in the distance, scouring the grounds for sepoys, unmindful of the weather, with Miss Blessed not far behind, one hand pulling a shawl tightly around her arms for warmth, and the other holding her bonnet down against a wind that sounded like the howling of Dartmoor's legendary demon hound. Miss Blessed always stopped to smile and wave at me.

On my visits to Amabel, Peter and Timothy would drag me by the hand up to the nursery, where I sat on the floor with them amid painted toy lions, tigers, and elephants, pretending that we were intrepid African explorers, like Speke and Burton, searching for the elusive source of the White Nile. While I realized I would never know the joy of playing with my own son like this, I couldn't fail to be cheered by Peter and Timothy, and their infectious enthusiasm soon had me forgetting, even for a few hours, the sadness that hung on my heart.

But those gray days soon came to an end, and the exiled sun returned in all its pomp and glory.

A sunny day in Devonshire is like no other in the world. After several weeks of low-hanging gray clouds that draw all color from the landscape, the sun seems to give it back a hundredfold. I know it is probably only an illusion caused by such a sharp contrast, but the very grass seemed greener, and in the garden the flowers seemed to spring out at you, their colors even more bright and vivid. Birdsong seemed sweeter, and I reveled in the smell of warm earth baking in the sun.

One morning, as I stood in the flower beds, snipping the most beautiful snapdragons for my basket, I found my thoughts straying to Drake, as they so often did against my will. One matter continued to plague me. If he was guilty as I thought, why hadn't he immediately leaped at my offer to sell him my share of the Raven Line? That was the opportunity he had been waiting for, yet he rejected it. Could I have misjudged the man after all?

"Oh, Nora . . ." I muttered with a sad shake of my head as I took my basket full of flowers back to the house.

It was just a little after three o'clock that afternoon, when Fenner came stomping into my sitting room, a frown on her normally placid face.

"Why the frown?" I asked her, as I finished arranging the flowers in a vase.

"It's very odd, madam, but I would swear the Masons are wearing new clothes."

"New clothes? Are you sure?"

Fenner looked down her long nose at me with her pelican stare. "I am a ladies' maid, madam," she informed me haughtily. "It is my business to know clothes."

"Hmph," I muttered. "Now that is interesting. I was told they had no money, and that's why they wanted to live here at Raven's Chase."

"Well, they've got some money somewhere, because these clothes are very well made." Suddenly, she fumbled in her pocket. "Madam, I almost forgot! It's a letter from America," she announced, waving the envelope in the air.

I rushed over at once, nearly stepping on poor Faust, who yowled in protest as he clung to my skirt with his claws. "Colin!" I cried, rudely snatching the letter from my poor maid, while the cat dislodged himself and went streaking off. "Thank you, Fenner. That will be all."

When she left, and I heard the door shut behind her, I slid a shaking finger under the envelope's flap to open the letter. Then I seated myself again, and read:

Dear Nora,
    Although I have been in New York City for several weeks, I'm afraid the news I have is not good. Forgive me for beginning this letter on such a disappointing note, but you know I have

never been one to hide the truth, no matter how unpleasant. So far, my investigation of the Masons has not met with success of the type we seek. I met with the solicitors Clement suggested, and they assured me that Mark Gerrick and Ella Mason were wed eleven years ago in this city. I have spoken with various of the family's neighbors, who all tell me the same story: Ella wed a young seaman without her father's consent and had a child by him. Everyone was soon told that her name was Mrs. Mark Gerrick, and her husband a sailor who went out to sea. Unless the Masons bribed half the neighborhood before leaving for England, I'm sure this part of their story is true. I'm afraid I must believe them.

I have also checked the records of St. John's Church, where Ella said they were married, and the records do indeed show that an Ella Mason and Mark Gerrick were married there in the presence of witnesses, whom I am now trying to locate. The minister who performed the ceremony is no longer there, but has a new parish in Boston, Massachusetts, some distance away. Have no fear. I am scheduled to depart for that city soon to find him. I promised to investigate this thoroughly, leaving no stone unturned, as it were, and I shall, though I am skeptical about what the Reverend Joseph Garrick (yes, odd how the names are similar, isn't it?) will have to tell me.

But, in all good conscience, I cannot offer you much hope, Nora. I'm sure you would share my deep sorrow and helplessness as I spent my days here trying to turn up some lead, some little shred of hope that will help me to prove the Masons are schemers out to secure the Gerrick fortune for themselves. Unfortunately, I can't.

As soon as I am finished speaking with the minister in Boston, I shall board a ship for home. So I should be back shortly after you receive this letter.

There were several more paragraphs concerning Amabel and the boys, expressing Colin's hope of seeing them soon, and urging me to give them his love.

I don't know how long I sat there, holding Colin's letter in my hand, and staring at it in a state of shock. All I could remember was feeling all hope slowly draining out of my body and leaving me stone cold on this warm afternoon.

So it was true. Ella Mason and Mark had been secretly married, and she had borne him a son he had never known. And Mark had lied to me by not telling me about Ella. Our entire marriage had been based on lies. Never in my life had I felt so alone, even when my father disowned me for marrying Oliver. Not even Colin's encouraging, strong words could buoy me up this time.

I was going to lose what was most precious to me—trust in my husband. I would be haunted for the rest of my life.

I was too numb for tears as I rose and started out on foot for the Little Chase. I needed to talk to someone, and only Amabel would understand.

When I arrived, she was upstairs in her sitting room, seated at a table strewn with shredded paper, a pot of paste, and several jars of paint. Amabel was engulfed in a huge white apron that protected her black dress from sticky fingers.

"Why, Nora," she greeted me with a pleasant smile, "I'm making papier-mâché fruit. Would you care to—?" Then she noticed my pallid face, and her smile died. "What on earth has happened? You're as white as my apron." And she hastily wiped her hands on a damp cloth and dried them.

"I received this from Colin just a short while ago," I murmured, stumbling into a chair and pulling the letter from my dress pocket.

As Amabel took it, she was looking at me with the queerest expression on her face. "You received a letter from my husband?"

"Why yes, didn't you?" And I knew in an instant that she hadn't. "I'm sure you'll be receiving one from him tomorrow, then," I said hastily, for I could tell she was hurt, though she tried to hide her feelings. "He just wrote to me first to prepare me for the bad news."

"Bad news?" she echoed.

I nodded. "Read it, and you'll understand."

Amabel leaned back in her chair, and I watched her face as

her eyes darted over first one page, then the other. Her expression changed from bewilderment to horror, then she smiled as she read the last paragraphs about herself and the boys.

"He says to give the boys his love," she murmured, her face softening.

"His dearest words are for you, Amabel," I pointed out.

She looked instantly apologetic. "Oh, do forgive me for being such a dunderhead," she said. "I was just so jealous that you received a letter from Colin and I didn't that I became quite uncharitable for a moment. Do forgive me, Nora."

I smiled.

Amabel sat up straight as she sighed and peeled the pages from her sticky fingers. "Well, it would appear that I am to gain a new set of relatives after all."

Taking a deep breath to keep from crying, I said, "It would appear so, unless, of course, Colin learns something from that minister. Odd, isn't it, that the names are so similar? Gerrick . . . Garrick."

"Perhaps he's some relative we know nothing about," Amabel speculated. Then she gave me a long, level look. "I don't mean to discourage you, Nora, but it does look as though the Masons are telling the truth. If Colin hasn't been able to find out anything to the contrary . . ."

I nodded my head vigorously. "I know, I know. Then it is hopeless." I looked at her in despair. "Why didn't Mark tell me about Ella, Amabel? Why didn't he tell me he already had a wife?"

"I don't know, Nora. But it's obvious he didn't love her, otherwise he would have said something to you about her."

"But that makes him sound so callous, so unfeeling. That's not the man I loved."

Amabel's blue eyes hardened, presaging a storm. "Mark could be cruel and callous at times, Nora. In a way, I'm not surprised he did this."

"Amabel!" I cried, wounded by her sharp, cruel words.

"Oh, come now, Nora," she shot back, "you know my

brother was no saint. God help me for speaking ill of the dead, but sometimes he could be reprehensible. He was rebellious, brooding, and a constant trial to Papa and especially poor Mama. And I'll never forgive him for packing Damon off to Goodehouse the way he did."

I rose angrily, feeling hurt and betrayed. "I refuse to dredge up old childhood hurts, Amabel. I came here expecting support, not abuse of my husband." I was nearly at the sitting room door before I felt a beseeching hand on my arm, restraining me.

"I'm sorry, Nora," Amabel said very softly, her black mood vanishing as abruptly as it had appeared. "It was cruel and inconsiderate of me to say those things. I know how much you loved Mark, and how hard this is for you to accept." Then she hugged me impulsively, and when she drew away, she said, "Will you stay for tea, and then dinner? We can talk, and I'm sure you don't want to go back to Raven's Chase just yet."

Although still smarting from her sharp words, I hated to hold a grudge, so I accepted her peace offering and agreed to stay for tea and supper. Just seeing Amabel's face light up with pleasure made me forget what she had said about Mark.

When Amabel chooses, she can be the most charming, delightful woman on the face of the earth, and she was outdoing herself trying to compensate for the harsh, cutting words she had said about Mark earlier. We spent the afternoon playing croquet, had tea, then played several rubbers of whist before dinner. After a lovely meal, of which I ate little, we spent the remainder of the evening listening to Amabel play the piano.

She played pleasant, lighthearted tunes this time, and while I sat there, I tried to appear absorbed in the lilting music, but the heavy pain in my heart was growing with every passing moment.

"What time is it now?" I muttered, when she finally sat back and began gathering her sheet music to put away.

As if in answer, the steeple clock on the mantel chimed nine times in quick succession.

"Nine o'clock already?" I cried, bolting to my feet. "I really must be getting back to the Chase before they send the men out after me."

Amabel looked disappointed as she rose from the piano. "Must you hurry off? I thought we could have coffee and ask Miss Blessed to join us."

"It's awfully late, Amabel."

"I can have someone drive you home. Say you'll stay."

Since I knew she wouldn't accept a refusal, I reluctantly agreed. "Oh, all right."

"Splendid. Would you mind asking Miss Blessed to join us? She should be upstairs, in her room."

So I took a lamp, left the music room, and started upstairs to find Miss Blessed, as Amabel had requested. The nurse's room was on the second floor, toward the rear of the house, so I had a long walk down several corridors as familiar to me as my own. Just as I turned a corner, I saw something so startling it caused me to spring back out of sight.

I had seen Damon Gerrick enter Miss Blessed's room.

For a moment, I was so shocked and alarmed all I could do was lean against the wall while my heart raced out of control. Then I regained my composure and peered around the corner.

The hallway was still and empty.

Had I imagined it? I wondered, with a shake of my head as I came out of hiding and started toward the nurse's room. No, I had seen Damon, however fleetingly, dash into his nurse's bedchamber, and I felt a sickness in the pit of my stomach. A gentleman did not enter a lady's bedchamber at night for a rubber of whist, and if the statuesque Miss Blessed was engaged in some sort of illicit liaison with her patient—a man not in full possession of his faculties—then her behavior was deplorable.

Nora, girl, I chided myself as I slowly walked toward the door, perhaps you're jumping to conclusions. Give Miss Blessed the benefit of the doubt.

But that confidence plummeted when I knocked and she

225

took several minutes to answer. When she did appear, she was clad in a long, white shift with her dark hair worn loose to her shoulders.

"Yes, Lady Raven?" she inquired, her beautiful voice edged with annoyance as she half closed the door behind her and kept one hand on the knob, as though concealing something inside.

"I'm sorry to disturb you, Miss Blessed," I said, wishing I had the ability to see through doors, "but Mrs. Trelawney asked me to invite you to have coffee with us in the drawing room."

She smiled, and something like relief flickered across her face. "Please thank Mrs. Trelawney for her kind invitation, but I'm afraid I've retired for the evening, and coffee tends to keep me awake."

"She'll be disappointed," I said, trying to return her smile and not succeeding very well. "Good night, Miss Blessed."

"Good night, Lady Raven."

As I turned and walked away, I heard the door close and the unmistakable sound of a key turning in the lock.

What should I do? I wondered, as I made my way back to the drawing room. Should I tell Amabel what I thought I saw, or keep silent? If I told her she might lose her temper and dismiss Miss Blessed without just cause and I would be responsible for Damon's losing the best nurse he had ever had.

But what if nurse and patient were lovers? I shivered in revulsion.

No, I told myself firmly, I had misinterpreted what I saw. Damon had a perfectly good reason for his nocturnal visit. It was none of my concern, and I had better keep out of it. Great harm could be done by jumping to conclusions.

"Is Miss Blessed joining us?" Amabel asked when I returned to the drawing room alone.

I shook my head. "She said she has retired for the evening."

Amabel shrugged and rang for coffee. Fifteen minutes later, a maid entered carrying a tray. We drank and talked for a while, mostly about Colin's letter, and I avoided all mention of

Drake Turner. Finally, when I found myself yawning repeatedly, I decided it was time to leave.

I rose and walked to the window, and when I saw there was a moon out, I decided to walk. Amabel wouldn't hear of it.

"I'll have one of the men take you home," she said.

"Don't bother," I insisted. "It's such a beautiful night, I'm going to walk."

Amabel gave me a reproving look. "But it's ten o'clock, Nora. You could fall, or . . . someone could accost you in the dark."

"Nonsense. This is Devonshire, not the streets of London, and I know my way as surely as old Bonnet."

"Please, Nora, I can't allow you to walk."

I grasped her arm and shook it. "Amabel Trelawney, this is one time you're not going to have your own way. I am going to take a short cut through the fields. I'll be at Raven's Chase in no time." She opened her mouth to protest, but I raised my hand and silenced her. "I don't want to hear another word. I am walking home. It will do me good."

Amabel sighed. "You're speaking in that stern, disapproving tone I remember so very well. All right, Nora, I shan't argue with you."

I thanked her and wished her good night as I started on my way, across the lawns toward the fields. Striding away from the Little Chase, I found the events of this day had taken their toll and drained me more than I had first realized. The night was perfect, warm and silvery, filled with the deep bass strummings of frogs and other night creatures.

But, as I hiked up my skirts and trudged on I found the going not as easy as I first imagined it. My breath was quick and labored, and my head was beginning to throb in time to the frogs' croaking. I found I needed to stop and rest quite frequently.

As I stood in the middle of a field bleached by moonlight, I could see deep pools of mist start to rise in the valleys, and I knew I must reach Raven's Chase before they rolled in and overtook me. I shivered, breathed deeply and forced myself to start walking again. All I had to do was pass by the copse, climb a slight rise, and I would be home, safe.

My step was bold as I hurried along, my skirt lifted high so it wouldn't swish through the grass and give the illusion that someone was stalking me. That very thought made me glance over my shoulder nervously, my heart beating in my throat.

"Keep thinking such thoughts and you'll frighten yourself to death, Nora, girl," I chided myself as I forged ahead. "Just a few more minutes, and you'll be home."

I purposely avoided looking into the dark depths of the copse as I hurried by, for I knew if I did my imagination would conjure a pair of red lupine eyes staring out at me, much the way a child imagines monsters dwelling in his cupboard, or under his bed, waiting to spring out at him once he's asleep. So, when it came out of the woods at me, I was totally unprepared.

If anyone asked me to recall what happened, to this day I could not. All I know is that one moment, there was nothing there, and the next, there was Mark, riding Odalisque.

Horse and rider came out of the shadows into the moon-light, and, though they were some distance away, I would have recognized the mare anywhere, with her finely chiseled features and arched tail. Mark sat tall in the saddle, wearing a dark coat and a high beaver hat pulled down low over his forehead. His face was in shadow.

That's all I remember. When I next regained consciousness, the damp scent of grass and earth was strong and sweet in my nostrils, and I awoke to find myself lying on my stomach where I had fallen. As I sat up and looked wildly around, I was alone, all alone.

I scrambled to my feet with a whimper and started running as fast as I could, not stopping for breath until I collapsed against the back door of Raven's Chase some moments later.

"There are no such things as ghosts," I babbled to myself as I let myself in and felt my way around the kitchen like a blind woman until I found a lamp. My trembling fingers managed to light it, and I went rushing upstairs to my room as quietly as an elephant crashing through the jungle.

I sighed in relief when I found Fenner had not waited up for me, for I don't think I could have faced her in my condition.

"Mark is dead," I muttered through chattering teeth, as my cold, stiff fingers undid the buttons on my dress and I pushed it off my body. "I imagined it, that's all. I just imagined it."

Then I rummaged through my bureau until I found a shift, a winter one of heavy flannel that would warm my shaking limbs, and I slipped it on. Tonight, my need for comforting was overwhelming, so I flung open the armoire, grabbed the first coat I touched, and hugged it to me for one long, agonizing moment. Just as I laid it down on the bed and was preparing to slide in beside it, my bedroom door, which I had forgotten to lock in my haste, flew open, startling me. There stood Drake.

He looked half dressed, for while he wore glossy black riding boots and tan whipcord breeches, his shirt was unbuttoned to the waist like some eighteenth-century buccaneer, and his hair was disheveled.

"Where in the hell have you been?" he growled, closing the door and entering my bedroom as though he had every right to be there. "I was just getting ready to ride over to the Trelawneys after you."

"How dare you come in here without knocking!" I sputtered, going rigid with anger as I stood up and faced him.

And then he saw the coat on my bed. His brows came together in puzzlement, then comprehension dawned with light-ninglike speed.

I defiantly searched his eyes and face for pity, but saw only deep sadness there, and it was more than I could bear. "Are you satisfied that you've humiliated me?" I cried, hating him for witnessing my shame.

"Nora," he whispered, rushing to take me into his arms. But words failed him, and all he could do was press my face helplessly into his shoulder. Drake's strong arms lashed me to him, and I could feel his ribs crushed against me, his lips pressed against my hair. He was holding me for dear life, as though I would disappear if he relaxed his grip, even for an instant.

"Let me go," I demanded, stiffening, trying to free myself. "There is nothing you can do for me, nothing."

"You're so wrong. There is much I can do for you," he whispered persuasively, "if you'll just let me."

I had little doubt of the "comfort" he was offering.

"I don't need anything you have to offer," I snapped, fear and panic giving me the strength of two as I struggled against him.

"Oh, but you do, Nora, more than you know."

Even as I fought, I knew it was useless, for the man was stronger than I and fighting him was like battering a mountain. With one arm secure around my waist, he held my head still with the other and began kissing me, quick, feather-light touches on my forehead, eyelids, and down my cheeks.

"Drake, please—!" I begged, as my senses seemed to snap to life at his skilled touch.

"Please what, Nora?" he whispered, his lips trailing along my arched throat. "Please continue? With pleasure." Then his mouth came down on mine, but with an unexpected gentleness.

My mind was shouting a warning to escape from him before it was too late, but my body had betrayed me and was already in his thrall. My skin tingled as though a delightful flame were running up my limbs, and when I closed my eyes, my head seemed to spin and take flight with a delicious giddiness. I felt myself sink against him when I should have pushed away and bolted for the sitting room door and safety.

"Nora," Drake said, my name sounding like a caress on his tongue, "look at me."

When I reluctantly opened my eyes and the giddiness subsided, I found myself staring into two deep sapphire whirlpools that seemed to draw me down into their hearts. There was none of the insincerity there that I had seen that afternoon in the library, when Drake had first attempted to seduce me. There

230

were no barriers between us this time. Drake Turner desired me, and I knew at that moment my desire matched his own.

"Lord, you are beautiful, Nora," he whispered urgently, his voice husky as he buried his face in my hair.

I caught my breath when I felt him push my shift off one shoulder, but just closed my eyes and clung to him as his lips brushed my skin in a lazy, heady circle.

"It's like white velvet, and that scent . . ." He inhaled deeply, savoring it. "The moors . . . the wind."

"Lies, lies, all honeyed lies," I taunted and laughed, testing him one final time.

He released me, and then as if he couldn't bear not touching me, grasped my wrists and held my hands against his heart. "I could never lie to you, ever again. Surely you know that by now." And he drew my hands up to his face, holding them against his cheeks, burning to my touch, while he closed his eyes and groaned.

"Do you want me, Nora?" His shaky whisper seemed to echo through the silent room as though it had been shouted. "Do you want me to stay?"

I never really answered him. Trembling, I slid my hands beneath his open shirt, feeling the wiry hairs of his chest beneath my fingertips, and the smooth, hard muscles of his shoulders as I locked my hands behind his neck and stood on tiptoe to reach his sweet mouth. When we parted, breathless and shaken, I drew him to the bed, ignoring Mark's coat, which would not be needed tonight after all.

From the moment of my surrender, I became Drake's alone. The past and the future no longer existed for me, just this immediate moment in time, and my world was bounded by four carved bedposts.

As Drake and I became lovers, he revealed a playful, sensual side I had never suspected. He turned the lamp down as low as a candle flame so our bodies became softly sculpted shadows to the eye, and he constantly whispered flirtatious, wicked, delightful things in my ear that engaged my mind, while his experienced touch teased and explored. I felt as though I had been awakened from the dead and responded to him utterly and without inhibition.

We turned to each other again and again in the wonder of discovery, until exhaustion finally overtook us and we reluctantly slept, our bodies fitted together as though we'd been lovers all our lives.

When I woke, I was alone in my bed, naked except for the sheet drawn over me. Mark's coat was gone, and I vaguely recalled Drake hanging it up in the armoire before dressing, kissing me on the forehead, and leaving at the first light of dawn.

I yawned and stretched, a languorous feeling washing over me as I recalled Drake's passionate lovemaking of the night before. I rolled over on my side and curled up against my pillow, savoring the memory.

Last night, I had been too preoccupied to draw the curtains, and now the morning sun poured in, bathing the room in a cruel light. At night, under a cloak of hushed darkness, the most adventurous occurrence is possible, but in the bright light of day, when illusion cannot stand close scrutiny, reality sets in with a resounding thud.

Delight was quickly replaced by guilt, and I sat bolt upright in bed, stunned by the enormity of what I had done. I had slept with my husband's enemy in the bed Mark and I had shared, and that realization made my whole body blush with shame.

I could make all the excuses I wanted for my behavior—Colin's letter had discouraged me, seeing Mark's ghost had been a shock—but I still could not justify my actions of the night before. As I lay there, Faust came padding in and bounded onto the bed, where he sat staring at me accusingly out of those slanted golden eyes so like my own. "I know what you did," they seemed to say. I chased him away, and when he streaked back into the sitting room, I couldn't stop thinking of Mark.

I recalled his warmth and consideration, and how he had given me back my self-respect after my first husband left it in tatters. After we were married, he encouraged me to write *The Call of the Curlew* and never once pressed me to have a child, though I knew he wanted one. Then, even after Gabriel was born, Mark always let me know that I was the most important person in his life. And now I had betrayed him in the worst possible way.

"How could I have let this happen?" I muttered to myself, shivering as I rose and picked up my shift off the floor. "I wasn't myself. I must have been weakened from seeing Mark's ghost."

I stood there silently as I tried to recall that nocturnal walk home by moonlight. I recalled glancing into the copse and when I looked up, the horse and rider had materialized out of the darkness. That's all I remembered, so I must have fainted. When I regained consciousness, I was lying on the ground, the specter gone.

"If you tell anyone, they're sure to think you're as mad as poor Damon," I muttered, pulling on my shift. Then I stopped short. "*Am* I going mad?" I wondered aloud. I thought of the time I had once visited Goodehouse, trembling at the memory of spiritless inmates dressed in gray, guarded by men with no life or feeling in their gray faces.

No, I wasn't going mad, I assured myself with conviction. My grief was just so overwhelming, I imagined that horse and rider last night. I so wanted to see Mark that my mind created him. Yet, there was something not quite right. about that apparition.

My thoughts were interrupted by Fenner, who greeted me with, "Good heavens, madam, we are the sleepy one today. Why, it's almost time for lunch."

"I got home quite late from Mrs. Trelawney's," was the only explanation I offered, and as I washed, I resolved not to say anything to anyone about my hallucination, not even Drake or Amabel. It would be my secret.

As Fenner dressed me, my eyes kept straying to Mark's

armoire, and I recalled something Drake had said to me last night, as I lay curled against him. "It's time you tried to put Mark's ghost to rest, don't you think?" I had replied, "I don't want to think about that just now." But now was the time.

"Fenner," I said, trying to keep the trembling out of my voice and failing, "I would like you to take all of Lord Raven's clothes from the armoire, pack them up and take them to Reverend Yellen for distribution to the needy."

My maid looked down her long nose at me and was silent for a moment. "Are you sure, madam?"

"No," I said with a tremulous smile, "but it must be done. I trust you will do as I request as soon as you finish dressing me."

"Yes, madam," was all she said.

As I went downstairs, I couldn't help but think of Drake last night. Needless to say, I was ambivalent about seeing him this morning, afraid of what I'd see in the depths of those icy blue eyes.

He was alone in the Garden Room, just finishing lunch when I walked in, my pulse fluttering nervously and cheeks stained warm pink.

"Good morning," he said with a gentle smile as he rose, "or should I say good afternoon? Have you eaten? I highly recommend Antoine's salmon mousse."

I felt suddenly shy and awkward, unable to face him or say a word, so I crossed the room to the French doors, where I could look out across the terrace and toward the garden. As I stood there, I heard the sound of his chair against the carpet as he rose, followed by footsteps, quick and light.

When I felt his hands drop onto my shoulders, I jumped and stepped away, causing Drake to say, "Nora? What's wrong?"

"What's wrong?" I cried, my voice high and skittish as tears blurred my eyes focused on the head gardener busily pruning roses. "My husband isn't in his grave six months and I—" I couldn't finish.

"Slept with his enemy?"

I closed my eyes and nodded. Then I did turn to face him, searching his eyes for any sign of triumph. "Why did you come to my room last night?"

"Because you hadn't returned from the Trelawneys' and I was concerned that something might have happened to you." His pale eyes didn't waver as he added, "I admit I took advantage of the situation, but you seemed to be in pain and needing comfort."

"But there are other means of offering comfort."

His mustache twitched and he smiled. "But I also wanted you. Is that so difficult for you to understand?"

Crossing my arms tightly, as if to put a physical barrier between us, I swallowed hard. "Why? Because I was Lord Raven's wife?"

Now I knew I had finally pushed him too far. An angry red flush raced up his neck and diffused into his face, and he reached out and grasped my wrists. "Will you stop it? I came to your room last night because I wanted *you* for yourself alone, not because you were once Raven's wife. I will admit that perhaps, in the beginning, I did want the Raven Line because I thought I would enjoy possessing what had once belonged to my rival." He gave me a little shake. "But that had nothing to do with last night, do you understand me?" When I did not answer him immediately, he looked almost desperate. "Do you believe me, Nora?"

At that moment, I realized in a blinding flash of clarity that I had allowed myself to fall into a most insidious trap. Before, I could maintain some semblance of objectivity about the man, but now, since allowing him to become my lover, that objectivity had become distorted, if not totally destroyed. It was like waking up one morning to discover you had gone blind overnight.

"I believe you," I said quietly.

When Drake smiled and tried to draw me to him, I stepped back and broke away, trying to exercise what little self-control remained. "But last night must never happen again," I warned him.

His arms fell to his sides and the light of hope went out of his eyes. "I see. It's Mark again, isn't it?"

"It will always be Mark," I replied wearily, as I turned away. Then, to cover the awkwardness of the moment, I fumbled in my pocket for Colin's letter. "Incidentally, I received this yesterday, and it does not contain promising news."

"I could tell you were upset about something," he said as he took it and scanned it. When he finished, he looked as worried as I felt. "Don't despair, Nora. Perhaps he will learn something from this Reverend Garrick fellow. Strange he has nearly the same last name as yourself."

"What could he possibly learn?" I demanded, losing all patience. "The church records even state that they were married in front of witnesses and the birth recorded."

"Just don't give up hope until Trelawney is here and telling you himself that all is lost."

But his words did not reassure me this time.

CHAPTER

11

In the warm, bright days that followed, I sequestered myself in my sitting room and wrote, because it was the only way I knew to try to ignore my growing attraction to Drake. I thought of myself as a mature, clear-eyed woman and much more worldly than a girl of sixteen, who, through inexperience, confuses desire and love. I had no such delusions. I knew two people became lovers for a wide variety of reasons, many of them having nothing to do with love, but whatever mine were, the results were totally unexpected and unwanted.

Many unanswered questions remained about Drake Turner. I still wondered if he had been the one to play such cruel tricks on me. Yet, I found myself growing increasingly doubtful of his guilt merely because these awakened feelings were clouding my judgment. That worried me.

I no longer trusted myself to be alone with Drake, for I could not deny that I was inexorably drawn to him, so I tried avoiding him as much as possible. My doors were kept locked at night as a precaution, though once, when I heard the knob turn ever so slowly, I nearly relented and rushed to open the door. I was falling under Drake's spell and it was becoming increasingly difficult to resist, though I could never let him know that.

One day, when Mrs. Harkins informed me that Mr. Turner had ridden off early the day before and not returned that night, I began to wonder about his mysterious comings and goings. Did he have another woman, someone in Sheepstor or Plymouth, perhaps? When I felt the first pangs of jealousy, I later laughed and chastised myself. Drake Turner's women were of no concern to me. Or so I thought.

I must confess I hadn't thought much about the Masons during this time, until the day I received the bills.

That fateful day, I was out in the garden with my basket, picking flowers, when Fenner came stomping out of the house, a look of outrage on her face.

"Madam," she called, "there is something you must see."

I straightened up and looked at her questioningly. "What is it, Fenner?"

She waved a handful of papers under my nose. "Bills, madam, bills, charged to the Gerrick account at several shops."

"Let me see them," I said.

"They're for clothing we never ordered, madam."

I stared at the bills, all from clothiers and dressmakers in either Sheepstor or Plymouth. "What's this? Two black day dresses, French kid slippers, a Norwich shawl . . ." I read another one. "Three pairs of trousers, riding boots, and two frock coats . . ." I regarded my maid with some asperity. "You're right. We've never ordered such clothes."

Fenner looked smug as she said, "Do you remember my telling you that I thought the Masons had new clothes?"

"Yes, and I paid you no mind."

"They must have ordered them and told the tradesmen to send these bills to you."

My cheeks seemed to grow suddenly hot as I stood there in the garden, staring at these bills, which, by my quick calculation, amounted to more than fifty pounds.

"Where *are* the Masons?" I demanded between clenched teeth.

"I believe they're having a picnic at the abbey," Fenner told me with great satisfaction.

Thrusting my basket into her hands, I said, "Take this inside for me, will you?"

As Fenner said, they were at the abbey, seated on the grass

before a blue checkered tablecloth spread with a feast courtesy of Mrs. Baker and Antoine. Brent seemed to be off chasing something up a hill, while his mother called words of warning for him not to stray too far. His uncle tossed his hair out of his eyes, laughed, and refilled the wineglasses.

When he saw me approach, he held the bottle up to me in a friendly salute. "Hello, Lady Raven. Won't you join us? It's such a beautiful day for a picnic."

Brent stopped when he saw me, and Ella turned to watch my approach with all the welcome a ram reserves for a wolf. All three of them were wearing garments I had not seen before.

I stopped at the edge of the tablecloth and towered over them. "What is the meaning of these?" I said, flinging the handful of bills atop their picnic lunch.

With a puzzled frown, Seth picked one up, stared at it, then looked up at me with his ingratiating smile. "Why, they're bills for our new clothes."

"Indeed. And who gave you the right to order them and have the bills charged to me?"

Seth just shrugged, and there was no remorse in him at all. "Since my nephew will soon inherit the Gerrick estate, we didn't think it was too forward to have the estate pay for our clothes, though it is somewhat in advance."

"It was my decision," Ella said coolly, sitting still, her eyes never leaving my face.

"I am not paying those bills," I insisted, then turned on my heel to leave.

"Well, we certainly can't pay them," Seth called after me. "We have no money."

I stopped and turned to face them again. "Then I suggest you do the obvious, Mr. Mason. Return your purchases."

"Lady Raven," Ella said. "I would suggest you pay those bills."

My brows rose. "And if I don't?"

Without uttering a word, she just smiled enigmatically and reached for her wineglass.

Visions of the ball rolling toward me down that darkened

corridor flashed through my mind for an instant. I turned and hurried back to the Chase.

The next day, the Masons began making good on their unspoken threats. A small photograph of Mark and myself disappeared from the mantel in the Chinese drawing room, and Mrs. Harkins informed me that one of two matching blue-and-white porcelain vases in the Ming Room had been broken, and that, when confronted, Ella Mason claimed she had accidentally knocked it over.

I, of course, confronted the Masons once again and accused them of committing these acts to annoy me, but, as expected, they denied it and accused me of being hysterical.

I was so angry and resentful of their presence, I even plotted with Mrs. Harkins for their forcible removal. She was going to have the maids pack the Masons' belongings one day while they were out, load the bags into a carriage, and then the footmen would bodily propel them into another carriage. But the doubts would gnaw at me once again. What if Brent was really Mark's son after all? What if he belonged here at Raven's Chase? Wasn't I obligated to let him stay here if his claim was justified?

So I told Mrs. Harkins to forget our plan.

During most of the Masons' campaign of retribution, Drake was nowhere to be found which was most annoying, since Hamish Pengelly, himself, came up from Plymouth with several associates for a conference, and, after waiting an entire afternoon, had to leave without seeing him. Then, about three days later, Drake suddenly appeared, though I wondered how long he would stay after Amabel summoned me over to the Little Chase with what was to be the surprise of my life.

As I came riding up on Curlew, I saw that a large bull's-eye target had been set up on the front lawn, and Miss Blessed and Nellie were applauding Peter and Timothy's efforts at archery, while Damon lazily watched from beneath the shade of a tree.

Amabel was not among their party, and when I asked Miss Blessed where she was, the nurse replied, "Inside, with a caller."

Puzzled, I dismounted while a footman held my horse, went inside, and was directed to the drawing room. As I was announced, I noticed that Amabel was sitting with another woman so beautiful that even Amabel was eclipsed.

She wore a modish gown of pale moss-green silk that could only have come from Paris. The gown accentuated her flawless ivory skin and sparkling blue eyes, and was the perfect foil for her hair, a blazing red-gold that could not be dimmed, even though partially hidden by a hat *à la casquette.* This woman had the kind of looks that kings lost kingdoms for, yet I sensed this confection had a brittle center.

Now both women rose, and Amabel said, "Nora, I'm so glad you could call. There's someone I'd like you to meet. This is my cousin by marriage, Lady Mary Janeaway, Marchioness of Eddington."

As I nodded to the marchioness, Amabel added, "I think you should know her maiden name was Mary Glover."

My eyes widened as I recalled Drake's words during our heated argument about the naming of the *Nancy Malone* after his mistress. *I want to name her the* Mary Glover, *after one of my mistresses.*

The marchioness saw my confusion and spoke in a voice that had the odd quality of being both soft and strong. "I can see you are bewildered, Lady Raven. Amabel explained your situation, and I felt I must come and speak to you personally."

"When you mentioned the name Mary Glover," Amabel said, "it sounded so familiar for some reason. I thought about it, and then remembered one of my cousins, Lord Eddington, married a woman named Mary Glover. So I wrote to her and asked if she had ever known Drake Turner."

I sank down onto the sofa, while our elegant visitor smiled graciously at me. "Amabel's letter so alarmed me, I felt it was my duty to come at once and talk to you." She smoothed her skirts and began. "I knew Drake Turner when he was just beginning to make a success of his company. He became quite infatuated with me, Lady Raven, and while I was flattered, I fear I did not return his feelings as intensely as he would have liked. I needed to make a good marriage, you see," she said matter-of-factly. "About that time, Eddie's—Lord Eddington's—cousin, Lord Raven, introduced me to him at a ball. We fell in love and announced our intentions to marry. Well, when Mr. Turner discovered this, he beame insufferable. He believed Lord Raven purposely introduced his cousin to me to keep Mr. Turner out of the family. And though I told him time and time again that I had no wish to marry him, that I never loved him, he became even more impossible."

I sat back in my seat, just letting the woman's words sink in a little at a time. "Then you were never Mr. Turner's—"

"Lady Raven!" The marchioness bristled, and turned an unbecoming shade. "I don't know what lies that man has told about me, but I can assure you that we were—that there was never anything between us except what existed in the poor man's mind."

"Forgive me for insinuating such a thing," I apologized.

Amabel smiled and said, "Don't you see, Nora? Drake Turner has never forgiven Mark for introducing Lady Eddington to my cousin. That, in addition to their rivalry in trade, has been fueling their discord all these years."

I sat there in silence, letting the full implication of her words sink in. No, I thought, Amabel is wrong about Drake.

Lady Eddington shook her head, and there was no fondness or regret in her soft-strong voice. "Drake Turner was a thoroughly unpleasant and disagreeable man. He probably still is."

Just then, a footman announced the unpleasant and disagreeable man himself, and when I glanced at Amabel in alarm, she explained, "I sent a message for Mr. Turner to join us. I see he gave us just enough time to tell you Lady Eddington's story."

As Drake came striding into the room, the marchioness rose and faced him squarely. When he saw her, he stopped and recoiled in shock, turning so pale I thought he was going to faint.

"Mary," he muttered thickly. "What are you doing here?"

"I'm the Marchioness of Eddington to you," she said with great hauteur and distaste. "I came here to tell these people the truth about you, Mr. Turner."

As I watched, Drake's face twisted into a mask of pain, then he just whirled around and strode out of the drawing room. I knew I must go after him, so, murmuring my hasty thanks to Lady Eddington, I went running out of the drawing room but, when I came flying out the front door, Drake was already mounted on Jester and cantering away.

"Drake, wait!" I shouted, scrambling into the saddle and kicking Curlew.

But he paid me no heed as he went galloping off, his rage deafening him to my entreaties. I chased him across the lawn, past the startled archers, over a low wall, and out across the fields I had crossed the night Mark's ghost appeared to me.

"Please, wait!" I called again, but my voice was drowned out by the thunder of hoofbeats.

He ignored me, as I suspected he would, but since Curlew was the faster horse, I was soon drawing alongside of Jester. Suddenly, I felt my stirrup give way, and with a cry of surprise, found myself airborne, with a bush spinning up to meet me.

When I next opened my eyes, I found myself staring at the sky, with Drake's arm cradling me as my head lolled against his shoulder.

"Nora, are you all right?" His voice was filled with desperation, as he patted my cheek to revive me, and I could tell the marchioness was the furthest thought from his mind.

"I—I think so," I murmured.

"Thank God! Now, is anything broken? Can you move your arms and legs?"

I did as he bade me, and thankfully, all of my limbs seemed in working order, though my arms and ribs felt sore, and I suspected I would be quite bruised tomorrow.

"Lucky for me that bush broke my fall," I murmured, nestling against him.

"Do you think you can stand?"

"Not yet," I lied.

I heard him sigh, then felt his lips brush my forehead as his arm tightened protectively about me.

But I realized I couldn't lie here forever in the middle of this field, so I made an effort to rise. With Drake's support, I managed to totter to my feet, and when I knew I would survive, I took a few tentative steps.

"Are you *sure* you're all right?" he demanded anxiously, his arms never leaving my waist.

I nodded, then looked up at him and said, "We must discuss Lady Eddington."

"I don't wish to discuss her with you or anyone else," he snapped. "Now, let's get you back to the Chase."

By the time Drake and I arrived, I was feeling much better, but he would hear nothing of my protests. He carried me to my room and insisted Miss Blessed be summoned to examine me. The nurse arrived along with an agitated Amabel, gave me as competent an examination as her training would allow and pronounced me fit, though bruised. She ordered me to bed for the rest of the day.

As soon as Miss Blessed departed, I rose, ignoring the ache in my ribs, and went in search of Drake.

I found him in the library, consuming more spirits than was prudent. When our eyes met, I said, "We must talk about Lady Eddington," and hobbled across the room, one hand pressed to my side to relieve the pain.

"What are you doing out of bed?" he growled.

"I'm going to stay right here until you tell me everything I want to know."

He came to my side, guided me to a wing chair, and hovered over me as I sat down with a sharp gasp of pain that caused him to wince sympathetically.

"It wasn't necessary for you to come downstairs and subject yourself to further hurt," he said gruffly.

I looked up at him, touched that he sounded more concerned than annoyed. "I didn't think you'd come to me, so I decided to come to you."

His mustache twitched and he murmured, "Obstinate woman." Then he went to the fireplace, rested his foot against the fender, and said, "Very well, Countess, since you are so curious about my former love. I fell in love with Mary Glover the moment I saw her. You've seen how beautiful she is. Well, I met her at a mutual friend's house, and she was speaking with a group of men when I walked into the room. Her voice was soft and melodious, and yet strong somehow."

I nodded and said a trifle wistfully, "She is very beautiful."

"I learned she came from an impoverished, though genteel, family, with a profligate brother who had run up huge gambling debts. So I thought she wouldn't be averse to a wealthy suitor."

Then Drake's face changed, becoming hard and ruthless once again. "I fell in love with her and wanted her desperately. And then Lord Raven introduced her to his cousin, the handsome, the wealthy, the titled Lord Thomas Janeaway, Marquess of Eddington. Who could compete with that? In addition to looks and wealth, he had a title, and no doubt her family pressured her into accepting his suit."

I could have pointed out that if Mary loved him as he thought, she would have wanted him no matter what, but men have to have their illusions. All I did was bow my head and say, "So you blame Lord Raven for bringing about the loss of your love."

"He introduced them deliberately, Nora," he growled. "He heard that I was courting her, and neatly stepped in. If she had never met Eddington, she would be my wife today."

And, judging by the bitterness in his voice and the rage in his eyes, his feelings for the exquisite Mary hadn't diminished with time. I should have spoken up and asked him if he still loved her, but my courage failed me, perhaps because I feared what his answer would be.

All I said was, "And that is why you hated my husband,"

from the depths of my chair. Then I hauled myself up. "I'm going back to my room. I'm quite fatigued."

"I didn't expect you to understand," he said stiffly. "Now, can you walk unassisted, or do you wish me to carry you?"

"I will manage," I replied, fighting against the pain, but he reached for me anyway, and carried me upstairs in silence.

When he left, I stared at the door and murmured, "I understand all too well, my friend, all too well."

By the third day I was feeling stiff, but able to dress and walk around without much pain or soreness. I was eating luncheon in my sitting room, passing a tidbit of ham now and then to Faust, when Drake walked in, his demeanor cool and his shaggy brows knotted.

I tensed, expecting him to start talking about Mary, but he surprised me by saying, "This is the stirrup leather from your saddle." When I took it and looked at him with a question on my face, he said, "Examine the break."

I sat back and did as he requested. "I don't understand," I said, puzzled, for I could see nothing wrong with it.

He came forward to show me. "Do you see how half the break is smooth, and the other half jagged, as though it's been torn?"

"Yes."

Blue eyes held mine. "It's been cut, Nora. Deliberately."

As we stared at each other, I felt the blood drain from my face and was thankful I was sitting down. My head fell back, and my voice was a hoarse croak as I said, "Cut? Deliberately?"

Drake nodded as he turned the leather in his hands. "Young Corman brought it to my attention. The poor man was ashen. The cut was made high up, so it would be undetected when the groom saddled your horse. And, with a sidesaddle, most of your weight would be on the left side, on your stirrup. So, when it broke, you'd lose your balance and fall."

I swallowed hard. "And be killed."

Drake said nothing, but the expression on his face mirrored his thoughts.

Suddenly, I lost all appetite, pushed my tray away and rose, ignoring Faust as he bawled impatiently for more food.

"Who?" I cried, knotting my fingers together.

Drake replied, "I asked Young Corman if he or any of the men had seen anyone lurking about the tack room, and he told me nearly everyone has been there at some time during the last week. Ella and Seth were there, trying to persuade Brent to ride . . . Damon was wandering about, as usual, with Miss Blessed, and even Mrs. Trelawney stopped by to borrow a new bit for her horse."

"So, any one of them could have done it."

Drake nodded.

The words "Nora will die" rang like a death knell through my mind, and I felt my control slipping away as raw fear took over, leaving me weak and trembling.

"It's Seth," I babbled, "It's got to be Seth. Or Ella."

"Not necessarily," Drake said.

"Who else then?" I demanded, whirling on him, my voice rising. "Amabel? My own sister-in-law?"

Drake came toward me, but I backed away. I was frightened and agitated, my breath coming quickly as I squeezed my fingers then rubbed my brow. "First the ball, then the study and Mark's ghost. And now—"

"What did you say?" Drake interrupted me sharply.

"Mark's ghost. I—I saw him the night I walked home from the Little Chase, the night you came to my room. It was Mark riding Odalisque."

Drake was at my side in an instant, his strong fingers biting into my arm. "Why didn't you tell me about this, Nora?"

"It—it was only a hallucination. I thought people would think I had gone mad, so I decided not to tell anyone."

He shook me. "Why didn't you trust me enough to tell me?"

"Because you bristle whenever I mention Mark's name."

"But there are no such things as ghosts, Nora, except those we create in our own minds. You know that. Come. You're going to show me exactly where this apparition appeared to you."

And he took me by the hand and dragged me off before I even had a chance to put on a bonnet or shawl.

Minutes later, we were standing by the copse, where the apparition had appeared.

"Now, tell me what happened," Drake demanded.

"I decided to walk home from the Little Chase," I began, trying to reconstruct that night in my mind. "It was as bright as daylight because the moon was out. It was very late, and I decided to walk home across the fields, rather than have someone drive me home."

"You weren't afraid?"

"Why should I be? I've walked between Raven's Chase and the Little Chase often enough without mishap." I stopped and pointed. "It happened right about there. I glanced up, and—and there was Odalisque standing there, with Mark on her back." I was so furious, I clenched my hands into fists. "Do you see why I didn't want to tell anyone about this? Even as I'm telling you now, it all sounds so preposterous. People would have thought me insane, if I told them." My voice trailed off and I calmed myself. "Then I must have fainted, and when I came to, the apparition was gone. That's all it was," I said bitterly, "the imaginings of a grief-stricken woman." Tears started streaming down my cheeks as I said, "Lord, how I wish it had been Mark."

This time, Drake did not put his arm around me or offer comfort He scowled, bit his lower lip, and looked puzzled. "Well, I happen to think your ghost was quite real, and I hope to be able to prove it."

Then he took me by the hand again and started leading me toward the spot where I had seen the apparition. When we came to it, he squatted down and stared at the ground, parting the grasses carefully with his hand, and touching the earth.

"Look," he said, with satisfaction. "Hoofprints. Not very distinct, but there are hoofprints here."

I bent over to look. "Of course there would be tracks here. I've ridden by the copse often enough, as has Amabel."

"True," he said, "but look at their pattern. If someone had circled the copse, there would be prints all along this line. As these go, it looks as though a horse came out of the copse, and just stood here for a moment, then turned and went back inside the grove."

What he said was true. There were no fresh tracks except those before us.

"Now," Drake said, looking up at me, "you told me Mark's horse was turned loose on the moors before you went to London. Would it be possible for someone to catch her?"

"I suppose so. She was spirited, but came when called."

Drake rose now, and stared off into space. "Suppose someone had caught her and has been hiding the mare for the express purpose of frightening you in just this way."

At first I was stunned, but it was the only logical explanation.

"Now," Drake continued, "why did you think the person on the horse was Mark?"

I pressed my fingers to my forehead. "Well, he was wearing top boots and breeches, and Mark's dark blue coat."

"But could you see his face?"

I suddenly felt very foolish. "No. He was too far away, and his high beaver hat was—" I stopped, for now I knew what had troubled me when I had first seen the apparition that night. "He was wearing a hat. Mark never wore a hat."

"But he had to that night, so you wouldn't see the impostor's face. Convenient, don't you think?" Drake looked at me for a moment, then added, "And how do you know it was even a man? Could it have been a woman?"

My lips formed the name, but I did not say it aloud: Amabel.

"It could fit, couldn't it?" he said. "Your sister-in-law is an excellent rider, and surely capable of catching the mare. All she had to do was find a place to hide the horse until she needed it."

I took a step back from him, not wanting to believe what he was suggesting. "But how could she have dressed in Mark's clothes, got Odalisque out of hiding, and beaten me to the copse? We had been having coffee together."

Drake had no answer.

"And why?" I asked aloud, but even as I said the words, I knew. "Peter's inheritance."

"What?" Drake demanded.

"Amabel confessed to me that she had read my journal and discovered that I planned to make Peter my heir. You see, if the Masons' claim is false, Timothy will inherit Raven's Chase upon Damon's death because Peter is illegitimate. I thought by leaving Peter the Raven Line and Mount Street house, I could compensate for the loss of his birthright. Raven's Chase would have been his, except for the accident of his birth."

"But why did you name him your heir when you're sure to marry again and have children of your own?"

"I have no plans ever to marry again," I said stiffly, and before Drake could comment, I continued, "Amabel would do anything for her children and family. The Gerrick name means everything to her."

"But what about Damon?" Drake asked. "Doesn't he stand to inherit if something happens to you?"

I shook my head. "Don't you remember my telling the Masons that, legally, he *is* Lord Raven, but I was granted custodianship of the estate? And, if the Masons' claim is true, then Brent would have to die before Damon could inherit. Except for the time the child was locked in the abbey cellars, nothing has happened to him." I dismissed Damon with a wave of my hand and sighed heavily. "No, Amabel must be the culprit." I shook my head in disbelief. "My own sister-in-law . . ."

Suddenly, Drake said, "Let's go back to the house."

When we arrived back at Raven's Chase, we went up to my bedchamber, and Drake strode over to the armoire, opening the doors and swinging them wide. He stopped short, his eyes widening incredulously. "What happened to your husband's clothes?"

"I had Fenner give them to Reverend Yellen, for distribution to the poor." Drake was staring at me with the oddest look on his face, a mixture of astonishment and pleasure. "Why are you looking at me that way?"

He stumbled over his words like a gawky schoolboy. "I— never mind. You've just destroyed evidence, that's all. We've already proved that the horse was not a ghost, and if your husband's clothes were still here, we could have seen if a dark blue coat was missing."

I nodded in sudden comprehension. "So you think someone took Mark's coat, hid Odalisque, then turned her loose when they were done with her."

"It certainly looks that way."

Suddenly, there came a knock at the door, and when I answered it, a frantic Fenner said, "Madam, Mr. Trelawney has returned from America and is waiting downstairs for you in the Chinese drawing room."

Colin, Amabel, and a short, gray-haired man dressed in the somber clothing of a minister rose when Drake and I entered the drawing room.

"Colin!" I cried, unable to restrain myself as I flung myself into his arms and hugged him as though he had been gone three years instead of three months.

"Nora, how are you?" he said, his eyes twinkling and his voice filled with laughter.

I stepped back to look at him, and his strength suddenly flowed through me again, as it always did. I felt like a marionette whose strings have suddenly been pulled, bringing it to life. My anxious eyes scanned his face for any sign of whether his news was bad or good, and when I saw his smile, I felt my own spirits soar.

"You've learned something," I said tentatively, squeezing my hands together until they hurt. "Was Ella Mason married to Mark? Is Brentwood his son?"

"Before I answer your questions, Nora, I'd like to introduce you to the Reverend Joseph Garrick, of Boston, Massachusetts."

The little old man who came forward looked comical, with his head of white hair that stood straight up, and tufts of white hair for eyebrows. He even had the cottony tufts growing out of his ears. But his gaze was forthright and his handshake firm, and when he spoke, his voice was as vigorous as a young man's.

"You must be the minister who married Mark and Ella," I said.

He nodded, his white eyebrows bobbing as he spoke. "Indeed I am."

My hopes plummeted, and I felt like screaming. "So, they were married after all."

"Don't jump to conclusions, Nora," Colin said mysteriously. "Would you summon the Masons, please?"

Puzzled, but knowing I could not rush Colin, I had one of the footmen summon Seth and Ella, and we all waited in silence, no one even daring to make small talk.

Finally, just as the suspense was becoming unbearable, there came a knock on the door and the Masons were shown in. Seth took one look at the Reverend Garrick and turned a ghastly shade of white.

But before he could recover himself, the little man said, "Why, Mr. Gerrick, how do you do? It's been a long, long time. Eleven years, I believe."

"Mr. Gerrick!" I cried, looking to Colin in appeal. "What does this mean? This isn't Mr. Gerrick."

Reverend Garrick turned to me and cocked his head to one side like a bemused finch. "But this is the man who called himself Mark Gerrick when I married him to this lady over here."

He pointed to Ella, who had also turned white. "I married them eleven years ago, on March 18, 1857. I'll never forget that date because our names are so similar that I thought we might be related."

"But these two are brother and sister!" I protested.

The reverend cast a disapproving look at Seth and shook his head in reproach. "Most improper. You can imagine my shock and dismay when Mr. Trelawney told me. It's quite illegal to marry a brother and sister, I can assure you."

"You're positive these are the people you married?" I asked.

The white brows rose, two dots above his eyes. "Lady Raven, I never forget a face, especially one belonging to someone I may be related to. Genealogy is a hobby of mine, you see, and when I thought I might be related to the distinguished Gerricks of Devonshire, I made a point of scouring records for years." The white brows bobbed, and he sighed in disappointment. "We're not related after all."

"When I met the Reverend Garrick in Boston," Colin explained, "I was startled to discover he remembered Mark Gerrick quite well. But when he began describing him— short, thin, with black hair always in his eyes—Mark sounded suspiciously like Seth Mason. That's why I had to persuade Reverend Garrick to come with me, to identify the man he had married."

Five pairs of eyes stared accusingly at the Masons. Seth just smiled his most charming smile, but Ella saw the futility of pretense and, for once, lost control.

"I told you it would never work!" she screamed at her brother, then whirled away from him.

Colin's eyes were fixed on Seth and they held no mercy. "I think you have some explaining to do, Mr. Mason."

Seth just shrugged, but his smile was now a little strained, and there was a shimmer of sweat on his brow. "We took a gamble and lost, that's all. There's nothing more to say."

"Oh, I think there is," Colin contradicted him. "I think you owe us an explanation of why you tried to swindle Lady Raven out of Raven's Chase."

"Ask Ella. In a way, she's the reason."

Ella, her composure regained, turned and stared down at us quite haughtily, as though conferring a great honor by telling us her story.

"When I was only eighteen, I met a soldier," she began. "I was innocent and he a smooth talker. He declared that he loved me, and we became lovers. In those days, I was much less cynical. When I discovered I was to have a child, he deserted me and I knew that I would never see him again. I faced a life of shame and was desperate, because I knew my father would cast me out of our home. Then, one day, I met Mark Gerrick through a cousin, as I told you. He dined with us and paid much attention to me, and when he left, Seth had an idea that would get me out of my predicament." She glanced at her brother. "He would pretend to be Mark Gerrick, and we would be married secretly." At our shocked looks, she added, "It was only in name, of course, a ruse designed to escape my father's wrath. He was a deeply religious, straitlaced man, and very proud."

Seth added, "I couldn't let my own sister be turned out into the cold, with nowhere to go, so I practiced copying Mark's handwriting from a note he had written to Ella, thanking her for dinner. Then we went away and were married in secret. Two friends served as witnesses and were sworn to secrecy." He addressed the Reverend Garrick. "We knew it was wrong, but we only did it to save Ella."

"Why was it necessary to go through a ceremony?" I demanded. "Why didn't you just tell your father Mark and Ella wed?"

"Because my father was a very shrewd man and would demand proof," Seth said, "which he did. I needed marriage lines to convince him."

Ella continued in her flat, emotionless tone. "It worked out splendidly. When I confessed my secret marriage to my father,

254

he was furious I had been deserted, but I persuaded him that Mark couldn't stand the responsibility of a child."

Seth said, "Then, when I heard that the *Neptune* had been shipwrecked and all aboard drowned, it was a stroke of fortune. No one questioned Ella, and our family's reputation was upheld."

I took a deep breath, my thoughts in a turmoil. "So, the letters you claimed your father received from Mark . . . that was all fabricated?"

Ella nodded. "My father believed him dead and didn't spare him another thought."

Seth said, "I had to find some way of explaining to you why Mark never contacted Ella once he returned home to England. That was as good a reason as any."

"But why did you come here, claiming to be Mark's wife?" I demanded of Ella. "Everyone knew you were a widow. There was no stigma attached to you or your child. You could have remained in New York."

"I can explain that," Colin cut in, stroking his beard. "During the course of my investigation, I discovered the Masons had fallen on hard times. Not only was the family business looted and burned in the draft riots of 1863, as Seth explained, but before that, in 1857, the store was forced out of business by a general economic collapse."

Seth nodded. "It was the same year we met Mark Gerrick."

"Your father spent years trying to recover," Colin went on, "but he just couldn't, and died a broken man. In addition, you, Mr. Mason, were dismissed from your newspaper in disgrace. You accused a high government official of corruption, without having any proof or verifying your sources of information. It became prudent for you to leave New York City quickly, and that's when, I believe, you heard of Mark's death. Am I right so far?"

The other man's eyes were filled with a grudging admiration. "You're a clever man, Trelawney. When I read of Lord

Raven's death, I wondered if we could claim a little share of his estate. We did have a little money left—barely enough to get us over here—but once that was gone, we'd be penniless, you see. It was a risk, of course, but we had to do something, or starve. And, faced with that, I'd take any risk." He raised his brows and smiled. "Wouldn't any of you? It was a perfect scheme," he went on, caught up in his own cleverness now, and feeling the necessity of revealing his brilliance to all of us. "Everything we told you was the truth, except for the fact that Mark and Ella were not really married. So, if anyone investigated, they would find that everything we said was true. One witness was killed at the Battle of Bull Run and the other went out West to seek his fortune. No one's heard from him in years."

"And that's why none of us could catch you in a lie," I muttered, astounded by the man's audacity and cleverness.

He nodded and flashed me a broad smile. "Precisely. The only flaw in the scheme was the Reverend Garrick here. Only he knew that I had impersonated Mark Gerrick, and who could have foreseen that he would remember me?"

"You didn't count on my memory for names and faces," the minister said, his voice heavy with admonition as his brows bobbed up and down.

"Exactly," Seth agreed blandly. "Who would bother to look up a minister who had married someone eleven years ago, then moved several hundred miles away? And even if they found him, what were the chances of his remembering the two people? Very unlikely. A minister performs many marriages in eleven years' time, and it's doubtful he could remember one couple out of hundreds."

"You didn't count on Colin Trelawney," Amabel said from across the room, her eyes sparkling with pride as she smiled at her husband.

"No, I didn't," Seth said, making a bow of acknowledgment in Colin's direction. "I gambled and lost."

"The gamble is going to garner you some time in prison, Mason," Colin said mercilessly.

"I think we've heard enough," a voice came from out of nowhere, and we all turned in surprise to see two men emerge from behind the lacquerware screen.

"Mr. Appleby . . . Mr. Squires," I murmured at seeing the two solicitors who had treated me so shabbily in London. "What are you doing here?"

"I had them accompany us," Colin explained. "I wanted impartial witnesses to what I was sure would be the Masons' confession."

Both men cast ignominious looks at Ella and turned to me with unctuous smiles on their faces, transferring their unwanted allegiance from Ella to me. "We owe you a profound apology, Lady Raven," Mr. Appleby said, "a profound apology. We cannot apologize enough for being taken in by these . . . these swindlers. And I assure you, they will pay."

Seth ran his hand through his wild dark hair and swallowed hard. "The entire scheme was my idea. I alone am responsible," he said heavily, "and I alone should be made to pay. Ella only did my bidding. She is not to blame." Ella, I noticed, did not disagree with him as he turned imploring brown eyes toward me. For the first time, they were devoid of bravado. "Do what you must, Lady Raven, but please, I'm begging you, leave Ella and Brent out of it."

I pressed my fingertips to my forehead, which had suddenly begun to throb. "I don't know what I'm going to do about you, Mr. Mason. I must have time to think."

But all I could think about was Mark. He had been returned to me. He had never married that woman, never had a child by her, never loved anyone but me.

I turned away from everyone and left the Chinese drawing room.

I informed Fenner I did not wish to be disturbed for the rest of the day and went to my sitting room to be alone with my tumultuous thoughts. As I sat in my favorite chair, holding Faust in my lap, I experienced a wide range of fluctuating emo-

257

tions. I hated the Masons for the grief they had subjected me to, yet felt a strange twisted pity when I recalled their sorry tale and guilty, frightened faces. I felt gratitude toward Colin for exposing them, and elation that all was finally resolved.

But my overriding emotion was bone-shaking relief—relief that Mark had been vindicated, relief that Raven's Chase was still mine, relief that there would be no more cruel tricks, ever again.

"It's over, cat," I murmured to Faust, touching my face to his soft fur.

I don't know how long I had been sitting there, when I heard a soft knock at the door. At first, I was irritated that my orders had been disobeyed, then relented, and went to see who was there.

It was Brent.

"Come in," I said. When he did so, I stopped and looked down at him. This was the moment I had long waited for, my moment of triumph, but all I could say was, "I've just learned you're not my husband's rightful son after all."

The boy let out a long-drawn-out sigh and looked both bemused and regretful as he reached up to pet Faust. "I feared that was the case," he said in his curious grown-up way. "Such a pity. I was beginning to enjoy living here. It's so much better than New York City."

I didn't know what to say.

There was pure childlike uncertainty and fear in his eyes as he said, "My mother and Uncle Seth made it all up, didn't they? I'm not really Lord Raven, am I?"

I nodded, but said nothing.

Suddenly, his face crumpled, and his eyes filled with tears. "My mother is going to go to jail, isn't she, and I'll never see her again, will I?" His confident, grating voice trembled as he said, "I—I couldn't bear that, Lady Raven, not seeing my mother ever again."

I stood there, stunned. All the time he had been here, Brent had sensed our weaknesses without ever revealing his own. He had picked us apart without giving quarter or showing an ounce of compassion for our feelings while he wounded us. Now he stood before me, a vulnerable child in dire fear of being separated from his mother, that most basic fear of all children. My need for vengeance evaporated like wood smoke.

"No; Brent," I said wearily, "your mother will not have to go to prison. I'll see that she doesn't."

He stared up at me, comprehending the gift I was giving him, and what it cost me. Then he flung himself against my skirts and clung to me as Peter or Timothy would.

I stroked his dark head and whispered, "Your mother needs you, you know. Why don't you go to her now?" And he dislodged himself and went running out of my sitting room.

No one disturbed me for the rest of the day, not even to bring me supper and, hours later, I dressed for bed. I was exhausted both mentally and physically, and looked forward to a good night's sleep. However, no matter how many sheep I counted, I just could not fall asleep.

The bottle of sleeping draft on the nightstand near my bed caught my eye, so I poured myself a glassful, held my breath, and swallowed the vile-tasting concoction. With a shudder, I set the glass down and settled in to enjoy a well-earned rest.

But no sooner had I settled myself back against the pillows, than the door to my sitting room opened, and there stood Damon.

The sight of him was so unexpected, I jumped and stared at him in indignation. "Damon, what are you doing here? You're confused again. This is not the Little Chase. Go home."

"I'm not going home, Nora."

I looked at him sharply. There was something quite different about the Damon Gerrick who stood before me now. Gone was the vacant stare from those blue eyes so like Amabel's, replaced with an uncanny intelligence I had never seen there before.

"What do you mean?" I inquired coldly, feeling suddenly uneasy.

His mouth twisted into a smile. "I mean, I am not leaving this room until you are dead."

CHAPTER
12

I swallowed hard, as I sat up with great effort and drew the sheet protectively about me. "You wish to kill me, Damon?"

"Yes," he replied conversationally, as he crossed the room to stand just a few feet away from me. "But before I did, I wanted to frighten you. I wish you could have seen yourself the night that ball came rolling toward you in the gallery. Your face was so-o-o white, and your eyes so-o-o round . . ."

"*You* did those terrible things to me?"

He giggled, and the eyes that had once seemed so vacant now glowed with malevolence as he looked down at me. "Surprised, Nora? Did you think poor, mad Damon incapable of such cleverness? Amabel, Angel, Nora . . . I fooled you all! And it was so simple. I grew up in Raven's Chase, so I know where all the keys are kept and which doors they open. And if a servant should pass me in the hall . . ." He shrugged. "It's just poor, mad Damon, lost again. We won't pay any attention to him."

I recalled the afternoon I had returned from a ride to find him wandering the halls aimlessly, but, like everyone else, I dismissed him without another thought. "So, you hid in the gallery and rolled the ball at me."

"I sometimes let myself in through the kitchen late at night. I knew you went to the gallery when you couldn't sleep, because I've seen you. It was easy enough for me to unlock the nursery and take the ball." His face fell in regret. "Though I do wish I could've seen your reaction to my handiwork in Mark's study."

As I thought of my ruined portrait and the words "Nora will die" scrawled in the dust, I felt a cold wave of horror ripple through me. If Damon had done that, then he must have been Mark's "ghost" the night I walked home. I took a deep breath to keep my voice steady as I said, "How did you manage to impersonate Mark that night?"

"That was my most ambitious and ingenious plan of all. First, I fed the horse oats until she would come when I called. It wasn't difficult, as she's very tame and often comes around to our stables for food. When I thought I would be needing her, I hid her away in the abbey cellars." Damon's face went absolutely still, and he muttered, "But that curious child almost discovered her, that's why I had to teach him a lesson by locking him in a cell down there." He grinned. "It worked, too. He never came snooping in the abbey again."

I let out my breath in a soft hiss as I recalled Amabel once going into a tirade about stolen oats. And Damon was the one who blew out Brent's candle and locked him in the abbey. Now, why hadn't Amabel mentioned seeing Damon out there that afternoon? Perhaps she noticed him, but thought nothing of it.

"Then I came here and helped myself to one of Mark's coats," he continued, his eyes never leaving my face lest he miss each wince, each sign of pain. "How provident it was you kept them. Then, when you came to Angel's room that night to invite her to coffee, I knew it was the perfect time. I dressed, got the horse, and waited in the copse for you to pass." He giggled again, a high-pitched sound that curdled my blood. "You should have seen your face then, Nora. Did you think you were going mad? I hope so."

I nodded, but only to humor him. "Why, Damon? Why did you do these things to me?"

He looked astonished that I didn't know. "Why, so Peter will inherit, of course. Amabel told me how you made my nephew your heir. I love my sister, Nora. We have always been as one. Whatever she wants, she must have."

"But Amabel would not have wanted you to harm me, Damon."

"Yes, she would, because you want her husband for yourself." His eyes widened until their whites showed. "She told me how you always smile at Colin and flirt with him, you baggage!"

"That's not true!" I cried, clutching at my sheet.

"It is true, and you must be punished."

Suddenly, a familiar black figure slid through the open sitting room door, padded silently across the carpet and bounded onto the bed where he promptly curled on my lap and started purring loudly, clamoring for attention, unmindful of the danger standing just a few feet away. I stroked Faust's thick soft fur with my cold, numb fingers while I furiously debated what to do.

I wondered how Damon was going to kill me, for he had no weapon as far as I could see, though a gun or knife could be concealed in his pockets. But if he shot or stabbed me, people would know my death was no accident.

"How are you going to kill me?" I demanded, my throat so dry I could barely speak.

"Since that fall from your horse didn't kill you . . ." He grinned again. "Yes, I was the one who cut your stirrup leather. But, since that failed, I had to come up with a better plan."

"And what is that?"

"Why, to let you kill yourself, of course."

I could feel my eyes widen in alarm. "What do you mean?"

His eyes slid down to the bottles of medicine at my bedside, and his mouth twisted into a smirk. "Angel told me about your medicines, so I took laudanum from her and put it in those bottles, lots and lots of laudanum, enough to kill a horse. I've been coming here almost every night, watching you, waiting for you to take it, but you never have. Until now. By the time anyone finds you, you'll be dead. Poor Nora. So bereft, so confused. She accidentally took too much of the wrong medicine."

Raw fear sent my heart hammering against my ribs, and my body broke out in a cold sweat. "No one will believe it."

"They thought Mark's death was an accident, didn't they?"

My hands stopped their rhythmic stroking and caught at the cat, causing Faust to wriggle and mew in protest. All I could do was stare at Damon. "You?"

"Yes, Nora. I was the one who knocked and slipped the note under the door for that foolish nursemaid. I was the one who tipped over the lamp. I was the one who locked Mark in until I was sure he was dead, then unlocked the door."

Time seemed to stop, and I felt nothing, as though my senses had gone numb. Then, the void was filled by white, blind rage, swirling through me with the ferocity of a hurricane, and I knew at that instant I was going to kill Damon Gerrick. With a scream of anguish, I picked up Faust and heaved the startled cat with all my strength at Damon's face.

Human scream of terror and feline yowl of surprise blended in ghastly harmony, and Damon staggered back, his arms flailing at the cat as the animal dug its claws into his shoulder and neck in an effort to keep his balance. I moved quickly, propelled by fury, and before Damon had a chance to dislodge the cat, I flung back the sheet and sprang from the bed, my eyes darting wildly about the room for a weapon, anything at all. They came to rest on the fireplace, and a poker in its holder. Just as Damon succeeded in freeing himself, I pushed the nightstand against his shins, felling him like a skittle, giving me time to rush for the poker.

Then I turned to face the man who had murdered my husband and son.

Damon was on his feet with the agility of the cat who was now serenely sitting in a corner, washing his whiskers as he watched us.

"Why?" I demanded hoarsely, between clenched teeth.

"Because I hated Mark. He sent me to that place. He stole Raven's Chase from me. I had to get it back."

I took a step forward. "You killed my baby. You killed my Gabriel. Now I'm going to kill you."

264

Damon tensed and crouched like a cornered animal, waiting to spring, his eyes riveted on the poker in fascination.

Just as I swung the weapon back and took two strides forward, my bedchamber door flew open, and there stood Drake and Colin.

"Nora!" Drake cried, stopping me in my tracks.

My hand trembled, the poker wavered, and clattered from my hands as I turned and wobbled toward him. "Damon—he killed Mark and Gabriel," I said as I sobbed and collapsed into his arms.

"We know that now," Drake said gently, his arm strong and comforting about me.

Meanwhile, a white-faced Colin and several burly footmen were approaching Damon as warily as they would a rabid dog. "It's all over now, Damon," Colin said soothingly. "You've got to come with me now."

Suddenly, I felt weak and nauseous. "Send for a doctor. He's poisoned me."

Drake blanched. "With what?"

"Laudanum."

"Good God!" As Drake swept me into his arms, I saw the men converge on Damon.

Happily for me, Drake's heroic efforts to save me were successful. After carrying me to the kitchen, I was given a noxious, but effective, mixture of mustard and warm water. What little of the laudanum was left in my stomach was diluted with hot coffee, then Drake kept me walking the floor, refusing to give up until I was out of danger. Later, the young doctor who came from Sheepstor assured me the antidote had been given in time. Damon thought the poison would take effect immediately, but in actuality, laudanum needs several hours to do its work. Because of his insane need to gloat and torment me, Damon had spoiled his own plan.

Needless to say, only the Masons and the servants would be

sleeping peacefully at Raven's Chase this night. A subdued Colin had gone off with Damon, bound and under guard, leaving Drake and me alone together in the Chinese drawing room.

"How did you know?" I demanded wearily, when I was finally allowed to sit down, the horrors of the night behind me.

"Miss Bridges' story haunted me," Drake said, looking drained and relieved as he sipped his sherry. "What if she were telling the truth? I asked myself. So, on one of my sojourns, I called upon her parents in Sheepstor. As luck would have it, she happened to be visiting them that day. I spoke with her at great length, and she impressed me with her sincerity. I believed her when she insisted someone slipped the note under her door. Once I assumed she was telling the truth, my suspects were narrowed to Mrs. Trelawney and her brother, the only two people home that night. I must admit Mrs. Trelawney was high on my list, and like everyone else, I dismissed Damon because of his illness. But when you told me about seeing Lord Raven's ghost, I wondered if it could have been a man." He smiled indulgently at me, as he reached over to touch my hand. "I wish you had told me about that incident sooner."

I squeezed his hand in return and looked away. "I told you I thought I imagined it."

"Today, events started happening too quickly, before I could confront Mrs. Trelawney. With the minister and those two solicitors here, I didn't get a chance to talk to Colin for a while. While you were up here, I finally got him alone and posed my theory that perhaps Damon was responsible. At first, he refused to believe me, and we almost came to blows. But," he added, admiration in his voice, "Trelawney's a fair man and heard me out. He thought I myself was the madman, at first. The one gap in my theory was Mrs. Trelawney's insistence that her brother had been with her the night of the fire. I began wondering if she was lying, just to protect Damon."

I felt myself go white. "Amabel knew he started the fire that killed Mark and Gabriel?"

He shook his head. "When Trelawney pressed her, she confessed she hadn't actually seen Damon that night, but when she asked her brother if he had been home, he replied yes. She had no reason to believe he was lying."

I leaned back in my chair and my voice trembled as I said, "I'll never forgive her, Drake."

"She loved her brother, Nora. When we love someone, we're often blind to their faults. Mrs. Trelawney didn't want to believe Damon committed that ghastly crime, so she put any suspicions right out of her mind. When things began happening to you, she sincerely believed the Masons or I were responsible. When she confessed to Trelawney and me that Damon actually wasn't with her the night of the fire, we knew you were in danger, and rushed over here just in time."

"And Miss Blessed? She never once suspected him?"

Drake leaned back in his chair and shook his head. "It seems she let her emotions get in the way of her professional judgment."

I thought of the afternoon I had happened upon the nurse and her patient up at the Eyrie, and the night I had seen Damon enter Miss Blessed's room. I was right. "They were lovers, then."

Drake nodded. "But she insisted he never gave any indication that he wasn't getting well. To her, he was progressing, but, in reality, he was just pretending."

I rose, trying to rub feeling into arms I was sure would never be warm again. "I hope Damon hangs for what he's done!"

"He's sick, Nora," Drake said gently. "He'll probably end his days in a place worse than Goodehouse."

"But he knew what he was doing!" I cried. "Only a sane man could have devised such a diabolical scheme."

"Miss Blessed assures me that not all mad people are raving lunatics. Some are quite cunning, like Damon."

"I almost killed him tonight, God help me." I wiped my eyes with a handkerchief. "In a way, Damon's won. Now I've got to live with the knowledge that my husband and son were murdered. An accident is bad enough, but at least it's something we can't control. But murder . . ." I was sobbing so hard I thought I'd never stop, when Drake took me in his arms and just held me.

I spent the next three days alone in my sitting room, with only Faust for company. Drake knew I needed to be alone, and did not try to see me, though I received message after frantic message from Amabel, and finally had to tell the butler not to relay messages from her.

In the end, I agreed to receive her because Colin asked me to, and I felt sorry for the changed man he had become. He, who had been our tower of strength for so long, had crumpled under the knowledge that his wife's bond with her brother had been stronger than her ties to him. But that was how the Gerricks were, obsessively faithful to their own.

When I reluctantly received her in the Chinese drawing room, she threw herself at my feet in a gesture that coming from anyone else would have been melodramatic and begged my forgiveness. I did forgive her, for I knew if I did not, the same hatred that had destroyed Damon would surely destroy me.

I even forgave Angel Blessed, who disappeared quietly out of our lives, leaving me only a note that said, "I was blinded by pride and love. I hope you can forgive me for that, because I shall never be able to forgive myself."

Then the day I had longed for arrived. The Masons were leaving.

As I turned from my sitting room window, where I had been watching the carriage pull up to the front door, Drake strode in. "The Masons would like to see you before they leave," he said.

My brows rose in astonishment. "After what they tried to do? I'm afraid I'm not that charitable and forgiving."

Drake's mustache twitched and I knew he was laughing at

me. "Oh, no? Yet, you refused to bring charges against them, and are even giving them passage back to America on a Raven ship. That's certainly the mark of a hardhearted woman, Nora Gerrick."

I shrugged. "I just want to be rid of them, that's all, not revenge."

"Come," he said, reaching for my hand. "It won't hurt to hear what they have to say."

"Must I?"

"Yes, you must."

They were waiting for me in the foyer, along with their bags. Seth smiled in his charming, easygoing way and seemed relieved that he wasn't going to prison.

"Thank you," he said, taking my hand and bringing it to his lips before I could pull away. "No hard feelings?"

"You ask too much, Mr. Mason," was my blunt reply.

A roguish sparkle lit his dark eyes as he tossed his hair out of his eyes. "Well, you can't blame a man for trying."

"I can, Mr. Mason."

He bowed. "Well, goodbye, Mrs. Gerrick. It has been a pleasure."

"Perhaps under different circumstances, I could say the same." Then I bristled as Ella came up to me. Her empty eyes were now filled with a sort of hopelessness, of wondering what was going to happen to her. I almost felt sorry for the woman.

"I have still another confession to make before I leave," Ella said. When I looked perplexed, she continued with, "I was the one who took your manuscript because I wanted to hurt you in return for your accusations that Brent frightened you with that ball. So I went to your rooms while you were out, and when I saw the papers lying on the table, I just took them and burned them in my fireplace."

"Thank you for confirming my suspicions," I replied, my voice tight and cold.

She didn't apologize, of course. All she said was, "At least you were lucky to be married to Mark Gerrick. I wish he had been my husband." And she turned and joined her brother by the door.

Finally, Brent stood before me, as fastidious as ever in his dark suit. "I hope you will be happy, Lady Raven," he said in his curiously adult manner. Then he bowed gravely, and the three of them passed through the front door and out of my life for good.

I breathed a deep sigh of relief as I turned to Drake. "So much for the Masons." And we slowly walked away like weary soldiers after a long campaign.

The day after the Masons left, I stood at my sitting room window, holding Faust to me and resting my cheek against his soft, warm fur. In the yard below, Jester came cantering beneath my window. Drake was on his back, his round hat pulled low over his forehead and a look of determination on his face as he rode by. He never glanced up once to see me standing there. I wondered just briefly where he was off to again, then turned away. I had other, more pressing problems to concern me.

The Masons had been vanquished, and Mark and Raven's Chase restored to me. The murder of my husband and son had been exposed, but I was still not free. My deep conflicting feelings for Drake still plagued me. I felt disloyal to my husband for the night Drake and I became lovers.

As I stroked the cat, I admitted that I had strong feelings for Drake, feelings that were growing stronger day by day. But was it because of a single night of passion, or something more substantial that could become deep and lasting?

"Oh, Faust," I murmured, "what am I going to do?"

Amabel and Colin joined me in the Garden Room for lunch, though Drake never appeared.

We were just finishing a refreshing lemon ice when Mrs. Harkins interrupted us. "Madam," she began, jingling her keys rapidly, "Mr. Turner is out front with a wagon, and he insists you come immediately. He says it's urgent."

Raising my brows in question, the three of us rose and hurried to the front door. There was Drake, trying to control a restive Jester, and, as Mrs. Harkins had said, with him was a large wagon pulled by a team of strong horses and driven by a farmer, who tipped his hat to us. I noticed there was a rather large object covered with oilcloth in the center of the wagon.

"What's this, Drake?" I asked as I came around to peer up into the wagon.

"See for yourself," he said, dismounting with a mysterious gleam in his eye. "It's for you."

"For me?" I murmured in surprise.

"Whatever can it be?" Amabel wondered aloud, as Drake and Colin helped me to climb into the wagon.

I looked at Drake again, but all he said was, "Go on. Don't you want to see what it is?"

With trembling fingers, I lifted an edge of the oilcloth and tugged it off to reveal a wooden carving of a woman.

"Why, it's a figurehead," Colin said, craning his neck to see. Then he gasped, "Why, Nora, it's you!"

He was right. The figurehead was of a woman whose good likeness of my face would have been recognizable even if the eyes weren't tilted and painted amber. The carver was so skilled and painstaking, my wild, curly hair seemed real as it flowed down the figurehead's shoulders.

"And look at her dress!" Amabel exclaimed. "Isn't that the one you wore in that portrait your father painted of you years ago?"

She was very perceptive. The dress was the cream-colored one from "The Edge of Experience," its folds so finely detailed they resembled soft fabric, not stiff wood.

I stared at Drake, speechless.

He smiled up at me. "When we were in Plymouth, and you were directing the refurbishing of the *Nancy Malone*, you were very efficient, Mrs. Gerrick, and thought of nearly everything." There was a mocking edge to his voice now. "However, you're still a touch green, because you neglected to commission a new figurehead for her. I felt *Lady Raven's Fortune* should have a likeness of her owner riding the waves with her at all times, for luck."

"But, how?"

"I borrowed the photograph of you in the Chinese drawing room. I knew you'd probably blame the Masons for stealing it, but I had to keep my project secret. Then I described the dress from your portrait to the carvers. That's where I've been disappearing to for days on end, to check on their progress and keep them working day and night. As you can see, it was well worth it."

"It's a masterpiece," Colin said in approval, sliding his arm around his wife's waist.

Then Drake and the driver helped me down from the wagon, and he held my hand. "Are you pleased?"

"Oh, Drake—" But I couldn't finish. I burst into tears, pulled away, and went running back into the house.

He wouldn't have found me seated on a bench in the library, tucked away behind the stacks, if my sniffs hadn't given me away.

"Nora, what's wrong?" he asked quietly, dropping down next to me and taking my hand. "I thought the figurehead would please you. If I had known you were going to be so upset—"

"It's not that. It's one of the most beautiful, thoughtful things that's ever been done for me."

He drew my hand to his lips. "It was the best way I could tell you that I love you and want you for my wife."

I stared at him in disbelief and dismay. "Don't you see, you're only making this even more difficult?"

His shaggy brows rose. "What can be so difficult about telling you I love you, and think those feelings are reciprocated?" When I didn't answer, he smiled. "I first fell in love with you the day you came to my house in Grosvenor Street, marched into my bedroom, and tried to slap me. You had charm and spirit. When you refused to sell me your half of the Raven Line after I bought out Belding and was *so* sure you'd sell it to me, I knew you were special."

"But I believed such horrible things of you, Drake."

"I can understand why, considering how I felt about your husband." He laced his fingers through mine, warming them. "My feelings for Mary died the moment I fell in love with you."

So Amabel had been wrong. But there was just one thing that puzzled me, and I couldn't resist saying, "Then why did you want to name the *Nancy Malone* after Mary?"

"Out of pique. I was so furious with you for buying that ship without consulting me, I wanted to bruise your pride in return, and what better way to do that than by naming your ship after another woman?"

"You succeeded admirably," I retorted dryly.

Then he explained how seeing Mary at the Little Chase had awakened so many powerful memories that, for a while, he thought he did still love her. When I confronted him later in the library, demanding to know about their past relationship, all the old bitterness toward Mark just came pouring out.

Drake reached over to stroke my cheek with his fingertips. "I'm sorry if I made you think I still cared for her." He shook his head. "What a fool I've been to waste my time loving someone who never loved me!"

Relieved and happy that at least one of us was free, I smiled as I squeezed his hand.

"We all make fools of ourselves. It's part of the human condition."

Now he rose and drew me to my feet. "You haven't answered my question, Nora. Will you marry me and share my life? You do realize we belong together, don't you, and we'll never know contentment if we're apart? Besides, you understand the ships, Nora, more than any woman I've ever known."

"So that's why you want me," I teased, "to gain my share of the Raven Line."

He shook his head in all seriousness. "If that were the case,

I would have bought it when you offered to sell. No, I want you for many reasons, and," he added softly, "if you'll invite me to your bedchamber, I'll explain some of them to you."

When he reached for me, I went willingly, with a soft groan of surrender, and abandoned myself to the feeling of weakness that washed over me. I wanted to experience it one last time.

But I managed to break away before my resolve was destroyed. "I can't, Drake."

"Nora!" he moaned, taking my face in his hands and forcing me to look at him. "I've told you Mary means nothing to me, so why are you turning away from me? I know you want me as much as I want you. Why are you denying it?" Then he released me as he answered his own question. "It's Mark again, isn't it?"

Nodding miserably, I squeezed my eyes shut so he wouldn't see them fill with tears.

"I thought you were on the verge of healing the day you told me you had given his clothes away. For the first time, I felt hope that you were ready to forget the past and make a future with me. But I can see I was wrong." He was silent for a moment, then said, "Will it always be Mark?"

"I—I don't know. I loved Mark so much, and I can't change the way I feel."

He shook his head, and there was that look of boyish wistfulness about him. "I just wish you could find it in your heart to feel the same about me."

"I do," I whispered, never feeling so torn and helpless, "but I must come to terms with my feelings for Mark, and I must do it alone. No one can help me this time, Drake, not even you."

His look of yearning was replaced by one of panic at the thought of losing me, and I knew he was fighting a battle of his own. Finally, he said, "What are you going to do?"

"I thought I'd go abroad for a while, far away from this house and all its memories."

"Where will you go?"

"I think it's best you don't know, Drake, for both our sakes."

Rebellion warmed his icy eyes. "Do you expect me to spend my days and nights wondering where you are, worrying how you are, never seeing you, never touching you?"

I nodded resolutely. "For a little while."

"And how long is 'a little while'?"

"I don't know. A month. A year. Until those feelings are sorted out. Until I can honestly say I want you for yourself, not as some substitute for Mark."

A muscle in his jaw twitched, and he stormed over to the mullioned window, his back turned. I knew he wasn't angry with me, but with fate and circumstances neither of us could control.

After a moment, he turned to face me. "Don't take too long, Nora," he warned, with that old, familiar arrogance, "or, by heaven, I'll find you wherever you are, and make sure you never leave me again."

That brought a smile to my lips. "Will you run the Raven Line for me?"

"If you trust me."

"You know I do, with all my heart."

I wanted to go to him, but just couldn't. I kept seeing Mark standing there, not Drake.

He read my mind and sighed in despair. "One day, when you can look at me and see Drake Turner, not your husband, then send for me."

I just hoped by that time it would not be too late.

My ultimate destination, highly recommended by Lewis Darwin, was a sprawling rented villa on beautiful Lake Como in Italy.

As I sat in the carriage and waited for my driver to swing open the iron gates, I had ample time to study the breathtaking view spread out before me. There was the lake itself, of course, shimmering blue in the hot afternoon sun as it mirrored the splendid mountains rising on all sides, and chestnut trees on the shore. In the road below the villa, a fine white dust rose beneath the hooves of a passing donkey, and, nearby, I could hear voices, one low and calm, speaking French, and another, more excited and rapid, speaking Italian.

I smiled as my driver returned and we rode up to the villa of pale yellow stucco, to where a huge Italian counterpart to Mrs. Harkins named Rosa nearly filled the doorway as she awaited my arrival. Later, when I was settled and had refreshed myself, I went for a short stroll around the grounds in the golden light of late afternoon. There was a spacious flagstone terrace, bordered by a low balustrade and stone urns of vines and oleander that softly perfumed the air. Toward the back was a high, thick wall of ilex, its burnished leaves gently rattling in the breeze.

Here, I was totally isolated from all that was familiar to me, like a cloistered nun. Mark and I had never visited this place on our travels, so it held no memories of times shared with him. No servants had accompanied me from England, not even faithful Fenner. I was attended only by Rosa, who also doubled as cook, several industrious village girls who came to clean, and a near-toothless gardener named Guido. He seemed to spend more time leaning on his rake and contemplating the horizon than working, but somehow, the work always got done, and the gardens were splendid. The servants' English was nonexistent, and my Italian only enough to make my most basic needs understood, so I even denied myself the pleasure of hearing the English language.

As August became September, with hazy mornings of lovely violet light cradled between the mountains, my quiet days did not vary.

I never left the villa, preferring the ilex-bordered solitude of the garden, where I could write in my journal or reflect undisturbed. Occasionally, as I looked out over the lake at little boats dipping and bending into the wind, I felt a twinge of homesickness, but then Guido, leaning on his rake, would grin and mumble, *"Bella! Bella!"* and the feeling would pass. I suspect I was gaining something of a reputation as a lady of mystery among the locals, for sometimes, as I was enjoying a cup of strong Italian coffee on the terrace, I would hear whisperings and rustlings in the bushes. When I rose to investigate, there came sounds of flight, and a moment later several black-haired boys could be seen racing away down the road toward their village, eager to boast to their friends that they had spied on the mysterious *"Signora inglese."*

During this sojourn, my manuscript was finally completed, but Lewis Darwin would have to wait until I returned to England to read it, for I had no desire to entrust my precious parcel to the mails. I could just imagine his reaction after reading it. *"Bravo,* my dear Nora," he would say in his raspy voice, "you have blossomed. The literary world will be at your *feet."* I smiled at that.

In the beginning, my thoughts were always of Mark and our son, and I often tortured myself wondering what might have been had Damon remained locked away in Goodehouse where he belonged.

Then another month passed, and I found myself gradually thinking more and more about Drake.

They were just fleeting thoughts at first, brief glimpses into the past as quick as a glance. I'd recall the way his icy eyes would suddenly warm when he looked at me, and how his mustache twitched just before he smiled. Gradually, those memories grew into entire senses. I found myself recalling the first time I had ever seen him, that morning at the crowded Plymouth train station as he scanned the horizon and impatiently consulted his pocket watch, and the day he scaled my garden wall, determined to see me. And I kept seeing his face when he brought the figurehead to me, as sure a declaration of love as a man could make.

But I never thought of that night we became lovers. That was my penance.

Time passed with agonizing slowness. Christmas came and went, unheralded and uncelebrated by me, which was no doubt unheard of in this staunchly Catholic country. New Year's Day suffered the same fate. Three weeks later, I spent the anniversary of my husband and son's murder sitting in my cold, barren garden, alone and haunted by memories.

And then, one night in February, Mark and Gabriel came to me in a dream and seemed to be saying goodbye. When I awoke to the thin morning sun streaming into my bedroom, the hard knot of pain in my heart was gone.

My father's words, all those months ago, now came back to me. "You can't recapture the past, Nora," he had warned me. "It's never quite the same country we left."

I finally realized that now, thanks to Drake. Perhaps I would occasionally visit that other country, but I no longer wanted to live there. I was finally free.

Now I jumped out of bed, slipped on my dressing gown, and called for Rosa at the top of my lungs. When she came to my room, she found me throwing clothes into trunks like a madwoman. Even with my limited command of her language, she understood the *"Signora inglese"* was leaving.

When I finally arrived in London, it was snowing lightly and I was exhausted from a long train ride across France and a rough Channel crossing, but still had to restrain myself from rushing to Drake's house in Grosvenor Street. It was of vital importance that he not see me in mourning tonight. So, as soon as I arrived at my house in Mount Street, I quickly changed into an evening gown of dark gold satin, secured my unruly hair back with amber combs, and left for Grosvenor Street.

When I arrived, however, I was informed by the startled butler that Mr. Turner was attending a performance of the opera at Covent Garden that evening. I could not bring myself to ask if he had gone alone, so I just got back into my carriage and had my driver hurry through slick, slushy streets to the opera house.

The crimson carpeted foyer was empty, and the usher who directed me to Mr. Turner's box warned me that *The Bohemian Girl* had already begun. But I was not going to be like poor Mr. Featherstone, waiting patiently until the performance was over before confronting Drake. I was hoping this was one interruption he would welcome. As I stood before that formidable closed door, my heart leaped into my throat and my nerve failed me. It had been over six months since we had last seen each other. What if he had given me up as hopeless? What if he had found another woman, an auburn-haired, blue-eyed enchantress, like Mary Glover?

"Then she who hesitates will be lost, Nora, girl," I muttered, as I swallowed hard, turned the knob, and went inside.

At first, going from light to dark blinded me and I just stood for a moment, dazed. Gradually, I could discern a solitary figure sitting there with his back toward me, and my heart leaped with joy and relief. He had waited for me after all.

I moved forward, and the soprano's soaring voice drowned out the soft swish of my satin train, so that when I placed my hand on Drake's shoulder, he started and turned in his seat, frowning in displeasure that someone should dare disturb him. When he saw me, his eyes widened, and an expression of incredulity flitted across his face.

"Nora?" he murmured in disbelief, as though I were some spirit that would vanish at any moment. Then he jumped to his feet, knocking over his chair with an alarming crash that earned us annoyed glances from his neighbors. He just stared at me in silence, demanding that I make the first move to declare myself.

"My darling, dearest Drake," I murmured, "I do love you so."

"Nora," he whispered, caressing my cheek with his fingertips, while his eyes never left mine. I could see tears of deep emotion in his eyes, and raw, unabashed love for the world to see. "No more ghosts?" he inquired.

"No more ghosts," I replied with conviction and knew there would never be a wall between us again.

279

Now a collective hiss of animosity rose from other patrons on both sides of Drake's box, and several dowagers eyed us disapprovingly through their opera glasses.

"We must leave of our own volition, my darling, before they ask us to," he said, his love for me so strong I felt it surround and strengthen me. "There is so much I have to say to you, and this is not the proper place."

"And what is the proper place?"

He grasped my hand and brought it to his lips. "Grosvenor Street?"

I smiled, nodded, and heard him catch his breath. Then I couldn't resist adding in a light and teasing voice, "What? Drake Turner leave the opera in the middle of a performance?"

"The opera be damned," was his reply.